# Midnight Never Come

### MARIE BRENNAN

orbit

www.orbitbooks.net

*This book is dedicated to two groups of people.*

*To the players of Memento:*
*Jennie Kaye, Avery Liell-Kok, Ryan Conner, and*
*Heather Goodman.*

*And to their characters, whose ghosts still haunt this story:*
*Rowan Scott, Sabbeth, Erasmus Fleet, and*
*Wessamina Hammercrank.*

ORBIT

First published in Great Britain in 2008 by Orbit

A CIP catalogue record for this book
is available from the British Library.

ISBN 978-1-84149-717-4

Typeset in Adobe Garamond
Printed and bound in the UK by CPI Mackays, Chatham ME5 8TD

Orbit
An imprint of
Little, Brown Book Group
100 Victoria Embankment
London EC4Y 0DY

An Hachette Livre UK Company
www.hachettelivre.co.uk

www.orbitbooks.net

# Acknowledgments

I owe a great debt of gratitude to the many people who helped me research this novel. During my trip to England, I was assisted by the following wonderful volunteers: from the Shakespeare's Globe Library and Archives, Victoria Northwood; from the National Trust, Kate Wheeldon at Hardwick Hall; and from Historic Royal Palaces, Alison Heald, Susan Holmes at the Tower of London, and Alden Gregory at Hampton Court Palace. (The rooftop scene is his fault.)

I'm also grateful to Kevin Schmidt, for the astrology in Act Three, and to Dr. William Tighe, who taught me everything I know about the Gentlemen Pensioners, and mailed me his dissertation to boot. He is not to be blamed for anything I got wrong.

Finally, I have to thank Kate Walton, for needing someone to keep her awake on a late-night drive to the airport back in June of 2006. It was the first of many fruitful midnight conversations about this story, and it wouldn't have been the same without her.

# Prologue

THE TOWER OF LONDON: *March 1554*

Fitful drafts of chill air blew in through the cruciform windows of the Bell Tower, and the fire did little to combat them. The chamber was ill lit, just wan sunlight filtering in from the alcoves and flickering light from the hearth, giving a dreary, despairing cast to the stone walls and meager furnishings. A cheerless place—but the Tower of London was not a place intended for cheer.

The young woman who sat on the floor by the fire, knees drawn up to her chin, was pale with winter and recent illness. The blanket over her shoulders was too thin to keep her warm, but she seemed not to notice; her dark eyes were fixed on the dancing flames, morbidly entranced, as if imagining their touch. She would not be burned, of course; burning was for common heretics. Decapitation, most likely. Perhaps, like her mother, she would be permitted a French executioner, whose sword would do the work cleanly.

Presuming the Queen's mercy permitted her that consideration. Presuming the Queen had mercy for her at all.

The few servants she kept were not there; in a rage she had sent them away, arguing with the guards until she won these

private moments for herself. As much as solitude oppressed her, she could not bear the thought of companionship in this dark moment, the risk of showing her weakness to others. And so when she waked from her reverie to sense another in the room, her anger rose again. Shedding the blanket, the young woman whirled to her feet, ready to confront the intruder.

Her words died, unspoken, and behind her the fire dipped low.

The woman she saw was no serving-maid, no lady attendant. No one she had ever seen before. A mere silhouette, barely visible in the shadows—but she stood in one of the alcoves, where a blanket had been tacked up to cover the arrow-slit window.

Not by the door. And she had entered without a sound.

"You are the Princess Elizabeth," the woman said. Her voice was a cool ghost, melodious, soft, and dark.

Tall, she was, taller than Elizabeth herself, and more slender. She wore a sleek black gown, close-fitting through the body but flaring outward into a full skirt and a high standing collar that gave her presence weight. Jewels glimmered with dark color here and there, touching the fabric with elegance.

"I am," Elizabeth said, drawing herself up to the dignity of her full height. "I have given no orders to accept visitors." Nor was she permitted any, but in prison as in court, bravado could be all.

The stranger's voice answered levelly. "I am not a visitor. Do you think this solitude your own doing? The guards allowed it because I arranged that they should. My words are for your ears alone."

Elizabeth stiffened. "And who are you, that you presume to order my life in such fashion?"

"A friend." The word carried no warmth. "Your sister means to execute you. She cannot risk your survival; you are a focal point for every Protestant rebellion, every disaffected nobleman who hates her Spanish husband. She must dispose of you, and soon."

No more than Elizabeth herself had already calculated. To be here, in the stark confines of the Bell Tower, was an insult to her rank. Prisoner though she was, she should have received more comfortable lodgings. "No doubt you come to offer me some escape from this. I do not, however, converse with strangers who intrude on me without warning, let alone make alliances with them. Your purpose might be to lure me into some indiscretion my enemies could exploit."

"You do not believe that." The stranger came forward one step, into a patch of thin, gray light. A cruciform arrow-slit haloed her as if in painful mimicry of Heaven's blessing. "Your sister and her Catholic allies would not treat with one such as I."

Slender as a breath, she should have been skeletal, grotesque, but far from it; her face and body bore the stamp of unearthly perfection, a flawless symmetry and grace that unnerved as much as it entranced. Elizabeth had spent her childhood with scholars for her tutors, reading classical authors, but she knew the stories of her own land, too: the beautiful ones, the Fair Folk, the Good People, whose many epithets were chosen to mollify their capricious natures.

The faerie was a sight to send grown women to their knees, and Elizabeth was only twenty-one. Since childhood, though, the princess had survived the tempests of political unrest, riding from her mother's inglorious downfall to her own elevation at her brother's hands, only to plummet again when their Catholic sister took the throne. She was intelligent enough to be afraid, but stubborn enough to defy that fear, to cling to pride when nothing else remained.

"Do you think me easier to cozen than my sister? Some say your kind are fallen angels, or in league with the devil himself."

The woman's laugh echoed from the chamber walls like

shattering crystal. "I do not serve the devil. I offer you a bond of mutual aid. With my help, you may be freed from the Tower and raised to your sister's throne. Your father's throne. Without it, your life will surely end soon."

Elizabeth knew too much of politics to even consider an offer without hearing it in full. "And in return? What gift — no doubt a minor, insignificant trifle — would you require from me?"

"Oh, 'tis not minor." The faintest of smiles touched the stranger's lips. "As I will raise you to your throne, you will raise me to mine. And when we both achieve power, perhaps we will be of use to each other again."

Every shrewd instinct and fiber of caution in Elizabeth warned her against this pact. Yet over her hovered the specter of death, the growing certainty of her sister's bitterness and hatred. She had her allies, surely enough, but they were not here. Could they be relied upon to save her from the headsman?

To cover her thoughts, she said, "You have not yet told me your name."

The fae paused. At last, her tone considering, she said, "Invidiana."

When Elizabeth's servants returned soon after, they found their mistress seated in a chair by the fire, staring into its glowing heart. The air in the chamber was freezing cold, but Elizabeth sat without cloak or blanket, her long, elegant hands resting on the arms of the chair. She was quiet that day, and for many days after, and her gentlewomen worried for her, but when word came that she was to be permitted to walk at times upon the battlements and to take the air, they brightened. Surely, they hoped, their futures — and that of their mistress — were looking up at last.

# Act One

*Time stands still with gazing on her face,*
*stand still and gaze for minutes, houres and yeares, to her giue place:*
*All other things shall change, but shee remains the same,*
*till heauens changed haue their course & time hath lost his name.*
        —John Dowland
            *The third and last booke of songs or aires*

*No* footfalls disturb the hush as the man—not nearly so young as he appears—passes down the corridor, floating as if he walks on the shadows that surround him.

His whisper drifts through the air, echoing from the damp stone of the walls.

"She loves me . . . she loves me not."

His clothes are rich, thick velvet and shining satin, black and silver against pale skin that has not seen sunlight for decades. His dark hair hangs loose, not disciplined into curls, and his face is smooth. As she prefers it to be.

"She loves me . . . she loves me not."

The slender fingers pluck at something invisible in his hands, as if pulling petals from a flower, one by one, and letting them fall, forgotten.

"She loves me . . . she loves me not."

He stops abruptly, peering into the shadows, then reaches up with one shaking hand to touch his eyes. "She wants to take them from me, you know," he confides to whatever he sees—or thinks he sees. Years in this place have made reality a malleable thing to him, a volatile one, shifting without warning. "She spoke of it again today. Taking my eyes . . . Tiresias was blind. He was also a woman betimes; did you know that? He had a daughter. I have no daughter." Breath catches in his throat. "I had a family once. Brothers, sisters, a mother and father . . . I was in love. I might have had a daughter. But they are all gone now. I have only her, in all the world. She has made certain of that."

He sinks back against the wall, heedless of the grime that mars *his fine clothing, and slides down to sit on the floor. This is one of the back tunnels of the Onyx Hall, far from the cold, glittering beauty of the court. She lets him wander, though never far. But whom does she hurt by keeping him close—him, or herself? He is the only one who remembers what this court was, in its earliest days. Even she has chosen to forget. Why, then, does she keep him?*

*He knows the answer. It never changes, no matter the question. Power, and occasional amusement. These are the only reasons she needs.*

*"That which is above is like that which is below," he whispers to his unseen companion, a product of his fevered mind. "And that which is below is like that which is above." His sapphire gaze drifts upward, as if to penetrate the stones and wards that keep the Onyx Hall hidden.*

*Above lies the world he has lost, the world he sometimes thinks no more than a dream. Another symptom of his madness. The crowded, filthy streets of London, seething with merchants and laborers and nobles and thieves, foreigners and country folk, wooden houses and narrow alleys and docks and the great river Thames. Human life, in all its tawdry glory. And the brilliance of the court above, the Tudor magnificence of Elizabetha Regina, Queen of England, France, and Ireland. Gloriana, and her glorious court.*

*A great light, that casts a great shadow.*

*Far below, in the darkness, he curls up against the wall. His gaze falls to his hands, and he lifts them once more, as if recalling the flower he held a moment ago.*

*"She loves me . . .*

*". . . she loves me not."*

RICHMOND PALACE, RICHMOND: *September 17, 1588*

"Step forward, boy, and let me see you."

The wood-paneled chamber was full of people, some hovering nearby, others off to the side, playing cards or engaging in muted conversation. A musician, seated near a window, played a simple melody on his lute. Michael Deven could not shake the feeling they were all looking at him, openly or covertly, and the scrutiny made him unwontedly awkward.

He had prepared for this audience with more than customary care for appearances. The tailor had assured him the popinjay satin of his doublet complemented the blue of his eyes, and the sleeves were slashed with insets of white silk. His dark hair, carefully styled, had not a strand out of place, and he wore every jewel he owned that did not clash with the rest. Yet in this company, his appearance was little more than serviceable, and sidelong glances weighed him down to the last ounce.

But those gazes would hardly matter if he did not impress the woman in front of him.

Deven stepped forward, bold as if there were no one else there, and made his best leg, sweeping aside the edge of his half-cloak for effect. "Your Majesty."

Standing thus, he could see no higher than the intricately worked hem of her gown, with its motif of ships and winds. A commemoration of the Armada's recent defeat, and worth more than his entire wardrobe. He kept his eyes on a brave English ship and waited.

"Look at me."

He straightened and faced the woman sitting beneath the canopy of estate.

He had seen her from afar, of course, at the Accession Day tilts and other grand occasions: a radiant, glittering figure, with beautiful auburn hair and perfect white skin. Up close, the artifice showed. Cosmetics could not entirely cover the smallpox scars, and the fine bones of her face pressed against her aging flesh. But her dark-eyed gaze made up for it; where beauty failed, charisma would more than suffice.

"Hmmm." Elizabeth studied him frankly, from the polished buckles of his shoes to the dyed feather in his cap, with particular attention to his legs in their hose. He might have been a horse she was contemplating buying. "So you are Michael Deven. Hunsdon has told me something of you—but I would hear it from your own lips. What is it you want?"

The answer was ready on his tongue. "Your Majesty's most gracious leave to serve in your presence, and safeguard your throne and your person against those impious foes who would threaten it."

"And if I say no?"

The freshly starched ruff scratched at his chin and throat as he swallowed. Catering to the Queen's taste in clothes was less than comfortable. "Then I would be the most fortunate and most wretched of men. Fortunate in that I have achieved that which most men hardly dream of—to stand, however briefly, in your Grace's radiant presence—and wretched in that I must go from it and not return. But I would yet serve from afar, and pray that one day my service to the realm and its glorious sovereign might earn me even one more moment of such blessing."

He had rehearsed the florid words until he could say them without feeling a fool, and hoped all the while that this was not some trick Hunsdon had played on him, that the courtiers would not burst into laughter at his overblown praise. No one laughed, and the tight spot between his shoulder blades eased.

A faint smile hovered at the edges of the Queen's lips. Meeting her eyes for the briefest of instants, Deven thought, *She knows exactly what our praise is worth.* Elizabeth was no longer a young woman, whose head might be turned by pretty words; she recognized the ridiculous heights to which her courtiers' compliments flew. Her pride enjoyed the flattery, and her political mind exploited it. *By our words, we make her larger than life. And that serves her purposes very well.*

This understanding did not make her any easier to face. "And family? Your father is a member of the Stationers' Company, I believe."

"And a gentleman, madam, with lands in Kent. He is an alderman of Farringdon Ward within, and has been pleased to serve the Crown in printing certain religious texts. For my own part, I do not follow in his trade; I am of Gray's Inn."

"Though your studies there are incomplete, as I understand. You went to the Netherlands, did you not?"

"Indeed, madam." A touchy subject, given the failures there, and the Queen's reluctance to send soldiers in the first place. Yet his military conduct in the Low Countries was part of what distinguished him enough to be here today. "I served with your gentleman William Russell at Zutphen two years ago."

The Queen fiddled idly with a silk fan, eyes still fixed on him. "What languages have you?"

"Latin and French, madam." What Dutch he had learned was not worth claiming.

She immediately switched to French. "Have you traveled to France?"

"I have not, madam." He prayed his accent was adequate, and thanked God she had not chosen Latin. "My studies kept me occupied, and then the troubles made it quite impossible."

"Good. Too many of our young men go there and come back

11

Catholic." This seemed to be a joke, as several of the courtiers chuckled dutifully. "What of poetry? Do you write any?"

At least Hunsdon had warned him of this, that she would ask questions having nothing to do with his ostensible purpose for being there. "She has standards," the Lord Chamberlain had said, "for anyone she keeps around her. Beauty, and an appreciation for beauty; whatever your duties at court, you must also be an ornament to her glory."

"I do not write my own, madam, but I have attempted some works of translation."

Elizabeth nodded, as if it were a given. "Tell me, which poets have you read? Have you translated Virgil?"

Deven parried this and other questions, striving to keep up with the Queen's agile mind as it leapt from topic to topic, and all in French. She might be old, but her wits showed no sign of slowing, and from time to time she would make a jest to the surrounding courtiers, in English or in Italian. He fancied they laughed louder at the Italian sallies, which he could not understand. Clearly, if he were accepted at court, he would need to learn it. For self-protection.

Elizabeth broke off the interrogation without warning and looked past Deven. "Lord Hunsdon," she said, and the nobleman stepped forward to bow. "Tell me. Would my life be safe in this gentleman's hands?"

"As safe as it rests with any of your Grace's gentlemen," the gray-haired baron replied.

"Very encouraging," Elizabeth said dryly, "given that we executed Tylney for conspiracy not long ago." She turned her forceful attention to Deven once more, who fought the urge to hold his breath and prayed he did not look like a pro-Catholic conspirator.

At last she nodded her head decisively. "He has your recommendation, Hunsdon? Then let it be so. Welcome to my Gentlemen Pensioners, Master Deven. Hunsdon will instruct you in your duties." She held out one fine, long-fingered hand, the hands featured in many of her portraits, because she was so proud of them. Kissing one felt deeply strange, like kissing a statue, or one of the icons the papists revered. Deven backed away with as much speed as was polite.

"My humblest thanks, your Grace. I pray God my service never disappoint."

She nodded absently, her attention already on the next courtier, and Deven straightened from his bow with an inward sigh of relief.

Hunsdon beckoned him away. "Well spoken," the Lord Chamberlain and Captain of the Gentlemen Pensioners said, "though defense will be the least of your duties. Her Majesty never goes to war in person, of course, so you will not find military action unless you seek it out."

"Or Spain mounts a more successful invasion," Deven said.

The baron's face darkened. "Pray God it never come."

The two of them made their way through the gathered courtiers in the presence chamber and out through magnificently carved doors into the watching chamber beyond. "The new quarter begins at Michaelmas," Hunsdon said. "We shall swear you in then; that should give you time to set your affairs in order. A duty period lasts for a quarter, and the regulations require you to serve two each year. In practice, of course, many of our band have others stand in for them, so that some are at court near constantly, others hardly at all. But for your first year, I will require you to serve both assigned periods."

"I understand, my lord." Deven had every intention of spending the requisite time at court, and more if he could manage it. One did not gain advancement without gaining the favor of those who granted it, and one did not do that from a distance. Not without family connections, at any rate, and with his father so new to the gentry, he was sorely lacking in those.

As for the connections he did have…Deven had kept his eyes open, both in the presence chamber and this outer room, populated by less favored courtiers, but nowhere had he seen the one man he truly hoped to find. The man to whom he owed his good fortune this day. Hunsdon had recommended him to the Queen, as was his privilege as captain, but the notion did not originate with him.

Unaware of Deven's thoughts, Hunsdon went on talking. "Have better clothes made, before you begin. Borrow money if you must; no one will remark upon it. Hardly a man in this court is not in debt to one person or another. The Queen takes great delight in fashion, both for herself and those around her. She will not be pleased if you look plain."

One visit to the elite realm of the presence chamber had convinced him of that. Deven was already in debt; preferment did not come cheaply, requiring gifts to smooth his path every step of the way. It seemed he would have to borrow more, though. This, his father had warned him, would be his lot: spending all he had and more in the hopes of *having* more in the future.

Not everyone won at that game. But Deven's grandfather had been all but illiterate; his father, working as a printer, had earned enough wealth to join the ranks of the gentry; Deven himself intended to rise yet higher.

He even had a notion for how to do it—if he could only find the man he needed. Descending a staircase two steps behind Hunsdon, Deven said, "My lord, could you advise me on how to find the Principal Secretary?"

"Eh?" The baron shook his head. "Walsingham is not at court today."

14

*Damnation.* Deven schooled himself to an outward semblance of pleasantry. "I see. In that case, I believe I should—"

His words cut off, for faces he recognized were waiting in the gallery below. William Russell was there, along with Thomas Vavasour and William Knollys, two others he knew from the fighting in the Low Countries. At Hunsdon's confirming nod, they loosed glad cries and surged forward, clapping him on the back.

The suggestion he had been about to make, that he return to London that afternoon, was trampled before he could even speak it. Deven struggled with his conscience for a minute at most before giving in. He was a courtier now; he should enjoy the pleasures of a courtier's life.

THE ONYX HALL, LONDON: *September 17, 1588*

The polished stone walls reflected the quiet murmurs, the occasional burst of cold, sharp laughter, echoing up among the sheets of crystal and silver filigree that filled the space between the vaulting arches. Chill lights shone down on a sea of bodies, tall and short, twisted and fair. Court was not often so well attended, but something was expected to happen today. No one knew what—there were rumors; there were always rumors—but no one would be absent who could possibly attend.

And so the fae of London gathered in the Onyx Hall, circulating across the black-and-white *pietre dura* marble of the great presence chamber. One did not have to be a courtier to gain entry to this room; among the lords and gentlewomen were visitors from outlying areas, most of them dressed in the same ordinary clothing they wore every day. They formed a plain, sturdy backdrop against which the finery of the courtiers shone all the more vividly. Gowns of cobwebs and mist, doublets of rose petals like armor, jewels of moonlight and starlight and other intangible riches: the fae who called the Onyx Hall home had dressed for a grand court occasion.

They had dressed, and they had come; now they waited. The one empty space lay at the far end of the presence chamber, a high dais upon which a throne sat empty. Its intricate network of silver and gems might have been the web of a spider, waiting for its spinner to return. No one looked at it openly, but each fae present glanced at it from time to time out of the corners of their eyes.

Lune looked at it more often than most. The rest of the time she drifted through the hall, silent and alone. Whispers spread fast; even those from outside London seemed to have heard of her fall from favor. Or perhaps not; country fae often kept their distance from courtiers, out of fears ranging from the well-founded to the ludicrous. Whatever the cause, the hems of her sapphire skirts rarely brushed anyone else's. She moved in an invisible sphere of her own disgrace.

From the far end of the hall, a voice boomed out like the crash of waves on rocky shores. "She comes! From the white cliffs of Dover to the stones of the ancient wall, she rules all the fae of England. Make way for the Queen of the Onyx Court!"

The sea of bodies rippled in a sudden ebb tide, every fae present sinking to the floor. The more modest — the more fearful — prostrated themselves on the black-and-white marble, faces averted, eyes tightly shut. Lune listened as heavy steps thudded past, measured and sure, and then behind them the ghostly whisper of skirts. A chill breeze wafted through the room, more imagined than felt.

A moment later, the doors to the presence chamber boomed

shut. "By command of your mistress, rise, and attend to her court," the voice again thundered, and with a shiver the courtiers returned to their feet and faced the throne.

Invidiana might have been a portrait of herself, so still did she sit. The crystal and jet embroidered onto her gown formed bold shapes that complemented those of the throne, with the canopy of estate providing a counterpoint above. Her high collar, edged with diamonds, framed a flawless face that showed no overt expression — but Lune fancied she could read a hint of secret amusement in the cold black eyes.

She hoped so. When Invidiana was not amused, she was often angry.

Lune avoided meeting the gaze of the creature that waited at Invidiana's side. Dame Halgresta Nellt stood like a pillar of rock, boots widely planted, hands clasped behind her broad back. The weight of her gaze was palpable. No one knew where Invidiana had found Halgresta and her two brothers — somewhere in the North, though some said they had once been fae of the alfar lands across the sea, before facing exile for unknown crimes — but the three giants had fought a pitched combat before Invidiana's throne for the right to command her personal guard, and Halgresta had won. Not through size or strength, but through viciousness. Lune knew all too well what the giant would like to do to her.

A sinuous fae clad in an emerald-green doublet that fit like a second skin ascended two steps up the dais and bowed to the Queen, then faced the chamber. "Good people," Valentin Aspell said, his oily voice pitched to carry, "today, we play host to kinsmen who have suffered a tragic loss."

At the Lord Herald's words, the doors to the presence chamber swung open. Laying one hand on the sharp, fluted edge of a column, Lune turned, like everyone else, to look.

17

The fae who entered were a pathetic sight. Muddy and haggard, their simple clothes hanging in rags, they shuffled in with all the terror and awe of rural folk encountering for the first time the cold splendor of the Onyx Hall. The watching courtiers eddied back to let them pass, but there was none of the respect that had immediately opened a path for Invidiana; Lune saw more than a few looks of malicious pity. Behind the strangers walked Halgresta's brother Sir Prigurd, who shepherded them along with patient determination, nudging them forward until they came to a halt at the foot of the dais. There was a pause. Then a sound rumbled through the hall: a low growl from Halgresta. The peasants jerked and threw themselves to the floor, trembling.

"You kneel before the Queen of the Onyx Court," Aspell said, with only moderate inaccuracy; two of the strangers were indeed kneeling, instead of lying on the floor. "Tell her, and the gathered dignitaries of her realm, what has befallen you."

One of the two kneeling fae, a stout hob who looked in danger of losing his cheerful girth, obeyed the order. He had the good sense not to rise.

"Nobble Queen," he said, "we hev lost ev'ry thing."

The account that followed was delivered in nearly impenetrable country dialect. Lune soon gave up on understanding every detail; the tenor was clear enough. The hob had served a certain family since time out of mind, but the mortals were recently thrown off their land, and their house burnt to the ground. Nor was he the only one to suffer such misfortune: a nearby marsh had been drained and the entire area, former house and all, given over to a new kind of farming, while a road being laid in to connect some insignificant town to some slightly less insignificant town had resulted in the death of an oak man and the leveling of a minor faerie mound.

When the last of the tale had spilled out, another pause ensued, and then the hob nudged a battered and sorry-looking puck still trembling on the floor at his side. The puck yelped, a sharp and nervous sound, and produced from somewhere a burlap sack.

"Nobble Queen," the hob said again, "we hev browt yew sum gifts."

Aspell stepped forward and accepted the sack. One by one, he lifted its contents free and presented them to Invidiana: a rose with ruby petals, a spindle that spun on its own, a cup carved from a giant acorn. Last of all was a small box, which he opened facing the Queen. A rustle shivered across the hall as half the courtiers craned to see, but the contents were hidden.

Whatever they were, they must have satisfied Invidiana. She waved Aspell off with one white hand and spoke for the first time.

"We have heard your tale of loss, and your gifts are pleasing to our eyes. New homes will be found for you, never fear."

Her cool, unemotional words set off a flurry of bowing and scraping from the country fae; the hob, still on his knees, pressed his face to the floor again and again. Finally Prigurd got them to their feet, and they skittered out of the chamber, looking relieved at both their good fortune and their departure from the Queen's presence.

Lune pitied them. The poor fools had no doubt given Invidiana every treasure they possessed, and much good would it do them. She could easily guess the means by which those rural improvements had begun; the only true question was what the fae of that area had done to so anger the Queen, that she retaliated with the destruction of their homes.

Or perhaps they were no more than a means to an end.

Invidiana looked out over her courtiers, and spoke again.

The faint hint of kindness an optimistic soul might have read into her tone before was gone. "When word reached us of this destruction, we sent our loyal vassal Ifarren Vidar to investigate." From a conspicuous spot at the foot of the dais, the skeletally thin Vidar smirked. "He uncovered a shameful tale, one our grieving country cousins dreamed not of."

The measured courtesy of her words was more chilling than rage would have been. Lune shivered, and pressed her back against the sharp edges of the pillar. *Sun and Moon,* she thought, *let it not touch me.* She had played no part in these unknown events, but that meant nothing; Invidiana and Vidar were well practiced in the art of fabricating guilt as needed. Had the Queen preserved her from Halgresta Nellt only to lay this trap for her instead?

If so, it was a deeper trap than Lune could perceive. The tale Invidiana laid out was undoubtedly false—some trumped-up story of one fae seeking revenge against another through the destruction of the other fellow's homeland—but the person it implicated was no one Lune knew well, a minor knight called Sir Tormi Cadogant.

The accused fae did the only thing anyone could, in the circumstances. Had he not been at court, he might have run; it was treason to seek refuge among the fae of France or Scotland or Ireland, but it might also be safety, if he made it that far. But he was present, and so he shoved his way through the crowd and threw himself prostrate before the throne, hands outstretched in supplication.

"Forgive me, your Majesty," he begged, his voice trembling with very real fear. "I should not have done so. I have trespassed against your royal rights; I confess it. But I did so only out of—"

"Silence," Invidiana hissed, and his words cut off.

So perhaps Cadogant was the target of this affair. Or perhaps not. He was certainly not guilty, but that told Lune nothing.

"Come before me, and kneel," the Queen said, and shaking like an aspen leaf, Cadogant ascended the stairs until he came before the throne.

One long-fingered white hand went to the bodice of Invidiana's gown. The jewel that lay at the center of her low neckline came away, leaving behind a stark patch of black in the intricate embroidery. Invidiana rose from her throne, and everyone knelt again, but this time they looked up; all of them, from Aspell and Vidar down to the lowliest brainless sprite, knew they were required to witness what came next. Lune watched from her station by the pillar, transfixed with her own fear.

The jewel was a masterwork even among the fae, a perfectly symmetrical tracery of silver drawn down from the moon itself, housing in its center a true black diamond: not the painted gems humans wore, but a stone that held dark fire in its depths. Pearls formed from mermaid's tears surrounded it, and razor-edged slivers of obsidian ringed the gem's edges, but the diamond was the focal point, and the source of power.

Looming above the kneeling Cadogant, Invidiana was a pitiless figure. She reached out her hand and laid the jewel against the fae's brow, between his eyes.

"Please," Cadogant whispered. The word was audible to the farthest corners of the utterly silent hall. Brave as he was, to face the Queen's wrath and hope for what passed for mercy in her, he still begged.

A quiet clicking was his answer, as six spidery claws extended from the jewel and laid needle-sharp tips against his skin.

"Tormi Cadogant," Invidiana said, her voice cold with formality, "this ban I lay upon thee. Nevermore wilt thou bear title or honor within the borders of England. Nor wilt thou flee

---

to foreign lands. Instead, thou wilt wander, never staying more than three nights in one place, neither speaking nor writing any word to another; thou wilt be as one mute, an exile within thine own land."

Lune closed her eyes as she felt power flare outward from the jewel. She had seen it used before, and knew some of how it worked. There was only one consequence for breaking such a ban.

Death.

Not just an exile, but one forbidden to communicate. Cadogant must have been plotting some treason. And this was a message to his coconspirators, subtle enough to be understood, without telling the ignorant that a conspiracy had ever existed in the first place.

Her skin shuddered all over. Such a fate might have been hers, had Invidiana been any more enraged by her failure.

*"Go,"* Invidiana snapped. Lune did not open her eyes until the hesitant, stumbling footsteps passed out of hearing.

When Cadogant was gone, Invidiana did not seat herself again. "This work is concluded for now," she said, and her words bore the terrible implication that Cadogant might not be the last victim. But whatever would happen next, it would not happen now. Everyone cast their gaze down again as the Queen swept from the room, and when the doors shut at last behind her, everyone let out a collective breath.

In the wake of her departure, music began to thread a plaintive note through the air. Glancing back toward the dais, Lune saw a fair-haired young man lounging on the steps, a recorder balanced in his nimble fingers. Like all of Invidiana's mortal pets, his name was taken from the stories of the ancient Greeks, and for good reason; Orpheus's simple melody did more than simply evoke the loss and sorrow of the peasant fae, and Cadogant's downfall. Some of those who had shown cruel amusement before now frowned, regret haunting their eyes. One dark-haired fae woman began to dance, her slender body flowing like water, giving form to the sound. Lune pressed her lips together and hurried to the door, before she, too, could be drawn into Orpheus's snare.

Vidar was lounging against one doorpost, bony silk-clad arms crossed over his chest. "Did you enjoy the show?" he asked, that same smirk hovering again on his lips.

Lune longed for a response to that, some perfect, cutting reply to check his surety that he stood in the Queen's favor and she did not. After all, fae had been known to suffer apparent disgrace, only for it later to be revealed as part of some scheme. But no such scheme sheltered her, and her wit failed. She felt Vidar's smirk widen as she shouldered past him and out of the presence chamber.

His words had unsettled her more than she realized. Or perhaps it was Cadogant, or those poor, helpless country pawns. Lune could not bear to stay out in the public eye, where she imagined every whisper spoke of her downfall. Instead she made her way, with as much haste as she could afford, through the tunnels to her own quarters.

The closing of the door gave the illusion of sanctuary. These two rooms were richly decorated, with a softer touch than in the public areas of the Hall; thick mats of woven rushes covered her floor, and tapestries of the great fae myths adorned her walls. The marble fireplace flared into life at her arrival, casting a warmer glow over the interior, throwing long shadows from the chairs that stood before it. Empty chairs; she had not entertained many guests lately. A doorway on the far side led to her bedchamber.

At least she still had this, her sanctum. She had lost the

Queen's favor, but not so terribly that she had been forced from the Onyx Hall, to wander like those poor bastards in search of a new home. Not so terribly as Cadogant had.

The very thought made her shiver. Straightening, Lune crossed the room to a table that stood by her bedchamber door, and the crystalline coffer atop it.

She hesitated before opening it, knowing the dreary sight that would meet her eyes. Three morsels sat inside: three bites of coarse bread, who knew how old, but as fresh now as when some country housewife laid them out on the doorstep as a gift to the fae. Three bites to sustain her, if the worst should happen and she should be sent away from the Onyx Hall—sent out into the mortal world.

They would not protect her for long.

Lune closed the coffer and shut her eyes. It would not happen. She would find a way back into Invidiana's favor. It might take years, but in the meantime, all she had to do was avoid angering the Queen again.

Or giving Halgresta any excuse to come after her.

Lune's fingers trembled on the delicate surface of the coffer; whether from fear or fury, she could not have said. No, she could not simply wait for her chance. That was not how one survived the Onyx Court. She would have to seek out an opportunity, or better yet, create one.

But how to do that, with so few resources available to her? Three bites of bread would not help her much. And Invidiana would hardly grant more to someone out of favor.

The Queen was not, however, the only source of mortal food.

Again Lune hesitated. To do this, she would have to go out of the Onyx Hall—which meant using one of her remaining pieces. That, or send a message, which would be even more dangerous. No, she couldn't risk that; she would have to go in person.

Praying the sisters would be as generous as she hoped, Lune took a piece of bread from the coffer and went out before she could change her mind.

RICHMOND AND LONDON: *September 18, 1588*

*So this,* Deven thought blearily as he fumbled the lid back onto the close stool, *is the life of a courtier.*

His right shoulder was competing with his head for which ached worse. His new brothers in the Gentlemen Pensioners had taught him to play tennis the previous night, in the high-walled chamber built for that purpose out in the gardens. He'd flinched inwardly at having to pay for entry, but once inside, he took to it with perhaps more enthusiasm than was wise. Then there was drinking and card games, late into the night, until Deven had little memory of how he had arrived here, sharing Vavasour's bed, with their servants stretched out on the floor.

An urgent need to relieve himself had woken him; in the bed, Vavasour slept on. Scrubbing at his eyes, Deven contemplated following his fellow's example, but told himself with resignation that he might as well put the time to use. Otherwise he would sleep until noon and then get caught up once more in the social dance; then it would be too late to leave, so he would stay another night, and so on and so forth until he found himself crawling away from court one day, bleary-eyed and bankrupt.

Checking his purse, he corrected that last thought. Perhaps not bankrupt, judging by his apparent luck at cards the previous night. But such winnings would not finance this life. Hunsdon was right: he needed to borrow money.

Deven suppressed the desire to groan and shook Peter Colsey awake. His manservant was in little better shape than he, having found other servants with whom to entertain himself, but fortunately he was also taciturn of a morning. He rolled off the mattress and confined himself to dire looks at their boots, his master's doublet, and anything else that had the effrontery to require work from him at such an early hour.

The palace wore a different face at this time of day. The previous morning, Deven had been too much focused on his own purpose to take note of it, but now he looked around, trying to wake himself up gently. Servants hurried through the corridors, wearing the Queen's livery or that of various nobles. Outside, Deven heard chickens squawking as two voices argued over who should get how many. Hooves thudded in the courtyard, moving fast and stopping abruptly: a messenger, perhaps. He bet his winnings from the previous night that Hunsdon and the other men who dominated the privy council were up already, hard at work on the business of her Majesty's government.

Colsey brought him food to break his fast, and departed again to have their horses saddled. Soon they were riding out in morning sunlight far too bright.

They did not talk for the first few miles. Only when they stopped to water their horses at a stream did Deven say, "Well, Colsey, we have until Michaelmas. Then I am due to return to court, and under orders to be better dressed when I do."

Colsey grunted. "Best I learn how to brush up velvet, then."

"Best you do." Deven stroked the neck of his black stallion, calming the animal. It was a stupid beast for casual riding—the horse was trained for war—but a part of the fiction that the

Gentlemen Pensioners were still a military force, rather than a force that happened to include some military men. Three horses and two servants; he'd had to acquire another man to assist Colsey. That still earned him more than a few glares.

By afternoon the houses they passed were growing closer together, clustering along the south bank of the Thames and stringing out along the road that led to the bridge. Deven stopped to refresh himself with ale in a Southwark tavern, then cocked his gaze at the sky. "Ludgate first, Colsey. We shall see how quickly I can get out, eh?"

Colsey had the sense not to make any predictions, at least not out loud.

Their pace slowed considerably as they crossed London Bridge, Deven's stallion having to shoulder his way through the crowds that packed it. He kept a careful hand on the reins. Travelers like him wended their way one step at a time, mingling with those shopping in the establishments built along the bridge's length; he didn't put it past the warhorse to bite someone.

Nor did matters improve much on the other side. Resigned by now to the slower pace, his horse drifted westward along Thames Street, taking openings where he found them. Colsey spat less-than-muffled curses as his own cob struggled to keep up, until at last they arrived at their destination in the rebuilt precinct of Blackfriars: John Deven's shop and house.

Whatever private estimate Colsey had made about the length of their visit, Deven suspected it was not short. His father was delighted to learn of his success, but of course it wasn't enough simply to hear the result; he wanted to know every detail, from the clothing of the courtiers to the decorations in the presence chamber. He had visited court a few times, but not often, and had never entered such an august realm.

"Perhaps I'll see it myself someday, eh?" he said, beaming with unsubtle optimism.

And then of course his mother Susanna had to hear, and his cousin Henry, whom Deven's parents had taken in after the death of John's younger brother. It worked out well for all involved; Henry had filled the place that might otherwise have been Michael's, apprenticing to John under the aegis of the Stationers' and freeing him to pursue more ambitious paths. The conversation went to business news, and then of course it was late enough that he had to stay for supper.

A small voice in the back of Deven's mind reflected that it was just as well; if he ate here, it was no coin out of his own purse. Why he should dwell on pennies when he was in debt for pounds made no sense, but there it was.

After supper, when Susanna and Henry had been sent off, Deven sat with his father by the fire, a cup of fine malmsey dangling from his fingers. The light flickered beautifully through the Venetian glass and the red wine within, and he watched it, pleasantly relaxed.

"Your place is assured, my son," John Deven said, stretching his feet toward the fire with a happy sigh.

Elizabeth's ominous words about Tylney had stayed in Deven's mind, but his father was right. There were graybeards in the Pensioners, some of them hardly fit for any kind of action. Unless he did something deeply foolish — like conspiring to kill the Queen — he might stay there until he wished to leave.

Some men did leave. Family concerns called them away, or a disenchantment with life at court; some broke their fortunes instead of making them. Seventy marks yearly, a Pensioner's salary, was not much in that world, and not everyone succeeded at gaining the kinds of preferment that brought more.

But then his father drove all money concerns from his mind, with one simple phrase. "Now," John Deven said, "to find you a wife."

It startled a laugh from him. "I have scarcely earned my place, Father. Give me time to get my feet under me, at least."

" 'Tis not me you should be asking for time. You have just secured a favorable position, one close to her Majesty; there will be gentlewomen seeking after you like hawks. Perhaps even ladies."

There certainly had been women watching the tennis matches the previous day. A twinge in Deven's shoulder made him wonder how bad a fool he had made of himself. "No doubt. But I know better than to rush into anything, particularly when I *am* serving the Queen. They say she's very jealous of those around her, and dislikes scandalous behaviour in her courtiers." The last thing he needed was to end up in the Tower because he got some maid of honor pregnant.

The best eye to catch, of course, was that of the Queen herself. But though Deven was ambitious, and her affection was a quick path to reward, he was not at all certain he wanted to compete with the likes of the young Earl of Essex. That would rapidly bring him into situations he could not survive.

"Marriage is no scandal," his father said. "Have a care for how you comport yourself, but do not stand too aloof. A match at court might be very beneficial indeed."

His father seemed likely to keep pressing the matter. Deven dodged it with a distraction. "If all goes as planned, my time will be very thoroughly employed elsewhere."

John Deven's face settled into graver lines. "You have spoken to Walsingham, then?"

"No. He was not at court. But I will do so at the first opportunity."

"Be wary of rushing into such things," his father said. Much of the relaxed atmosphere had gone out of the air. "He serves an honorable cause, but not always by honorable means."

Deven knew this very well; he had done some of that work in the Low Countries. Though not the most sordid parts of it, to be sure. "He is my most likely prospect for preferment, Father. But I'll keep my wits about me, I promise."

With that, his father had to be satisfied.

LONDON AND ISLINGTON: *September 18, 1588*

Leaving the Onyx Hall was not so simple as Lune might have hoped. In the labyrinthine politics of court, someone would find a way to read her departure as suspicious, should she go out too soon after Invidiana's sentencing of Cadogant. Vidar, if no one else.

So she wandered for a time through the reaches of the Onyx Hall, watching fae shy away from her company. It was an easy way to fill time; though the subterranean faerie palace was not so large as the city above, it was far larger than any surface building, with passages playing the role of streets, and complexes of chambers given over to different purposes.

In one open-columned hall she found Orpheus again, this time playing dance music; fae clapped as one of their number whirled around with a partner in a frenzied display. Lune placed herself along the wall and watched as a grinning lubberkin dragged a poor, stumbling human girl on, faster and faster. The mortal looked healthy enough, though exhausted; she was probably some maidservant lured down into the Onyx Hall for brief entertainment, and would be returned to the surface in the end, disoriented and drained. Those who had been there for a long time, like Orpheus, acquired a fey look this girl did not yet have.

Their attention was on the dance. Unobserved, Lune slipped across to the other side of the hall and out through another door.

She took a circuitous route, misleading to anyone who might see her passing by, but also necessary; one could not simply go straight to one's destination. The Onyx Hall connected to the world above in a variety of places, but those places did not match up; two entrances might lie half the city apart on the surface, but side-by-side down below. It was one of the reasons visitors feared the place. Once inside, they might never find their way out again.

But Lune knew her path. Soon enough she entered a small, deserted chamber, where the stone walls of the palace gave way to a descending lacework of roots.

Standing beneath their canopy, she took a deep breath and concentrated.

The rippling, night-sky sapphire of her gown steadied and became plainer blue broadcloth. The gems that decorated it vanished, and the neckline closed up, ending in a modest ruff, with a cap to cover her hair. More difficult was Lune's own body; she had to focus carefully, weathering her skin, turning her hair from silver to a dull blond, and her shining eyes to a cheerful blue. Fae who were good at this knew attention to detail was what mattered. Leave nothing unchanged, and add those few touches — a mole here, smallpox scars there — that would speak convincingly of ordinary humanity.

But building the illusion was not enough, on its own. Lune reached into the purse that hung from her girdle and brought forth the bread from her coffer.

The coarsely ground barley caught in her teeth; she was careful to swallow it all. As food, she disdained it, but it served its own purpose, and for that it was more precious than gold. When the last bit had been consumed, she reached up and stroked the nearest root.

With a quiet rustle, the tendrils closed around and lifted her up.

She emerged from the trunk of an alder tree that stood along St. Martin's Lane, no more than a stone's throw from the structures that had grown like burls from the great arch and surrounding walls of Aldersgate. The time, she was surprised to discover, was early morning. The Onyx Hall did not stand outside human time the way more distant realms did—that would make Invidiana's favorite games too difficult—but it was easy to lose track of the hour.

Straightening her cap, Lune stepped away from the tree. No one had noticed her coming out of the trunk. It was the final boundary of the Onyx Hall, the last edge of the enchantments that protected the subterranean palace lying unseen below mortal feet; just as the place itself remained undiscovered, so would people not be seen coming and going. But once away from its entrances, the protections ended.

As if to hammer the point home, the bells of St. Paul's Cathedral rang out the hour from within the tightly packed mass of London. Lune could not repress the tiniest flinch, even as she felt the sound wash over her harmlessly. She had done this countless times before, yet the first test of her own protections always made her nervous.

But she was safe. Fortified by mortal food against the power of mortal faith, she could walk among them, and never fear her true face would be revealed.

Settling into her illusion, Lune set out, walking briskly through the gate and out of London.

The morning was bright, with a crisp breeze that kept her

cool as she walked. The houses crowding the lane soon spaced themselves more generously, but there was traffic aplenty, an endless flow of food, travelers, and goods into and out of the city. London was a voracious thing, chewing up more than it spat back out, and in recent years it had begun to swallow the countryside. Lune marveled at the thronging masses who flooded the city until it overflowed, spilling out of its ancient walls and taking root in the formerly green fields that lay without. They lived like ants, building up great hills in which they lived by the hundreds and thousands, and then dying in the blink of an eye.

A mile or so farther out, it was a different matter. The clamor of London faded behind her; ahead, beyond the shooting fields, lay the neighboring village of Islington, with its manor houses and ancient, shading trees. And along the Great North Road, the friendly, welcoming structure of the Angel Inn.

The place was moderately busy, with travelers and servants alike crossing the courtyard that lay between the inn and the stables, but that made Lune's goal easier; with so many people about, no one took particular notice of one more. She passed by the front entrance and went toward the back, where the hillside was dominated by an enormous rosebush, a tangled, brambly mass even the bravest soul would be afraid to trim back.

This, too, had its own protections. No one was there to watch as Lune cupped a late-blooming rose in her hand and spoke her name into the petals.

Like the roots of the alder tree in London, the thorny branches rustled and moved, forming a braided archway starred with yellow blossoms. Inside the archway were steps, leading down through the earth, their wood worn smooth by countless passing feet. Charmed lights cast a warm glow over the interior. Lune began her descent, and the rosebush closed behind her.

The announcement of her name did not open the bush; it only told the inhabitants someone had come. But visitors were rarely kept waiting, outside or in. By the time Lune reached the bottom of the steps, someone was there.

"Welcome to the Angel, my lady," Gertrude Goodemeade said, a sunny smile on her round-cheeked face as she bobbed a curtsy. " 'Tis always a pleasure to see you here. Come in, please, please!"

No doubt the Goodemeade sisters gave the same friendly greeting to anyone who crossed their threshold—just as, no doubt, more courtiers came here than would admit it—and yet Lune did not doubt the words were sincere. It was in the sisters' nature. They came from the North originally—brownies were Border hobs, and Gertrude's voice retained traces of the accent—but they had served the Angel Inn since its construction, and supposedly another inn before that, and on back past what anyone could remember. Many hobs were insular folk, attached to a particular mortal family and unconcerned with anyone else, but these two understood giving hospitality to strangers.

The edges of the tension that had frozen Lune's back for days melted away in the warmth of the brownies' comfortable home.

Lune suffered Gertrude to lead her into the cozy little chamber and settle her onto a padded bench at one of the small tables. "We haven't seen you here in some time," Gertrude said. She was already bustling about, embroidered skirts swishing with her quick movements, fetching Lune a cup of mead without asking. It was, of course, exactly what Lune craved at that moment. The talents of brownies were homely things, but appreciated all the same.

One brownie, at any rate. Lune opened her mouth to ask where Gertrude's sister was, then paused at sounds on the staircase. A moment later her question was answered, for Rosamund entered, wearing a russet dress that was the twin of Gertrude's save for the embroidery on its apron — roses instead of daisies — just as her cheerful face mirrored that of her sister.

Behind her came others who were less cheerful. Lune recognized the haggard male hob immediately; the others were less familiar, having mostly pressed their faces into the floor of the Onyx Hall when she last saw them.

Gertrude made a sympathetic sound and hurried forward. For a short time the room seemed overfull, wall-to-wall with hobs and pucks and a slender, mournful-faced river nymph Lune had missed among them the first time. But no brownie would suffer there to be confusion or standing guests for long; soon enough a few of the strangers were ensconced at the tables with bread fresh out of the oven and sharp, crumbly cheese, while the more tired among them were bundled off through another door and put to bed.

Lune wrapped her fingers around her mead and felt uncomfortable. She had dismissed her illusion of mortality — she would have felt odd maintaining it inside, as if she had kept a traveling cloak on — but the bite of human bread she had eaten still made her proof against church bells, iron horseshoes, and other anti-faerie charms. How the refugees had gotten to the Angel from the Onyx Hall, she did not know, but she doubted it had been so easy. Rosamund must have been present at court, though. Lune chided herself for not studying the crowd more closely.

Gertrude had not forgotten her. Moments later, the smell of roasted coney filled the room, and Lune was served along with the others. The food was simple, prosaic, and good; one could easily imagine mortals eating the same thing, and it made the elaborate banquets of the court seem fussy and excessive.

*Perhaps,* Lune thought, *this is why I come here. For perspective.*

Would it be so bad, to leave the court? To find a simpler life, somewhere outside of London?

It would be easier, certainly. In the countryside, there was less need to protect oneself against mortal tricks. Peasant folk saw fae from time to time, and told stories of their encounters with black dogs or goblins, but no one made trouble of it. Or rarely, at least. They generally only tried to lay creatures who made too much a nuisance of themselves. And out there, one was well away from the intrigues of the Onyx Court.

Next to Lune on the bench, a tuft-headed sprite began to sniffle into his bread.

Wherever these rural fae had come from, it was not far enough to save them from Invidiana.

No, she could not leave London. To be subject to the tides of the court, but unable to affect them...

There was another choice, of course. Across the boundary of twilight, down the pleasant paths that led neither to Heaven nor Hell, and into the deeper reaches of Faerie, where Invidiana's authority and influence did not reach. But few mortals ever wandered so far, and for all the dangers they posed to fae, Lune would not leave them behind. Mortals were endlessly fascinating, with their brief, bright lives, and all the passion that fueled them.

Rosamund began to shepherd the others off, murmuring about baths and nice soft beds. Gertrude came by as the sprite vacated Lune's bench. "Now then, my lady—forgive me for that. Poor things, they were starved to the bone. Was it just a bite to eat you were looking for, and a breath of good country air?"

Her apple-cheeked face radiated such friendly helpfulness that Lune shook her head before she could stop herself. On the instant, Gertrude's cheerful demeanor transformed to concern. "Oh, dearie. Tell us about it."

Lune had not meant to share the story, but perhaps it was appropriate; she could hardly ask for aid without explaining at least some of why she needed it, and the Goodemeades were generally ignorant of politics. They might be the nearest fae who had *not* already heard.

"I am disgraced at court," she admitted.

She tried to speak as if it were of small moment. Indeed, sometimes it was; if everyone who angered Invidiana suffered Cadogant's fate, there would soon be no court left. But she stood upon the edge of a knife, and that was never a comfortable place to be.

Gertrude made a sympathetic face. "Queen's taken a set against you, has she?"

"With cause," Lune said. "You listen to the talk in the mortal inn, do you not?"

The brownie dimpled innocently. "From time to time."

"Then you know they fear invasion by Spain, and that a great Armada was only recently defeated."

"Oh, we heard! Great battles at sea, or some such."

Lune nodded, looking down at the remnants of her coney. "Great battles. But before them and after, great storms as well. Storms for which we paid too high a price." She had confessed the details only to Invidiana, and would not repeat them; that would only deepen the Queen's wrath. But she could tell Gertrude the shape of it. "I was Invidiana's ambassador to the folk of the sea, and did not bargain well enough. She is displeased with the concession I promised."

"Oh dear." Gertrude paused to assimilate this. "What was so dreadful, then? I cannot imagine she wants us to be invaded; surely it was worth the price."

37

Lune pushed her trencher away, painting a smile over her ever-present knot of worry. "Come, you do not want to talk of such things. This is a haven away from court and its nets—and long may it remain so."

"True enough," the brownie said complacently, patting her apron with plump but work-worn fingers. "Well, all's well that ends well; we don't have any nasty Spanish soldiers trampling through the Angel, and I'm sure you'll find your way back into her Majesty's good graces soon enough. You have a talent for such things, my lady."

The words returned Lune to her original purpose. "I hesitate to ask you this," she admitted, looking at the doorway through which the last of the refugees had vanished. "You have so many to take care of now—at least until they can be settled elsewhere. And I wonder Rosamund could even bring them here safely."

Her reluctance had exactly the desired effect. "Oh, is that all?" Gertrude exclaimed dismissively, springing to her feet. The next Lune knew, the brownie was pressing an entire heel of bread into her hands. It was not much different from what the Goodemeades had served, but any fae could tell one from the other at a touch. Mortality had a distinctive weight.

Looking down at the bread, Lune felt obscurely guilty. The maidservants of the Angel put out bread and milk faithfully; everyone knew that. And Invidiana taxed the Goodemeades accordingly, just as she taxed many country fae. Many more rural humans than city folk put out food for the fae, yet it was in the city that they needed it most. The Onyx Hall shut out the sounds of the bells and other such threats, but to venture into the streets unfed was an assurance of trouble.

She needed this. But so did the Goodemeades, with their guests to take care of.

"Go on, take it," Gertrude said in a soft voice, folding her hands around the bread. "I'm sure you'll find a good use for it."

Lune put her guilt aside. "Thank you. I will not forget your generosity."

MEMORY: *May–August 1588*

*I*n villages and towns all along the coast of England, piles of wood awaited the torch, and men awaited the first sight of the doom that was coming to devour them.

In the crowded harbor of Lisbon, the ships of the *Grande y Felicícisma Armada* awaited the order that would send them forth, for God and King Philip, to bring down the heretic queen.

In the waters that separated them, storms brewed, sending rain and heavy winds to lash the lands on both sides of the English Channel.

The Armada was a greater thing in story than it was in reality. The five hundred mighty ships that would bear an unstoppable army to England's shores, their holds crammed with implements of torture and thousands of Catholic wet nurses for the English babics who would be orphaned by the wholesale slaughter of their parents, were in truth a hundred and thirty ships of varying degrees of seaworthiness, crewed by the dregs of Lisbon, some of whom had never been to sea before, and commanded by a landsman given his posting only a few months gone. Disease and the depredations of the English scourge Sir Francis Drake had taken their toll on God's weapon against the heretics.

But the worst was yet to come.

In this, the quietest month of the year, when all the experienced seamen had assured the Duke of Medina-Sidonia that the waters would be calm and the winds fair for England, the storms did not subside; instead, they grew in strength. Gales drove the ships back when they tried to progress, and scattered the weaker, less seaworthy vessels. Fat-bottomed merchantmen, Mediterranean galleys unsuited to the blasts of the open sea, lumbering supply ships that slowed the pace of the entire fleet: the Great and Most Fortunate Armada was a sorry sight indeed.

Delays had slain what remained of May; June rotted away in the harbor of La Coruña, while sailors sickened and starved, their victuals fouled by the green wood of the barrels they were kept in. The commanders of the fleet found new terms by which to damn Drake, who had burned the seasoned barrel-staves the previous year.

In July they sailed again, obedient to God's mission.

Red crosses waved on white flags. The banner of Medina-Sidonia's ship carried the Virgin and a crucified Christ, and the motto *Exsurge, Domine, et judica causam tuam!* Monks prayed daily, and even sailors were forbidden to take the Lord's name in vain.

Yet none of it availed.

Beacon fires flared along the coast of England: the Spanish had been sighted. The wind favored the English, and so did the guns; the trim English ships refused boarding engagements, dancing around their ungainly enemy, battering away with their longer guns while staying out of Spanish range. Like dogs tearing at a chained bear, they harried the Spanish up the coast to Scotland, while the storms kept up their merciless assault.

Storms, always storms, every step of the way.

Storms struck them in the Orkneys, and again off the Irish coast, as the Armada fought to crawl home. From Lisbon into the Channel, around all the islands of England, Scotland, and Ireland—everywhere the fleet went, the wrath of sky and sea pursued.

Sick unto death with scurvy and typhus, maddened by starvation and thirst, the sailors screamed of faces in the water, voices in the sky. God was on their side, but the sea was not. Ever fickle, she had turned an implacable face to them, and all the prayers of the monks could not win her goodwill.

For a deal had been struck, in underwater palaces spoken of only in sailors' drunken tales. The sea answered to powers other than man's, and those powers—ever callous to human suffering—had been persuaded to act in favor of the English cause, against their usual disinterested neutrality.

So it was that the skies raged on command and alien figures slipped through the water, dancing effortlessly around the foundering vessels, luring men overboard and dragging them under, discarding many to wash up, bloated and rotting, on the Irish shore, but keeping a few for future amusement. It was difficult to say who had the more unfortunate fate: those who died, or those who lived.

In Spain, bells rang out in premature celebration, while his most Catholic Majesty awaited news of his most holy mission.

In England, the heretic queen rallied her people, while reports trickled in from Drake and the Lord Admiral, speaking of English heroism.

In the turbulent waters of the Atlantic, the remnants of the Armada, half their number lost, captured, or sunk, limped homeward, and took with them the hopes of a Spanish conquest of England.

THE ONYX HALL, LONDON: *September 18, 1588*

The mortal guise fell away from Lune like a discarded cloak the moment the alder tree grew shut around her, and she concealed the bread within the deep folds of her skirts. Those who wished to, would find out soon enough that she had it, and where she had obtained it, but she would hide it as best she could. Plenty of lesser courtiers would come begging for a crumb if they knew.

Some of them might smell it on her; certain fae had a nose for mortality. Lune hurried through the Onyx Hall to her chambers, and tucked the heel of bread into her coffer as the door closed behind her.

With it safely stowed, she rested her hands upon the inlaid surface of the table, tracing with one fingertip the outline of its design. A mortal man knelt at the foot of a tower; the artisan had chosen to show only the base of the structure, leaving to the imagination which faerie lady had caught his heart, and whether she returned his love.

It happened, sometimes. Not everyone played with mortals as toys. Some, like hobs, served them faithfully. Others gave inspiration to poets and musicians. A few loved them, with the deathless passion of a faerie heart, all the stronger for being given so rarely.

But mortals were not Lune's concern, except insofar as they might provide her with a route to Invidiana's favor.

She lowered herself onto the embroidered cushion of a stool. With deliberate, thoughtful motions, Lune began to remove the jeweled pins from her hair, and laid each one on the table to represent her thoughts.

The first she laid down glimmered with fragments of starlight, pushing the boundaries of what she, as a courtier in disgrace, might be permitted to adorn herself with. *A gift,* Lune thought. A rare faerie treasure, or a mortal pet, or information. Something Invidiana would value. It was the commonest path to favor, not just for fae but for humans as well. The difficulty was, with so many gifts being showered at the Queen's feet, few stood out enough to attract her attention.

A second pin. The knob at the end of this one held the indigo gems known as the sea's heart. Lune's fingers clenched around it; she had dressed for court in a rush, and had not attended to which pins she chose. Had Vidar seen it? She prayed not. Bad enough to have lost the Queen's goodwill by that disastrous bargain with the folk of the sea; worse yet to wear in her hair their gift to the ambassador of the Onyx Court.

Dame Halgresta certainly had not seen it; of that, Lune could be sure, because she was not bleeding, or dead.

She set it down on the table, forcing her thoughts back to their task. If not a gift, then what? A removal of an obstacle, perhaps. The downfall of an enemy. But who? The ambassador from the Courts of the North had quit the Onyx Hall in rage after the execution of the mortal Queen of Scots, accusing Invidiana of having engineered her death. There were enemies aplenty in that coalition of Seely and Unseely monarchs, the courts of Thistle and Heather and Gorse. To move against them, however, Lune would have to go there herself: a tedious journey, with no assets or allies waiting for her at the end.

As for other enemies, she was not fool enough to think she could take action against the Wild Hunt and live.

Lune sighed and pulled a third pin from her hair.

Silver locks spilled free as she did so, sending the remaining pins to the floor. Lune left them where they fell, fingering the snowflake finial of the one in her hand. Give the Queen something she wanted, or remove something that stood between her and what she wanted. What else was there?

Amusement. The Queen was a cold woman, heartless and cruel, but she could be entertained. Her favorite jests were those that accomplished some other goal at the same time. Even without that, though, to amuse the Queen...

It was a slim enough thread, but the last thing she could grasp for.

Lune held the snowflake pin, pressing her lips together in frustration. The outlines of her options were simple enough; the difficulty lay in moving from concept to action. Everything she thought of was weak, too weak to do her much good, and she was not positioned to do more. The trap of courtly life: those in favor were the best positioned to gain favor, while those who fell out of it were often caught in a spiral of worsening luck.

She would not accept it. Running her thumb over the sharp, polished points of the snowflake, Lune disciplined her mind. How could she better her position in the Onyx Court?

"Find Francis Merriman."

Lune was on her feet in an instant, the snowflake pin reversed and formed into a slender dagger in her hand. Her private chambers were charmed against intruders, a basic precaution in the Onyx Hall, and no one would break those protections unless they had come to do her harm.

No one, save the slender figure in the shadows.

Lune let out her breath slowly and relaxed her grip on the dagger, though she did not put it aside. "Tiresias."

He was often where he should not be, even where he *could* not be. Now he crouched in the corner, his slender arms wrapped around his knees, his pale, ethereal face floating in the darkness.

Lune avoided Invidiana's mortal pets for a varied host of reasons: Orpheus for fear of the effect his music might have on her; Eurydice for her ghost-haunted eyes; Achilles for the barely contained violence that only the Queen's will held in check. Tiresias was different. She did not fear the gift for which he was named. Sometimes Lune doubted even Invidiana could tell which visions were true, which mere constructs of his maddened brain.

No, it was the madness itself that gave her pause.

He was older than the other pets, they said, and had survived longer than any. Achilles died so often that one of the quickest routes to Invidiana's favor, if only briefly, was to find another mortal with a gift for battle fury and bring him to court; she was forever pitting the current bearer of that name against some foe or another, just for an evening's entertainment. They fought well, all of them, and sooner or later died bloodily.

They rarely survived long enough to suffer the effects of the Onyx Hall.

Tiresias survived, and paid the price.

He had flinched at her sudden movement, fear twisting his face. Now he looked up at her, searchingly. "Are you real?" he whispered.

He asked the question incessantly, no longer able to distinguish reality from his own delusions. It made for great sport among the crueler fae. Lune sighed and let the dagger revert to a pin, then laid it on the table. "Yes. Tiresias, you should not be here."

He shrank farther back into the shadows, as if he would meld into and through the wall. Perhaps he could, and that was how he arrived in such unexpected places. "Here? 'Tis nothing more than a shadow. We are not here. We are in Hell."

Lune moved away from the table, and saw his eyes linger on

the coffer behind her. A few bites of mortal bread could not lift the faerie stain from his soul; after untold years in the Onyx Hall, she doubted anything could. If he set foot outside, would he crumble to dust? But he hungered for mortality, sometimes, and she did not want him thinking of the bread she had. "Go back to your mistress. I have no patience for your fancies."

Tiresias rose, and for a moment Lune thought he might obey. He wandered in the wrong direction, though—neither toward the door, nor the coffer. The back of his sable doublet was torn, a thin banner of fabric fluttering behind him like a tiny ghost of a wing. Lune opened her mouth to order him away again, but stopped. He had said something, which she had overlooked in her fright.

Moving slowly, so as not to startle him, Lune approached Tiresias's back. He would always have been a slender man, even had he lived as a normal human, but life among the fae had made him insubstantial, wraithlike. She wondered how much longer he would last. Mortals could survive a hundred years and more among the fae—but not in the Onyx Hall. Not under Invidiana.

He was fingering the edge of a tapestry, peering at it as if he saw something other than the flooded shores of lost Lyonesse. Lune said, "You spoke a name, bade me find someone."

One pale finger traced a line of stitchery, moonlight shining down upon a submerged tower. "Someone erred, and thus it sank. Is that not what you believe? But no—the errors came after. Because they misunderstood."

"Lyonesse is ages gone," Lune replied, with tired patience. She might not have even been there, for all the attention he paid to her. "The name, Tiresias. Who was it you bade me find? Francis Merriman?"

He turned and fixed his sapphire gaze on her. The pupils of

his eyes were tiny, as if he stared into a bright light; then they expanded, until the blue all but vanished. "Who is he?"

The innocence of the question infuriated her, and in her distraction, she let him slip past. But he did not go far, halting in the center of the room, reaching for some imagined shape in the air before him. Lune let her breath out slowly. Francis Merriman: a mortal name. A courtier? A likely chance, given the political games Invidiana played. No one Lune knew of, but they came and went so quickly.

"Where can I find him?" she asked, trying to keep her voice gentle. "Where did you see him? In a dream?"

Tiresias shook his head violently, hands scrabbling through his black hair, disarranging it. "I do not dream. I do not dream. Please, do not ask me to dream."

Lune could imagine the nightmares Invidiana sent him for her own entertainment. "I will do nothing to you. But why should I seek him?"

"He knows." The words came out in a hoarse whisper. "What she did."

Her heart picked up its pace. Secrets—they were worth more than gold. Lune tried to think who Tiresias might mean. "She. One of the ladies? Or—" Her breath caught. "Invidiana?"

Bitter, mocking laughter greeted the suggestion. "No. Not Invidiana; that is not the point. Have you not been listening?"

Lune swallowed the desire to tell him she would start listening when he said something of comprehensible substance. Staring at the seer's tense face, she tried a different tack. "I will search for this Francis Merriman. But if I should find him, what then?"

Slowly, one muscle at a time, his body eased, until his hands hung limp at his sides. When he spoke at last, his voice was so clear she thought for a heartbeat that he was in one of his rare lucid periods—before she listened to his words. "Stand still, you ever-moving spheres of Heaven. . . ." A painful smile curved his lips. "Time has stopped. Frozen, cold, no heart's blood to quicken it to life once more. I told you, we are all in Hell."

Perhaps there had never been any substance in it to begin with. Lune might be chasing an illusion, pinning too much hope on the ramblings of a madman. Not everything he said came from a vision.

But it was the one possibility anyone had offered her, and the only one she was likely to receive. Her best hope otherwise was to bargain her bread for information that might be of aid. There were plenty of courtiers who would have use for it, playing their games in the world above.

When she made her bargains, she would ask after this Francis Merriman. But secretly, so she did not betray her hand to the Queen. Surprise might count for a great deal.

"You should go," she murmured, and the seer nodded absently, as if he had forgotten where he was, and why. He turned away, and when the door closed behind him, Lune returned to her table and collected the scattered pins that had fallen from her hair.

There were possibilities. She simply had to bring one to fruition.

And quickly, before the whirlpools of the court dragged her down.

RICHMOND PALACE, RICHMOND: *September 29, 1588*

". . . You shall be retained to no person nor persons of what degree or condition, by oath, livery, badge, promise, or otherwise, but only to her Grace, without her special license . . ."

Deven suppressed a grimace at those words. How strictly were they enforced? It might hamstring his plans for advancement at court, if the Queen were jealous with that license; he would be bound to her service only, without any other patron. Certainly some men served other masters, but how long had they petitioned to be allowed to do so?

Hunsdon was still talking. The oath for joining the Gentlemen Pensioners was abominably long, but at least he did not have to repeat every word of it after the band's captain; Deven only affirmed the different points that Hunsdon outlined. He recognized Elizabeth as the supreme head of the Church; he would not conceal matters prejudicial to her person; he would keep his required quota of three horses and two manservants, all equipped as necessary for war; he would report any fellow remiss in such matters to the captain; he would keep the articles of the band, obey its officers, keep secrets secret, muster with his servants when required, and not depart from court without leave. All enumerated in elaborately legalistic language, of course, so that it took twice as long to say as the content warranted.

Deven confirmed his dedication to each point, kneeling on the rush matting before Hunsdon. As ordered, he had dressed himself more finely, driving his Mincing Lane tailor to distraction with his insistence that the clothing be finished in time for today's Michaelmas ceremony. The doublet was taffeta of a changeable deep green, slashed with cloth-of-silver that blithely violated the sumptuary laws, but one visit to court had been enough to show Deven how few people attended to those restrictions. The aglets on his points were enameled, as was the belt that clasped his waist, and he was now a further fifty pounds in debt to a goldsmith on Cheapside. Listening to Hunsdon recite the last words, he prayed the expense would prove worthwhile.

"Rise, Master Deven," the baron said at last, "and be welcome to her Majesty's Gentleman Pensioners."

The Lord Chamberlain settled a gold chain about his shoulders when he stood, the ceremonial adornment for members of the band. Edward Fitzgerald, lieutenant of the Gentlemen Pensioners, handed him the gilded poleax he would bear while on duty, guarding the door from the presence chamber to the privy chamber, or escorting her Majesty to and from chapel in the morning. Deven was surprised by the heft of the thing. Ceremonial it might be, and elaborately decorated, but not decorative. The Gentlemen Pensioners were the elite bodyguard of the monarch, since Elizabeth's father Henry, eighth of that name, decided his dignity deserved better escort than it had previously possessed.

Of course, before Deven found himself using the gilded polearm, any attacker would have to win through the Yeomen of the Guard in the watching chamber, not to mention the rest of the soldiers and guardsmen stationed at any palace where the sovereign was in residence. Still, it was reassuring to know that he would have the means to defend the Queen's person, should it become necessary.

It meant that *he* was not purely decorative, either.

His companions toasted their newest member with wine, and a feast was set to follow. In theory, the entire band assembled at court for Michaelmas and three other holidays; in practice, somewhat less than the full fifty were present. Some were assigned to duties elsewhere, in more distant corners of England or even overseas; others, Deven suspected, were at liberty for the time being, and simply had not bothered to come. A man might be docked pay for failure to attend as ordered—that was in the articles he had sworn to obey—but a rich enough man hardly need worry being fined a few days' wages.

Despite the revelry, Deven's mind kept returning to the question of patronage. His eyes sought out Hunsdon, across the laughing, boisterous mass of men that filled the chamber where they dined. The officers of the band sat at a higher table — Hunsdon and Fitzgerald, plus three others who were the company's standard bearer, clerk of the check, and harbinger.

He could ask Hunsdon. But that would be tantamount to telling the baron that he intended to seek another master.

Surely, though, that would come as no surprise. Hunsdon knew who had secured Deven's position in the Gentlemen Pensioners.

Deven reached reflexively for his wine, grimaced, then grinned at himself. He did not know how he was going to handle his patronage, but one thing he *did* know: making any plans about such things while this drunk was not wise. Attempting to ask delicate questions of his captain would be even less wise. Therefore, the only course for a wise man to follow was to go on drinking, enjoy the night, and worry about such matters on the morrow.


RICHMOND PALACE, RICHMOND: *September 30, 1588*

Deven had been among military men; he should have expected what the morrow would bring. William Russell, who either possessed the constitution of an ox or had not drunk nearly as much as he appeared to the previous night, arrived in his chamber at an hour that would have been reasonable had Deven gone to bed before dawn, and rolled him forcibly out of bed. "On your feet, man; we can't keep the Queen waiting!"

"Nnnnnngh," Deven said, and tried to remember if there

was anything in the articles that forbade him to punch one of his fellows.

Between the two of them, Colsey and Ranwell, his new manservant, got him on his feet and stuffed him into his clothes. Deven thought muzzily that someone had arranged for a Michaelmas miracle; he didn't have a hangover. Round about the time he formed up with the others for the Queen's morning procession to chapel, he realized it was because he was still drunk. And, of course, Fitzgerald had assigned him to duty that day, so he was on display in the presence chamber when the inevitable hangover came calling. He clung grimly to his poleax, tried to keep it steady, and prayed he would not vomit in front of his fellow courtiers.

He survived, though not happily, and passed the test to which he had been put. Moreover, he had his reward; the Queen emerged from her privy chamber just as he was handing off his position to Edward Greville, and she gifted him with a nod. "God give you good day, Master Deven."

"And to you, your Majesty," he answered, bowing reflexively; the world lurched a little when he did, but he kept his feet, and then she was gone.

The Queen remembered his name. It shouldn't have pleased him so much, but of course it did, and that was why she did it; Elizabeth had a way of greeting a man that made him feel special for that instant in which her attention lighted upon him. Even his headache did not seem so bad in the aftermath.

It came back full force as he left, though. Handing off his poleax to Colsey, he suffered Ranwell to feed him some concoction the man swore would cure even the worst hangover; less than a minute later his stomach rebelled and he vomited it all back up. "Feed me that again," Deven told his new servant, "and you'll find yourself sent to fight in Ireland."

Colsey, who still did not appreciate having to share his master with an interloper, smirked.

Deven cleaned his mouth out and took a deep breath to fortify himself. He wanted little more than to collapse back into bed, but that would never do, so instead he addressed himself to the business at hand.

It made no sense to ask Hunsdon about the permissibility of acquiring another patron, if he did not have such a man already friendly to him. Deven hoped he did, but until that was confirmed, best not to broach the subject with Hunsdon at all.

Squaring his shoulders, Deven gritted his teeth and went in search, hangover and all.

But luck, which had preserved him through the morning's ordeal, was not on his side in this matter. The Principal Secretary, he learned, was ill and thus absent from court. His inquiries led him to another man, ink-stained and bearing a thick sheaf of papers, who was attending the meetings of the privy council in Walsingham's absence.

Deven made bold enough to snatch a moment of Robert Beale's time. After introducing himself and explaining his business, at least in broad outline, he asked, "When might the Principal Secretary return to court?"

Beale's lips pressed together, but not, Deven thought, in irritation or offense. "I could not say," the Secretary said. "He requires rest, of course, and her Majesty is most solicitous of his health. I would not expect him back soon—for some days at least, and possibly longer."

*Damnation, again.* Deven forced a smile onto his face. "I thank you for your time," he said, and got out of Beale's way.

He could hardly go asking favors of a man on his sickbed. He could send a letter—but no. Better not to press the matter.

As much as it galled him, he would have to wait, and hope the Principal Secretary recovered soon.

THE ONYX HALL, LONDON: *October 20, 1588*

Tens of thousands of mortals lived in London, and more in the towns and villages that surrounded it. In the entirety of England, Lune could not begin to guess how many there were.

Except to say there were too many, when she was trying to find a particular one.

She had to be discreet with her inquiries. If Tiresias was to be trusted—if he truly had a vision, or overheard something while lurking about—then this Francis Merriman knew something of use. It followed, then, that she did not want to share him with others. But so far discretion had availed her nothing; the mortal was not easily found.

When a spindly little spriteling came to summon her before Vidar, her first thought was that it had to do with her search. There was no reason to think that, but the alternatives were not much more appealing. Concealing these thoughts, Lune acknowledged the messenger with a nod. "Tell the Lord Keeper I will come when I may."

The messenger smiled, revealing sharp, goblinish teeth. "He demanded your immediate attendance."

Of course he did. "Then I will be pleased to come," Lune said, rising as she mouthed the politic lie.

In better times, she might have made him wait. Vidar's exalted status was a new thing, and Lune had until recently been a lady of Invidiana's privy chamber, one of the Queen's intimates—inasmuch as she was intimate with anyone. That freedom was gone now; if Vidar said to leap, then leap she must.

And of course he kept her dangling. Vidar's rise to Lord Keeper had made him a most desirable patron, rich in both wealth and enchantment, and now his outer chamber thronged with hopeful courtiers and rural fae begging some favor or another. He might have demanded her immediate attendance, but he granted audience to a twisted bogle, two Devonshire pisgies, and a travel-stained faun in Italian dress before summoning Lune into the inner chamber.

He lounged in a chair at the far end of the room, and did not rise when she came in. Some fae held to older fashions of clothing, but he closely followed current styles; the crystals and jet embroidered onto his doublet winked in the light, an obvious mimicry of Invidiana's clothing. Rumor had it the black leather of his tall, close-fitting boots was the skin of some unfortunate fae he had captured, tortured, and executed on the Queen's behalf, but Lune knew the rumors came from Vidar himself. It was ordinary doeskin, nothing more. But the desire for that belief was telling enough.

She gave him the curtsy rank demanded, and not a hair more. "Lord Ifarren."

"Lady Lune." Vidar twiddled a crystal goblet in his bony fingers. "How good of you to come."

She waited, but he did not offer her a seat.

After a leisurely study of her, Vidar set aside the goblet and rose. "We have known one another for a long time, have we not, my lady? And we have worked together in days past—to mutual benefit, as I weigh it. It pains me to see you thus fallen."

As a stag in season was pained to see a rival fall to a hunter's arrow. Lune cast her gaze modestly downward and said, " 'Tis kind of you to say it, my lord."

"Oh, I have a mind to offer you more kindness than just a sympathetic word."

She instantly went on guard. Lune could think of nothing Vidar might gain by offering her true help, but that did not mean he *would* not. As cut off as she had been from the inner circles of court gossip, he might have some gambit in play she did not see. But what would she have to offer him?

No way to find out, save to walk farther into his trap. "I would be most glad to hear anything your lordship might extend to me."

Vidar snapped his fingers, and a pair of minor goblins hurried to his side. At his gesture, they began unlacing the points of his sleeves, drawing them off to reveal the black silk of his shirt underneath. Ignoring them, Vidar asked, "You once lived for an extended period of time among mortals, yes?"

"Indeed, my lord." He raised one needle-thin eyebrow, and she elaborated. "I was a waiting-gentlewoman to Lady Hereford—as Lettice Knollys was known, then. Her Majesty bid me thence to keep a daily eye upon the mortal court, and report to her its doings."

The skeletal fae shuddered, a twitchy, insectlike motion. "Quite a sacrifice to make on the Queen's behalf. To live, day and night, under a mask of mortality, cut off from all the glory of our own court…Ash and Thorn. I would not do it again."

It might be the first sincere statement he had made since Lune entered. Vidar's own mortal masquerade, the one that had earned him his new position, had been more sporadic than sustained, and he had not enjoyed it. She said temperately, "I was pleased to serve her Majesty in such a capacity."

"Of course you were." He let the cynical note hang in the air, then offered, "Wine?"

Lune nodded, and took the cup a goblin brought to her. The wine was a fine red, tasting of the smoky, fading light of autumn, the flamboyant splendor of the leaves and their dry rustle underfoot, the growing bite of winter's chill. She recognized it from the first sip: surely one of the last remaining bottles brought as a gift to Invidiana when Madame Malline le Sainfoin de Veilée replaced the old ambassador from France. Some years hence, that had been. Madame Malline had remained at the Onyx Court when the ambassador from the Courts of the North departed, but relations were strained. There would be no more such gifts, not for a long time.

"You might," Vidar said, breaking her reverie, "have a chance to serve her Majesty again."

She failed to hide entirely the sharp edge that put on her interest. "Say on."

"Return to the mortal court."

The blunt suggestion made her breath catch. To live among mortals again...it was exhausting, dangerous, and exhilarating. Few fae had the knack for it, or even a liking. No wonder Vidar had sent for her.

But what purpose did he have in mind? Surely not her former assignment, Lettice Knollys. If the fragments of gossip Lune had heard were correct, she was no longer at court; she was in mourning for the death of her second husband, the Earl of Leicester.

She took another sip of wine. This one burned more than the first. "Return, my lord? To what end?"

"Why, to gather information, as you did before." Vidar paused. "And, perhaps, to gain access to—even leverage over—a certain individual."

She had concerned herself too much of late with fae politics: the bargain with the folk of the sea, the raids of alfar ships, the never-ending tensions with the Courts of the North. Lune cursed herself for not keeping a closer eye on the doings of mortals: she did not know who was prominent now, whom she might be dispatched to trouble. She might not even recognize the name Vidar gave. "And who might that be, my lord?"

"Sir Francis Walsingham."

Cut crystal dug into her fingers.

Lune said carefully, "I believe I recognize that name."

"You should. He has lasted quite a long time, for a mortal, and risen high. Principal Secretary to Queen Elizabeth, he is now." Vidar gestured, and a goblin brought him his wine cup again. "Have you ever met him?"

"He did not come to court until after I had ceased my masquerade." Though she knew who he was, enough to be afraid.

"You will find him easily enough. The mortal court is at Richmond now, but they will shift to Hampton Court before long. You can join them there."

Lune handed off her goblet to a servant. The wine tasted too much of regret, and impending loss. "My lord, I have not yet said I would undertake this task."

A thin, predatory smile spread across Vidar's face. In a purring voice, he said, "I do not think you have a choice, Lady Lune."

As she had feared. But which was the greater risk: refusal or acceptance? Whatever honey Vidar used to coat it, she was not being offered this assignment out of a desire to see her redeem her past mistakes. Walsingham was not merely Principal Secretary; he was one of the foremost spymasters of Elizabeth's court. And his Protestantism was of a puritan sort, that assumed all fae to be devils in disguise. Any attempt to approach him, much less keep watch over him, might result in him catching her out, and if he caught her out...

Only mortal food given in tithe to the fae protected glamours and other magics. A short period of imprisonment could have disastrous results.

Food. Lune said, "Such masquerades are costly, Lord Ifarren. To maintain a plausible presence at court, one must be there every day. Mortal bread—"

"You will have it," Vidar said dismissively. "A spriteling will bring it to you each morning—or evening, if you prefer."

He had capitulated far too easily. "No. Such a plan leaves no margin of safety. Were I to be bidden to some duty elsewhere and missed the messenger, we would risk exposure. A whole loaf at a time, or more than one." A whole loaf, eaten only when needed, could cover quite a long journey in mortal disguise. Long enough, perhaps, to reach safety in another land.

If worse should truly come to worst.

Vidar's cynical eye seemed to see her thoughts. "You overestimate her Majesty's trust in you. But a week could be arranged. On Fridays, perhaps. Mortals assume we favor that day; we might as well oblige their fancies. And then you need not fear their holy day. I take it by this hard bargaining that you have agreed?"

Had she? Lune met Vidar's gaze, searching the flat blackness of his eyes for some hint of—something. Anything. Any crumb of information that might guide her.

She could not even be certain these orders came from Invidiana. Vidar might have concocted them, as a means of removing her permanently.

No. Even he would not endanger the Onyx Court in such fashion, to risk her true nature being revealed.

...Or would he? His desires were no secret in the higher circles of court. Even Invidiana knew her councillor coveted her throne. Where the Wild Hunt would destroy the Queen and tear the Onyx Hall down stone by stone, scattering her court to the four winds, Ifarren Vidar was more subtle; he would leave all as it was, but claim the Crown for himself. If he could but find a way.

Was this it? Was Lune to become a pawn in some hidden scheme of his?

If so — if she could discover the pattern of it, and inform Invidiana —

There was more than one route to favor.

Lune spread her skirts, and gave him no more humble a curtsy than she had before. Humility would be more suspicious to him than pride. "I am most grateful for the chance to be of service to her Majesty."

"Of course." Vidar eyed her with satisfaction. "Would it please you to be seated, Lady Lune? I have prepared a description of the role you are to take —"

"Lord Ifarren." She took pleasure in interrupting him. "My task is to be as you said? To gather information, and gain access to Sir Francis Walsingham?"

"And leverage, of whatever sort may offer itself."

Nothing would *offer* itself, but she might create something. But that was neither here nor there. "Then I will create my own role, as her Majesty trusted me to do in the past."

Displeasure marred the line of his mouth. "Her Majesty likewise trusted you to bargain sharply against the sea people."

Lune damned the day she had ever been sent beneath the waves. Vidar had not been there, with the task of convincing the inhabitants of an alien land that the doings of mortal nations were their concern. Fae they might be, but unlike their landbound brethren, the mermaids and roanes and other denizens of the sea had not adopted current customs of courtly rule. And their idea of interaction with humans involved shipwrecks and the occasional lover, not politics. She had been lucky to find *anything* they wanted.

But to say so would sound peevish and weak. Instead she said, "You disdain mortal life, Lord Ifarren. Would you ride a horse raised by one who detested animals?"

"I know Walsingham," Vidar said.

"And I will most humbly hear your advice where he is concerned. But you asked for me because there is none in the Onyx Court more talented at this art than I. When I approach the mortal court, I will do so on my own terms."

The challenge hung in the air between them. Then Vidar waved one hand, as if it did not matter. "So be it. I will inform you of the court's movements. And *you* will inform *me* of your chosen role, before you go to join them."

"I will need some bread before then."

"Why?"

Now he was the one sounding peevish. Lune said calmly, "To familiarize myself with the situation, my lord. I have not been among that court in many years."

"Oh, very well. Now get out of my sight; I have other things to attend to."

Lune made her curtsy and withdrew. If Vidar had meant to position her where she would fail, she had at least escaped one trap. And with the allotment she would be given, she could afford to trade her own bread to other fae for information.

Once upon a time, she had clawed her way up from insignificance to favored status, by shrewd trading and well-timed service. If she had done it once, she could—and would—do so again.

HAMPTON COURT PALACE, RICHMOND: *October 14, 1588*

Deven rode into the spacious Base Court of the palace and dismounted almost before his bay gelding came to a halt. The

61

October air had picked up a distinct chill since sunset, nipping at his cheeks, and his fingers were cold inside his gloves. There was a storm building, following in the aftermath of the day's gentle autumn warmth. He tossed his reins to a servant and, chafing his hands together, headed for the archway that led deeper into the palace.

Stairs on his left inside the arch led upward to the old-style Great Hall. No longer the central gathering place of the monarch and nobles, at Hampton Court the archaic space was more given over to servants of the household, except on occasions that called for great pageantry. Deven passed through without pausing and headed for the chambers beyond, where he could find someone that might know the answer to his question.

The Queen was not using that set of rooms as her personal quarters, having removed to a different part of the sprawling palace, but despite the late hour, a number of minor courtiers were still congregated in what was sometimes used as the Queen's watching chamber. From them, he learned that Elizabeth was having a wakeful night, as she often did since the recent death of her favorite, the Earl of Leicester. To distract herself, she had gone to a set of rooms on the southern side of the Fountain Court to listen to one of her ladies play the virginals.

The door was guarded, of course, and Deven was not in that elite rank of courtiers who could intrude on the Queen uninvited. He bowed to his two fellows from the Gentlemen Pensioners, then turned to the weary-eyed usher who was trying unsuccessfully to stifle a yawn.

"My most sincere apologies for disturbing her Majesty, but I have been sent hither to bring her a message of some importance." Deven brought the sealed parchment out and passed it over with another bow. "It was Sir James Croft's most express wish that it be given to her Grace as soon as may be."

The usher took it with a sigh. "What does the message concern?"

Deven bit back the acid response that was his first reflex, and said with ill-concealed irritation, "I do not know. 'Tis sealed, and I did not inquire."

"Very well. Did Sir James wish a reply?"

"He did not say."

"Wait here, then." The usher opened the door and slipped inside. A desultory phrase from the virginals floated out, and a feminine laugh. Not the Queen's.

When the usher reemerged, he had something in his hand. "No response to Sir James," he said, "but her Majesty bids you carry these back to the Paradise Chamber." He held out a pair of ivory flutes.

Deven took them hesitantly, trying to think of a way around embarrassing himself. He failed; the usher gave him a pitying smile and asked, "Do you know the way?"

"I do not," he was forced to confess. Hampton Court had grown by stages; now it was a sprawling accretion of courtyards and galleries, surpassed in England only by Whitehall itself, which his fellows reassured him was even more confusing to explore.

"The quickest path would be through these chambers to the Long Gallery," the usher said. "But as they are in use, go back to the Great Hall..."

It wasn't as bad as he feared. A pair of galleries ran north to south through the back part of the palace, connecting to the Long Gallery of the south side, with the chambers where Elizabeth had chosen to reside for this visit. At the most southeasterly corner of the palace, and the far end of the Long Gallery, lay the Paradise Chamber.

Deven unlocked the door and nearly dropped the flutes. The candle he bore threw back a thousand glittering points of light; raising it, he saw that the dark chamber beyond was crammed to the walls with riches beyond words. Countless gems and trifles of gold or silver; tapestries sumptuously embroidered in colored silks; pearl-studded cushions; and, dominating one wall, an unused throne beneath a canopy of estate. The royal arms of England decorated the canopy, encircled by the Garter, and the diamond that hung from the end of the Garter could have set Deven up in style for the rest of his life.

He realized he had stopped breathing, and made himself start again. No, not the rest of his life. Ten years, maybe. And ten years' fortune would not do him much good if he were executed for stealing it.

The entire contents of the room, though...

No wonder they called it Paradise.

He set the flutes on a table inlaid with mother-of-pearl and backed out again, locking the door on the blinding wealth within, before it could tempt him more. *They would hardly miss one small piece, in all that clutter....*

Perhaps it was his own guilty thoughts that made him so edgy. When Deven heard a sound, he whirled like an animal brought to bay, and saw someone standing not far from him.

After a moment, he relaxed a trifle. Rain had begun to deluge the world outside, obscuring the moon, and so the Long Gallery was lit only by his one candle, not enough to show him the figure clearly, but the silhouette lacked the robe or puffed clothing that would mark an old courtier or a young one. Nor, he reminded himself, did he have anything to feel guilty about; he had done nothing more than what he was ordered to, and no one, servant or otherwise, could hear the covetous thoughts in Deven's mind.

But that recalled him to his duty. Though the Queen was not present, surely he also had a duty to defend that which was hers. "Stand fast," he said, raising the candle, "and identify yourself."

The stranger bolted.

Deven gave chase without thinking. The candle snuffed out before he had gone two strides; he abandoned it, letting taper and holder fall so he could lunge for the door through which the stranger had vanished. It stood just a short distance from the Paradise Chamber, and when he flung himself through it, he found himself on a staircase, with footsteps echoing above him.

The stranger was gone by the time he reached the third floor, but the steps continued upward in a secondary staircase, cramped and ending in a half-height door that was obviously used for maintenance. Deven yanked the door open and wedged himself through, into the cold, drenching rain.

He was on the roof. To his right, low crenellations guarded the drop-off to the lower Paradise Chamber. He looked left, across the pitched sheets of lead, and just made out the figure of the stranger, running along the roof.

Madness, to give chase on a rooftop, with his footing made uncertain by rain-slicked lead. But Deven had only an instant to decide his course of action, and his blood was up.

He pursued.

The rooftop was an alien land, all steep angles and crenellated edges, with turrets rising here and there like masts without sails. The path the stranger took was straight and level, though, unbroken by chambers, and that was what oriented Deven in his fragmentary map of Hampton Court: they were running along the roof of the Long Gallery, back the direction he had come.

In his head, he heard the usher say, *The quickest path would be through these chambers…*

The gallery led straight toward the room where Elizabeth sat with her ladies, whiling away her sleeplessness with music.

Deven redoubled his efforts, flinging caution to the wind, keeping to his feet mostly because his momentum carried him forward before he could fall. He was gaining on the stranger, not yet close enough to grab him, but nearly—

Lightning split the sky, half-blinding him, and as thunder followed hard on its heels Deven tried too late to stop.

Brick cracked him across the knees, halting his stride instantaneously. But his weight carried him forward, and he pitched over the top of the crenellations, hands flying out in desperation, until his left fingers seized on something and brought him around in a shoulder-wrenching arc. His right hand found brick just in time to keep him from losing his grip and falling a full story to the lower rooftop below.

He hung from the crenellations, gasping for air, with the rain sending rivers of water through his hair and clothes to puddle in his boots.

His left shoulder and hand ached from the force of stopping his fall, but Deven dragged himself upward, grunting with effort, until at last he could hook one foot over the bricks and get his body past the edge. Then he collapsed in the narrow wedge where the pitch of the roof met the low wall of the crenellations and let himself realize he wasn't about to fall to his death.

*The stranger.*

Deven twisted to look over the wall, onto the roof of the chambers where Elizabeth listened to the virginals. He saw no sign of the intruder anywhere on the rain-streaked lead, and no hatches hung open in the turrets that studded the corners of the extension; through the grumble of the storm, he heard a faint strain of music. But that meant nothing save that no one had been hurt yet.

Even if Deven could have made the jump down, he could not burst in on the Queen, soaked to the bone and with his doublet torn, its stuffing leaking out like white cotton entrails. He hauled himself to his feet, wincing as his bruised knees flared, and began his limping progress back along the Long Gallery, to the door that had led him up there to begin with.

His news, predictably, caused a terrible uproar, and soon a great many people were roused out of bed, but the intruder had vanished without a trace. Some time later, no longer dripping but still considerably damp, Deven found himself having to relate the story to Lord Hunsdon, from his arrival at Hampton Court that night up to the present moment.

"You saw nothing of his face?" Hunsdon asked, fingers tapping a worried beat on the desk before him.

Deven was forced to shake his head. "He wore a cap low on his head, and we stood some ways apart, with only one candle for light. He seemed a smallish fellow, and dressed more like a laborer than a gentleman, but beyond that I cannot say."

"Where do you think he went, after you lost him?"

The chambers there connected at their corner to the courtiers' lodgings that ringed the Base Court; from there, the man might have run nearly anywhere, though the soaring height of the Great Hall would have forced him to circumnavigate the courtyard if he wished to go somewhere else. There was no good access to the ground; everything was at least two stories. With rope, he might have gone through a second-floor window, but they found no such rope, nor sign of a very wet man coming in anywhere.

The last Deven had seen of the man was when they reached the end of the gallery, and the stranger...leapt over the edge.

No, not quite. The man had leapt, yes, but upward, into the air—not as a man would jump if he intended a landing on a pitched roof below.

After that, his memory only offered him the flapping of wings.

He shook his head again, shivering in his damp, uncomfortable clothes. "I do not know, my lord. Out into the gardens, perhaps, and from thence into the Thames. Or perhaps there was a boat waiting for him." How he would have gotten from a second- or third-floor roof to the gardens, Deven could not say, but he had no better explanation to offer.

Nor, it seemed, did Hunsdon. The baron's mouth was set in a grim line. "It seems the Queen is safe for now. But we shall stay alert for future trouble. If you see the fellow again..."

Deven nodded. "I understand, my lord." He might walk past the man in the street and not know him. But Deven believed now, as he had not truly before, that the Queen's enemies might stage threats against her life. His duty was more than simply to stand at her door with a gold-covered ax.

He prayed such a threat would not come again. But if it did, then next time, he would be more effective in stopping it.

MEMORY: *July 12, 1574*

The sleeping man lay in an untidy sprawl on his bed. The covers, kicked aside some time earlier, disclosed an aging body, a sagging belly usually hidden by the peasecod front of his doublets, and his dark hair was thinning. He was still fit enough—not half so far gone as some other courtiers—but the years were beginning to tell on him.

In his mind, though, in his dreams, he was still the young man he had been a decade or two before.

Which suited very well the purposes of the being that came to visit him that night.

How it slipped in, no observer could have said. Under the edge of the door, perhaps, or out of the very stuff of shadows. It showed first as a stirring in the air, that coalesced into an indistinct shape, which drifted gently through the chamber until it reached the bed.

Hovering over the sleeping man, the figure took more distinct shape and color. A fluttering linen chemise, freed from the constraints of bodice and kirtle and the usual court finery. Auburn hair, flowing loose, its tips not quite brushing the man below. A high forehead, and carmined lips that parted in an inviting smile.

The man sighed and relaxed deeper into his dream.

Robert Dudley was hunting, riding at a swift canter through open fields, pursuing hounds that gave the belling cry of prey sighted. At his side rode a woman, a red-haired woman. He thought, faintly, that she had been someone else a moment ago—surely it was so—but now she was younger, her hair a darker shade of red.

And they were not riding, they were walking, and the hounds had vanished. A pleasant stream laughed to itself, hidden somewhere in the reeds to one side. The sunlight was warm, casting green-gold light down through the trees; up ahead the landscape opened into a grassy meadow, with something in it. A structure. A bower.

Curtains fluttered invitingly around the bed that stood within.

Clothing vanished at a thought, leaving skin upon skin, and together they tumbled into bed. Auburn hair cascaded around him, a second curtain, and Robert Dudley gazed adoringly into the face of Lettice Knollys, all logic and reason crumbling before the onslaught of passion that overwhelmed him.

Easy enough, to fan the flames of an early flirtation into a conflagration. He would not remember this upon waking, not as anything more than an indistinct dream, but it would serve its purpose nonetheless. And if Lettice Knollys were in truth Lettice Devereux, Lady Hereford, and wed elsewhere, it did not matter. Dudley did not have to marry her. He had only to give his heart, turning it from the target at which it had ever been fixed: his beloved Queen Elizabeth.

Robert Dudley, Earl of Leicester, moaned deep in his throat as he writhed on the bed, aware of nothing but the dream that suffused his mind. Above him hovered the ghostly form of Lettice Knollys, perfect as she had never been, even in the blossom of her youth.

The scholars of Europe spoke of demons they called succubi. But more than one kind of creature in the world wielded such power, and not all served the devil.

Some served a faerie Queen, and did her bidding with pleasure, dividing from the mortal Queen her most loyal and steadfast admirer.

A man might die of such surfeit. The ghostly figure lost its definition, fading once more into indistinct mist, and with an unfulfilled sigh the Earl of Leicester subsided into dreamless sleep.

There would be other nights. The creature that visited him considered itself an artist. It would work upon him by slow degrees, building his desire until he thought of no one else. And when his heart turned away from the mortal Queen, and the creature's work here was done. . . .

There would be other mortals. Invidiana always had use for this creature's talents.

WHITEHALL PALACE, WESTMINSTER: *November 3, 1588*

Deven stood in front of the polished mirror and ran one hand over his jaw, checking for stubble. Colsey had shaved him that morning, and his hair was newly trimmed into one of the more subdued styles currently fashionable; he wore a rose-red doublet with a falling collar, collected from the tailor only yesterday when the court completed its move into Whitehall, and even his low shoes were laced with silk ribbons. He looked better than he had when he was first presented to the Queen, but felt very nearly as inadequate.

From behind him, Colsey said, "Best you get moving, master."

The reminder was appreciated, though a little presumptuous—Colsey occasionally forgot he was not Deven's father, to order him about. It made Deven take a deep breath and turn away from his blurred reflection in the mirror, setting himself toward the door like a man at the tilt.

Tilting. He had thought about entering the upcoming Accession Day jousts, but knew it would be a waste of his time and coin; certainly one could catch the Queen's eye by performing well, but he was at best indifferent with the lance. He would have to content himself with the usual pageantry of the Gentlemen Pensioners, who would make a brave show around Elizabeth during the celebrations.

He had a hard time focusing on pageantry, though, when his feet were leading him toward a real chance for success at court.

He fingered the tabs at the bottom of his new doublet and

wondered if it looked too frivolous. A useless thought—he had not the time to go change—but he was second-guessing himself at every turn today.

Deven gritted his teeth and tried to banish his nerves.

Several men were in the chamber when he arrived, and a number more came and went. Such was the inevitable consequence of absence from court, even with someone like Beale to cover one's duties. But Deven was expected, and so he waited very little before being ushered into the chamber beyond, where the Principal Secretary sat behind a small mountain of paper.

Deven advanced halfway across the floor and then knelt on the matting. "Master Secretary."

Sir Francis Walsingham looked tired in the thin November sunlight that filtered through the palace's narrow windows. They had not been lying, when they said he was ill; the marks of it showed clearly. Deven had met him twice before—the rest of their dealings had been through intermediaries—and so he had sufficient basis for comparison. Walsingham was dark complected for an Englishman, but his skin had a pale, unhealthy cast to it, and there were circles under his eyes.

"I am glad," Deven said, "that God has seen fit to restore you to health."

Walsingham gestured for him to rise. "My illness was unfortunate, but 'tis past. Beale tells me you have some matter you would beg of me."

"Indeed." He had expected more small talk beforehand, but given the pile of work facing Walsingham, perhaps he should not be surprised the man wished to cut directly to what was relevant. That encouraged Deven to speak plainly, as he preferred, rather than larding his words with decoration, which seemed to be a substantial art form at court.

He clasped his hands behind his back and began. "I wished

to thank you in person for your good office in securing for me the position I now hold in the Gentlemen Pensioners."

" 'Tis no great matter," Walsingham said. "You did me good service among the Protestants in the Low Countries, and your father has much aided her Majesty in the suppression of seditious pamphlets."

"I am glad to have been of service," Deven answered. "But I hope my use might not end there."

The dark eyes betrayed nothing more than mild curiosity. "Say on."

"Master Secretary, the work I did on your behalf while on the continent made it clear to me that the defense of her Majesty—the defense of England—depends on many types of action. Some, like armies and navies, are public. Others are not. And you are clearly a general in the secret sort of war."

The Principal Secretary's lips twitched behind their concealing beard. "You speak of it in poetic terms. There is little of poetry in it, I fear."

"I do not seek poetry," Deven said. "Only a chance to make my mark in the world. I have no interest in following my father in the Stationers' Company, nor does Gray's Inn hold me. To be utterly frank, my desire is to be of use to men such as yourself, who have the power and the influence to see me rewarded. My father earned the rank of gentleman; I hope to earn more."

And that, he hoped, would strike a sympathetic chord. Walsingham had been born to a family with far greater connections than Deven's own, but he had earned his knighthood and his position on the privy council. Whether Deven could strike a target so high, he doubted—but he would aim as high as he could.

Or perhaps his words would turn, like a knife in his hands, and cut him. Walsingham said, "So you serve, not out of love for England and her Queen, but out of ambition."

Deven quelled the urge to flinch and salvaged what he could. "The two are not in conflict with one another, sir."

"For some, they are."

"I am no dissident Catholic, Master Secretary, nor a traitor tied to the purse strings of a foreign power, but a good and true-hearted Englishman."

Walsingham studied him, as if weighing his every virtue and vice, weakness and use, with his eyes alone. He was, in his way, as hard to face as Elizabeth.

Under the sharp edge of that gaze, Deven felt compelled to speak on, to lay on the table one of the few cards he possessed that might persuade the Principal Secretary and undo the damage of his own previous words. "Have you heard of the incident at Hampton Court?" Walsingham nodded. Of course he had. "Then you know 'twas I who came across the intruder."

"And pursued him over the rooftops."

"Even so." Deven's fingers had locked tight around each other, behind his back. "You have no reason to believe me, Master Secretary—but ambition was the farthest thing from my mind that night. I pursued that man without concern for my own safety. I do not tell you this out of pride; I wish you to understand that, when I had only an instant to think, I thought of the Queen's safety. And when the man was gone—vanished into the night—I blamed myself for my failure to catch him.

"I have no wish to run across rooftops again. But you, Master Secretary, are dedicated to making such things unnecessary, by removing threats before they can approach so near to her Grace. That is a task to which I will gladly commit myself. I had rather be of more use to the Queen and her safety than simply standing at her door with a gold ax in my hands."

He hadn't meant to speak for so long, but Walsingham had let him babble without interruption. A shrewd move; the more

Deven spoke, the less planned his words became, and the more inclined he was to speak from the heart. He just hoped his heart sounded more like a fervent patriot than a callow, idealistic boy.

Into the silence that followed his conclusion, the Principal Secretary said, "Then you would do what? Fight Catholics? Convert their faithful? Spy?"

"I am sworn to her Majesty's service here at court," Deven said. "But surely you have need of men here, not to find the information, but to piece together what it means." He offered up an apologetic smile. "I—I have always liked puzzles."

"Have you." The door creaked behind Deven; Walsingham waved away whoever it was, and then they were alone again. "So the short of it is, you would like to solve puzzles in my service."

And to benefit thereby—but Deven was not fool enough to say that again, even if they both heard those words still hanging in the air. He hesitated, then said, "I would like the chance to prove my worth in such matters to you."

It was the right answer, or at least a good one. Walsingham said, "Inform Beale of your wishes. You shall have your chance, Michael Deven; see you do not squander it."

He was kneeling again almost before the words were finished. "I thank you, Master Secretary. You will not regret this."

# Act Two

There is no treasure that doeth so vniuersallie profit, as doeth a good Prince, nor anie mischeef so vniuersallie hurt, as an yll Prince.
— Baldesur Castiglione
The Courtyer

*The chamber is a small one, and unfurnished; whatever lay here once, no one claims it now. There are rooms such as these in the Onyx Hall, forgotten corners, left vacant when their owners died or fled or fell from favor.*

*For him, they feel like home: they are neglected, just as he is.*

*He came in by the door, but now he cannot find it again. Instead he wanders to and fro, from one wall to another, feeling the stone blindly, as if the black marble will tell him which way to go, to be free.*

*One hand touches the wall and flinches back. He peers at the surface, leaning this way and that, as a man might study himself in a mirror. He stares for a long moment, then blanches and turns away. "No. I will not look."*

*But he* will *look; there is no escape from his own thoughts. The far wall now draws his eye. He crosses to it, hesitant in his steps, and reaches out until his fingers brush the stone, tracing the image he sees.*

*A face, like and unlike his own. A second figure, like and unlike her. He spins about, but she is not there with him. Only her likeness. Only in his mind.*

*Against his will, he turns back, wanting and not wanting to see.*

*Then he is tearing at the stone, pulling at the mirror he imagines until it comes crashing down, but that brings him no respite. All about him he sees mirrors, covering every wall, standing free on the floor, each one showing a different reflection.*

*A world in which he is happy. A world in which he is dead. A world in which he never came among the fae, never renounced his mortal life to dwell with immortal beings.*

*A world in which…*

*He screams and lashes out. Blood flowers from his fist; the silvered glass is imaginary, but it hurts him just the same. Beyond that one lies another, and soon he is lurching across the room, breaking the mirrors, casting them down, pounding at them until they fall in crimson fragments to the floor. His hands strike stone, again and again, lacerating his flesh, cracking his delicate bones.*

*Until he no longer has the will to fight, and sinks into a crouch in the center of the chamber, mangled fingers buried deep in his hair.*

*All around him, the pieces of his mind reflect a thousand broken other lives.*

*He could see much, if he looked into them. But he no longer has the will for that, either.*

*"There are no other lives," he whispers, trying to make himself believe it, against all the evidence of his eyes. "What is over and done cannot be redone. 'Tis writ in stone, and will not fade."*

*His bleeding hands drift downward and begin to write strange, illegible hieroglyphs upon the floor. He must record it. The truth of how it went. Else those who come after will be lost in the maze of mirrors and reflections, never knowing reality from lies.*

*It will not matter to them. But it matters to him, who tried for so long to tell the truth of the futures he saw. That gift has turned traitor to him, bringing nothing more than pain and despair, and so he takes refuge in the past, writing it out amidst the shattered pieces of a hundred might-have-beens.*

HAMPTON COURT PALACE, RICHMOND: *January 6, 1590*

The winter air carried a crisp edge the sunlight did little to blunt, but for once there was hardly more than a breeze off the Thames, scarcely enough to stir the edge of Deven's cloak as he hurried through the Privy Garden. He passed bare flowerbeds protected beneath layers of straw, squinting at the brightness. He had been assigned to serve the Queen at supper for the Twelfth Night feast, but that duty hardly precluded one from participating in the merriment. Deven had no idea how many cups of hippocras he had downed, but it felt like a dozen too many.

Nor was he the only one who had overindulged, but that was to his advantage. Deven had not risen at this ungodly hour without reason. With so many courtiers and the Queen herself still abed, he could snatch a few moments for himself, away from prying eyes—and so could the one he was hurrying to meet.

She was waiting for him in the Mount Garden, standing in the lee of the banqueting house, well-muffled in a fur-trimmed cloak and gloves. The hood fell back as Deven reached for her face, and lips met cold lips in a kiss that quickly warmed them both.

When they broke apart, Anne Montrose said, a trifle breathlessly, "I have been waiting for some time."

"I hope you are not too cold," Deven said, chafing one slender hand between his own. "Too much hippocras, I fear."

"Of course, blame the wine," she said archly, but smiled as she did so.

" 'Tis a thief of men's wits, and of their ability to wake." Frost glittered on the ground and the bare branches of trees like ten thousand minuscule diamonds, forming a brilliant setting for the gem that was Anne Montrose. With her hood fallen back,

81

her unbound hair shone palest gold in the sun, and her wide eyes, a changeable gray, would not have looked out of place on the Queen of Winter that featured prominently in last night's masque. She was not the greatest beauty at court, but that mattered little to him. Deven offered her his arm. "Shall we walk?"

They strolled sedately through the hibernating gardens, warming themselves with the exercise. It was not forbidden for them to be seen together; Anne was the daughter of a gentleman, and fit company for him. There were, however, difficulties. "Have you spoken to your mistress?" Deven asked.

He was hesitant to broach the topic, which might ruin the glittering peace of this morning. It had weighed heavy upon him, though, since he first voiced it to Anne, some months prior. The increased duties of winter court and the neverending ceremonies of the Christmas season had prevented them from doing more than exchange brief greetings whenever they passed, and now he fretted with impatience, wanting an answer.

Anne sighed, her breath pluming out in a cloud. "I have, and she has promised to do what she may. 'Tis difficult, though. The Queen does not like for her courtiers to marry."

"I know." Deven grimaced. "When Scudamore's wife asked permission, the Queen beat her so badly she broke Lady Scudamore's finger."

"I am glad I do not serve *her*," Anne said darkly. "The stories I hear of her temper are dreadful. But I am not the one who will bear the brunt of her wrath; she cares little what a gentlewoman in service to the Countess of Warwick does. You, on the other hand..."

*Marriage is no scandal,* his father had said, when he went into service at court, over a year ago. *Get thee a wife,* his fellows in the band had said. It was the way of the world, for men and women to marry—but not the way of the Queen. She remained virginal and alone, and so would she prefer her courtiers to be.

"She is envious," Anne said, as if she had heard that thought. "There is no love in her life, and so there should be none in the lives of those who surround her—save love for her, of course."

It was true as far as it went, but also unfair. "She has had love. I do not credit the more sordid rumors about her and the late Earl of Leicester, but of a certainty she was fond of him. As they say she was of Alençon."

"Her froggish French prince. That was politics, nothing more."

"What would you know of it?" Deven said, amused. "You could not have been more than ten when he came to England."

"Do you think the ladies of court have ceased to gossip about it? Some say it was genuine affection, but my lady of Warwick says not. Or rather, she says that any affection the Queen may have felt was held in check by her awareness of politics. He was, after all, Catholic." Anne reflected on this. "I think it was desperation. Mary was old when she married; Elizabeth would have been older, in her forties. It was her last chance. And, having lost it, she now vents her frustration on those around her who might find happiness with another."

The breeze off the Thames was picking up, forging a sharper edge. Anne shivered and pulled up the hood of her cloak. Deven said, "Enough of the Queen. I am one of her Gentlemen Pensioners; she calls me fair, gives me minor gifts, and finds me amusing at times, but I'll never be one of her favorites. She cannot take much offense at the prospect of my marriage." It had been Mary Shelton, chamberer to her Majesty, not John Scudamore of the Pensioners, who suffered the broken finger.

Anne laughed unexpectedly from within the depths of her hood. "So long as you do not get me with child, and end up in the Tower for it, like the Earl of Oxford."

"We would run away, first." It was a romantic and stupid thing to say. Where would they go? The only places he knew were London and Kent, and the Netherlands. The former were too near the Queen's grasp, and the latter, no refuge at all. But Anne favored him with an amused smile, one he could not help returning.

All too soon, though, frustration returned to plague him, as it so often did. They walked a little way in silence; then Anne, sensing his mood, asked, "What troubles you?"

"Practicalities," he confessed. "A growing awareness that my ambition and I dwell in separate spheres, and I may well never ascend to meet it."

Her gloved hand rose and tucked itself into the crook of his elbow. "Tell me."

This was why he loved her. At court, a man must always watch what he said; words were both currency and weapons, used to coax favor from allies and strike down enemies. And the ladies were little better; Elizabeth might forbid her women to engage heavily in politics, but they kept a weather eye on the Queen's moods, and could advance the causes of petitioners when they judged the moment right—or hinder them. Even those without the Queen's ear could carry tales to those who had it, and a man might find his reputation poisoned before he knew it, from a few careless words.

He never felt the need for such caution with Anne, and she had never given him cause, not in the year he had known her. She had said once, last autumn, that when in his company she could be at ease, and he felt the same. She was not the greatest beauty at court, nor the richest catch, but he would gladly trade those for the ability to speak his mind.

"I look at Lord Burghley," he said, approaching the subject from a tangent. "Much of what Walsingham does is built on foundations laid by Burghley, and in fact the old baron still maintains his own links with agents and informants. When Burghley dies, or retires from her Majesty's service—which won't happen until after the Second Coming—his son Robert will inherit his barony, his offices, and his agents."

When he paused, Anne said, "But you are not Robert Cecil."

"Sidney might have been—he was married to Walsingham's daughter, before either of us came to court—but he's dead. And I am not sufficiently in Walsingham's affections to take his place, nor ever likely to be."

Anne squeezed his arm reassuringly. They were walking too close together, her farthingale shoving at his leg with every stride, but neither of them moved to separate. "Do you need to be?"

"To do what Walsingham does? Yes. I haven't the wealth to support such an enterprise, nor the connections. Beale and I are forever passing letters and petitions up and down the chain, obtaining licenses for foreign travel, pardons for prisoners who might be of use, requests for gifts or pensions to reward those who have been of service. They do not often receive payment, but the important thing is that they believe they might. I cannot promise that and be believed. And even if I could...I am not in the Queen's councils." Deven's mouth twisted briefly in inarticulate frustration. "I am the son of an unimportant gentleman, distinguished enough by my conduct in the Netherlands to be rewarded with a position at court, pleasing enough to be granted the occasional preferment—but nothing more. Nor ever likely to be."

That speech, delivered in a low monotone from which familiarity had leached all the passion, carried them back to the center of the garden where the banqueting house stood. The morning was upon them in full; the Queen would be waking soon, and he had to be there for the honor guard when she processed to chapel for the service of Epiphany. But the chambers of the palace were close and stuffy, too full of people flocking to the winter court; out here the air was clean and simple, and he did not want to leave.

Anne turned to face him and took his gloved hands in her own, buff-colored leather against brown. "You are twenty-seven," she pointed out. "The men you speak of are *old* men. They achieved their positions over time. How old was Walsingham, when Elizabeth made him her Secretary?"

"Forty-one. But he had connections at court—"

"Also built over time."

"Not all of them. Much of it is a matter of family: fathers and sons, brothers and cousins, links by marriage—"

Her fingers tightened fractionally on his, and Deven caught himself. "I'll not lay you aside for political advantage," he promised.

The words brought a smile to her face that warmed her gray eyes. "I did not think you would."

"The true problem is the Queen. I do not speak against her," he added hastily, and could not restrain a quick glance around, to reassure himself they were alone in the garden. "I am her loyal servant. But her preference is for those of families she knows—often those bound to her already by ties of blood. Of which I am not one."

Anne relinquished his hands so she could straighten her hood. "Then what will you do?"

He shrugged. "Be of use to Walsingham, as much as I can be. Hope that he will reward me for my service."

"Then I have something for you."

Deven cast a startled glance at her, then frowned. "Anne, I have told you before—'tis neither meet nor safe for you to carry tales."

"Gossip is one of the great engines of this court, as you well know. I am not listening at keyholes, I promise you." She was a tallish woman, the top of her hood at eye level for him, and so she did not have to tilt her head back much to look at him; instead she tilted it to the side, eyes twinkling. "Are you not the least bit curious?"

He was and she knew it. "You will find a way to tell me, regardless."

"I could be more subtle, but this is so much easier." Anne folded her hands demurely across the front of her cloak. "'Tis a minor thing, to my eyes, but I never know when some minor thing fits into the greater patterns you and your master see. You are aware of Doctor Dee?"

"The astrologer? He had an audience with the Queen a month gone, at Richmond."

"Do you know the substance of it?"

Deven shook his head. "He was at court only a day or two, and I did not speak to him."

"My lady of Warwick tells me 'tis some difficulty with his house and books. Someone despoiled them while he was abroad; he seeks redress. You may expect to see more of him, I should think—or at least to hear people arguing on his behalf."

"People such as your countess?"

"I thought you did not want me carrying tales." She laughed as he mock-scowled at her. "I imagine your master knows of his situation—they are friends, are they not?—but I can learn more if you would like."

This, he was unpleasantly aware, was often how espionage worked. Few of those who fed Walsingham information did so in an organized and directed fashion, deliberately infiltrating places where they did not belong, or masquerading as that which they were not. Most of the intelligence that reached the Principal Secretary came from men who simply kept their eyes and ears open, and wrote to him when they saw or heard something of interest.

Men, and the very rare woman.

As if she had heard that thought—he must be as transparent as glass to her—Anne said, "'Tis not as if I were offering to return information from the court of the Holy Roman Emperor, or the Pope's privy closet. I will simply tell you if Doctor Dee calls on the countess again."

"I cannot ask a woman to spy," Deven said. "It would be infamous."

"'Tis listening, not spying, and you are not asking me. I do it of my own free will. Consider it a dowry of an intangible sort, paid in advance." Anne took his hand again, and tugged him a step forward, so they stood in the shadow of the banqueting house. There she cupped his jaw in her gloved fingers and kissed him again. "Now I must return; my lady will be rising."

"As will mine," Deven murmured, over the rapid beating of his heart. "You will tell me what the countess says—whether the Queen would be angry at the thought of our marriage?"

"I will," Anne promised. "As soon as I may."

MEMORY: *December 21, 1581*

ℳany parts of the subterranean palace consisted of adjoining chambers, one opening into the next with never a break. Some were arranged around cloistered courtyards of sculpture or night-blooming plants; others connected via long galleries, hung with tapestries and paintings of rich hue.

But there were other passages, secret ones. Few fae ever saw them, and almost no mortals.

The man being escorted through the tunnel was a rare exception.

Of the other mortals who had been brought that way, most were attractive; those who were not held influential positions at court or in trade, and compensated for their lack of handsomeness by their use. This one was different. His cowl taken from him, his clipped, mutilated ears were bared for all to see, and though he was not old, cunning and suspicion — and at the moment, fear — robbed his face of any beauty. Nor was he a powerful man.

He was no one. But he knew a little of faeries, and now his investigations had brought him here, to a world whose existence he had never so much as suspected.

A door barred the way at the end of the passage, bronze-bound and painted black. One of the escorting fae, a hunched, goblinish thing, raised his bony-knuckled hand and knocked. No response came through the door, but after a moment it swung open on oiled hinges, as if of its own accord.

The chamber into which the mortal man stepped was as sumptuous as the corridor outside was bleak. The floor was bare of either rushes or carpets, but it was a fine mosaic in marble, strange figures that he would have liked to study more closely. Cool silver lights gleamed along the walls; out of the corner of his eye, he thought he saw wings moving within their depths. The walls were likewise marble, adorned at regular intervals by tapestries of colored silk studded here and there with jewels. The ceiling was a masterwork display of astrological notation, reflecting the current alignment of the stars far above.

But all this richness was dominated into insignificance by the curtain before him.

Was it black velvet, worked elaborately in silver? Or cloth-of-silver, painstakingly embroidered with black silk? His escort, his guards, stood between him and it, as if he would have approached to examine it. Some of the gems encrusting the fabric appeared to be diamonds, while others were more brilliant and alive than any diamonds he had ever seen. Pearls as large as hummingbird eggs weighted its bottom edge. The curtain alone displayed wealth only the crowned heads of Europe could hope to equal, and not even all of them.

He was not surprised when one of his escorts kicked him in the back of the knee, forcing him to the floor.

The stone pressed hard and cold against his knees as he waited.

And then a voice spoke from behind the curtain.

"You seek after magic, Edward Kelley."

"I do." The words came out rusty and faint on the first try; he wet his lips and said it again. "I do. And I have found it."

Found more than he had ever dreamed of.

A soft sound came from behind the curtain, a cool laugh. The voice was melodious and controlled, and if the face that accompanied it was anything to match, she must be the most beautiful faerie lady to ever call England home.

Lady—or queen? Even among fae, he doubted such riches were common.

The lady spoke again from her concealment. "You have found only the meanest scraps from the table of magic. There is more, far more. You wish to know the secrets of creation? We have them bound in books. You wish to transform base metal into gold? 'Tis child's play, for such as us."

Faerie gold. It turned to leaves or stones before long—but

90

a man could do a great deal with it, while it still shone. And though it was a poor substitute for true transformation, the Philosopher's Stone, learning of it might advance his alchemical work.

Yes, there was a feast here for him.

"I would be your ladyship's most humble student," he said, and bowed his head.

"I am sure," the lady said. "But you must know, Edward Kelley—all gifts carry a price. Especially those from fae."

He was a learned man. Some believed fae to be devils in different guise. Others placed them midway between Heaven and Hell: above men in the hierarchy of creation, but below the celestial forces that served God.

Regardless of the explanation, all agreed that to strike a bargain with their kind was a dangerous business. But having seen this much, no man who laid claim to intellectual curiosity could be expected to turn back.

He had to swallow before his voice would work. "What price would you demand?"

"Demand?" The lady seemed offended. "I will not ask for your soul, or your firstborn child. I merely have a request of you, that I think you will find it easy enough to grant."

That was more ominous than a straightforward demand would have been. He waited, eyes on the hanging pendants of pearls, to hear more. They did not quite touch the floor, and in the shadows beyond he thought he could see just the hem of a glittering skirt.

At length the lady said, "There is a mortal scholar known as Doctor John Dee."

Kelley nodded, then remembered the lady could not see him. "I know of him."

"He seeks to speak with angels. For this purpose he has

contracted the services of a man named Barnabas Saul. My request is that you take Saul's place. The man is nothing more than a charlatan, a cozener who seeks to take advantage of Doctor Dee. We will arrange for him to be discredited, and you will replace him as scryer."

"And then?" Kelley knew it would not end there. "Once I am in Dee's confidences — assuming I can make it there —"

" 'Tis easily arranged."

"Then what would you have me do?"

"Nothing damaging," the hidden lady assured him. "He will never speak to angels, whatever scryer he contracts to assist him. But 'tis in our interests that he should think he has done so. You will describe visions to Dee, when he asks you to gaze into the crystal. You may invent some if you wish. From time to time, one of my people will visit you in that glass, and tell you what to say. And in exchange, we will teach you the secrets you wish to learn."

Kelley had never met the man; what did he care if Dee was led astray by faeries? Yet it made him nervous all the same. "Can you promise me the things I say will not harm him? Can you give me your word?"

All around him, the silent fae of his escort stiffened.

Silence from behind the curtain. Kelley wondered how badly he had offended. But if the lady fed him visions that would incite Dee to treason, or something else harmful...

"I give you my word," the lady said in a clipped, hard tone unlike her previous voice, "that I will give no orders for visions that will harm Doctor John Dee. If you lead him astray with your own invention, that is no fault of ours. Will that suffice, Edward Kelley?"

That should be enough to bind her. He hoped. He dared not press for more. Yet he had one further request, unrelated to the first. "I am most grateful," he said, and bowed his head again. "You have already given me more than I ever dreamed of, bringing me here. But though it be presumptuous of me, I do have one more thing to ask. Your voice, lady, is beauty itself; might I have the privilege of gazing upon your face?"

Another silence, though this time his escort did not take it as strongly amiss.

"No," the lady said. "You shall not see me tonight. But on some future day—if your service pleases—then perhaps, Edward Kelley, you shall know who I am."

He wanted to see her beauty, but she had surmised correctly; he also wanted to see whom he was serving. But it was not to be.

Was he willing to accept that, in exchange for what the fae might teach him?

He had answered that question before he ever agreed to accompany them beneath the streets of London.

Edward Kelley bowed until his forehead touched the cold marble and said, "I will serve you, Lady, and go to Doctor Dee."

The Onyx Hall, London: *February 5, 1590*

The night garden of the Onyx Hall had no day garden with which to contrast, but still it bore that name. It was enormous, comparable in size to the great presence chamber, but very different in character; in place of cold, geometric stone, there was instead the softness of earth, the gentle arch of branches. The quiet waters of the Walbrook, the buried river of London, bisected the garden's heart. Paths meandered through carefully arranged beds of moonflower, cereus, and evening primrose;

angel's trumpet wound its way up pillars and around fountains. Here and there stood urns filled with lilies from the deeper reaches of Faerie. Night lasted eternally here, and the air was perfumed with gentle scents.

Lune breathed in deeply and felt something inside her relax. As much as she enjoyed living among mortals, it was exhausting beyond anything else she knew. Easy enough to don human guise for a trip to Islington and back; living among them was a different matter. Being in the Onyx Hall again was like drinking cool, pure water after a long day in the sun and wind.

The ceiling above was cloaked in shadow, and spangled with brilliant faerie lights: tiny, near-mindless creatures below even a will-o'-the-wisp—barely aware enough to be called fae. The constellations they formed changed from time to time, as much a part of the garden's design as the flowerbeds and the delicate streams that rippled through them. Their shape now suggested a hunter, thrown through the air from the antlers of a stag.

That was troubling. There must have been some recent clash with the Wild Hunt.

Lune was not the only one in the garden. A small clutch of four fae had gathered a little distance away, under a sculpted holly tree. A black-feathered fellow perched in the branches, while two ladies gathered around a third, who sat on a bench with a book in her hands. Whatever she was reading aloud to them was too quiet for Lune to hear, but it sparked much mirth from her audience.

Footsteps on the flagstones made her turn. Lady Nianna Chrysanthe hurried to her side, saying breathlessly, "You must have come early."

"I finished my business sooner than expected." Vidar had not questioned her nearly as closely as he might have. Lune was not sure whether to find that worrisome, or merely a sign that he was not as competent as he liked to believe. "What do you have for me?"

The honey-haired elfin lady cast a glance around, then beckoned Lune to follow. They went deeper into the garden, finding their own bench on which to sit. They were still within sight of the group beneath the holly tree, and now another pair at the edge of a fountain, but the important thing was that no one could overhear them.

"Tell me," Nianna whispered, more out of excitement than caution, "what does—"

"Give me your news first," Lune said, cutting her off. "Then I will tell you."

Pushing Nianna was dangerous. Lune's work among mortals had gone some way toward restoring her status, but not her former position in the privy chamber, and Nianna alone of her former companions there deigned to speak with her much at all. Lune did not want to lose her most reliable source of information. But she knew Nianna, and knew how far the lady could be pushed. Nianna pouted, but gave in. "Very well. What do you wish me to begin with?"

Lune pointed at the faerie lights in their constellation. "How stand matters with the Wild Hunt?"

"Not well." Nianna deflated a little. Her slender fingers plucked at the enameled chain that hung from her girdle. "There are rumors they will ally at last with the Courts of the North—"

"There have always been such rumors."

"Yes, but this time they seem more serious. Her Majesty has formed a provisional agreement with Temair. A regiment of Red Branch knights, to fight the Wild Hunt—or the Scots, or both—if she uses her influence on the mortal court to affect events in Ireland on their behalf. They're willing to consider it, at least; the unanswered question is how much aid she would have to give them in return."

Lune let her breath out slowly. Red Branch knights; they would be quite an asset, if Invidiana could get them. The English fae could hold their own against Scotland, even if the red-caps along the Border took the other side, but the Wild Hunt was, and always had been, a very different kind of threat. The only thing that kept them at bay so far was their absolute refusal to fight this war on any mortal front. And Invidiana was not foolish enough to leave the safety of the Onyx Hall, buried in the midst of mortal London, and meet them on their own terms.

"Has there been an active threat from the Hunt?"

"An assassin," Nianna said dismissively. "A Catholic priest. I believe he is still strung up in the watching chamber, if you wish to see him."

She did not. Would-be assassins, and their punishments, were a common occurrence. "But from the *Hunt*?"

"That is why everyone thinks they may have a true alliance with the Courts of the North."

If true, it was worrisome. The Scottish fae had no compunctions about using mortals in the fight; they had been forming pacts with witches for years and sending them south to cause trouble. The leaders of the Hunt all claimed kingship over one corner of England or another; they might have decided they wanted lands and sovereignty badly enough to look the other way while their allies soiled their hands with mortal tools.

Lune doubted it, but she wasn't in a position to judge. "What else?"

Nianna put a painted fingernail to her lip, considering. "Madame Malline has been asking around, attempting to discover how the bargain with the folk of the sea was struck.

I do not know what the Cour du Lys would want with such knowledge, but there must be something. You should stay away from her."

That, or barter with her. If she could do it in a way that wouldn't anger Invidiana. "Continue."

"That is all I know about her aims. Let me see... there have been a few more fae in from country areas, complaining that their homes have been destroyed." Nianna dismissed this with a wave. She had been a lady of the privy chamber to Invidiana for a long time; the travails of country folk were insignificant to her. "Oh yes, and a delegation of muryans from Cornwall—they just arrived; no one knows yet what they want. What else? Lady Carline has a new mortal she's stringing along. She might get to keep him for a time; Invidiana has taken Lewan Erle back to her bed, so her attention is elsewhere. Or not."

Bedroom politics did not interest Lune. They might be of consuming fascination to some, but they rarely affected the matters she attended to. What had she not yet asked about? "The Spanish ambassador?"

"Don Eyague is still here, and has hosted a few visitors. The rumor is that he is being courted by a growing faction in Spain that are dissatisfied with living in a Catholic nation. But I do not know what they intend; I doubt they have the numbers or resources to make any kind of substantial change to the mortal government, even if they decided to mimic her Majesty. For all I know, they may be considering emigration—here, or to the Low Countries. Who can say?"

Fae rarely emigrated, but no matter. Lune had only one question left for Nianna. She glanced casually toward the pair of fae at the nearby fountain, to make sure they were not listening. The lady sat on the stone coping of the edge, framing herself and her red silk gown prettily against the elaborate grotesque that spouted water in five directions, while the gentleman stood and read to her from a book. The sight momentarily distracted her; it looked like the same book the others had been reading beneath the holly tree.

Upon that thought, the book burst into flame.

The gentleman cried out in shock and dropped the burning pages. Lune caught a fleeting glimpse of something streaking across the garden; she turned to track it and saw the book the others held also catch fire. Silhouetted briefly atop the pages was a tiny, glowing, lizard-shaped creature. Then the salamander darted down again, and vanished amidst the flowers of the garden. A trail of smoke showed briefly where it went; then it was gone.

Lune asked, very carefully, "What was that?"

"I did not see, but I believe it was a sal—"

"I am not asking about the creature. What did it just burn?"

"Oh." Nianna tittered, then hid it guiltily behind her hand. "A mortal book. It has been ever so popular at court, but it seems her Grace does not find it amusing."

Lune rolled her eyes and seated herself once more on the bench. "Ah. Would this be that poem called *The Faerie Queene*?"

"You know of it?"

"The Queen—the mortal Queen—likes it greatly, so of course every courtier who wishes to curry favor must be seen with a copy, or heard quoting it at every suitable occasion." And a few that were not so suitable; Lune was growing heartily tired of the work. "I am not surprised Invidiana dislikes it."

"Well, it *is* very inaccurate. But would she not like that? After all, if the mortals knew the truth, they would come down here with crosses and priests and drive us out."

Nianna was a brainless fool. The insult was not that it was inaccurate; no one expected accuracy out of poets. Peasants might know the truth about fae—to an extent—but poets took that truth, dried it out, ground it to powder, mixed it with strange chemicals, and used it to dye threads from which to weave a tapestry that bore only the most passing of resemblances to real fae and their lives.

No, the insult was that the Faerie Queen of the title was a transparent symbol for Elizabeth. That would be what Invidiana could not stand.

The gentleman at the fountain was now extemporaneously composing a poem, in a very loud voice, about the swift and merciless wrath of the Queen. He was not very good. Lune ignored him and asked Nianna, "What of Francis Merriman?"

"What?" Nianna had been attending to the poem. "Oh, yes. A few people have heard that name."

"They have?" Lune restrained her eagerness. She had not forgotten her conversation with Tiresias, over a year ago. There was no Francis Merriman in Elizabeth's court, at least not yet. She suspected she would find him there—perhaps Elizabeth herself was the one whose secret Merriman held?—but she had to consider other possibilities. "Who knows of him?"

Nianna began to count the names off on her jeweled fingers. "That wretched Bobbin fellow...Lady Amadea Shirrell...one or two others, I think. It does not matter. They all said the same thing. Tiresias mentioned the name to them, at one time or another. Some of them looked for him, but no one turned anything up."

Hope vanished like a pricked soap bubble. Lune quelled a frustrated sigh; she did not want Nianna to think the matter too important to her. She already had a time of it, impressing upon the lady the merit of keeping her inquiries discreet, lest

Invidiana catch wind of them before Lune had this mortal in hand.

Nianna's words reinforced her growing conviction that she was simply too early. Tiresias was a seer. When he was not raving in confusion about things that never existed, he spoke of the future. Francis Merriman might not even have been born yet.

But when he did appear, Lune intended to be the first to find him.

"Lady Lune," Nianna breathed, plucking at her sleeve, "I have gathered information for you, as you asked—told you all the news of the court, and answered all your questions. Will you not tell me now of my love?"

*Ah yes.* Lune said, "He will meet you Friday next, at the tavern called The Hound, that lies near Newgate."

Many fae at court had mortal friends or lovers. Some knew their companions were fae; a great many more did not. John Awdeley, a clerk of the chaundry at Whitehall Palace, did not know, and so Nianna required assistance in arranging assignations with him, in such a time and place as she could keep up her pretense of being a maidservant in a London mercer's house.

She did not love him, of course, but she was infatuated with him for now, and being fae, now was all that mattered.

Lune answered Nianna's subsequent questions with rapidly diminishing patience; she had no interest in describing the state of Awdeley's beard, nor recounting how many times he had asked after his maidservant love. "Enough," she said abruptly, when Nianna asked for the seventh time whether he had shown any favor to other women, and if so, their names and stations, so she might curse them and teach them the foolishness of being rival to a fae. "I do not follow the man his every waking moment; I have little to do with him. And our bargain was not that I would recount his doings to you, down to the contents of his supper. You have your meeting with him, and I the latest news of the court. Now begone with you."

Nianna drew herself up in a graceful, offended ripple. "How dare you speak so dismissively to me? Who do you think you are?"

"Who am I?" Lune smiled, giving it a malicious edge. "While you trail after Invidiana, carrying her gloves and her fans and enduring the brunt of her wrathful moods, I eat mortal bread every day and report to her the secret doings of Elizabeth's court. I am, moreover, your pander to this mortal you have set your sights upon. What aid I give you there, I can revoke. Turning his thoughts to another woman would be easy."

The lady hissed, all warmth of manner instantly gone. "Your body would be floating in Queenhithe by the next morning for fish and gulls to peck at."

"Would it?" Lune met her gaze unblinking. "Are you sure?"

The specter of the Queen was so easy to invoke. And while Invidiana certainly did not come to the aid of every fae who claimed the possibility, she took no offense at being so named; it served her purposes to be a figure of terror to her courtiers. She even made good on the threats occasionally, simply to keep everyone guessing. The threats would lose their meaning if they never bore teeth.

Nianna backed down, but not graciously. Lune might have to find a new informant to keep her abreast of matters. She would not have antagonized Nianna so, but the conference with Vidar had put her back up, and left her with no patience for the lady's passing mortal infatuation.

They parted on coldly courteous terms, and Lune wandered through the garden alone. Two faerie lights drifted loose from the constellation above and floated about her shoulders. Lune brushed them away. Since losing her position in the privy chamber, she had not the rank or favor to merit such decoration, and did not want anyone carrying tales of her presumption. By the time they reached the ears of those in power, the casual wanderings of two faerie lights would be a halo of glory she had shaped and placed on her own head.

The conversation with Nianna left her weary. She had intended to spend more time in the Onyx Hall, to see for herself how the patterns of alliance and power had shifted, but all that talk of Awdeley had turned her thoughts back to the mortal court. Nianna's infatuation was simple to understand. Lune herself spent a great deal of time feigning just such an attachment.

Her feet sought out the chamber of the alder roots. She had a brief leave from the duties of her masquerade; she would go to Islington and rest herself at the Angel, under the friendly care of the Goodemeades, before returning to the life and duties of Anne Montrose.

RICHMOND PALACE, RICHMOND: *February 12, 1590*

The Christmas season had gone, and with it went a great deal of gaiety and celebration. While some privileged courtiers continued to dwell at Hampton Court nearby — the Countess of Warwick among them — the core of Elizabeth's court removed to Richmond, a much smaller palace, and more used for business than pleasure.

Deven would not have minded, were it not that he no longer saw Anne even in passing. The entire corps of Gentlemen Pensioners was obliged to attend the Queen at Christmas, and the increased numbers did not lighten anyone's load; indeed, the extra effort required to organize the full band during the elaborate ceremonies of the season was draining. Life at Richmond was simpler, if more austere, and free time easier to come by.

Easier to come by, and easier to spend: Deven found himself often closeted with Robert Beale, Walsingham's secretary. As much as the common folk might like to believe that the defeat of the Armada ended the threat from Spain, they were not so lucky, as the reports pouring in from agents abroad showed. Philip of Spain still had his eye fixed on heretic England and its heretic Queen.

"Did you hear," Beale said, laying down a paper and rubbing his eyes, "that Essex wants command of the forces being sent to Brittany?"

The room was small enough that the fire made it stuffy; Deven took advantage of Beale's pause to set down his own reading and unbutton the front of his doublet so he could shrug out of it. The green damask was pulling apart at the shoulder, but the garment was comfortable, and Fitzgerald had not assigned him to duty today. He had not even bothered with a collar or cuffs that morning; he had slipped from his quarters to here in a state of half-dress, intending to spend the entire day cloistered away from court ritual.

He laid the doublet over an unused chair and dragged his thoughts back to what Beale had said. "You're ahead of me, as usual," Deven admitted, returning to his seat. "I did not even know the Brittany expedition had been agreed to."

"It hasn't, but it will be."

Deven shook his head. "The Queen will never let him go. She's overfond of that one."

"Which means he will be insufferable with frustration. The

man should be allowed to go abroad and kill things; it might cool his hot head."

"If these reports are accurate, he will have his chance soon enough." Deven scowled at the note in his hands. Someone had got hold of a message in cipher, and Walsingham had passed it to his steganographer Thomas Phelippes. The report Phelippes had returned to them was written in a clear hand, and Deven's fledgling Spanish was sufficient to interpret it; the problem must be in the message itself. "I doubt the accuracy of this one, though, unless Philip plans to arm every man, woman, child, and cow in Spain."

"Forget Spain." The voice came from behind Deven; he twisted in his chair in time to see Walsingham closing the door behind himself.

The Principal Secretary's face looked pinched, and his words were startling. Forget Spain? They were the Great Enemy; Deven would no more expect Walsingham to forget Spain than for Philip to forget Elizabeth.

"Not you, Robin," Walsingham said, as the Secretary moved to set down the papers in his hand. Beale sighed and kept them. "I have a task for you, Deven."

"Sir." Deven rose and bowed, wishing he had at least kept his doublet on. His breeches, only loosely laced on in the absence of a doublet to be tied to, threatened to flap at the waist.

Walsingham ignored his state of undress. "Ireland."

"Ireland?" He sounded foolish, repeating the Principal Secretary's statement, but it was entirely unexpected. "What of it, sir?"

"Fitzwilliam has accused Perrot of treason — of conspiring with Philip to overthrow her Majesty."

Sir John Perrot was a name Deven had only recently become familiar with; one of Walsingham's men, he had returned a year and a half before from a stint as Lord Deputy in Ireland. Fitz-william, then, must be Sir William Fitzwilliam, his successor.

Beale had been listening, not reading; now he said, "Impossible."

Walsingham nodded. "Indeed. And this is why, Deven, you will turn your thoughts from Spain to Ireland. Fitzwilliam has a grievance with Perrot; he resents that Perrot sits on the privy council and advises her Majesty on Irish affairs, and resents more that the lords in Ireland have taken to writing him directly, bypassing Fitzwilliam's own authority. I am not surprised by his antagonism. What surprises me is the form it has taken. Why this accusation, and why now?"

Deven didn't want to voice the thought that had come into his head, but no doubt Walsingham had already thought the same. "The answers to that, sir, most likely lie in Ireland."

He did not want to go. Aside from the general unpleasantness of traveling to Ireland, it would take him away from court and Anne, neither of which he wanted to leave for long. But he could not pledge his service to Walsingham, and then balk when asked to serve him elsewhere. It would be a mark of the Secretary's trust; Beale himself had been sent on diplomatic missions before.

But Walsingham was shaking his head. "It may come to that, but not yet. I suspect some cause here at court. Fitzwilliam is Burghley's man; I doubt Burghley has goaded him to this, but there may be factional forces I am not seeing. Before I send you anywhere, I will have you look about court. Who shows an interest in Ireland? Who is formulating petitions regarding affairs there, that have not yet reached the privy council?"

"It might have nothing to do with Ireland. Perhaps this strike has entirely to do with Perrot, and Fitzwilliam is simply a convenient route to it."

Beale nodded at this, but Walsingham again shook his head. "I do not think so. Keep your eyes open, certainly, for anything regarding Perrot—but Ireland is your focus. Search out anything I may have missed."

"Yes, sir." Deven bowed again and reached for his doublet.

*"Anything,"* Walsingham repeated, as Deven quickly looped his points through the waist of the doublet and started on the buttons. "Even things in the past—years past. Whatever you may find."

"Yes, sir." Dressed enough to go out once more, Deven took his leave. He would have to find Colsey and put himself together properly, starting with a doublet that wasn't coming unsewn. His quiet day in private, it seemed, would have to wait.

HAMPTON COURT PALACE, RICHMOND: *February 13, 1590*

The banked coals in the fireplace cast a dim, sullen glow over the bedchamber, barely enough to highlight its contents: the chests containing clothes and jewels, the bed heaped with blankets, the pallets of sleepers on the floor.

Anne Montrose lay wakeful, eyes on the invisible fretwork of the ceiling above, listening to her companions breathe. A gentle snore began; the countess had drifted off. One of the other gentlewomen made quiet smacking noises and rolled over. A few sparks flared up the chimney as a glowing log end crumbled under its own weight. The snoring ceased as the countess lapsed into deeper sleep.

Silent as a ghost, Anne rolled back her own blankets and stood.

The rushes pricked at her bare feet as she stole across the floor. The hinges did not creak when she opened the door;

she took particular care to keep them well oiled at all times. A muted thud was the only sound to betray her when she left.

Midnight had passed already, and the palace lay sleeping. Even the courtiers indulging in illicit trysts had retired by now. The dark cloak she wore was symbolic as well as practical; it served as a useful focal point for the minor charm she called up. Anyone who might be awake would not see her unless she wanted them to.

By the thin bars of light that came in through the courtyard windows, she made her way along the gallery and to the privy stair that led down to the gardens. Snow had dusted the ground during the day. In the moonlight, their shoulders and heads capped with white, the heraldic beasts that marked out the squares of the Privy Garden seemed even stranger than usual, like frosted gargoyles that might leap into motion without warning. She cast sidelong glances at them as she passed, but they remained lifeless stone.

Up ahead, the banqueting house loomed tall and sinister in the Mount Garden, surrounded by trees pruned carefully into grotesques. And on the far side of that, murmuring to itself under a thin shell of ice, the Thames.

A figure waited for her in the shadows of the Water Gallery, just above the river's edge.

"You are late."

Lune kept the illusion of Anne Montrose over her features; she did not want the nuisance of reconstructing it. She did not have to think like a human, though, and so she stood barefoot on the icy ground, the cloak now flapping free in the wind off the river.

"I am not late," she said, as a bell ringer inside the palace clock tower began to toll the second hour after midnight.

Vidar smiled his predatory smile. "My mistake."

Why Vidar? Ordinarily he dispatched a minor goblin to bring her bread. Lune supposed she would learn the answer soon enough, but she would not satisfy him by asking. Instead she held out one hand. "If you please. I am near the end of my ration."

She was unsurprised when Vidar did not move. "What matters that? Unless you expect a priest to leap out of the river and bid you begone, in the name of his divine master, you are in no immediate danger of being revealed."

Months before, Lune had snatched a few days of solitude for herself, pleading an ill kinswoman in London to cover for her absence. Those days spent wearing her true face had allowed her to shift the schedule of her ration; the goblins delivered it on Fridays, but she ate it on Tuesdays. The margin of safety might be important someday. But Vidar did not know that, and so she feigned the apprehension she should have felt, hearing him come so close to naming the mortal God to her face.

"My mistress may wake and find me gone," she said, sidestepping Vidar's jibe. "I should not tarry."

He shrugged his bony shoulders. "Tell her you slipped off for a tryst with that mortal toy of yours. Or some other tale. I care not what lie you give her." He settled his back against the brickwork of the Water Gallery, arms crossed over his narrow chest. "What news have you?"

Lune tucked her reaching hand back inside her cloak. So. Again she was unsurprised; she knew she was hardly the Onyx Court's only source of information regarding the mortals. But it meant something, that Vidar considered the matter pressing enough to seek her out here. Like the mistress he strove to emulate and eventually unseat, he rarely left the sanctuary of the Onyx Hall.

"Sir John Perrot has been accused of treason," she said,

allowing the pretense that Vidar did not already know. "He is a political client of Walsingham's, and so the Principal Secretary is moving to defend him. Deven has been assigned to investigate: who is taking an interest in Irish affairs, and to what end." That Deven and Walsingham both were at Richmond, she did not say. The Countess of Warwick had been bidden there the other day to attend the Queen, by which fortunate chance Lune had been able to learn of Deven's assignment; Vidar would be displeased if he knew how rarely she saw him at the moment. He was her link to Walsingham. Without him, she had very little.

Vidar tapped a sharp fingernail against a jeweled clasp that held the sleeve of his doublet closed. "Has your toy asked you to tell him of what you hear?"

"No, but he knows I will do it regardless." Lune's eyes went from the tapping fingernail to Vidar's face, his sunken eyes hidden in shadow. "Is the accusation our doing?"

The fingernail stopped. Vidar said, "You are here to do the bidding of the Queen, not to ask questions."

How the removal of Perrot would advance Invidiana's bargaining with the Irish fae, Lune could not guess, but Vidar's attempt to dodge the question told her it would. "The better I understand the Queen's intentions, the better I may serve her."

She startled a bitter but honest laugh out of Vidar. "What a charming notion — understanding her intentions. Dwelling among mortals has made you an optimistic fool."

Lune pressed her lips together in annoyance, then smoothed her features out. "Have you instructions for me, then? Or am I simply to listen and report?"

Vidar considered it. Which, again, told her something: Invidiana was permitting him some measure of discretion in this matter. He had not come here just as a messenger. And that told her why it was Vidar, and not a goblin, bringing her bread tonight.

She tucked that information away, adding it to her meager storehouse of knowledge.

"Seek out the interested parties," he said, the words guarded and thoughtful. "Assemble a list of them. What they desire, and why, and what they would be willing to do in exchange."

Then no bargain had yet been settled with the Irish fae. If it had been, Lune would be assigned more specifically to cultivate a particular faction. Had the accusation of Perrot been simply a demonstration of Invidiana's power, to convince the Irish of her ability to deliver on her promises?

She could not tell from here, and Lady Nianna, even when feeling friendly, was not enough to keep her informed. It was pleasant to dwell among mortals, close enough to the center of the Tudor Court to bask in its glory without being caught in its net, and to enjoy the illusion of freedom from the ever more vicious intrigues of the Onyx Court, but she could never forget that it was an illusion. Nowhere was safe. And if she ever let that slip her mind, she would discover what it meant to truly fall from favor.

"Very well," Lune said to Vidar, allowing a note of boredom to creep into her voice. Let him think her careless and inattentive; it was always better to be underestimated. "Now, my bread, if you will."

He remained motionless for a few breaths, and she wondered if he would try to extort some further service out of her. But then he moved, and drew from inside his cloak a small bundle of velvet.

Holding it just short of her extended hand, Vidar said, "I want to see you eat it now."

"Certainly," Lune replied, easily, with just a minor note of surprise. It made no difference to her; adding a week of protection now would not negate the remnant she still enjoyed. Vidar must suspect her of hoarding the bread, instead of eating it. Which she had done, a little, but only with great care. The last thing she wanted was to see her glamour destroyed by a careless invocation to God.

The bread this time was coarse and insufficiently baked. Whether Vidar had chosen it from among the country tithes, or Invidiana had, or someone else, it was clear the chooser meant to insult her. But it did the job whether it was good bread or bad, so Lune swallowed the seven doughy bites, if not with pleasure.

The instant she was done, Vidar straightened. "There will be a draca in the river from now on. If anything of immediate import develops, inform it at once."

This time Lune failed to completely hide her surprise, but she curtsied deeply. "As my lord commands."

By the time she straightened, he was gone.

RICHMOND PALACE, RICHMOND: *March 3, 1590*

As much as Deven would have liked to present Walsingham with a stunning revelation set in gold and decorated with seed pearls, after a fortnight of investigating the Irish question, he had to admit defeat.

It wasn't that he had learned nothing; on the contrary, he now knew more than he had ever expected to about the peculiar subset of politics that revolved around their neighbor island to the west. Which included a great deal about the Irish Earl of Tyrone, and the subtleties of shiring Ulster; there were disputes there going back ages, involving both Sir John Perrot and the current Lord Deputy Fitzwilliam.

But it all added up to precisely nothing Walsingham would not have known already.

So Deven laid it out before his master, hoping the Principal Secretary would make something of it he could not. "I will keep listening," he said when he was done, and tried to sound both eager and determined. "It may be there is something I have missed."

For this conference he had been permitted into Walsingham's private chambers for the first time. They were not particularly splendid; Deven knew from Beale the financial difficulties the Principal Secretary faced. He had understood from his earliest days at court that many people there were in debt, but the revelation of Walsingham's own finances had disabused him of any lingering notion that the heaviest burdens lay on ambitious young men such as himself. A few hundred pounds owed to a goldsmith paled into insignificance next to tens of thousands of pounds owed to the Crown itself.

Of course, Elizabeth herself was in debt to a variety of people. It was the way of the world, at least at court.

But Walsingham did not live in penury, either. His furnishings were understated, like his clothing, but finely made, and the chamber was well lit, both from candles and the fire burning in the hearth to drive away the damp chill. Deven sat on a stool near that fire, with Walsingham across from him, and waited to see if his master saw something he did not.

Walsingham rose and walked a little distance away, hands clasped behind his back. "You have done well," he said at length, his measured voice giving nothing away. "I did not expect you to discover so much about Tyrone."

Deven bent his head and studied his hands, running his thumb over the rough edge of one fingernail. "You knew about these matters already."

"Yes."

He could not entirely suppress a sigh. "Then what was the purpose? Simply to test me?"

Walsingham did not respond immediately. When he did, his voice was peculiarly heavy. "No. Though you have, as I said, performed admirably." Another pause; Deven looked up and found the Principal Secretary had turned back to face him. The firelight dancing on his face made him look singularly unwell. "No, Michael—I was hoping you might uncover something more. The missing key to a riddle that has been troubling me for some time."

The candor in his voice startled Deven. The admission of personal failure, the use of his given name—the choice of this chamber, rather than an office, to discuss the matter—Beale had said before that Walsingham had an occasional and surprising need to confide in others about sensitive matters. Others that included Beale.

Others that had not, before now, included Deven.

"Fresh eyes may sometimes see things experienced ones cannot," he said, hoping he sounded neither nervous nor intrusive.

Walsingham held his gaze, as if weighing something, then turned away. His hand trailed over a chess set laid out on a table; he picked up one piece and held it in his hand, considering. Then he set it down on a smaller table next to Deven. It was a queen, the black queen. "The matter of the Queen of Scots," he said. "Who were the players in that game? And what did they seek?"

The non sequitur threw Deven for a moment—from Ireland to Scotland, with no apparent connection. But he was accustomed by now to the unexpected ways in which Walsingham tested his intelligence and awareness, so he marshaled his thoughts. The entire affair had begun when he was very young—possibly before, depending on how one counted it—and had ended before he came to court, but the Scottish queen had more influence on English policy than most courtiers could aspire to in their lives, and her echoes were still felt.

"Mary Stewart," he said, picking up the chess piece. It was finely carved from some wood he could not identify, and stained dark. "She should be considered a player herself, I suppose. Unless you would call her a pawn?"

"No one who smuggled so many letters out through the French embassy could be called a pawn," Walsingham said dryly. "She had little with which to fill her time but embroidery and scheming, and there must be limits to the number of tapestries and cushions a woman can make."

"Then I'll begin with her." Deven tried to think himself in her place. Forced to abdicate her throne and flee to a neighboring country for sanctuary—sanctuary that became a trap. "She wanted...well, not to be executed, I imagine. But if we are considering this over a longer span of time, then no doubt she wished her freedom from confinement. She was imprisoned for, what, twenty years?"

"Near enough."

"Freedom, then, and a throne—any throne, from what I hear. English, Scottish, probably French if she could have got it back." Deven rose and crossed to the chessboard. If Walsingham had begun the metaphor, he would continue it. Selecting the white queen, he set her down opposite her dark sister. "Elizabeth, and her government. They—you—wished security for the Protestant throne. Against Mary as a usurper, but there was a time, was there not, when she was considered a possible heir?"

Walsingham's face was unreadable, as it so often was, particularly when he was testing Deven's understanding of politics. "Many people have been so considered."

He hadn't denied it. Mary Stewart had Tudor blood, and Catholics considered Elizabeth a bastard, incapable of inheriting the throne. "But it seems she was a greater threat than a prospect. If I may be so bold as to say so, my lord, I think you were one of the leading voices calling for her removal from the game."

The Principal Secretary did not say anything; Deven had not expected him to. He was already considering his next selection from the chessboard. "The Protestant faction in Scotland, and their sovereign, once he became old enough to rule." The black king went onto the table, but Deven placed him alongside the white queen, rather than the black. "I do not know James of Scotland; I do not know what love he may bear his late mother. But she was deposed by the Protestant faction, and branded a murderess. They, I think, did not love her."

Having mentioned the Protestants, the next components were clear. Deven hesitated only in his choice of piece. "Catholic rebels, both in England and Scotland." These he represented with pawns, one black and one white, both ranged in support of the black queen. It would be a mistake to assume the rebels all unlettered recusant farmers, but ultimately, whatever their birth, they were pawns of the Crowns that backed them. "Their motives are clear enough," he said. "The restoration of the Catholic faith in these countries, under a Catholic queen with a claim to both thrones."

What had he not yet considered? Foreign powers, that backed the rebels he had depicted as pawns. They did not fit the divide he had created, using black pieces for the Scots and white for the English; in the end he picked up the two black bishops. "France and Spain. Both concerned, like the rebels, with the restoration of Catholicism. France has long invested her men and munitions in Scotland, the better to bedevil us, and Spain sent the Armada as retaliation for Mary Stewart's execution."

Walsingham spoke at last. "More a pretext than an underlying cause. But you have them rightly placed."

The pieces were arrayed on the table in a strange, disorganized game of chess. On one side stood the black queen with her two bishops, a pawn, and a second pawn from the white; on the opposing side, the white queen and the black king. Had he missed anyone? The English side was grievously outnumbered. But that was a true enough representation. She had Protestant allies, but none whose involvement in the Scottish matter was visible to Deven.

The only group he still wondered about was the Irish, with whom this entire discussion had begun. But he did not know of any involvement on their part, nor could he imagine any that made sense.

If he had failed the test, then so be it. He faced Walsingham and made a slight bow. "Have I passed your examination, sir?"

By way of reply, Walsingham took a white knight and laid it on the English side. "Her Majesty's privy council," he said. Then he moved the white queen out into the center, the empty space between the two. "Her Majesty."

Dividing Elizabeth from her government. "She did not wish the Queen of Scots to be executed?"

"She was of two minds. As you observed, Mary Stewart was a potential heir, though one who would never be acceptable to those of our Protestant faith. Her Majesty also feared to execute the anointed sovereign of another land."

"For fear of the precedent it would set."

"There were those who sought our Queen's death, of course,

regardless of precedent. But if one Queen may be killed, so may another. Moreover, you must not forget they were kinswomen. Her Majesty recognized the threat to her own safety, and that of England, but she was most deeply reluctant."

"Yet she signed the execution order in the end."

Walsingham smiled thinly. "Only when driven to it by overwhelming evidence, and the patient effort of us her privy councillors. Bringing that about was no easy task, and her secretary Davison went to the Tower for it." At Deven's started look, he nodded. "Elizabeth changed her mind in the end, but too late to prevent Mary's execution; Davison bore the weight of her wrath, though little he deserved it."

Deven looked down at the table, with the white queen standing forlornly, indecisively, between the two sides. "So what is the riddle? Her Majesty's true state of mind regarding the Queen of Scots?"

"There is one player you have overlooked."

Deven bit his lip, then shook his head. "As much as I am tempted to suggest the Irish, I do not think they are who you mean."

"They are not," Walsingham confirmed.

Deven studied the chess pieces once more, both those on the table and those unused on the board, then made himself close his eyes. The metaphor was attractive, but easy to get caught in. He mustn't think of knights, castles, and pawns; he must think of nations and leaders. "The Pope?"

"Ably represented by those Catholic forces you have already named."

"A Protestant country, then." Mustn't think in black and white. "Or someone farther afield? Russia? The Turks?"

Walsingham shook his head. "Closer to home."

A courtier, or a noble not at court. Deven could think of

many, but none he had cause to connect to the Scottish Queen. Defeated, he shook his head. "I do not know."

"Nor do I."

The flat words brought his head up sharply. Walsingham met his gaze without blinking. The deep lines that fanned out from his eyes were more visible than ever, and the gray in his hair and beard. The vitality of the Principal Secretary's intellect made it easy to forget his age, but in this admission of defeat he looked old.

Not defeat. Walsingham would not be outplayed. But it seemed he had, for the moment, been stymied. "What do you mean?"

Walsingham gathered his long robe around him and sat once more, gesturing for Deven to do the same. "Her Majesty had little choice but to execute Mary Stewart; the evidence against her was unquestionable. And years in the assembling, I might add; I knew from previous experience that I would need a great deal. Yet for all the efforts of the privy council, and all that evidence, it was a near thing—as her treatment of Davison shows."

"You think someone else persuaded her in the end? Or was arguing against it, and turned her back after her decision?"

"The former."

Deven's mind was racing, pursuing these new paths Walsingham had opened up. "Not anyone on the Catholic side, then." That ruled out a good portion of Europe, but fewer in England, even with some educated guesses as to who was a closeted papist.

"There is more." Walsingham steepled his ink-stained fingers, casting odd shadows over his weary face. "Some of the evidence against the Queen of Scots fell too easily into my hands. There are certain strokes of good fortune that seem too convenient, certain individuals whose assistance was too timely. Not just at the end, but throughout. During the inquiry into her husband's death, she claimed that someone had forged the letters in that casket, imitating her cipher in order to incriminate her. An implausible defense — but it may have been true."

"Someone among the Protestant Scots. Or Burghley."

But Walsingham shook his head before the words were even out. "Burghley has long had his agents, as did Leicester, before his death. But though we have not always been free with the knowledge we gain, I do not think they would, or could, have kept such an enterprise concealed from me. The Scots are a better guess, and I have spent much effort investigating them."

His tone said enough. "You do not think it was them, either."

"It does not end with the Queen of Scots." Walsingham rose again and began to pace, as if his mind would not allow his tired body to remain still. "That was the most obvious incident of interference, and the longest, I think, in the founding and execution. But I have seen other signs. Courtiers presenting unexpected petitions, or changing stances that had seemed firmly set. Or the Queen herself."

Elizabeth, not Mary. "Her Grace has always been of a... mercurial temperament."

Walsingham's dry look said he needed no reminder. "Someone," the Secretary said, "has been exercising a hidden influence over the Queen. Someone not of the privy council. I know my fellows there well enough; I know their positions. These interventions I have seen have, from time to time, matched the agenda of one councillor or another...but never one consistently."

Deven respected Walsingham enough to believe that evaluation, rather than assume someone had successfully misled him for so long. Yet someone must have, had they not? Incredible as it was, someone had found a way to play this game without being uncovered.

The Secretary continued. "It would seem our hidden player has learned, as we all have, that to approach the Queen directly is less than productive; he more often acts through courtiers—or perhaps even her ladies. But there are times when I can think of no explanation save that he had secret conference with her Majesty, and persuaded her thus."

"Within the last two years?"

Walsingham's dark gaze met Deven's again. "Yes."

"Ralegh."

"He is not the first courtier her Majesty has taken to her bosom without naming him to the council; indeed, I sometimes think she delights in confounding us by consulting others. But we know those individuals, and account for them. It is not Ralegh, nor any other we can see."

Deven cast his mind over all those with the right of access to the presence and privy chambers, all those with whom he had seen the Queen walk in the gardens. Every name he suggested, Walsingham eliminated. "But your eye is a good one," the Secretary said, with a wry smile. "There is a reason I took you into my service."

He had been pondering this matter since Deven's appearance at court? Since before then, from the sound of it; Deven should not be surprised to find himself a pawn in this game. Or, to switch metaphors, a hound, used to tease out the scent of prey. Yet a poor hound he was turning out to be. Deven let his breath out slowly. "Then, my lord, by your arguments, there are a number of people it cannot be, but a great many more who it *might* be. Those you can set aside are a few drops against an ocean of possibilities."

"Were it not so," Walsingham said, his voice flat once more, "I had found him out years ago."

Accepting this rebuke, Deven hung his head.

"But," the Secretary went on, "I am not defeated yet. If I cannot find this fellow by logic, I will track him to his lair—by seeing where he moves next."

Now, at last, they were coming to the true reason Walsingham had picked up that first chess piece and asked about the Queen of Scots. Deven did not mind playing the role of the Secretary's hound, when set to such a compelling task. And he even knew his quarry. "Ireland."

"Ireland," Walsingham agreed.

With these recent revelations in mind, Deven tried to see the hand of a hidden player in the events surrounding Perrot, Fitzwilliam, and Tyrone. Yet again the muddle defeated him.

"I do not think our player has chosen a course yet," Walsingham said when he admitted this. "I had suspected him the author of the accusation against Perrot, but what you have uncovered makes me question it. There are oppositions to that accusation I did not expect, that might also be this unknown man's doing."

Deven weighed this. "Then perhaps he is playing a longer game. If, as you say, he manipulated events surrounding the Queen of Scots, he has no aversion to spending years in reaching his goal."

"Indeed." Walsingham passed a hand over his face, pinching the bridge of his nose. "I suspect he is laying the foundations for some future move. Which is cautious of him, and wise, especially if he wishes his hand to remain unseen. But his caution also gives us time in which to track him."

"I will keep listening," Deven said, with more enthusiasm than he had felt when he said it before. Now that he knew what to listen *for,* the task was far more engaging. And he did not want to disappoint the trust Walsingham had shown him, revealing this unsolved riddle in the first place. "Your hidden player must be good, to have remained unseen for so long, but everyone makes mistakes eventually. And when he does, we will find him."

Memory: *December 1585*

The man had hardly stepped onto the dock at Rye when he found two burly fellows on either side of him and a third in front, smiling broadly and without warmth. "You're to come with us," the smiler said. "By orders of the Principal Secretary."

The two knaves took hold of the traveler's elbows. Their captive seemed unassuming enough: a young man, either clean-shaven or the sort who cannot grow a beard under any circumstances, dressed well but not extravagantly. The ship had come from France, though, and in these perilous times that was almost reason enough on its own to suspect him. These men were not searchers, authorized to ransack incoming ships for contraband or Catholic propaganda; they had come for him.

He was one man against three. The captive shrugged and said, "I am at the Secretary's disposal."

"Too right you are," one of the thugs muttered, and they marched him off the dock into the squalid streets of Rye.

With their captive in custody, the men rode north and west, under a gray and half-frozen sky. Three cold, miserable days brought them to a private house near the Palace of Placentia in Greenwich, and the next day brought a knock at the door. The leader muttered, "Not before time, either," and went to open it.

Sir Francis Walsingham stepped through, shaking out the folds of his dark cloak. Outside, two men-at-arms took up station on either side of the door. Walsingham did not look back to them, nor at the men he had hired, though he unpinned the cloak and handed it off to one of those men. His eyes were on the captive, who had risen and offered a bow. It was difficult to tell whether the bow was meant to be mocking, or whether the awkwardness of his bound hands led to that impression.

"Master Secretary," the captive said. "I would offer you hospitality, but your men have taken all my possessions—and besides, the house isn't mine."

Walsingham ignored the sarcasm. He gestured for the two thugs to depart but their leader to remain, and when the three of them were alone in the room, he held up a letter taken from the captive, its seal carefully lifted. "Gilbert Gifford. You came here from France, bearing a letter from the Catholic conspirator Thomas Morgan to the dethroned Queen of Scots—a letter that recommends you to her as a trustworthy ally. I trust you recognize what the consequences for this might be."

"I do," Gifford said. "I also recognize that if those consequences were your intent, you would not have come here to speak privately with me. So shall we skip the threats and intimidation, and move on to the true matter at hand?"

The Principal Secretary studied him for a long moment. His dark eyes were unreadable in their nest of crow's-feet. Then he sat in one of the room's few chairs and gestured for Gifford to take the other, while Walsingham's man came forward and unbound his hands.

When this was done, Walsingham said, "You speak like a man who intends to offer something."

"And you speak like one who intends to negotiate for something." Gifford flexed his hands and examined them, then laid them carefully along the arms of the chair. "In plain terms, my position is this: I come bearing that letter of recommendation, yes, and have every intention of putting it to use. What I have not yet determined is the use to which I will put it."

"You offer your services."

Gifford shrugged. "I have taken stock of the other side. No doubt you have a file somewhere detailing it all, Douai, Rome, Rheims—"

"You became a deacon of the Catholic church in April."

"I would be disappointed if you did not know. Yes, I studied at their seminaries, and achieved some status therein. Had I not, Morgan would not now be recommending me to Mary Stewart. But if you know of those things, you also know of my conflicts with my supposed allies."

"I am aware of them." Walsingham sat quietly, with none of the fidgeting that marked lesser men. "You mean to say, then, that these conflicts of yours were a sign of true disaffection, and that your recent status was achieved in order to gain their trust."

Gifford smiled thinly. "Perhaps. I would like to be of use to someone. I have no particular passion for the Catholic faith, my family notwithstanding, and I judge your cause to be in the ascendent. Though perhaps my willingness to switch sides is reason enough for you not to trust me. I am no ideologue for anyone's faith, yours included."

"I deal with men of the world as much as with ideologues."

"I am glad to hear it. So that is my situation: I was sent to find some way to restore secret communications for Mary Stewart, so that her allies here and abroad might be able to plot her release once more. If you wish to block that communication, you can stop me easily enough—but then they will find someone else."

"Whereas if I make use of you, I will know what is being said."

"Assuming, of course, that I am the only courier, and not sent to distract you from the real channel of communication."

The two men sat silently, watched by the third, while the fire crackled and gave out its warmth. There was no illusion of warmth between Walsingham and Gifford—but there was opportunity, and in all likelihood both preferred that to warmth.

"You have been publicly arrested," Walsingham said at last. "What will you tell Morgan?"

"He's a Welshman. I will tell him I told you that I came here to advance the interests of the Welsh and English factions against the Jesuits."

"Whereupon I, favoring any sort of internal strife among my enemies, released you to proceed about that business."

Gifford smiled mockingly.

Walsingham weighed him for a long moment, his shrewd eyes unblinking. At last he said, "You will keep me informed as you make contact with the Queen of Scots, so that we may devise a way to keep her correspondence under our eye." He took up the letter from Morgan and passed it back to Gifford. "Go to Finch Lane, near Leadenhall Market. There is a man there named Thomas Phelippes. You will give him this letter, and keep in his company until I send you onward. The delay will not be remarked; the Scottish woman's residence is being moved, and until it is settled once more no one will expect you to contact her. Phelippes will return the letter to you when you go."

Gifford accepted the letter and tucked it away. "May this be profitable to us both."

But when they released him, he did not proceed as instructed to Leadenhall. The time for that would come, but he had other business first.

The house he sought out stood hard by the fishy stench of Billingsgate, but despite its location, its windows and doors were boarded up. By the time he arrived there, he had shaken off the Secretary's men who had been following him, and so he entered the tiny courtyard alone.

Dusk was falling as he knelt with fastidious care on the ground and ran his long fingers around the edge of one flagstone. With a small grimace of effort, he pried it from its rest, revealing not dirt beneath, but a vertical passage, with a ladder propped against one wall. When the flagstone settled back into place above him he reached out, found smooth stone, and laid his lips on it in a grudging kiss.

A whisper of sound as the stone shifted, and a rush of cool light.

He stepped through into a place which both was and was not beneath the courtyard of the house near Billingsgate. As he did so, the last vestiges of the facade that was Gilbert Gifford fell away, and with a disturbingly fluid shrug, a new man revealed himself.

He had cut it very fine; much longer and his protection would have faded. He had underestimated how cursedly slow travel could be, when confined to slogging along ordinary roads on ordinary horses, and food not specifically given in offering did nothing to maintain his facade. But he had reached the Onyx Hall in safety, and he could explain away his delay in getting to Phelippes.

First, he would report to his Queen.

With one last rippling shiver that shook off the lingering stain of humanity, Ifarren Vidar set off deeper into the Onyx Hall, to tell of his work against the Scottish woman, and to prepare himself for more time spent imprisoned in mortal guise.

RICHMOND PALACE, RICHMOND: *March 6, 1590*

The draca was not the only fae around Elizabeth's court. Lune was the only one living as a human, but others came and went, to gather secrets, visit lovers, or simply play tricks. Sometimes she knew of their presence; other times she did not.

But she assumed, even before she left the Onyx Hall to lay the groundwork for Anne Montrose's entrance, that someone had been set to watch her. With the endless peregrinations of Elizabeth's court, it was necessary; they could not spend more than a month or two in one residence before it became fouled by habitation, and the Queen's whim could send everyone packing on a moment's notice. The sprites and goblins assigned to bring Lune bread on Fridays had to know where to find her.

That was hardly the watcher's only purpose, though. She never let herself forget that someone else was reporting back on her actions.

Since Vidar's appearance at Hampton Court, Lune had conducted herself with even more care than usual. Her ostensible purpose there was to monitor Walsingham and gain access to him via Deven, but she might at a moment's notice be asked to take action on the Irish affair. A less subtle fae might charm one or more courtiers into behaving as desired; Lune knew her value lay in her ability to work through human channels. Invidiana did not want her influence over the mortal court betrayed by indiscreet use of faerie magic.

So she gathered secrets, and tallied favors, and waited to see what would happen, one eye ever on the few tiny scraps of information about her own court she was able to glean from her contacts.

The draca in the river was useful. Water spirits were often garrulous, and this one was no exception; it might not have access to the daily life of the Onyx Court—it never went past the submerged entrance in the harbor of Queenhithe—but it spoke to other water-associated fae, and even (it claimed) to the Thames itself, which was the lifeblood of London. More news came its way than one might expect. When surprisingly warm and sunny weather descended on them one afternoon, Anne Montrose persuaded the countess to go out along the river, and Lune spent nearly an hour talking to the draca, learning what it knew.

When Elizabeth summoned the countess to attend her at Richmond, the draca followed them downriver. Lune never used it to send word to Vidar and Invidiana, but one blustery day in March, the draca gave her a warning: Vidar himself would bring her bread that night.

Lune was not surprised—she had expected she might see him again, given the apparent importance of Ireland to both courts at present—but she might have been startled, if she came upon him unawares. She thanked the draca, rewarded it with a gold earring purloined from the countess, and went about her business as if nothing were unusual.

Someone was always watching.

Richmond was smaller, and more difficult to sneak around in. Lune left the countess's chamber well in advance of her appointed rendezvous, and sacrificed her careful illusion of Anne Montrose for the purpose of disguise. It was possible to turn mortal eyes away, but tiring; far easier to appear as someone who had a right to be up and about, even at odd hours. A servant of the household in this part of the palace; a man-at-arms in that part, though she impersonated men badly and would not have wanted to attempt a conversation as one.

One careful stage at a time, she made her way outside and into the night.

When at Hampton Court, she met her courier along the river; here, the appointed meeting place lay within the shadows of the orchard. She ducked beneath the drooping, winter-stripped branches of a willow and, straightening, discarded her appearance of mortality entirely.

The fae who waited for her there was not Vidar.

Lune swore inwardly, though she kept her face smooth. A change of plans? A deliberate deception on Vidar's part? Or just the draca lying for its own amusement or self-interest? It did not matter. Gresh, one of her more common contacts, was waiting for her.

"Your bread," he grunted, and tossed it at her without ceremony. Like most goblin fae, he was a squat and twisted thing; ceremony would have been a painful mockery on him. Lune sometimes thought that was why so few of them occupied places of importance in the Onyx Court. In addition to their chaotic and unrefined natures, which disrupted the elegance Invidiana prized, they did not look the part. Mostly they operated as minions of the elfin fae, or stayed away from court entirely.

But elegance and beauty were not the only things that mattered; Dame Halgresta and her two brothers proved that. Raw ugliness and power had their places, too.

Lune caught the bread and examined it; she had been shorted on her ration more than once. The lump was large enough to make up the requisite seven bites, though, and so she tucked it away in her purse. "So what you got?" Gresh asked, scratching through the patchy, wiry hairs of his beard. "Make it quick—just the important stuff—got better things to do with my time than sit under some drippy tree listening to gossip." He glared up at the willow's swaying branches as if personally offended by them.

She had spent much of the day planning out what she would say to Vidar, how she would answer the questions she anticipated him asking. Faced with only Gresh, she felt rather deflated. "The Earl of Tyrone is likely to come before the privy council again soon," she said. "If her Majesty wishes to take some action, that would be an opportune time; he is an ambitious man, and a contentious one. He can be bought or provoked, as needed."

Gresh picked something out of his beard, examined it, then threw it away with a disappointed sigh. "What about what's-his-face? The one you supposed to be watching. Not the Irish fellow."

"Walsingham may be my assignment," Lune said evenly, "but he is not the only way to advance our Queen's interests at court. I began with the most significant news."

"Planning to bore me with insignificant news?"

"*Less* significant is not the same as *insignificant*."

"Dunna waste time arguing; just get on with it."

Tedious experience had taught her that Gresh could neither be charmed nor intimidated into better behavior. It simply wasn't in his nature. Lune swallowed her irritation and went on. "Walsingham continues to defend Sir John Perrot against the accusation of treason. His health has been poor, though. If he has to take another leave of absence, Robert Beale will likely stand in for him with the privy council, as he has done before, but while Beale will follow his master's wishes, he will be less effective of an advocate for Perrot."

Gresh scrunched his brows together in either pain or intense thought, then brightened. "Walserthingy, Wasserwhatsit... oh, right! Something I was supposed to ask you." He feigned a pensive look. "Or should I make you wait for it?"

Lune didn't bother to respond to that; it would only amuse him more.

"Right, so, Water-whoever. Got some mortal fellow dangling that serves him, right?"

"Michael Deven."

"Sure, him. How loyal's he?"

"To me?"

"To his master."

She hadn't expected that question. To buy herself time, Lune said, "He has been in Walsingham's service since approximately a year and a half ago—"

Gresh snorted, a phlegmy sound. "Ain't asking for a history. Would your mortal pup betray him?"

Her nerves hummed like harpstrings brought suddenly into tune. Lune said carefully, "It depends on what you mean by betrayal. Would he act directly against Walsingham's interests?" She didn't even have to ponder it. "No. Deven, like his master, is dedicated to the well-being of England and Elizabeth. At most, his opinion on how to serve that well-being might differ from Walsingham's. I suppose if it differed enough, and he thought the situation critical enough, he might take action on his own. But a direct betrayal? Never. The most he has done so far is indiscreetly share some information he should have kept secret."

"That so?" Gresh greeted this with an eager leer. "Like what?"

Lune kept her shrug deliberately careless. "Matters I have already shared with her Majesty. If you are not privy to them, that is no concern of mine."

"Aw, c'mon." The goblin pouted—a truly hideous sight. "No new scraps you could toss the way of this poor, bored soul?"

Why was he pressing? "No. I have nothing new to report."

It could have been the wind that stirred the branches of the willow. By the time she realized it wasn't, the knife was already at her throat.

"Really," Vidar breathed in her ear, his voice soft with malice. "Would you care to rethink that statement, Lady Lune?"

Gresh cackled and did a little dance.

She closed her eyes before they could betray her. More than they already had. With sight gone, her other senses were sharpened; she heard every quiet tap as the willow's bare branches met and parted, the chill whistling of the damp spring breeze. Frost left a hard crust on the ground and a hard scent in the air.

The edge against her throat rasped imperceptibly across her flesh as she inhaled, its touch light enough to leave the skin unbroken, firm enough to remind her of the blade's presence.

"Have you heard something to the contrary, Lord Ifarren?" she asked, moving her jaw as little as possible.

His left arm was wrapped around her waist, nails digging in hard enough to be felt through the boning of her bodice. Vidar was taller than her, but with his skeletal build, he weighed about the same. What would Gresh do, if she tried to fight Vidar?

There was no point in trying. Even if she got the knife away from him, what would she do? Kill him? Invidiana had been known to turn a blind eye to the occasional murder, but Lune doubted this one would go unremarked. If she could even best the faerie lord.

He laughed silently; she felt it where his body pressed against her back. "How very evasive an answer, Lady Lune." Vidar pronounced her title like a threat. "I have heard something very interesting indeed. I have heard that you spoke with that mortal toy of yours."

"I speak with him often." The words came out perfectly unruffled, as if they stood in ordinary discourse.

"Not so often as you might. You should have told me he was at Richmond without you."

"My apologies, my lord. It was an oversight."

Another silent laugh. "Oh, I am sure. But this recent conversation — that is the one that interests me. A little whisper has said he told you something of import." His grip tightened around her waist, and the knife pressed closer. "Something you have not shared."

She knew the conversation he meant. There was no way the draca could have heard it; they stood in the palace kennel at the time, well away from the river. What manner of fae could have overheard them without being seen?

A black dog, perhaps — some skriker or brash. Hidden in among the hounds. But how much had it heard?

Not everything, or Vidar would not be here now, forcing the information out of her. But she had to be very careful of what she said.

She opened her eyes. Gresh had vanished, his duty done; if he was eavesdropping, that would be Vidar's problem.

"Sir Francis Walsingham," she said, "has begun to suspect."

Vidar went still against her back. Then his arm uncurled; the elfin lord kept the knife against her throat as he circled around to stand in front of her. His black eyes glittered in the near-total darkness.

"What did you say?" he whispered.

She wet her lips before she could suppress the nervous movement. "The Principal Secretary has begun to suspect that someone unknown to him has a hand in English politics."

"What has he seen?"

The question lashed out like a whip. But it was easier for Lune to retain her composure, even with the knife still against her skin, now that her body was not pressed to Vidar's in violently intimate embrace. "Seen? Nothing. He suspects only." She had to give him more than that. "The recent events concerning Ireland have caught his attention. He is beginning to look back at past matters, such as the Queen of Scots."

Vidar's shoulders rose fractionally with tension. Lune knew that one would worry him.

"And what," Vidar said, his voice now hard with control, "will he do with his suspicions?"

Lune shook her head, then froze as she felt the knife scrape her throat once more. "I do not know. Deven does not know. Walsingham spoke of it only briefly, and that in a confused fashion. He has not been well; Deven thinks this a feverish delusion brought on by overwork."

She stood motionless, briefly forgotten as Vidar considered her words. The black dog—if that was the watcher in question—could not have heard them over the racket the other hounds were making. He had only seen them talking, and surmised from her reaction that whatever Deven spoke of was important. Vidar's sharp reaction to her first declaration had made that plain.

Which meant that she could afford to bend the truth—within limits.

Vidar's gaze sharpened and turned back to her. "So," he said. "You learned of this—a clear and immediate threat to the Queen's grace and the security of our people—and you chose to keep the information to yourself." His lips peeled back from his teeth in mockery of a smile. "Explain why."

Lune sniffed derisively. "Why? I should think it obvious, even to you. This is the kind of situation that makes people stop thinking, sends them into a blind panic wherein they strike out at the perceived threat, thinking only to destroy it. Which might be a terrible waste of opportunity."

"Opportunity." Vidar relaxed his arm; the knife moved away,

though it still glimmered in his hand, unsheathed and ready. "Opportunity for Lady Lune, perhaps—at the expense of the Onyx Court, and all the fae who shelter under its power."

She wondered if this rhetoric came from their habit of copying mortals. The greater good of the Onyx Court, and the faerie race as a whole, was occasionally deployed as a justification for certain actions, or an exhortation to loyalty. It might have carried more force had it not been only an occasional device—or if anyone had believed it to be more than empty words. "Not in the slightest," she said, keeping her voice even and unperturbed. "I am no fool; what gain could there possibly be for me, betraying her Majesty in such a manner? But I am better positioned than any to see which direction Walsingham moves, what action he takes. And I tell you that quick action would be inadvisable here. Far better to watch him, and to move subtly, when fortune should offer us a chance." She allowed herself an ironic smile. "Even should he uncover the times and places in which we have intervened, I hardly expect he will imagine fae to be the culprits."

And that was true enough. But Vidar's malicious smile had returned. "I wonder what her Majesty would think of your logic?"

Beneath the facade of her composure, Lune's heart skipped several beats.

"I might not tell her." Vidar examined the point of his dagger, scraping some imagined fleck of dirt off it with one talonlike fingernail. "It would be a risk to me, of course—if she found out... but I might be willing to offer you that mercy, Lady Lune."

She had to ask; he was waiting for it. "At what price?"

His eyes glittered at her over the blade in his hands. "Your silence. At some point in the future, I will bid you keep some knowledge to yourself. Something commensurate with what I do for you now. And you will be bound, by your word, to keep that matter from the Queen."

She could translate that well enough. He was binding her to be his accomplice in some future bid to take the Onyx Throne.

Yet what was her alternative? Say to him, *So tell the Queen, and be damned,* and then warn Invidiana of Vidar's ambition? She knew of it already, and he had not said anything specific enough to condemn him. At which point Lune would be dependent on nothing more than the mercy of a merciless Queen.

Lune kept from grinding her teeth by force of will, and said in a voice that sounded only a little strained, "Very well."

Vidar lowered the knife. "Your word upon it."

He was leaving nothing to chance. Lune swallowed down bile and said, "In ancient Mab's name, I swear to repay this favor with favor, of commensurate kind and value, when you should upon a future occasion ask for it, and to let no word of it reach the Queen."

That, or remove him as a threat before he ever had occasion to ask. *Sun and Moon,* Lune thought despairingly, *how did I reach such a state, that I should be swearing myself to Vidar?*

The dagger vanished as if it had never been. "Excellent," Vidar said, and smiled that toothy smile. "I look forward to hearing your future reports, Lady Lune."

OATLANDS PALACE, SURREY: *March 14, 1590*

Standing at attention beside the door that led from the presence chamber to the privy chamber, Deven fixed his eyes on the far wall and let his ears do the work. It was a tedious duty, and a footsore one—shifting one's weight was frowned upon—but it did afford him a good opportunity to eavesdrop. He had come to suspect that Elizabeth's penchant for conversing in a variety of languages was as much an obfuscatory tactic as a demonstration of her learning; her courtiers were a polyglot assortment, following the lead of their Queen, but few could speak every language she did. He himself was often defeated by her rapid-fire speech, but he had enough Italian now to sift out the gist of a sentence, and his French was in fine practice. So he stared off into the distance, poleax held precisely upright, and listened.

He listened particularly for talk of Ireland.

A hidden player, Walsingham had said. Deven had already calculated that any such player must either have the right of entrée to the presence chamber — likely the privy chamber as well — or else must have followers with such a right. The former made more sense, as one could not effectively influence the machinery of court at a distance for long, but he couldn't assume it too firmly.

Unfortunately, though a great many people were barred from entry, a great many were not. Peers of the realm, knights, gentlemen — even some wealthy merchants — ambassadors, too. Could it be one of them? Neither the Spanish nor the French would have reason to urge Mary's execution on Elizabeth, and they had little enough reason to care what happened in Ireland, though part of the accusations against both Perrot and the Earl of Tyrone were that they had conspired with the Spanish.

But ambassadors came and went. If Walsingham was correct, this player had been active for decades. They made poor suspects, unless the true players were their more distant sovereigns — but those were already on the board, so to speak.

Round and round Deven's thoughts went, while out of the corners of his eyes he watched courtiers come and go, and he eavesdropped on every scrap of conversation he could.

A tap on his brocade shoulder roused him from his reverie. Focusing so much on the edges of the room, he hadn't paid any attention to what was in front of him.

William Tighe stood before him, ceremonial polearm in hand. On the other side of the doorway, John Darrington was changing places with Arthur Capell. Deven relaxed his stance and nodded thanks to Tighe.

As he stepped aside, he saw something that distracted him from the endless riddle in his mind. Across the chamber, the Countess of Warwick laid aside her embroidery hoop and rose from her cushion. She made a deep curtsy to Elizabeth, then backed away. Transferring the poleax to his left hand, Deven moved quickly to the outer door, where he bowed and opened it for the countess.

He followed her out into the watching chamber, past the Yeomen of the Guard and usher at that door, and as soon as they passed out of earshot he said, "Lady Warwick. If I could beg a moment of your time?"

She looked mildly surprised, but nodded and gestured for him to walk at her side. Together they passed out of the watching chamber, filled with those courtiers hoping for an opportunity to gain entrance to the more restricted and privileged domain beyond. Deven waited until they had escaped those rapacious ears before he said, "I humbly beg your pardon for troubling you with this matter; I am certain there are many other, more pressing cares that demand your ladyship's time. But I am sure you can understand how affection drives a man's heart to impatience. Have you any sense yet how her Majesty's disposition lies, with respect to my desire?"

It was far from the most elaborate speech he had ever delivered at court, yet he seemed to have puzzled the countess. "Your desire?"

"Mistress Montrose, your waiting-gentlewoman," Deven said. "She tells me she has asked your ladyship to discern which way the wind blows with the Queen—whether her Grace would be angered by the notion of our marriage."

Her step slowed marginally. Working in Walsingham's service, Deven had questioned a variety of dubious men; he had learned to read body language very well. What he read in her hesitation chilled him. "Master Deven . . . she has made no such request of me."

They walked on a few more strides, Deven's legs carrying him obediently onward, because he had not yet told them to do otherwise.

"No such request," he repeated, dumbly.

The look she gave him was guarded, but compassionate. "If you wish it, I can discover her Majesty's inclination on the matter. I am sure she would not object."

Deven shook his head, slowly. "No . . . no. That is . . . I thank you, my lady." The words came out by rote. "I may ask for your good office in this matter later. But I . . . I should speak to Anne."

"Yes," the countess said softly. "I imagine you should. God give you good day, Master Deven."

OATLANDS PALACE, SURREY: *March 15, 1590*

He did not seek out Anne until the next day. He spent the evening alone in his chamber, sending Ranwell off on a spurious errand. Colsey waited on him alone that night, and was permitted to stay because he would keep his mouth shut.

The place his thoughts led him was not pleasant, but he could not avoid it. And delay would not improve matters. When he had leisure the following afternoon, he went in search of Anne.

She was not with the countess; she had been assigned other tasks that day. Oatlands was a small palace compared with Hampton Court or Whitehall, yet it seemed the proverbial haystack that day, and Anne the needle that kept eluding his search. Not until nearly dusk did he find her, when he went again to check the countess's own chambers, and found her making note of a delivery of books.

He stopped on the threshold, his movement suddenly arrested, and she looked up from her paper. The smile that lit her face made him hope it was all a simple misunderstanding—but he did not believe it.

"We must speak," he said without preamble.

Anne put down the pen and bit her lip. "The countess may return soon; I should—"

"She will forgive you this absence."

A thin line formed between her pale brows, but she rose from her seat. "Very well."

He would not have this conversation inside; there were always ears to overhear, whether they belonged to courtiers or servants of the household. Anne fetched a cloak. Deven had not thought to bring one for himself. Together they went out into the orchard, where the trees only intermittently protected against the spring wind.

Anne walked with him in silence, granting him the time he needed. The words were prepared in his mind, yet they did not come out easily. Not with her at his side.

"I spoke with the countess today."

"Oh?" She seemed guardedly curious, no more.

"About the Queen. About—you, and me, and the matter of our marriage." His cheeks and lips were going cold already. "That was the first she heard of it."

Anne's step slowed, as the countess's had before her.

Deven made himself turn to face her. His gut felt tight, like he was holding himself together by muscle alone. "If you do not wish to marry me, all you need do is say so."

The words were spoken, and she did not immediately dispute them. Instead she dropped her chin, so that her hood half-concealed her face. That gesture, too, spoke clearly to him. He waited, trying not to shiver, and almost missed it when she whispered, "'Tis not that I do not wish to. I cannot."

"Cannot?" He had resigned himself to her cooled affections, or tried to; now he seized on this word with mingled hope and confusion. "Why?"

She shook her head, not meeting his gaze.

"Does your father not approve?"

Another shake of her head. "I — I have no father."

"Are you promised already to another? *Wed* to another, God forbid?" Again she denied it. Deven groped for other possible reasons. "Are you Catholic?"

A wild, inappropriate laugh escaped her, then cut off abruptly. "No."

"Then in God's name, why not?"

He said it louder than he meant to. Anne flinched and turned away, presenting her cloaked back to him. "I —" Her voice was ragged, like his, but determined. He knew well how strong her will was, but it had never been turned against him before. "I am sorry, Michael. You deserve an explanation, and I have none. But I cannot marry you."

The strained beats of his heart marked the time as he stared at her, waiting for further words, that were not forthcoming. "Now, or ever?"

Another painfully long pause. "Ever."

That flat declaration drained the warmth out of him faster than the bitter air ever could. Deven swallowed down the first three responses that came to his tongue; even now, in his bafflement and pain, he did not want to hurt her, though the urge flared within him. Finally he said, hearing the roughness in his own voice, "Then why did you let me believe you would?"

She turned back at last, and the tears that should have been in her eyes were absent. She had a distant look about her, and though it might simply be how she showed pain, it angered him. Had this meant nothing to her?

"I feared you would leave me, when you knew," she said. "You are your father's heir, and must marry. I did not wish to lose you to another."

The words were too manipulative. He was expected to protest, to tell her there was no other in his heart, and though it was true he would not say it. "If you wished me to stay, then you should not have kept me like a fish on a hook. I believed you trusted me more than that—as I trusted you."

Now tears sparkled at the corners of her eyes. "Forgive me."

He shook his head, slowly. There was some riddle here he could not solve, but he had not the will to untangle it. If he stayed any longer, he would say something he would regret.

Turning, he left her in the dead wilderness of the orchard, with her cloak rippling in the cold wind.

OATLANDS PALACE, SURREY: *March 19, 1590*

The countess was a kind woman, as ladies of the court went. She kept a weather eye not just on the Queen she served, but on the women who served her in turn. It did not escape her that a problem had arisen between her waiting-gentlewoman Anne Montrose and Michael Deven of the Gentlemen Pensioners, andfollowing the revelation of that problem, the two of them had fallen out.

Lune would have preferred Lady Warwick to be less concerned for her well-being. As it was, she almost resorted to faerie magic to convince her human mistress to leave her be. Anne Montrose needed to be upset, but not *too* upset, lest the countess pry too closely; hidden behind that mask, Lune had to shake off the practiced habits of her masquerade, and figure out what to do next.

She cursed herself for the misstep. Originally she had fostered his worry about Elizabeth's possible jealousy because it provided a convenient delaying tactic; their romance was useful, but she could not possibly afford to go through with an actual marriage. And he was not, unfortunately, the sort of courtier to indulge in an illicit affair for years on end without worrying about scandal. It would have been easier if he were. But he soon made it clear he wished to wed her, and so she had to find ways of putting him off.

She should have expected he would speak to the countess directly. She should have known, the first time she lied and said she had asked her mistress to look into the matter, that a time would come when she must produce an answer.

It was a problem she could not solve as Anne Montrose, because Anne loved Deven; the mortal woman she pretended to be would marry him and be done with it. As Lune, her one bitter consolation was that Deven was unlikely to spot fae manipulation at court, now that the nearest fae manipulator had become estranged from him.

But what now? She had no answer to that all-important question. Walsingham had other confidants—Robert Beale, Nicholas Faunt—but if she approached them in her current guise, all she would do was rouse suspicion. The more effective course of action, in the long term, would be to retreat and return under a different glamour and persona, but with the Principal Secretary searching for evidence of Invidiana's hand, Lune could not afford the months it would take to reintegrate herself to any useful extent.

She might have no choice but to resort to more direct methods: concealment, eavesdropping, theft of papers, and other covert activities. To do so would require extensive use of charms, and so as far as she was concerned they were a last resort—but she might be at that point. Vidar expected her to provide information, and soon.

Deven's absence left a palpable hole in her life. Their duties often kept them apart, but it had become habit to seek out occasions to meet, even if they saw each other only in passing, exchanging a smile while going opposite ways down a gallery or through a chamber. Now she avoided him, and he her. Being near each other was too uncomfortable.

What would she do without him? Not until he was gone did she realize how much she had depended on him. She saw Walsingham twice, at a distance, and fretted over what the Principal Secretary might be doing.

What Deven might be doing. He was, as he had said, Walsingham's hound.

She lay awake late into the night the following Thursday, staring into the darkness as if it would provide an answer. And so she was awake when the countess rose from her bed and reached for a dressing gown.

Anne Montrose whispered, "My lady?"

"I cannot sleep," the countess murmured back, pulling on the padded, fur-trimmed gown. "I need air. Will you walk with me?"

Anne shed her blankets and helped her mistress, fetching a coif to keep her head and ears warm outside. They both slipped on overshoes, then exited the chamber, leaving the other gentlewomen undisturbed.

Deep in the recesses of her mind, where Anne Montrose gave way to Lune, the faerie thought: *Something is wrong*.

The countess did not walk quickly, but she moved with purpose, through the palace and toward the nearest exterior door. Anne followed her, squinting to see in the near-total darkness, and then they were outside, where the air rested unnaturally still.

In the silence, she thought she heard a sound.

Music.

Music intended only for the countess's ears.

Anne Montrose's face took on a wary, alert expression her mistress would have been surprised to see—had she eyes for anything other than the miniature stone tower of the herber up ahead.

Who would summon her? Who would play a faerie song, to lure the Countess of Warwick from her bed and into the shadows of night?

They rounded the herber, and found someone waiting for them.

Orpheus's rangy body was wrapped tenderly around the lyre, his fingers coaxing forth a melody that was still all but inaudible, to all but its intended target. The countess sank to the ground before him, heedless of the damp that immediately soaked into and through her dressing gown; her mouth hung slack as she gazed adoringly up at the mortal musician and listened to his immortal song.

Heavy footsteps squelched in the wet soil behind Lune, and again, as with Vidar, she realized the truth too late.

The countess was not the target. She was merely the lure, to draw Lune outside, away from mortal eyes.

Lune flung herself to the left, hoping to evade the one behind her, but hands the size of serving platters were waiting for her. She dropped to the ground—the fingers clamped shut above her shoulders, just missing their grip—but then a boot swung forward and struck her squarely in the back, sending her face-first into the dirt.

Two paces away, the countess sat serenely, oblivious to the violence, held by the power of Orpheus's gift.

A knee planted itself in Lune's back, threatening to snap her spine with its sheer weight. She cried out despite herself, and heard a nasty chuckle in response. Her arms were twisted up and back, bound together with brutal efficiency; then her captor hauled her up by her hair and flung her bodily against the stone wall of the herber.

Coughing, stumbling, eyes watering with pain, Lune could still make out the immense and hated bulk of Dame Halgresta Nellt.

"You fucked up, slut," the low, rocky voice growled. Even through the venom, the pleasure was unmistakable. "The Queen forgave you once—Mab knows why. But she won't forgive you this time."

Lune forced her lungs to draw in air. "I haven't," she managed, then tried again. "Vidar knows. Everything I know. What goes on here. I report to him."

Halgresta hadn't come alone. Six goblins materialized out of the shadows, armed and armored and ready to catch Lune if she tried to run—as if she could outrun a giant. She had to talk her way out of this.

Talk her way out, with Halgresta. It would be like using a pin to dismantle an iron-bound door.

The giantess grinned, showing teeth like sharpened boulders. "Vidar knows everything, eh? Well, he does now. But not from you."

What? What had Vidar learned? How had he gotten someone closer to Walsingham than she had?

"You lost your toy, bitch." Halgresta's voice struck her like another blow, knocking all the wind out. "You lost that mortal of yours."

*Deven.*

The stabbing pain in her ribs was subsiding; Lune didn't think anything was broken. She made herself stand straighter, despite her awkwardly bound arms. "I am not finished," she said, with as much confidence as she could muster. "Deven is only one route to Walsingham. There are other ways to deal with the problem—"

Halgresta spat. The wad of spittle hit the countess's shoulder and slid down, unnoticed; Orpheus's melody was still ghosting through the air, plaintive and soft. "Right. Other ways. And other people to take care of them. You? You're coming back to the Onyx Hall."

"Let me talk to Vidar," Lune said. Had she reached such a nadir that he seemed like a thread of hope? Yes. "I am sure he and I can reach an accord."

The giantess leaned forward, until her ugly, stony face was the only thing Lune could see, almost invisible in the darkness. "Maybe you and Vidar could," Halgresta growled. "Who knows what plots you and that spider have hatched. But he's not the one who told me to bring you in.

"The Queen is."


St. Paul's Cathedral, London: *April 7, 1590*


Sir Philip Sidney, late husband of Sir Francis Walsingham's daughter, had been buried in a fine tomb in St. Paul's Cathedral when he died in 1586.

Now the tomb was opened again, to receive the body of Sir Francis Walsingham.

The ceremony was simple. The Principal Secretary had died in debt; his will, found in a secret cabinet in his house on Seething Lane, had requested that no great expenditure be made for his funeral. They buried him at night, to avoid attracting the attention of his creditors.

And so there was no great procession, no men-at-arms wearing matching livery—not even the Queen. She had quarreled often with Walsingham, but in the end, the two respected one another. She would have come if she could.

Deven stood alongside Beale and others he knew more distantly: Edward Carey, William Dodington, Nicholas Faunt. Some small distance away stood the pale, grieving figures of Ursula Walsingham and her daughter Frances. The gathering was not large.

The priest's voice rolled sonorously on, his words washing over Deven and vanishing up into the high Gothic reaches of the cathedral. The body was placed in the tomb, and the tomb closed over it.

The body. Deven had seen death, but never had he so much difficulty connecting a living man to the lifeless flesh he left behind.

He could not believe Walsingham was dead.

The priest pronounced a benediction. The gathered mourners began to depart.

Standing rooted to his spot, eyes fixed on the carved stone of the tomb, Deven thought bleakly, *Master Secretary—what do I do now?*

# Act Three

O heauens, why made you night, to couer sinne?
By day this deed of darknes had not beene.
— Thomas Kyd
The Spanish Tragedie

*They dance in intricate patterns, coming together and parting again, skirts and long sleeves swaying a counterpoint to their rhythm. But his ears cannot hear the music, or the sound of their laughter. His world has wrapped him in silence. To his eyes, those around him are ghosts: they dance beneath the earth, which is the realm of the dead, and the dead have no voices with which to speak. Aeneas fed his ghosts blood, and Odysseus, too, but no such heroes exist here. There is no blood that might quicken their voices to life once more.*

*He hovers against a pillar, entranced and afraid, and the other ghosts stare at him. No —not ghosts. He remembers now. They are alive. They speak, but he cannot hear them. Only whispers, ghost sounds, unreal.*

*They wonder why he does not speak to them. That is what the living do; they talk, they converse, they prove their existence with words. But where Tiresias was blind, the man who bears his name is mute. He cannot —dares not —speak.*

*His jaw aches from being clenched tightly shut. Words beat within him like caged birds, terrified, desperate, fighting to break free, and when he keeps them trapped within, they stab at him with talons and beaks, until he bleeds from a thousand unseen wounds. He cannot speak. If he makes a sound, the slightest sound—*

*Are you real? He is desperate to know. If they are real... if he could be sure, then perhaps he would have the courage.*

*No. No courage. It died, broken on the rack of this place. He sees too much of what will come —or what came, what might come, what could never be. He no longer believes in a difference. A difference would mean his choices matter. His choices, and his mistakes. Everyone's mistakes.*

151

*Fire. Fire and ash and blood fill his vision. The dance vanishes. The walls are broken open, stones shattered, the sky brought down to fight the earth. He presses his hands against his head, his eyes, harder, harder, slams himself against the pillar—did he cry out? Fear grips him by the throat. No sound. No sound. Certain words are the wrong words; the only safe words are no words.*

*They stare at him and laugh, but he hears nothing.*

*The silence chokes him. Perhaps he should speak, and be done with it.*

*But no. He cannot do it; he lacks the strength. Too much has been lost. The man he needs is gone, gone beyond recall. Alone, mute, he has no will to act.*

*She has seen to that.*

*He curls up on the stone, not knowing where he lies, not caring, and wraps his trembling hands around his throat. The birds want to fly. But he must keep them safe, keep them within, where they will harm no one but him.*

*None of this is real. But dreams have the power to kill.*

THE TOWER OF LONDON: *April 9, 1590*

The light hurt Lune's eyes, but she refused to let it show. "Tiresias. The Queen's seer. Will you bid—" No, not bid. She had no right to demand such things. "Will you beg him to visit me?"

A harsh laugh answered her. Sir Kentigern Nellt's voice rumbled an octave below his sister's, and was twice as ugly. It matched the rest of him, from his rough-hewn face to the cruelty of his spirit. Whether he even bothered to pass along her requests, Lune did not know, but she had to ask.

Vidar first; she was already in debt to him, but she would have promised more to get out of this cell. He did not come, though. Nor did Lady Nianna, which was no surprise. Lune had been on good terms with the previous Welsh envoy, the bwganod Drys Amsern, but the Tylwyth Teg changed their ambassadors regularly; they did not like anyone to remain for too long under the corrupting influence of the Onyx Court. Amsern was gone. And the Goodemeades had no political influence with which to aid her.

The seer was the last person she could think to ask for.

At a gesture from Sir Kentigern, her goblin jailers heaved on the heavy bronze door of her cell and swung it shut once more.

The resulting blackness was absolute. Her protection against human faith had long since worn off; beyond that, she could not tell how long she had been there. Nor when, if ever, she would get out. The Onyx Hall did not extend beyond the walls of London, but the Tower lay within those walls, and it, too, had its reflection below. These cells were used for people Invidiana was very displeased with. And while a mortal died quickly if you

153

deprived him of food—even more quickly, without water—it was not so with fae. Wasting away might take years.

Sitting in the darkness, Lune thought, *Sun and Moon. When did I become so alone?*

She missed...*everything.* The entire false life she had constructed for herself, torn away in an instant. She missed Anne, which made no sense; Anne had never been real.

But it reminded her of memories long buried. Not just her recent time at Elizabeth's court; that distant, mist-shrouded age—how long ago?—before she came to the Onyx Hall. Lune could no longer recall where she lived then, nor who was around her, but she knew that life had been different. Gentler. Not this endless, lethal intrigue.

She was so very tired of intrigue. Tired of having no one she could honestly call "friend."

"Too much mortal bread," Lune whispered to herself, just to break the silence. A year of it had changed her, softened her. Made her regret the loss of such mortal things as warmth and companionship. She was inventing memories now, losing herself in delusion like Tiresias, pining for a world that could never be.

It wasn't true, though. There *were* fae like that, fae who could be friends. The Goodemeades were living proof of its possibility.

Not in the Onyx Hall, though.

And if Lune wanted to survive, she could not afford to indulge such fancies. She gritted her teeth. To escape the intrigue, first she had to scheme her way free. The only way out was through.

Keys rattled outside her cell. The lock clanked and thunked, and then the familiar protest of the hinges as the door swung open. Light flooded through. Lune stood, using the wall to steady herself, and looked flinchingly toward the opening, raising her gaze a degree at a time as her eyes could bear the light.

A figure came through. Not twisted enough for a goblin. Not tall enough for Kentigern. But not Tiresias, either. The sihouette had a broad, triangular base: a woman, in court dress.

"Leave the door open," an accented and melodious voice said. "She will not flee."

The goblin outside bowed, and stepped back.

Lune's eyes were adjusting at last. Her visitor moved to one side, so she was no longer backlit, and with a confused shock Lune recognized her. "Madame," she said, and sank into a curtsy.

The ambassador from the Cour du Lys seemed all the more immaculate for her dirty surroundings, wearing a crystalline gown in the latest fashion, her lovely copper hair curled and swept up under a pert little hat. Malline le Sainfoin de Veilée eyed Lune's filthy skin with distaste, but inclined her head in greeting. "The *chevalier* has given me permission to speak with you, and a promise of discretion."

Kentigern would probably keep that promise, if only because he was not subtle enough to seek out a buyer for his information. "Is discretion needed, *madame ambassadrice?*"

"If you choose to accept the bargain I offer you."

Lune's mind felt as rusty as the door hinges. That the French envoy was offering her help, she could understand, but why? And what did she want in return?

Madame Malline did not explain immediately. Instead she snapped her jeweled fingers, and when a head appeared in the doorway—a sprite belonging to the embassy, not the goblin jailer—she spoke imperiously in French, demanding two stools. A moment later these were brought in, and Madame

Malline arrayed herself on one, gesturing for Lune to take the other.

When they were both seated, and Madame Malline had arranged her glittering skirts to her satisfaction, she said, "You may know I am in negotiations with your Queen, regarding the conflict with the Courts of the North, and which side my king will take. You, Lady Lune, are not valuable enough as a bargaining piece to be worth much in that debate, but you are worth a little. I am prepared to offer Invidiana certain concessions of neutrality—minor ones, nothing more—in exchange for your freedom from this cell."

"I would be in your debt, madame," Lune said reflexively. Sitting in the light, on a cushioned stool, had warmed up the stiff muscles of her mind. She remembered now how she might repay that debt.

She hoped the ambassador meant something else.

"Indeed," the French fae murmured. "I know of you, Lady Lune, though we have not spoken often. You have more between your ears than fluff; you would not have survived for so long were it not so. You know already what I will ask."

Lune wished desperately for a bath. It seemed a trivial thing, her unwashed state, when laid against her political predicament, but the two were not unconnected; grimy, with her hair straggling around her face in strands dulled from silver to gray, she felt inferior to the French elf. It would undermine her in the bargaining that must come.

But she would do her best. "My Queen," Lune said, "also knows what you will ask. I would be foolish indeed to betray her."

Madame Malline dismissed this with a wave of one delicate hand. "*Certainement,* she knows. But she, knowing, permitted me to come here. We may therefore conclude that she does not see it as a betrayal."

"What we may conclude, *madame ambassadrice,* is that it amuses her to grant me enough rope with which to hang myself." Lune gestured at the walls of her cell. "That I have been kept here means she has not made up her mind to destroy me. This might be her way of making her decision: if I tell you more than she wishes me to, then she will declare it treason and execute me."

"But then the bird would already have flown, *non*? I would have the information she does not wish me to have. Unless you suggest she would strike you dead even as you speak."

Invidiana could do it, with that black diamond jewel. But she had not used it on Lune, and the envoy had a point; by the time Lune was dead, the information would already have been passed on. And despite everything, Lune did not think Invidiana would breach protocol so inexcusably as to kill a foreign ambassador on English soil. She often bent the rules of politics and diplomacy until they wept blood, but to break them outright—especially during such negotiations—would ensure an alliance against her that even the Onyx Court could not survive.

It was a slim enough thread on which to hang her life. But what was her alternative? Invidiana might yet decide to kill her anyway—or worse, forget her. One day the door would cease to open, and then Lune would dwindle to nothingness, alone in the dark, screaming away her final years inside a stone box.

"I am willing to negotiate," she said.

*"Bon!"* Madame Malline seemed genuinely pleased. "Let us speak, then. I will have wine brought, and you will tell me—"

"No." Lune cut her off as the French elf raised her hand to summon a servant again. She stood and straightened her skirts, resisting the urge to brush dirt off them. It wouldn't help, and it would make her look weak. "You secure my release, and *then* I tell you what I know."

The warmth in the ambassador's smile dwindled sharply at the insinuation. She could not be surprised, though; distrust and suspicion were the daily bread of the Onyx Court. And indeed, she played the same card in return. "But once you are free of this cell, what is to reassure me *I* will have what *I* seek?"

Lune had not expected so obvious a trick to succeed, but it had been worth a try. "I will tell you some things now, and more once I am free."

Madame Malline pursed her full lips, considering it. "Tell me, and I will see to it you are moved to a better cell, and so on from there."

The alternative was to give her word, and Lune's half of the bargain was necessarily too vague for that to work. "Very well."

Servants appeared again. One sprite poured the wine, while another bowed deeply and presented Lune with a platter of fresh grapes. She made herself eat these slowly, as if she did not really need them. Negotiations were not over. She still could not afford to look weak.

"The folk of the sea," she said when the sprites had bowed and retreated to the edge of the room. "They take offense if you call them fae, and in truth I do not know if they are. 'Tis a question for philosophers to debate. I went among them for politics."

Madame Malline nodded. "The mortal Armada, yes."

"They are a secretive people; they do not welcome commerce with outsiders, and reckon themselves to have little care what goes on above the surface of the water. Indeed, in some cases they bear hostility toward those who live on land." Such as, for example, the Cour du Lys, the strongest faerie court in the north of France. Lune did not know what offense had been committed there, but she knew there had been one. She would have to be careful not to offer the ambassador any information that might be useful in healing that breach.

But her explanations had to seem natural and unaffected. "They would not speak directly to anyone who lives on the surface," Lune said, "but they will talk to our river nymphs, sometimes. We had occasional contact through the estuary at Gravesend. It was through this that Invidiana arranged for my embassy. They agreed to let me come among them; I do not know what she promised them for that concession."

"Did you go alone?" the envoy asked.

"Two of the estuary nymphs accompanied me, their tolerance for saltwater being higher than their riverbound sisters. Beyond that, I was served by the folk of the sea."

"And how did you go among them?"

She could still feel the air whistling past her cheeks, the gut clench of fear that this had all been some cruel jest of Invidiana's. Lune closed her eyes, then made herself open them and meet Madame Malline's gaze. "I leapt from the cliffs of Dover. And that, *madame ambassadrice,* is all I will say for now." She rose, stepped clear of her stool, and spread her soiled skirts in a curtsy. "If you would know more, then show me what you can do on my behalf."

Madame Malline studied her, then nodded thoughtfully. "*Oui,* Lady Lune. I will do so. And I look forward to hearing the continuation of your tale."

A moment later she was gone, and the door closed again, blocking out all light. But a stool stayed behind, a promise of assistance to come.

St. James' Palace, Westminster: *April 10, 1590*

*In the end, his urine came forth at his mouth and nose, with so odious a stench that none could endure to come near him.*

The report crumpled abruptly in Deven's hand; he made his fingers unclench. Laying the paper on the table, he smoothed it out, and suppressed the urge to fling it in the fire.

Walsingham was barely in his tomb, and already the Catholics were rejoicing, and spreading damnable rumors in their glee. They made of the Principal Secretary's death something so utterly vile—

The paper was creasing again. Deven snarled and turned his back on it.

He did so in time to see Beale enter the room. The older man looked as if he had not slept well the previous night, but he was composed. Beale's gaze flicked past Deven to the battered report.

"They saw him as their chief persecutor," he said quietly, brushing a strand of graying hair out of his eyes. "So terrible a figure cannot die like an ordinary man, and so they invent stories, which confirm their belief that he was an atheist and font of rank corruption."

Deven's jaw ached as he moved it, from having been clenched so tight. "No doubt there will be a festival in Spain, when the news reaches Philip."

"No doubt." Beale came farther into the room, sought out a chair and sank into it. "While here we mourn him. The English Crown has lost a great supporter. A great man."

*At the moment when we need him the most.*

The thought was casual, reflexive—and then the implications struck him.

His jerk of movement drew Beale's eye. "Indeed," Deven said, half to himself. "The Catholics are very glad of it. But he said he did not think the guilty party was Catholic."

Beale frowned. "'Guilty party'?"

Deven turned to face him, driven by a sudden energy. "He must have spoken of it to you—he held you in great trust. A hidden player, he told me, scarcely a month gone. Someone with a hand in our court, who operates in secret."

"Ah," Beale said, and his frown deepened. "Yes."

"Do you doubt him?"

"Not entirely." Beale's hands moved to straighten the papers scattered over the desk, as if they needed something to do while his brain and mouth were otherwise occupied. "He told you of the Queen of Scots, I presume? In that matter, I agree with him. I was closely involved with certain parts of that affair, and I do believe someone was influencing the Queen. Regarding the recent events with Perrot...I am not so sure."

Disregarding this latter part, Deven said, "But you do believe there is such a player."

"Or was. He may be gone now."

"Walsingham set me to hunt this man. He hoped fresh eyes might see what his could not. And now he's dead."

The paper shuffling stopped, as Beale saw the mark he aimed at. "Deven," he said, clearly choosing his words with care, "Sir Francis has—had been sick for a long time. Think of his absence last year. This is not a new-sprung development, risen out of nowhere in the last month."

"But if the hidden player *is* still around, and is involved with the Irish matter—"

"If, if," Beale said impatiently. "I am not convinced of either. And even were it so, why not eliminate *you*? After all, you are the one up to your eyebrows in the trouble surrounding Perrot. If anyone was about to uncover the secret, it would be you."

Deven snorted. "I do not have so high an opinion of myself as to think I pose a greater threat than Walsingham. If I did not uncover it, someone else would, and pass it along to him."

Beale rose and came around the corner of the table to take him by the shoulders. "Michael," the older secretary said, soft but firm. "I know it would be easier to believe that someone poisoned or cursed Sir Francis, and brought about his untimely death. But he was a sick man, one who had shaken off illness often before in his determination to continue his work. He could not do so forever. God willed it that his time should end. That is all the explanation there is."

The grip on his shoulders threatened his self-control. Just a short month before, Deven had seen before himself a bright and intriguing future, with both a patron and a wife to lend it purpose. Now he had no prospect of either.

All he had was the duty the Principal Secretary had laid upon him.

Deven stepped back, out of Beale's hands. His voice came out steadier than he expected as he said, "No doubt you are right. But it does not answer the matter of this hidden player. You do not know if he is still around, but you also do not know that he is gone. I intend to find out. Will you help me?"

Beale grimaced. "As I may. Sir Francis's death has put matters into disarray. If anything is to be preserved of the work he has done, the agents and informers he acquired, I'll have to find someone else to take them on."

This broke through the desolate fog that had gripped Deven's mind. He had not thought of that, but of course Beale was right; only someone well placed on the privy council could make good use of Walsingham's people. "Did you have someone in mind?"

"Burghley has made overtures, which I expected. But Essex also expressed an interest."

"Essex?" Deven knew it was disrespectful, but he could not repress a snort. "He hasn't the patience for intelligence work." Or the mind.

"No, he hasn't. But he married Sir Francis's daughter."

*"What?"*

Beale sighed heavily, sitting once more. "In secret. I don't know when, and I don't know if Sir Francis knew. But Essex told me, as a means of strengthening his position." His tired eyes shifted back up to Deven. "Do not tell the Queen."

"And risk her throwing a shoe at me? I think not." Essex had been her favorite since his stepfather Leicester's death, though God alone knew why. The Queen's affection was easy enough to understand; she was in her late fifties, and Essex not yet twenty-five. But Deven did not believe the man held much affection for his sovereign. Elizabeth might still be admired for her wit and political acumen, but not for her beauty, and Essex did not seem the type to love her mind. His affection would last precisely as long as the tangible rewards of her favor.

"Unfortunately," Beale went on, "when all is said and done I cannot pass on everything intact, even if Burghley or Essex concedes the ground to the other. Too much of it was in Sir Francis's head, and never committed to writing. Even I do not know who all his informants were."

With that, Deven could not help. Walsingham had never shared all his secrets with anyone, and now, without a proper patron, Deven lacked the influence to be of use politically. He would have to scrabble hard for favor and preferment.

Unless...

If Walsingham was right, and the hidden player had occasional direct access to the Queen, then Elizabeth certainly knew who it was. But was she pleased with that situation? Knowing her distaste for being managed by her councillors, no. If Deven could uncover the man's identity, and use the knowledge to break his influence....

He hadn't Essex's beauty. But he did not want the burden of being Elizabeth's favorite; all he wanted was her favor.

This might earn it for him.

Deven settled himself back into his chair, and shoved the report of Catholic rumors aside without looking at it. "Tell me," he said, "what you know of the hidden player."

THE ONYX HALL, LONDON: *April 9–12, 1590*

The improvements to her circumstances came one tantalizing step at a time. First it was the stool, left in her cell, followed shortly by a torch and a pallet on which to sleep. Then removal to a better cell, one that did not lie at the roots of the White Tower. To earn that one, Lune had to tell Madame Malline of her leap from the cliffs of Dover, plummeting three hundred feet into the choppy waters of the English Channel. It was no jest: the strangely shimmering pearl she'd been given to swallow permitted her to survive underwater, though not to move with the grace of her nymph escorts, or the merfolk who waited for her below.

The merfolk. The roanes. The evanescent sprites born from the spray of the crashing waves. Stranger things, in deeper waters. She did not see the Leviathan itself, but lesser sea serpents still occasionally haunted the Channel between England and France.

Were the folk of the sea fae? What defined fae nature? They were alien, enchanting, disturbing, even to one such as Lune. No wonder mortals told such strange stories of them.

But they were little touched by human society. That, she told Madame Malline, was the most difficult thing about them. Those fae who dwelt in the cracks and shadows of the mortal world did so because of their fascination with humans and human life. The Onyx Court was only the most vivid proof of that fascination, the most intensive mimicry of mortal habits. The folk of the sea were more like the inhabitants of deeper Faerie, less touched by the currents of change. But at least those who dwelt in Faerie breathed air and walked on the earth; beneath the waves lay a world where up and down were little different from north or east, where events flowed according to inscrutable rhythms.

Even speaking of them, she fell back into the metaphors of speech she had acquired there, likening everything to the subtle behavior of water.

That information got Lune into a more comfortable cell. A primer on the diplomacy of underwater society took her back to her own chambers, where she lived under house arrest, with Sir Prigurd Nellt instead of Sir Kentigern commanding the guards that bracketed her door.

Then came the final negotiation, the one she had been anticipating for some time.

"Now," Madame Malline said when they had dispensed with the pleasantries, "you know what I wish to hear. Stories of how you went to the sea, what you found there—these are interesting, and I thank you for them. But I have shown you my goodwill in helping you thus far, and the time has come for you to repay it."

They were seated by the fire in Lune's outer chamber, with

glasses of wine at hand. Not the fine French vintage Vidar had offered the day he set Lune on Walsingham's trail, but a good wine nevertheless. Lune could almost ignore the way her chambers had been ransacked after her downfall, her charms breached, her jewels and her little store of mortal bread stolen away by unknown hands.

*"Au contraire, madame ambassadrice,"* Lune said, dropping briefly into the envoy's own tongue to soften the rudeness she was about to offer. "Secure my freedom; have the guards removed from my door. Then I will give you the information you seek."

Madame Malline's smile was beautiful and utterly without warmth. "I do not think so, Lady Lune. Should I do so, there would be nothing save gratitude that binds you to help me further. And though grateful you may be, when weighed against your fear of angering Invidiana..." She lifted her wine goblet in one graceful, ringed hand, and her smile turned just the faintest bit malicious. *"Non.* You will tell me, and take your chances with your Queen."

All as Lune had expected. And, in a way, as she had needed.

"Very well," she said, letting the words out reluctantly. "You wish to know, then, what I agreed to. What price I offered them, in exchange for their assistance against the Spanish Armada."

*"Oui."*

"Peace," Lune said.

One delicately plucked eyebrow arched upward. "I do not understand."

"The folk of the sea do not ignore everything that goes on in the air. I do not know who spread the rumors; perhaps a draca or other water spirit eavesdropped on someone's indiscreet conference, then spoke to another, and so on until the news flowed downriver and reached them. Invidiana intended to make war against the folk of the sea. And the concession I offered them was an agreement to abandon that course."

Madame Malline studied her, eyes narrowed and full lips pursed. At last she said, meditatively, "I do not believe you."

Lune met her gaze without flinching. "It is true."

"Your Queen has an obsession with mortal ways, mortal power. Even her wars against the Courts of the North have their origin in mortal affairs, the accusation that she sabotaged the Queen of Scots. There is no human court out on the water. Why should Invidiana desire power over the folk of the sea? What cares she for what they do beneath the surface?"

"She cares nothing for it," Lune said. "But she cares a great deal for what the folk of the sea can do about mortals *on* its surface. Had her Majesty's plans moved more quickly, we would not have had to negotiate for their assistance against the Armada, but she was not yet fully prepared to assert sovereignty over the undersea. If she had done so . . . imagine what she could do, were they bound to obey her." Lune paused, to let Madame Malline consider it. Break the back of Spanish shipping. Give fair weather to English vessels, and foul to their enemies. Strike coastal areas with crippling storms.

The ambassador's mind quickly moved ahead to the next complication. "But you have told me yourself that they are not organized, they have no *Grand Roi*—that you had to bargain with a dozen nobles of one sort or another to reach any agreement. Even the Courts of the North have unified themselves more than that. Your Queen could not hope to control the oceans."

"She would not need to. A small force would do. They are highly mobile, the folk of the sea, and adapt with speed; a few dedicated, obedient groups would be able to wreak quite enough havoc to suit her purposes."

Lune took advantage of the pause to reach for her own wine and conceal her face behind the rim. Madame Malline was staring into the fire, clearly working through the ramifications of this. Searching for a way to turn it to the benefit of the Cour du Lys. They had their own conflicts with Spain, with Italy, with heathen fae across the Mediterranean Sea.

Surely Madame Malline could work out why Lune would fear Invidiana's retaliation, once she had spoken.

The French elf's eyes finally moved back to Lune's face. "I see," the ambassador said, her voice slightly breathless. "I thank you, Lady Lune. Your Queen has listeners on this room, of course, but I have paid them off. For your honesty, I will do more than have you freed; I will also protect you from her retaliation. She will hear from her spies that you told me a persuasive lie. I cannot promise it will be enough, but it is all I may do."

Lune smoothed the lines of worry from her own face. Rising from her seat, she curtsied to the envoy. "You have my most humble thanks, *madame ambassadrice*."

THE STRAND, OUTSIDE LONDON: *April 13, 1590*

The list Beale gave Deven was depressingly short.

Gilbert Gifford had been granted a handsome pension of a hundred pounds a year for his work in passing along the letters of the Queen of Scots, but Thomas Phelippes had reported more than two years ago that he'd been arrested by French authorities and slung in prison. So far as Beale knew, Gifford was still there. By all accounts, he was as untrustworthy and mercenary a man as Walsingham had ever hired; rumors said he'd later tried to arrange Elizabeth's murder with Mendoza, the former Spanish ambassador to England. He might well have been serving another master. But Deven could not very well question him when he was in a French jail. And his cousin among the Gentlemen Pensioners, though a dubious character in his own right, was not useful to Deven.

Henry Fagot was another informer Walsingham had suspected of coming too easily to hand, but he was even less accessible than Gifford; no one knew who he had been. He had passed information out of the French embassy some six or seven years before, but hid behind a false name. The potential suspects, of course, were long gone from England.

And those were his two strongest prospects. From there, the list degenerated even more. Some individuals were dead; others were gone; others weren't individuals at all, but rather suspicions of "someone in the service of Lord and Lady Hereford," or leads even less concrete than that.

This was the information Walsingham had not given him, for fear of prejudicing his mind and leading his thoughts down paths others had already explored. Having considered it, Deven had to agree; the past would not give him the answer. He had to look at the present. If Walsingham was right, and the player was still active, with a hand in the Irish situation... a great many ifs, as Beale said. But what other lead could he follow?

Nothing save his suspicions about Walsingham's death. And Beale had argued well against those.

Carrying a message from a council meeting at Somerset House to St. James' Palace, his cloak pulled tight around him in feeble protection against a driving rainstorm, Deven abruptly remembered Beale's words.

*"I know it would be easier to believe that someone poisoned or cursed Sir Francis..."*

Poison, no. But Deven could think of at least one man who

might have the capacity to bring about a man's death through infernal magic.

Doctor John Dee.

He raised his head, heedless of the water that streamed down his face, and stared blindly through the gray curtain of rain. Dee. A necromancer, they said, who trafficked with demons and bound spirits to his will. But also Walsingham's friend; would Dee have betrayed him so foully?

There were other problems. Dee had been on the continent for six years—six crucial years, in the tale of the Queen of Scots. But Fagot's work in the embassy had begun around the time that Dee departed. And Gifford, too, had conveniently shown up in that time.

Could they have been working for the astrologer, while he was abroad?

Someone had persuaded Elizabeth, possibly by meeting with her in person. Dee could not have done that, unless someone had gone to a great deal of effort to fabricate rumors about his travels with Edward Kelley. It was a stretch to imagine the man working so effectively through intermediaries. And what would Dee care about events in Ireland?

Deven shook his head, sending water flying. Beneath him, his bay gelding kept stolidly putting one foot down after another, ignoring both the rain and the preoccupation of his rider. Too many questions without answers—but it was the strongest possibility yet. Before his departure for the continent, Dee had spun out grand visions of England's destiny in the world, with Elizabeth upon the throne. The Queen of Scots would have been an obstacle to those visions, one he might take steps to remove.

And perhaps his difficulties now stemmed, at least in part, from Elizabeth's disillusionment over how she'd been managed into killing her Scottish cousin.

What did Deven know about Dee's activities now, the positions and benefits for which he was petitioning the Crown?

The answers came obediently to mind—and with them, something else. The reason why he knew those answers.

Anne.

*"'Tis listening, not spying, and you are not asking me. I do it of my own free will."*

Yes, she had volunteered information on Doctor Dee quite eagerly. Deven knew all about the man's penury, the theft of books and priceless instruments from his house at Mortlake, the dispute with his wife's brother over the ownership of that house. Even Burghley's attempts to get Dee's confederate Edward Kelley back to England, so he could put his Philosopher's Stone to work producing gold for Elizabeth. Information Deven had taken in and set to one side, because he could not see what to do with it.

The thought of Anne twisted like a knife in him. They hadn't spoken since that confrontation in the orchard; shortly thereafter, according to the Countess of Warwick, Anne had begged and received permission to leave her service. Deven did not know why, nor had he asked; the subject was too painful, the unresolved questions between them too sharp. These thoughts, however, cast the entire situation in a new and unpleasant light.

What she could possibly be doing in Dee's service, he did not know. But if Dee were the player...

More ifs. He had so few names to chase, though. And going after Dee directly would not be wise.

Was he thinking of this because he truly suspected Anne, and thought finding her would accomplish something? Or did he just wish to see her again?

"A bit of both," he admitted out loud, to no one in particular. The gelding flicked his ears, scattering droplets of rain.

By the time he arrived at St. James' Palace, drenched and shivering, he had made up his mind. He stopped to change clothes only because it would not do to drip on the floor of a peer.

The Countess of Warwick frowned when Deven asked what reason Anne had given for leaving. "She did not speak of your argument, though I suspect that played a part. No, she named some other cause...."

Deven stood in his wet hair and dry clothes, and tried not to chafe with impatience.

"'Tis hard to recall," the countess admitted at last, looking embarrassed. "I am sorry, Master Deven. An ailing family member, perhaps. Yes, I remember, that was it—her father, I believe."

*"I have no father,"* Anne had said, when he asked her why she could not marry.

So either she had lied to the countess, or to him. And she had lied to him before.

He put on a look of solicitous concern. "I am very sorry to hear it. Perhaps it was concern for her father that led to our troubles. Do you know where her family lives? I have been given a leave of absence from my duties; I might call upon her, to offer my sympathies if nothing else."

The countess's confusion melted away, and she smiled indulgently at him, no doubt thinking of young love. "That would be very kind of you. She is London-born, from the parish of St. Dunstan in the East."

Little more than a stone's throw from Walsingham's house, south and west along Tower Street. Deven would have ridden to Yorkshire, but he need not go far at all.

"I thank you, my lady," Deven said, and left with all the haste decency would allow.

THE ONYX HALL, LONDON: *April 14, 1590*

Though almost everything of value had been stripped from Lune's chambers following her disgrace, her gowns remained. No one, apparently, wanted to be seen wearing the clothing of a traitor imprisoned beneath the White Tower.

She dressed herself in raven's feathers, simple but elegant, with an open-fronted collar and cuffs that swept back from her hands in delicate lacework. Now, of all times, she wanted to show her loyalty to Invidiana by wearing the Queen's colors. The plain pins holding up her silver hair were her only adornment; humility, alongside loyalty, would be her watchword tonight.

When she was ready, she took a steadying breath, then opened the door to her chamber and stepped outside.

"Are you ready?" Sir Prigurd asked in his resonant bass voice, and waited for her brief curtsy. "Come along, then."

Two guards accompanied them through the palace. Lune was not taken to the presence chamber. A good sign, or a bad one? She could only speculate. Prigurd led her onward, and soon Lune knew where they were going.

The Hall of Figures was a long gallery, sunken below the usual level of the rooms by the depth of a half-flight of stairs. Statues lined it on both sides, ranging from simple busts to full figures to a few massive works large enough to fill a small chamber on their own. Some were made by mortal artisans, others by fae; some had not been crafted at all, unless the basilisk could be called a crafter.

Lune prayed the stories were not true, that Invidiana kept a basilisk in some hidden confine of the Onyx Hall.

Prigurd and the guards stayed on the landing at the top of the stairs. Lune went down alone. As her slipper touched the floor, she saw movement out of the corner of her eye; she flinched despite herself, thinking of basilisks.

No monster. In her distraction, she had simply taken the man for a statue. The mortal called Achilles had more to recommend him to Invidiana than just his battle furies; his nearly naked body might have been a sculpted model for the perfection of the human form.

He took her by the arm, his hard fingers communicating the violence that always trembled just below the surface. Lune knew better than to think it directed at her, but she also knew better than to think herself safe from it. She offered no resistance as Achilles led her down the gallery, past the watching statues.

A chair had been placed partway down the Hall of Figures, and a canopy of estate erected above it. Before Lune came anywhere near it, she sank gracefully to her knees — as gracefully as she could, with Achilles still holding one arm in an iron grip.

"Bring her closer."

The mortal hauled Lune to her feet before she could stand on her own, towed her forward a few steps, and shoved her down again.

The moments passed by in silence, broken only by breathing, and a scuff at the entrance to the gallery as Sir Prigurd shifted his weight.

"I am given to understand," Invidiana said, "that you have been telling Madame Malline lies."

"I have," Lune said, still kneeling in a sea of raven feathers. "More than she realizes."

A few more heartbeats passed; then, on some unspoken signal from the Queen, Achilles released Lune's arm. She remained kneeling, her eyes on the floor.

Invidiana said, "Explain yourself."

There was no point in repeating the early steps of it; Invidiana knew those already. She might even know what Lune had said at the end. But that was the part she wished to hear, and so Lune related, in brief, honest outline, the lie she had told the ambassador. "She believed me, I think," Lune said when she was done. "But if she does not, 'tis no matter; the lie tells her nothing she can use."

"And so you gained your freedom," Invidiana said. Her voice was as silken and cold as a dagger of ice, that could kill and then melt away as if it had never been. "By slandering your own sovereign."

Lune's heart thudded painfully. "Your Majesty—"

"You have spread a lie that will damage my reputation in other lands. You have given the *ambassadrice du Lys* information about the undersea that might be turned against England. You have sold details of a royal mission, for the sake of your own skin." The whip crack of her words halted. Invidiana murmured the next part softly, almost intimately. "Tell me why I should not kill you."

Feathers crumpled in her fingers, their broken shafts stabbing at her skin. Lune's heart was beating hard enough to make her body tremble. But she forced herself to focus. Invidiana was angry, yes, but the anger was calculated, not heartfelt. A sufficiently good reply might please the Queen, and then the rage would vanish as if it had never been.

"Your Majesty," she whispered, then made her voice stronger. "When those in other lands hear that you dream of extending your control over the folk of the sea, they will fear you, and this is no bad thing. As for Madame Malline, indeed, I *hope* she tells her king what I have said, and he attempts to pursue it; if he threatens war undersea, thinking to win himself some concession thereby, then we will have the pleasure of watching those proud and powerful folk destroy him. Moreover, by satisfying her with this lie, I have ended her prying questions, that might otherwise have uncovered the truth of my embassy, and the secrets I have kept on your Grace's behalf."

Having offered her political reasons, Lune risked a glance upward. A flash of white caught her eye, and she found herself meeting an unfocused sapphire gaze. Tiresias knelt now at Invidiana's feet, leaning against her skirts as a hound might, with her spidery fingers tangled in his black hair. He wore no doublet, and the white of his cambric shirt blazed in the darkness of the hall.

She swallowed and lifted her chin higher, fixing her attention just below Invidiana's face. "And if I may be so bold as to say it, your Majesty—no fae who cannot find a way to benefit herself while also serving the Onyx Throne belongs in your court."

Invidiana considered this, one hand idly stroking Tiresias's hair. He leaned into the touch, as if there were no one else present.

"Pretty words," the Queen said at last, musingly. She tightened her grip on Tiresias, dragging his head back until he gazed up at her, mouth slackened, throat exposed and vulnerable. The Queen gazed down into her seer's eyes, as if she could see his visions there. "But what lies behind them?"

"Your Grace." Lune risked the interruption; silence might kill her just as surely. "I will gladly return to the service I left. I told Dame Halgresta I had other options available to me; give me my freedom, and I will discover all you wish to know about Walsingham."

Tiresias laughed breathlessly, still trapped by Invidiana's hand. "A body in revolt, the laws of nature gone awry. It cannot happen. Yet the stories say it did, and are not stories true?" One hand rose, as if seeking something; it faltered midair, came to rest below the unlaced collar of his shirt. "Not those that are lies."

His words hardened Invidiana's black eyes. She trailed one fingernail down the seer's face; then her hand moved to hover near the jewel in the center of her bodice, the black diamond edged by obsidian and mermaid's tears. The sight transfixed Lune with fear. But when the Queen scowled and returned her attention to Lune, she left the jewel where it was pinned. "Walsingham is no longer a problem. You may be. But I am loathe to cast aside a tool that may yet have use in it, and so you will live."

Lune immediately bent her head again. "I am most grateful for—"

"You will live," Invidiana repeated in honeyed, venomous tones, "as a warning to those who might fail me in the future. Your chambers are no longer your own. You may remain in the Onyx Hall, but for hospitality you will be dependent upon others. Anyone giving you mortal food will be punished. If hands turn against you, I will turn a blind eye. Henceforth you are no lady of my court."

The words struck like hammer blows on stone. Lune's hands lay slack and nerveless in her lap. She might have wept—perhaps Invidiana wanted tears, begging, a humble prostration on the floor, a display of sycophantic fear. But she could not bring herself to move. She stared, dry eyed, at her Queen's icy, contemptuous face, and tried to comprehend how she had failed.

"Take her," the Queen said, her voice now indifferent, and

this time Achilles truly did have to drag Lune to her feet and out of the hall.

MEMORY: *April 6, 1580*

*It* began as a trembling, a rattling of cups and plates on sideboards, a clacking of shutters against walls.

Then the walls themselves began to shake.

People fled into the streets of London, fearing their houses would fall on them. Some were killed out there, as stones tumbled loose and plummeted to the streets. Nothing was exempt: a masonry spire on Westminster Abbey cracked and fell; the Queen felt it in her great chamber at Whitehall; across all of southern England, bells tolled in church steeples, without any hand to ring them.

God's judgment, the credulous believed, was come to them at last.

The judgment, though, did not come from God — nor was it intended for them.

Out in the Channel, the seabed heaved and the waves rose to terrifying heights. The waters swamped all under, with no respect for country; English, French, and Flemish, all drowned alike as their ships foundered and sank.

Some few were close enough to see the cause of the tremor, in the short moments before their death.

The bodies struck the waves with titanic force. Those few, hapless sailors saw colossal heads, hands the size of cart horses, legs thicker than ancient trees. Then the waters rose up, and they saw nothing more.

At Dover, a raw white scar showed where a segment of the cliff had cracked and fallen in the struggle.

In the days to come, mortals on both sides of the Channel would feel the aftershocks of the earthquake, little suspecting that beneath the still unsteady waves, terrible sea beasts were tearing at the corpses of Gog and Magog, the great giants of London, who paraded in effigy through the streets of the city every Midsummer at the head of the Lord Mayor's procession.

Rarely did the conflicts of fae become so publicly felt. But the giants, proud and ancient brothers, had long refused to recognize any Queen above them, and Invidiana did not take kindly to rebellion. Some said she had once been on friendly terms with them, but others scoffed; she had no friends. At most, they might have once been useful to her.

Now their use had ended.

Giants could not be disposed of quietly. She sent a legion of minions against them, elf knights and hobyahs, barguests and redcaps from the north of England, and the brutal Sir Kentigern Nellt to lead them. On the cliffs of Dover the battle had raged, until first one brother and then the other fell to their opponents. In a final gesture of contempt, Nellt hurled their bodies into the sea, and shook the earth for miles around.

While the mortals cowered and prayed, the warriors laughed at their fallen enemies. And when the waves had subsided and there was no more to see, they retired to celebrate their bloody triumph.

TOWER WARD AND FARRINGDON WITHOUT, LONDON:
*April 15, 1590*

A monumental stone Elizabeth gazed down on Deven as he rode up Ludgate Hill toward the city wall, making him feel like a small boy that had been caught shirking his duties. He had leave from the lieutenant of the Gentlemen Pensioners to be absent that day, but still, he breathed more easily when he and Colsey passed through the gate, with its image of the Queen, and into London.

The rains that had deluged the city of late had washed it moderately clean for once. The smaller streets were still a treacherous sludge of mud, but Deven kept to wider lanes, where cobbled or paved surfaces glistened after their dousing. Only when he turned north onto St. Dunstan's Hill did he have to be careful of his horse's footing.

In the churchyard, he halted and tossed his reins to Colsey. He cleared the steps leading to the church door in two bounds, passing a puzzled laborer who was scrubbing them clean, and went inside.

The interior of the church was murky, after the rain-washed brilliance outside. Deven's eyes had not yet adjusted when he heard a voice say, "How may I be of service, young master?"

The words came from up ahead, on his left. Deven turned his head that way and said, "I seek a parishioner of yours, but I do not know where the house lies. Can you direct me?"

"I would be glad to. The name?"

His vision had cleared enough to make out a balding priest. Deven said, "The Montrose family."

The priest's brow furrowed along well-worn lines. "Montrose...of this parish, you said?"

"Yes. I am searching for Anne Montrose, a young woman of gentle birth, who was until recently in service to the Countess of Warwick."

But the priest shook his head after a moment of further thought and said, "I am sorry, young master. I have no parishioners by that name. Perhaps you seek the church of St. Dunstan in the West, outside the city walls, near to Temple Bar?"

"I will ask there," Deven said mechanically, then thanked the priest for his assistance and left. The countess would not have confused the two parishes. Yet some vain hope made him ride a circuit around St. Dunstan's, asking at all the churches that stood near it, then cross the breadth of the city again to visit the other St. Dunstan's, which he had passed on his way in from Westminster that morning.

Only one church, St. Margaret Pattens, had any parishioners by the surname of Montrose: a destitute family with no children above the age of six.

Colsey stayed remarkably silent through this entire enterprise, given how Deven had told him nothing of the day's purpose. When his master emerged from St. Dunstan in the West, though, the servant said tentatively, "Is there aught I can do?"

The very hesitance in Colsey's voice told Deven something of his own expression; in the normal way of things the man never hesitated to speak up. Deven made an effort to banish the blackness he felt to somewhere less public, but his tone was still brusque when he snapped, "No, Colsey. There is not."

Riding back along the Strand, he wrestled with that blackness, struggling to shape it into something he could master. Anne Montrose was false as Hell. She had lied to her mistress about her home and her family. Doubtless she was not the only one at court to have hidden inconvenient truths behind a falsehood or two, but in light of the suspicions Deven had formed, he could not let the trail die there.

The ghost of Walsingham haunted his mind, asking questions, prodding his thoughts. So Anne was false. What should be his next step?

Trace her by other means.

Hunsdon looked dubious when he heard Deven's request. "I do not know...Easter will be upon us in a week. 'Tis the duty of her Majesty's Gentlemen Pensioners to be attendant upon her during the holiday. *All* of them."

Deven bowed. "I understand, my lord. But never in my time here has every single member of the corps been present at once, even at last month's muster. I have served continually since gaining my position, taking on the duty periods of others. This is the first time I have asked leave to be absent for more than a day. I would not do so were it not important."

Hunsdon's searching eye had not half the force of Walsingham's, but Deven imagined it saw enough. He had not been sleeping well since the Principal Secretary's death—since his rift with Anne, in truth—and only the joint efforts of Colsey and Ranwell were keeping him from looking entirely unkempt. No one could fault him in his performance of his duties, but his mind was elsewhere, and surely Hunsdon could see that.

The baron said, "How long would you be absent?"

Deven shook his head. "If I could predict that for you, I would. But I do not know how long I will need to sort this matter out."

"Very well," Hunsdon said, sighing. "You will be fined for your absence on Easter, but nothing more. With everyone—or at least most of the corps—coming to court, finding someone to replace you until the end of the quarter should not be difficult. You have earned a rest, 'tis true. Notify Fitzgerald if you intend to return for the new quarter."

If this matter occupied him until late June, it was even worse than he feared. "Thank you, my lord," Deven said, bowing again.

Once free of Hunsdon, he went straightaway to the Countess of Warwick again.

She had taken Anne on as a favor to Lettice Knollys, the widowed Countess of Leicester, who had last year married for the third time, to Sir Christopher Blount. A question to her new husband confirmed that his wife, out of favor with Elizabeth, was also out of easy reach; she had retired in disgrace to an estate in Staffordshire. Blount himself knew nothing of Anne Montrose.

Deven ground his teeth in frustration, then forced himself to stop. Had he expected the answer to offer itself up freely? No. So he would persist.

Inferior as Ranwell's personal services were to Colsey's, the newer servant could not be trusted with this. Deven sent Colsey north with a letter for the countess, and made plans himself to visit Doctor John Dee.

THE ONYX HALL, LONDON: *April 18, 1590*

Lune's own words mocked her, until she thought she heard them echoing from the unforgiving walls of the palace: *No fae who cannot find a way to benefit herself while also serving the Onyx Throne belongs in your court.*

It was true, but not sufficient. Lune did not believe for an instant that Invidiana was angry at the lie she had given Madame Malline; that was simply an excuse. But the Queen had set her mind against Lune before that audience ever happened — before Lune ever went to the Tower. Would anything have changed that?

Ever since she went undersea, her fortunes had deteriorated. The assignment to Walsingham had seemed like an improvement, but only a temporary one; in the end, what had it gained her?

Time among mortals. A stolen year, hovering like a moth near the flame of the human court. A lie far preferable to the truth she lived now.

Living as an exile in her own home, hiding in shadows, trying to keep away from those who would hurt her for political advancement or simple pleasure, Lune missed her life as Anne with a fierce and inescapable ache. Try as she did to discipline her mind, she could not help thinking of other places, other people. Another Queen.

Elizabeth had her jealousies, her rages, and she had thrown her ladies and her courtiers in the Tower for a variety of offenses. But for all that her ringing tones echoed from the walls of her chambers, threatening to chop off the heads of those who vexed her, she rarely did so for anything short of genuine, incontrovertible treason.

And despite those rages, people flocked to her court.

They went for money, for prestige, for connections and marriages and Elizabeth's reflected splendor. But there was more to it than that. Old as she was, contrary and capricious as she was, they loved their Gloriana. She charmed them, flattered them, wooed them, bound them to her with charisma more than fear.

What would it be like, to love one's Queen? To enjoy her company for more than just the advantage it might bring, without concern for the pit beneath one's feet?

Lune felt the eyes on her as she moved through the palace, never staying long in one place. A red-haired faerie woman, resplendent in a jeweled black gown that spoke of a rapid climb within the court, watched her with a sharp and calculating eye. Two maliciously leering bogles followed Lune until to escape them she had to dodge through a cramped passageway few knew about and emerge filthy on the other side.

She kept moving. If she stayed in one place, Vidar would find her. Or Halgresta Nellt.

Without mortal bread, going into the city was impossible. But when she heard a familiar, heavy tread, she ran without thinking; the nearest escape lay in the Threadneedle Street well, one of the exits from the Onyx Hall.

Luck afforded her this one sign of favor; with no sense of what hour it was in the mortal city, Lune found herself above ground in the dead of night. She wasted no time in flinging a glamour over herself and dodging into the shadows of a tiny lane, where she waited until she was certain the giantess had not followed.

It was a dangerous place to be. One of the nearest things to an inviolable rule in the Onyx Hall forbade drawing too much attention among mortals. Night allowed more freedom of movement than day, but without bread or milk, she would be limited to a goblin's skulking mischief.

Or she could flee.

Like a needle pointing to the north star, her head swiveled unerringly to look up Threadneedle, as if she could see through the houses to Bishopsgate and the road beyond. Out of London.

Invidiana wanted her to stay and suffer. But did she have to?

Wherever Lune had been before she came here, London was her home now. Some few fae migrated, even to foreign lands, but she could no more leave her city to live in Scotland than she could dwell among the folk of the sea.

She looked back at the well. Dame Halgresta lacked the

patience to lie in wait; whether she had been chasing Lune, or simply passing by, she would be gone now.

Lune stepped back out into Threadneedle Street, laid her hand on the rope, and descended down the well, back into the darkness of the Onyx Hall.

MORTLAKE, SURREY: *April 25, 1590*

Deven rode inattentively, his eyes fixed on the letter in his hand, though he knew its contents by heart already.

> *I arranged a position for Mistress Montrose with Lady Warwick at the request of her cousin, a former waiting-gentlewoman in my own service, Margaret Rolford.*

Colsey was no fool. He knew why his master had searched London from one end to the other; he asked the next logical question before he left Staffordshire, knowing that otherwise he would have to turn around and go back. The answer was waiting in the letter.

> *Margaret Rolford lives now in the parish of St. Dunstan in the East.*

The manservant had that answer waiting, too. "No Rolfords, either. Not there, nor in Fleet Street. I checked already."

No Margaret Rolford. No Anne Montrose. Deven wondered how Margaret had come into Lettice Knollys's service, but it wasn't worth sending again to Staffordshire to ask; he no longer believed he would uncover anything useful by that route. Anne seemed to have come from nowhere, and to have vanished back to the same place.

He scowled and tucked the letter into his purse.

Cottages dotted the land up ahead, placid and pastoral, with a modest church spire rising above them. Had he reached the right village? Deven had given both his servants a day's liberty and ridden out alone; Colsey would not approve of him coming here. So he himself had to flag down a fellow trudging along the riverside towpath with a basket on his back and ask, "Is this the village of Mortlake?"

The man took in his taffeta doublet, the velvet cap on his head, and bowed as much as the weight of the basket would allow. "Even so, sir. Can I direct you?"

"I seek the astrologer Dee."

He half-expected his words to wipe the pleasant look from the man's face, but no such thing; the fellow nodded, as if the scholar were an ordinary citizen, not a man suspected of black magic. "Keep along this road, sir, and you'll find him. There's a cluster of houses, but the one you want is the largest, with the extra bits built on."

The villager caught the penny Deven tossed, then quickly sidestepped to regain control of his burden as it slipped.

Deven soon saw what the man had meant. The "extra bits" were extensions easily as large as the house to which they had been added, making for a lopsided, rambling structure that encroached on the cottages around it. Flagstone paths connected that building to several nearby ones, as if they were all part of the same complex. And none of it was what Deven expected; nothing about the exterior suggested necromancy and devilish conjurations.

He dismounted, looped his horse's reins around a fence post, and knocked at the door. It was opened a moment later by a maidservant, who promptly curtsied when she found a gentleman on the step.

A twinkling later he was in the parlor, surreptitiously eyeing the unremarkable furnishings. But he did not have long to look; soon an older man with a pointed, snow-white beard entered.

"Doctor Dee?" Deven offered him a polite bow. "I am Michael Deven, of the Queen's Gentlemen Pensioners, and formerly in service to Master Secretary Walsingham. I beg your pardon for the imposition—I should have sent a letter in advance—but I have heard much of you from my master, and I hoped I might beg assistance from such a learned man."

His nerves hummed as he spoke. If his suspicions were correct, he was foolish to come here, to expose himself thus to his quarry. But he had not been able to talk himself out of this journey; the best he could do was to deliberately omit to send a letter, so that Dee would have no warning of his coming.

But what did he expect to find? There were no mystic circles on the floor, no effigies of courtiers awaiting burial at a crossroads or beneath a tree. And Dee did not flinch at Walsingham's name. The man might be the hidden player, but it was increasingly difficult for Deven to believe he might have killed Walsingham by foul magic.

"Assistance?" Dee said, gesturing for Deven to take a seat.

Deven contrived to look embarrassed; he might as well put his flush to use. "I—I have heard, sir, that you are as able an astrologer as dwells in England. I am sure your time is much occupied by working on behalf of the Queen's grace, but if you might spare a moment to help a young man in need...."

Dee's alert, focused eyes narrowed slightly at this. "You wish me to draw up a horoscope? To what end?"

Glancing away, Deven permitted himself a nervous, self-deprecating laugh. "I — well, that is — you see, there's a young woman."

"Master Deven," the astrologer said in unpromising tones, "I do occasionally calculate on behalf of some of her Majesty's court, but not often. I am no street corner prophet, predicting marriage, prosperity, and the weather for any who pass by."

"Certainly not!" Deven hastened to reassure the man. "I would not even ask, were it simply a matter of 'will she or won't she.' But I have run into difficulty, and having tried everything at my disposal, I am at a loss as to how to proceed." He had to skirt that part carefully; he did not want to give Dee any more information than necessary. Assuming the man had not already heard his name from Anne. "I am sure you have many more important researches to occupy your time — I would be more than happy to fund them in some small part."

The words were perfectly chosen. Dee would have taken offense at the suggestion of being paid for his work; no doubt the man wanted to distinguish himself as no common magician. But an offer of patronage, no matter how fleeting and minor, did not go amiss, especially given the astrologer's financial difficulties.

Dee's consideration did not take long. "A horary chart is simple enough to draw up. I imagine, by your flushed complexion, that the matter is of some urgency to you?"

"Indeed, sir."

"Then come with me; we can answer your question directly."

Deven followed his host through the cottage and into one of the extensions, where he stopped dead on the threshold, awed into silence by the sight that greeted him. The room was lined with shelves, a great library that dwarfed those held by even the most learned of Deven's own acquaintances. Yet it had an air of recent abuse, that called to mind what Anne had said about Dee's troubles; there were blank stretches of shelving, scars on the woodwork, and a conspicuous lack of reading podiums or other accoutrements he expected of a library.

Dee invited him over to the one table the room still held, with a stool on either side of it and a slew of paper on top. The papers were swept away before Deven could attempt to read them, and fresh sheets brought out, with an inkwell and a battered quill.

"First," Dee said, "we pray."

Startled, Deven nodded. The two men knelt on the floor, and Dee began to speak. His words were English, but they did not come from the Book of Common Prayer; Deven listened with sharp interest. Not Catholic, but perhaps not entirely Church of England either. Yet the man apparently considered prayer a requisite precursor to any kind of mystical work.

None of it was what he had expected.

When the prayer was done, they sat, and Dee sharpened his quill with a penknife. "Now. What is the question you wish answered?"

Deven had not formulated its precise wording in his mind. He said, choosing his words with care, "As I said, there's a young gentlewoman. She and I have had difficulties, that I wish to smoothe over, but she has gone away, and despite my best efforts I cannot locate her. What…" He reconsidered the question before it even came out of his mouth. "How may I find her again?"

Dee sat with his eyes closed, listening to this, then nodded briskly and began marking out a square on the paper that lay before him.

After watching the astrologer work for a few minutes, Deven said hesitantly, "Do you not wish to know my date of birth?"

"'Tis not necessary." Dee did not even look up. "For a horary chart, what matters is the moment at which the question was formulated." He selected a book from a stack on the floor behind him and consulted it; Deven glimpsed orderly charts of numbers and strange symbols, some of them marked in red ink.

He waited, and tried not to show his relief. That had worried him the most, the prospect of giving Dee such information about himself. A magician might do a great deal with that knowledge. As it stood now, he might be any ordinary gentleman, asking after any ordinary woman; he had not even mentioned Anne's name.

But had she mentioned his?

Dee worked in silence for several minutes, examining the chart in the book, making calculations, then noting the results on the square horoscope he sketched out. It did not take long. Soon Dee leaned back on his stool and studied the paper, one hand idly stroking his pointed white beard.

"Be of good cheer, Master Deven," Dee said at last in absent, thoughtful tones at odds with his words. "You will see your young woman soon. I cannot say when, but look you here—the Moon is in the Twelfth House, and the Stellium of Mars, Mercury, and Venus—her influence has not yet passed out of your life."

Deven did not look where the ink-stained finger pointed; instead he watched Dee. The chart meant nothing to him, while the astrologer's pensive expression meant a great deal. "Is there more?"

The sharp eyes flicked up to meet his. "Yes. Enemies threaten—her enemies, I think, but they may pose a danger

191

to you as well. The gentlewoman's disposition is obscure to me, I fear. Conflict surrounds her, complicating the matter. Death will send her into your path again."

Death? A chill touched Deven's spine. Was that a threat? He did his best to feign the concern of the lovestruck man he pretended to be, while searching for any hint of malice in the other's gaze. Perhaps the chart really did say that. He wished he knew something of astrology.

Deven bent over the paper, lest Dee read too much out of his own expression. "What should I do?"

"Be wary," the philospher said succinctly. "I do not think the woman means you harm, but she may bring harm your way. Saturn's presence in the Eighth House indicates authority is set against this matter, but the Trine with Jupiter..." He shook his head. "There are influences I cannot read. Allies, perhaps, where you do not expect them."

It might be nothing more than a trick, something to send him running in fear. But at the very least, it did not sound like the kind of horoscope an impatient man might invent to placate a lovelorn stranger. Either it was a coded warning, or it was genuine.

Or both.

"I thank you, Doctor Dee," he said, covering his thoughts with courtesy. "They say knowledge of the stars helps prepare a man for that which will come; I only hope it shall be so with me."

Dee nodded, still grave. "I am sorry to have given you such ill tidings. But God guides us all; perhaps 'twill be for the best."

Recalling himself, Deven removed his purse and laid it on the table. It was more than he had meant to pay, but he could not bring himself to fish through it for coins. "For your researches. I pray they lead you to knowledge and good fortune."

THE ONYX HALL, LONDON: *April 25, 1590*

A clutch of chattering hobs and pucks passed through the room, laughing and carefree. All the fae of England were abuzz with the preparations for May Day, and the courtiers were no exception. Every year they took over Moor Fields north of the wall, enacting charms and enchantments that would keep mortals away. And if a few strayed into their midst, well, May Day and Midsummer were the two occasions when humans might hope for kindlier treatment at fae hands. Even the cruelty of the Onyx Court subsided for a short while, at those great festivals.

Lune watched them go from her perch high above. The chamber had a great latticework of arches supporting its ceiling, and it was upon one of these that she rested, her skirts tucked up around her feet so they would not trail and attract notice. It was an imperfect hiding place; plenty of creatures in the palace had wings. But it gave her a brief respite both from malicious whispers, and from those who sought to harm her.

When all around her was silent, she lowered herself slowly to the floor. Her gown of raven feathers was suitable for hiding, and she had long since discarded her velvet slippers; the pale skin of her bare feet might betray her, but it was much quieter when she moved. She lived like a rat in the Onyx Hall, hiding in crevices, stealing crumbs when no one was looking.

She hated every heartbeat of it.

But hatred was good; anger was good. They gave her the energy to keep fighting, when otherwise she would have given up.

She would not let her enemies defeat her like this.

Lune slipped barefoot out of the chamber, down a passageway

that looked all but disused, lifting the ragged hem of her skirts so they would not leave traces in the dust. Until she began her rat's life, she had never realized how many forgotten corners the palace held. It was enormous, far larger than any mortal residence, and if it served the function of both hall and city to the fae that dwelt therein, still it was more than large enough for their needs.

Up a narrow staircase and through a door formed of interwoven hazel branches, and she was safe—as safe as she could get. No one seemed to know of this neglected chamber, which meant she had already bypassed one part of Invidiana's sentence upon her, that she be dependent on others for a place to lay her head. This place was hers alone.

But someone else had found it.

Lune's body froze, torn between fight and flight, assuming on the instant that it was Vidar. Or Dame Halgresta. Or one of their servants. Her hands flexed into claws, as if that would be of any use, and her bare feet set themselves against the dusty floor, ready to leap in any direction.

She saw no one. But someone was there.

Lune knew she should run. That was life these days; that was how she survived. But the chamber's scant furnishings, some of them scavenged from elsewhere in the palace, could not possibly be concealing the tall, heavy form of the Captain of the Onyx Guard, and if it were just some goblin minion...

She should still run. Lune was no warrior.

Instead she moved forward, one noiseless step at a time.

No one crouched behind the narrow bed, with its mattress stuffed with straw. No one stood in the shadow of a tall mirror that had been there when Lune found the room, its crystalline surface so cracked and mazed that nothing could be seen in its depths. No one waited between the cobwebbed, faded tapestries and the stone walls.

She paused, listening, and heard nothing. And yet...

Guided by instinct, Lune knelt and looked into the space beneath the bed.

Tiresias's face stared back at her, pale and streaked with tears.

Lune sighed in disgust. Her tension did not vanish entirely, but a good deal of it evaporated; she had never once seen the madman attack anyone. And he did not look like he was spying; he looked like he was hiding.

"Come out from under there," she growled. How had he fit? Small as he was, she never would have expected the seer could curl up in that narrow space. He shook his head at her words, but the violation of even this tenuous sanctuary angered Lune; she reached under the bed and dragged him out bodily. Invidiana was unlikely to execute her simply for manhandling one of her pets.

Emerging into the dim light, Tiresias gave her a twisted smile that might have been meant to be bright. "Not everything is found so easily," he said gravely. "But if one's cause is good...you might do it."

"Get out," Lune spat. She barely restrained herself from striking him, venting the anger she dared not release on anyone else in the Onyx Hall. "You are one of *her* pets, *her* tools. For all I know, she sent you to me — and anything you say might be a trap she has laid. Everything is a trap, with her."

He nodded, as if she had said something deeply wise. "One trap begets another." Hiding under the bed had sent his hair into disarray, strands tangling with the tips of his eyelashes, twitching when he blinked. "Would you like to break the traps? All of them?"

Lune laughed bitterly, retreating from him. "Oh, no. I will not hear you. One deranged, pointless quest is enough—or would this be the same one? Will you tell me again to seek Francis Merriman?"

Tiresias had begun to turn toward the door, as if to wander off mid-conversation, but his motion arrested when she said that, and he pivoted back to face her. "Have you found him?"

"Have I found him," she repeated, flat and unamused. "No. I have not. He is no one at the mortal court—no gentleman or lord, no wealthy merchant, no officer serving in any capacity. He is not a poet or playwright or painter in the city, nor a prisoner in the Tower. If he lives in some future time that you have foreseen, then I doubt me I will be here to see him come, unless my fortune changes a great deal for the better. If he lives now, then he is no one of any note, and I have no reason to seek him." She glared at him, full of fury, as if all her fall in station were his fault. It was not, but she could and did blame him for how long she had spent chasing a vain, false hope. "I believe you invented Francis Merriman, out of your own mad fancies."

"Perhaps I did." It came out unutterably weary, heavy with resignation. He glanced down, his delicate shoulders slumping under a familiar weight of pain. "Perhaps only Tiresias is real."

The words stole the breath from her body. Anger died without warning, as his meaning became clear. "You," Lune whispered, staring at him. "*You* are Francis Merriman."

His eyes held lifetimes of wistful sadness. "Long ago. I think."

Invidiana's pets, with their classical names, each one collected for a special talent. Lune had given little thought to where they came from, who they were before they fell into the shadows of the Onyx Court. And how long had Tiresias been there? After so many years, who would bother to recall Francis Merriman?

Except him. And not always then. "Why?" Lune asked, hands lifting in wordless confusion. "You scarcely even remember who you were. What changing tide brought you to speak that name again?"

He shook his head, hair falling forward like a curtain too short for him to hide behind. "I do not know."

"'Twas in my chamber," Lune said, remembering. "I was considering my situation. I asked myself how I might better my standing in the Onyx Court—and then you spoke. Do you remember?"

"No." A tear glimmered at the edge of his sapphire eye.

A swift step brought her close; she took him by the arms and shook him once, restraining the urge to violence. Could she have avoided her downfall, had she seen what lay under her very eyes? "Yes, you *do*. Madman you may be, but 'twas no accident you said those words. You said you knew what she did. Who?"

"I cannot." His breath caught raggedly in his throat, and he twisted in her grip. "I cannot. If I—" He shook his head, convulsively. "Do not ask me. Do not make me do this!"

He tore himself free and stumbled away, catching himself against the wall. Lune studied his back for a moment, noting in pitiless detail the trembling of his slender shoulders, the whiteness of his fingers where they pressed against the stone. He feared something, yes. But her *life* hung in the balance; she could not stay ahead of her enemies forever.

If the price of her survival was forcing him to speak, then she would not hesitate.

"Francis Merriman," she said, enunciating the name with soft precision. "Tell me."

The name stiffened his whole body. He might have done anything in that moment; Lune tensed, wondering if he would strike her. Instead he whispered, almost too faint to hear, "Forgive me, Suspiria. Forgive me. 'Tis all I can do for you now. Forgive me..."

His voice trailed off. Francis Merriman lifted his head and turned back to face her, and Lune saw the transcendent effort of his will push back the fogs and shadows of untold years among the fae, leaving his eyes drawn and strained, but clear. The resulting lucidity, the determination, frightened her more than his madness ever had.

With a deliberate motion, he reached out and gripped Lune's arms, fingertips digging into the thin tissue of her sleeves.

"Someone must do it," he said. "I have known that for years. You have asked, and you have little left to lose; therefore I lay it upon you. You must break her power."

Lune wet her lips, willing herself not to look away. "Whose power?"

"Invidiana's."

The instant he spoke the name, a paroxysm snapped his head back, and his hands clenched painfully on Lune's arms. She cried out and reached for him, thinking he would collapse, but he kept his feet and brought his head down again. Six points of red had blossomed in a ring on his brow, flowers of blood, and they poured forth crimson ribbons as he spoke rapidly on, through gritted teeth. "I saw, but did not *understand*—and neither did she. 'Tis my fault she formed that pact, and we have all suffered for it, fae and mortals alike. You must break it. 'Twas not right. She is still c—"

The words rasped out of him, ever wilder and more strained, until the only thing keeping him on his feet was their mutual grip and the splintering remnants of his will. Now his voice died in an agonized cry, and his legs gave way. He slipped free of Lune's hands and crumpled bonelessly to the floor, his face a mask of blood.

The only sound in the room was the pounding of Lune's heart, and the ragged gasping of her own breath as she stared down at him.

*I cannot,* he had said, when she demanded he speak. *If I— If I do, I will die.*

Lune remembered where she was. In a chamber of the Onyx Hall, with the Queen's mad seer lying bloody and dead at her feet. She ran.

MORTLAKE AND LONDON: *April 25, 1590*

A man might not be thought strange if he took an early supper before riding the eight miles back to London, nor if he spoke cheerfully of his purpose in coming to Mortlake. Deven's observations on his way in were true; though some in the village were suspicious of Dee's conjurations, casual chatter over his food revealed that the astrologer often served as a mediator in local problems, settling disputes and offering advice.

Deven was not sure what to think.

The delay meant a late start back to London, though, and full dark came well before he reached the Southwark end of London Bridge. The bankside town offered many inns, but without a manservant it would be irritating, and Deven was in no mood to stop yet; his mind was too full of thoughts. Though the great bell at Bow had long since rung curfew, he bought his way through the Great Gate House that guarded the bridge, trading on his coin and his status as a gentleman and a Gentleman Pensioner.

Dee could not have murdered Walsingham by black magic. Deven simply did not believe it. But did that mean that Walsingham had died of purely natural causes, as Beale insisted, or merely that Deven had pinned his suspicions on the wrong man? The astrologer might still be the hidden player, without being a murderer. Was he working with Anne, or not? And if so, how much stock—if any—should Deven put in the man's predictions?

He thought he was keeping at least marginally alert for movement around him. Cloak Lane was deserted, empty of others who like him were braving the curfew, but there might be footpads; alone, without a manservant, Deven had no intention of being taken by surprise.

Yet he was, when a figure stumbled abruptly out of the blackness of a narrow alley.

The bay horse reared, as surprised as his rider, and Deven fought to control the beast with one hand while reaching for his sword with the other. Steel leapt free, his gelding's hooves thudded into the unpaved street, and he raised his blade in readiness to strike—

—then the figure lifted its face, and Deven recognized her. *"Anne."*

She shied back from him, hands raised as if to defend herself. The sword was still in his hand. Deven scanned Cloak Lane quickly, but saw no one else.

Dee had spoken of enemies and conflict.

He had said that death would send Anne into his path again.

She was backed against the shuttered wall of a shop, like an animal brought to bay. The sight slipped under his defenses, sparking sympathy against his will. Deven compromised; he dismounted, so as not to loom over her, but kept the sword out, relaxed at his side. "Anne. 'Tis me—Michael Deven. Is someone chasing you? Are you in trouble?"

She had changed, since last he saw her; the bones of her face stood higher, as if she had lost weight, and her hair looked paler than ever. Her clothing was a sad imitation of a gentlewoman's finery, and—she must be running from someone—she stood barefoot in the dirt.

"Michael," she whispered. The whites of her eyes stood out starkly in her stricken face. She started to say something, then shook her head furiously. "Go. Leave me!"

"No," he said. "You are in trouble; I know it. Let me help you." A foolish offer, yet he had to make it. He extended his left hand, as if toward a wild horse that might bolt.

"You *cannot* help me. I have told you that already!"

"You have told me nothing! Anne, in God's name, what is going on?"

She flinched back at his words, hands flying up to defend her face, and Deven's blood froze as she changed.

Hair—silver. Gown—black feathers, trembling with her. And her face, imperfectly warded by her hands, refined into otherworldly beauty, high-boned and strange, with silver eyes wide in horror and fear.

The creature that had been wearing Anne Montrose's face stood a moment longer, pressed against the wall like she expected to be struck down on the spot.

Then she cried out and fled into the darkness of the city.

THE ANGEL INN, ISLINGTON: *April 25, 1590*

The veil of glamour she threw over herself as she ran covered her imperfectly, a bad attempt at a human seeming, until she was nearly to Aldersgate. Then the bells tolled and it shredded away like mist, leaving her exposed. Lune fled the city as if the Wild Hunt were at her heels.

She fled north, without pausing to consider her course, and arrived panting at the rosebush behind the Angel Inn.

What she would tell them, she did not know. But she cried out until the doorway revealed itself, then threw herself down the steps to the room below.

Both of the Goodemeades were there, Rosamund catching her as she came through. "My lady," the brownie said in surprise, then looked up at her face. All at once her expression changed; the concern stayed, but steely determination rose up behind it. "Gertrude," she said, and the other brownie moved.

At a gesture, the rushes and strewing herbs covering the floor whisked away into tidy piles, revealing the worn wooden boards beneath. Then these groaned and flexed aside, and where they parted Lune saw more stairs, with lights blooming into life below. She had no chance to ask questions, and no mind to frame them; the hobs hurried her through this secret door, and the boards grew shut behind them.

The room below held two comfortable beds and a hearth now flickering with fire, but no other inhabitants. Rosamund led her to one bed and got her to sit, putting Lune at eye level with the little brownie. Her face still showed concern, and determination, and a sharp-eyed curiosity that was new.

"Now, dear," she said in a gentle voice, holding Lune's hands, "what has happened?"

Lune drew in a ragged, shuddering breath. She hadn't thought about what to say, what story she would offer them to explain her distracted state; too much had happened, Invidiana, the seer, Michael. All her wary instincts failed. "Tiresias is dead."

Soft gasps greeted her statement. "How?" Rosamund whispered. Her plump fingers trembled in Lune's. "Who killed him?"

Lune could not suppress a wild, short laugh. "He did. He knew it would mean his death, yet still he spoke."

The sisters exchanged startled, sorrowful looks. Tears brimmed in Gertrude's eyes, and she pressed one hand to her heart. "Ah, poor Francis."

"What?" Lune snatched her hands from Rosamund's, staring at Gertrude. "You knew who he was?"

"Aye." Gertrude answered her, while Rosamund pressed one kind hand against Lune's shoulder, to keep her from rising. "We knew. Francis Merriman...we remember when he bore that name, though precious few others do. And if he died as you say..."

Rosamund finished her sentence. "Then he has betrayed her at last."

The brownie did not have to try hard to keep Lune in place; her knees felt like water, trembling from her headlong flight, with Deven's oath and the tolling of the bells still reverberating in her bones. Lune dug her fingers into the embroidered coverlet. "How—"

"The jewel," Rosamund said. "The one she wears on her bodice. We've suspected for ages that she laid it on him, not to speak of certain things, on pain of death. 'Twas the only explanation we could find for his silence. And we could not ask him to speak—not when it would carry such a price."

Lune remembered the six points of blood appearing on his brow, where the claws of the jewel had touched. Never before had she seen its power strike home.

She swallowed down the sickness in her throat. *She* had asked him to speak. Forced him.

"Lass," Gertrude said, coming forward to lay a hand on Lune's other shoulder, so she was hemmed in by both sisters. "I would not question you, so soon after his death, but we must know. What did he say?"

His blazing, lucid eyes swam in her vision. Lune shivered, feeling suddenly closed in; the brownies let her go when she tried to rise, and she went toward the hearth, as if its flames could warm the cold spot in the pit of her stomach. "He told me to break her power. That she...that she had formed some kind of pact. And that it was harming everyone, both mortal and fae."

She did not see the sisters exchange a glance behind her back, but she felt it. Standing in the hidden room beneath their home, Lune's sense finally gathered itself enough for her to wonder. The Goodemeades helped those in need—that was why she had come to them—but otherwise they stayed out of the politics of the Onyx Court. Everyone knew that.

Everyone who had not heard their questions, had not seen the alert curiosity in Rosamund's eyes.

They paid more attention than anyone credited.

"This pact," Rosamund said from behind Lune. "What did he tell you about it?"

Lune shivered again, remembering his hoarse voice, desperately grinding out words through the pain that racked him. "Very little. He...he could barely speak. And it struck him down, the—the jewel did—before he could tell me all. She misinterpreted some vision of his." Hands wrapped tightly around her elbows, she turned and faced the Goodemeade sisters. "What vision?"

Gertrude shook her head. "We do not know. He never spoke of it to us."

"But this pact," Lune said, looking from Gertrude to Rosamund. Their round, friendly faces were unwontedly solemn, but also wise. "You know of that, don't you?" The sisters exchanged glances again, a silent and swift communication. "Tell me."

A flicker of wings burst into the room before they could speak. Lune twitched violently at the motion; her nerves were frayed beyond endurance, and the fear-inspired energy that drove her this far had faded. But the little brown bird settled on Gertrude's hand, flirting its reddish tail, and she saw it was merely a nightingale—not even a fae in changed form.

But it must have been touched by fae magic, for it chirped energetically enough, and the brownies both nodded as if they understood. They asked questions of it, too, questions that stirred more fear in Lune's heart—"Who?" and "How many?" and "How long before they arrive?"

And then, after another burst of birdsong, "Tell us what he looks like."

Finally Gertrude nodded. "Thank you, little friend. Keep watch still, and warn us when they draw near."

The nightingale launched itself into the air, flew to an opening in the wall Lune had not attended to before, and vanished.

Rosamund turned once more to Lune. "They are searching for you, my lady. A half-dozen soldiers, and that horrible mountain Halgresta. They cannot know you are here, I think, but they always suspect us when someone's in trouble. Never fear, though; we are good at turning their suspicions aside."

"But it also seems," Gertrude added, "that we have a visitor skulking around our rosebush. Tell me, are they aware of that nice young man you were with at the mortal court?"

"Nice young…" Lune's heart stuttered. "Yes, they are."

Gertrude nodded decisively. "Then we must take care of him, too."

Delay had cost him any hope of keeping the silver-haired creature in sight. But she left a trail: raven feathers, shed from her gown as she fled.

Deven followed them through the cramped and twisted streets of London. The woman eschewed Watling Street, Old Change, Cheapside, instead making her way northwest by back lanes, until he found a feather beneath the arch of Aldersgate itself.

The gate should have been shut for the night, but the heavy doors hung open, the guards there blinking and disoriented.

The trail led north. Mounted now, Deven should have lost sight of the black feathers in the night, but their faint glimmer drew his eye. By the time he reached Islington, he had a fistful of the things, iridescent and strange.

The last feather he found impaled on the thorn of a rosebush behind the Angel Inn.

Light showed here and there along the inn's back wall, and he knew they would still welcome a traveler at the front. But the woman could not have gone that way—

*Unless,* his mind whispered uneasily, *she put on Anne's face again.*

The feathers rustled in his fist. Despite himself, Deven paced around the rosebush, as if he would find some other sign. The thorned branches stood mute.

The hairs on the back of his neck rose. Deven glanced up at the sky, but it stood clear from one horizon to the next, with not a cloud in sight. Why, then, did he feel a thunderstorm approaching? He drew his blade again, just for the comfort of steel, but it did him little good. Something was coming, and every nerve screamed at him to run.

"Master Deven! This way, quickly!"

He spun and saw a woman beckoning from a doorway that glowed with warm, comforting light. He was on the staircase before he realized the doorway stood in the rosebush, in the comfortable tavern before he considered that he had just passed underground, through the opening in the floor before he asked himself, *Who is this woman? And why did you just follow her?*

"There," a northern accent said with satisfaction, from somewhere in the vicinity of his belt. "I wouldn't normally resort to charms, but we couldn't rightly stand there and argue. My apologies, Master Deven."

The sword trembled in his hand.

The woman who had lured him below was joined by a second, just as short, and alike as only a sister could be. They wore tidy little dresses covered with clean, embroidered aprons, and their apple-cheeked faces spoke of friendliness and trust—but they came only to his belt, and were no more human than the figure silhouetted in front of the fire, her hair shining like silver washed with gold.

"Michael," she breathed.

He retreated a step, risked a glance over his shoulder, saw that the floor had grown shut behind him. Leveling his swordpoint at the three of them, Deven said, "Come no closer."

"Truly," one of the little women said, the one with roses embroidered on her apron, "there's no need for that. We brought you below, Master Deven, because there are some rather unpleasant people coming this way, and you will be safer down here. I promise, we mean no harm."

"How in *God's* name am I supposed to believe that?"

All three cringed, and one of the women gave a muffled

squeak—the one with the daisies on her apron. "Now, now," the rose woman said, a trifle more severely. "That isn't very gentlemanly of you. Not to mention that we shouldn't like to see our house pop up out of the ground without so much as a by-your-leave, or an apology to the folk above. We are fae, Master Deven; surely you must know what that means."

Ominous thudding answered before he could; all four of them looked up. "They're at the rosebush," the daisy woman said, and then a snarl reverberated through the chamber, deep and hard, like thunder in an ugly storm.

*"Open, in the name of the Queen."*

The two short ones exchanged glances. "I am the better liar," the daisy woman said, and the rose woman answered, "but they will be suspicious if they do not see us both." She fixed Deven with a stare that was no less effective for coming from a creature so small. "You will put up your sword, good master, and refrain from invoking certain names while in our house. We are protecting you from what's above, which is good for both you and us. Once we have gotten rid of these nuisances, we shall answer any question you have."

"As many as we know the answers to," the daisy woman corrected her. "Come, we must hurry."

Upon which the two of them whisked off their aprons, mussed their hair, yawned theatrically, and hurried up the stairs, looking for all the world as if they had just been roused from bed.

The floor stretched open to let them pass, then shut again, like a cellar without a door.

Deven said, half to himself, "What..."

"Hush," the silver-haired creature hissed. She had not spoken since uttering his name, and now her attention was not more than half on him; she still looked upward, listening as heavy boots clomped across the floor.

"Where is she?" The voice he had heard before. It made Deven feel as if his bones were grinding together.

"I beg your pardon, Dame Halgresta—" The words were punctuated by a yawn. "We had just retired for the night. Would you like some mead?"

A clanking splash, as of a metal tankard being knocked to the floor. "I would not. *Tell me where she is.*"

The other sister: "Who?"

"Lady—" The deep voice cut off in a noise something between a growl and a laugh. "Lady no more. The bitch Lune."

Deven glanced across the hidden room at his involuntary companion. The silver-haired woman shivered unconsciously, her hands rising to cup her elbows. Upstairs, the two sisters parried the stranger's questions with a masterful blend of innocence, confusion, and well-timed misdirection. No, they had not seen the lady—beg pardon, the woman Lune. Aye, of course they would say if they had; were they not the Queen's loyal subjects? No, they had not seen her in some time—very rarely at all, since she went to the mortal court.

At that, finally, the fae woman looked across the room at him. Her eyes shone unmistakably silver, no common gray... but the set of them was familiar, from many a fond study.

Neither of them dared speak, with danger so near above. Instead they stared at each other, until the fae woman— Lune—broke and turned away.

He had not listened to the rest of the conversation above. More heavy footsteps, lighter voices trying to press the departing visitor to take some sweetmeats, or ale for the ride back to the city. Then silence, and the feeling of oppression lifted.

Deven decided to risk it. Crossing the floor, he approached Lune as closely as he dared, and in a voice pitched to carry no further than her ears, he said, "What has become of Anne Montrose?"

The pointed chin lifted a fraction. Her voice equally soft, Lune said, "She was always thus, beneath the mask."

He turned away, realized the sword was still in his hand, sheathed it. And then they waited for the sisters to return.

"Dame Halgresta's gone," Rosamund said to Lune, when they came downstairs again. "I presume you listened? They know nothing of Francis's death; someone saw you flee the palace, is all. Be careful, my lady. She very much wishes to kill you."

Gertrude nudged her sister in the ribs while tying her daisy-flowered apron back on. "Manners, Rosamund. Now that we haven't got that awful giantess breathing down our necks, we should take care of our guest."

"Oh! Of course!" Rosamund made a proper curtsy to Deven. "Welcome to our house, Master Deven. I am Rosamund Goodemeade, and this is my sister Gertrude. And this is the Lady Lune."

Ever since she and Deven had lapsed into silence, Lune's attention had been fixed on the fireplace, the safest target she could find. Now she said wearily, "He knows." She turned to find the brownies wide-eyed and a little nervous. Relaxing her arms from their tight positions across her body, she added, "He drove the glamour from me when I was on my way here."

His blue eyes might have been shuttered against a storm, so little could she read out of them. Walsingham's service had taught him well—but he had never used such defenses against her before. Well, she could not blame him. "So there you have it, Master Deven," Lune said to him, hearing her own voice as if it belonged to a stranger. "There are faeries at the mortal court. Though most of them come in secret, and do not disguise themselves as I did."

A muscle worked in his jaw. When Deven spoke, it sounded almost nothing like his natural voice, either. "So 'twas you all along. I suspected Dee."

Gertrude said in confusion, "She was what all along?"

"The hidden player," Lune said, still looking at Deven. "The secret influence on English politics that his master Walsingham has begun to suspect."

Bitterness twisted the corner of his mouth. "You were under my eyes, the entire time."

Lune matched him with her own sour laugh. "'Tis a night for such things, it seems. You are both right and wrong, Master Deven. I was a lead to your hidden player—not the player herself. There are two Queens in England. You serve one; you seek the other."

Her words broke through the stoic facade he had constructed while they waited, revealing startlement beneath. "*Two* Queens..."

"Aye," Rosamund said. "And that may be the answer to the question you asked us, Lady Lune, before we were interrupted."

It was enough to distract her from Deven. "What?"

Gertrude had scurried off to the far end of the room while they spoke. Something bumped the back of Lune's farthingale; she looked down to see the brownie pushing a stool almost as tall as she was. "If we're going to have this conversation," Gertrude said, with great firmness, "then we will sit while we do so. I've been on my feet all day, baking and cleaning, and you two look about done in."

"I have not said I will stay," Deven said, with another glance over his shoulder to the sealed top of the staircase.

Lune smiled ironically at him. "But you will. You want answers—you and your master."

"Walsingham is *dead*." In the time it took him to say that, two strides ate up the distance between them and Deven was in her face, his anger beating at her like the heat from the fire. "I suppose I have you to thank for that."

Her knees gave out; she dropped without grace onto the stool Gertrude had put behind her. "He—what? Dead? When?"

"Do not pretend to be innocent," he spat. "You knew he was looking for you, for evidence of your Queen's hand. He was a threat, and now he's dead. I may be the world's greatest fool—you certainly played me as such—but not so great a fool as that."

Rosamund's hand closed over the silk of his right sleeve, drawing his fingers back from the sword hilt they had unconsciously sought. "Master Deven," the brownie said. The man did not look down at her. The uneven shadows of firelight turned his face monstrous, warping the clean lines of his features. "Lady Lune was imprisoned when your master died. She could not have killed him."

"Then she gave the order for it to be done."

Lune shook her head. She could not hold Deven's gaze; she felt naked, exposed, confronting him while wearing her true face. He would not have glared at Anne with such anger and hate. "I did not. But if he's dead . . . how?"

"Illness," Deven said. "Or so it was made to seem."

Walsingham had often been sick. He might have died by natural means. Or not. "My task," she said, staring fixedly at the battered feathers of her skirt, "was to watch over Walsingham, to know what he was about. And, if I could, to find a means of influencing him."

Deven met this with flat disgust. "Me."

"He is—was—an astute man," Lune said, dodging Deven's implicit question. She could not explain her choice, not now. "I believe my Queen feared he was coming near the truth. You may be right to blame me, Master Deven, for I told Vidar—a fae lord—what the Principal Secretary was about. After I was taken from Oatlands, he may have taken steps to remove that threat. But I never ordered it."

Gertrude had Deven's other sleeve now, and the gentle but insistent tugging from the brownies got him to back up a step, so that he no longer towered over Lune on the stool. "Why?" Deven asked at last. Some of the anger had gone from his voice, replaced by bewilderment. "Why should a faerie Queen care what happens in Ireland, or what became of Mary Stewart?"

"If you will sit," Gertrude said, returning with patient determination to her point of a moment before, "we may be able to answer that question."

When they were all seated, with mugs of mead in their hands—the brownies' family name, Deven realized, was more than mere words—the rose-flowered woman, Rosamund, began to speak.

"My lady," she said, bobbing her curly head at Lune. "How long have you been at the Onyx Court?"

Lune had straightened the remnants of her feathered gown and smoothed her silver hair, but her bare feet were still an incongruous note, the slender arches freckled with mud. "A long time," she said. "Not so long as Vidar, I suppose, but Lady Nianna and Lady Carline are more recently come than I. Let me see—Y Law Carreg was the ambassador from the Tylwyth Teg then...."

It reminded Deven powerfully of his early days at Elizabeth's court. A flood of names unknown to him, currents of alliance and tension he could not read. Somehow it made the notion more real, that there truly was another court in England.

When Lune's recitation wound down, Rosamund said, "And how long has Invidiana been on the throne?"

The elfin woman blinked in astonishment. "What manner of question is that?" she said. "An age and a day; I do not know. We are not mortals, to come and go in measured time." And indeed, Deven realized, in all her explanation of her tenure at court, she had not once named a date or span of years.

The sisters looked at each other, and Gertrude nodded. Rosamund said, with simple precision, "Invidiana became the Queen of faerie England on the fifteenth day of January, in the mortal year fifteen hundred and fifty-nine."

Lune stared at her, then laughed in disbelief. "Impossible. That is scarcely thirty years! I myself have been at the Onyx Court longer than that."

"Have you?" Gertrude said, over the top of her mead.

The elfin woman's lips parted, at a loss for words. Deven had been quiet since they sat down, but now he spoke. "That is the day Elizabeth was crowned Queen."

"Just so," Rosamund answered.

Now he was included in Lune's disbelieving stare. "That is not possible. I *remember*—"

"Most people do," Gertrude said. "Not specific memories, tied to specific mortal years—no, you're quite right, we do not measure time so closely. Perhaps if we did, more fae would notice the change. The Onyx Court as such has only existed for thirty-one years, perhaps a bit longer, depending on how one considers it. Vidar has been there longer. But all your memories of Invidiana's reign do not go further back than that. You just believe they do, and forget what came before."

Rosamund nodded. "My sister and I are some of the only ones who remember what came before. Francis was another. She let him remember on purpose, I believe, and we were with him when it happened; he kept us from forgetting. Of the others who know, every last one now rides with the Wild Hunt."

Lune's silver eyes widened, and she set her mug down with careful hands. "They claim to be kings."

"And they were," Gertrude confirmed. "Kings of faerie England, one corner of it or another. Until Elizabeth became Queen, and Invidiana with her. In one day—one moment—she deposed them all."

Deven had not forgotten where the conversation began. "But why? This cannot be usual for your kind." It was not usual for *his* kind, to be sitting in a hidden cellar of a faerie house, speaking with two brownies and an elf. His mead sat untouched on the table before him; he knew better than to drink it. "Why the connection?"

"We are creatures of magic," Rosamund said, as casually as if she were reminding him they were English. "And in its own way, a coronation ceremony *is* magic; it makes a king—or a queen—out of an ordinary mortal. Gertrude and I have always assumed Invidiana took advantage of that ritual to establish her own power."

Lune's voice came from his right, unsteady and faint. "But she did more than that, didn't she? Because there was a pact."

"'Pact?'" The word chilled Deven. "What do you mean?"

For a moment, he thought he perceived both sorrow and horror in her expression. "Do you recall me asking after a mortal named Francis Merriman?" Deven nodded warily. "He was under my eyes, as I was under yours. He...died tonight. He told me of a pact formed by Invidiana, my Queen, that he said was harming mortals and fae alike. And he begged me to break it."

Deven said, "But a pact..."

"Must be known to both parties," Rosamund finished for

him. "Any fae with an ounce of political sense knows that Invidiana regularly interferes with the mortal court, and uses that court to control her own people. And from time to time a mortal learns that he or she has dealings with fae — usually someone enough in thrall that they will not betray it. But if what Francis said is correct . . . then someone on the other side knows precisely what is going on."

The words were trembling in Deven's throat. He let them out one by one, fearing what they meant. "The Principal Secretary . . . he told me of a hidden player. And he believed that player did — not often, but at times — have direct access to her Majesty."

He missed their reactions; he could not bring himself to look up from his clenched fists. The suggestion was incredible, even coming from his own mouth. That Elizabeth might know of faeries — not simply know of them, but traffic with them. . . .

"I believe it," Lune whispered. "Indeed, it makes more sense than I like."

"But *why*?" Frustrated fear and confusion boiled out of Deven. "Why should such a pact be formed? What would Elizabeth stand to gain?"

An ironic smile touched Lune's thin, sculpted lips. "The keeping of her throne. We have worked hard to ensure it, at Invidiana's command. The Queen of Scots you have already named; Invidiana took great care to remove her as a threat. Likewise with other political complications. And the Armada . . ."

Her sentence trailed off, but Gertrude finished it, quite cheerfully. "You have Lady Lune to thank for those storms that kept the Spanish from our shores."

The bottom dropped out of Deven's stomach. Lune said, "I negotiated the treaty only. I have no power to summon storms myself."

He desperately floundered his way back to politics, away from magic. "And your Queen gained her own throne in return."

The black feathers he'd collected along the way had fallen from his hand at some point after he came downstairs. Lune had the broken tip of one in her fingers, and with it was tracing invisible patterns on the tabletop, her gaze unfocused. "More than that," she said, distant with thought. "Elizabeth is a Protestant."

Rosamund nodded. "Whereas Mary Tudor and Mary Stewart were both Catholics."

"What means that to you? Surely you cannot be Christian."

"Indeed, we are not," Lune said. "But Christianity can be a weapon against us—as you yourself have seen." Nor had Deven forgotten; he would use it again, if necessary. "Catholics have rites against us—prayers, exorcisms, and the like."

"As does the Church of England. And many puritan-minded folk call your kind all devils; surely that cannot be to your advantage."

"But the puritans are few in number, and the Church of England is a new-formed thing, which few follow with any ardor. 'Tis a compromise, designed to offend as few as possible as little as possible, and it has not existed long enough for its rites to acquire true power. The Book of Common Prayer is an empty litany to most people, form without the passionate substance of faith." Lune laid the feather tip down on the table and turned her attention to him. "This might change, in years to come. But for now, the ascendancy of your Protestant Queen is a boon to us."

He could taste his pulse, so hard was his heart beating. The chessboard in his mind rearranged itself, pieces of new colors adding themselves to the fray. Walsingham had surely never dreamed of this. And when Beale heard...

*If* Beale heard.

In personal beliefs, Walsingham had been a Protestant reformer, a "puritan" as their opponents called them; he would have loved to see the Church of England stripped of its many remaining papist trappings. But Walsingham was also a political realist, who knew well that any attempt at sweeping reformation would provoke rebellion Elizabeth could not survive. Beale, on the other hand, was outspoken about his beliefs, and often agitated for puritan causes at court.

Should Beale ever hear that Elizabeth, the great compromiser of religion, had formed a pact with a *faerie queen*—

England was already at war with Catholic powers. She could not fight another one within her own borders.

Deven looked from Rosamund, to Gertrude, to Lune. "You said this Francis Merriman of yours begged you to break the pact."

Lune nodded. "He said it was a mistake, that both sides had suffered for it." Her hesitation was difficult to read; the silver eyes were alien to him. "I do not know the effects of this pact, but I know Invidiana. I can imagine why he wanted me to break it."

"Do you intend to do so?"

The question hung in the air. This deep underground, there was no sound except their breathing, and the soft crackling of the fire. The Goodemeade sisters had their lips pressed together in matching expressions; both of them were watching Lune, whose gaze lay on the broken feather tip before her.

Deven had known Anne Montrose—or thought he had. This silver-haired faerie woman, he did not know at all. He would have given a great deal to hear her thoughts just then.

"I do not know how to," Lune said, very controlled.

"That is not what I asked. I do not know the arrangements

of your court, but two things I can presume: first, that your Queen would not want you to interfere with this matter, and second, that you are out of favor with her. Else you would not be here, barefoot and in hiding, with her soldiers hunting you out of the city. So will you defy her? Will you try to break this pact?"

Lune looked to the Goodemeades. The brownies' faces showed identical resolution; it was not hard to guess what they thought should be done.

But what he was asking of her was treason.

Deven wondered if Walsingham had ever felt such compunctions, asking his agents to betray those they professed to serve.

Lune closed her eyes and said, "I will."

MEMORY: *January 14–15, 1559*

*D*espite the cold, people packed the streets of London. In the southwestern portions of the city, in the northeast — in all those areas removed from the center — men wandered drunkenly and women sang songs, while bonfires burned on street corners, creating islands of light and heat in the frozen air, banners and the clothing of the wealthy providing points of rich color. Everywhere in the city was music and celebration, and if underneath it all many worried or schemed, no such matters were permitted to stain the appearance of universal rejoicing.

The press was greatest in the heart of the city, the great artery that ran from west to east. Crowds packed so tightly along the route that hardly anyone could move, save a few lithe child thieves who took advantage of the bounty. Petty Wales, Tower Street, Mark Lane, Fenchurch, and up Gracechurch Street; then the course straightened westward, running down

Cornhill, past Leadenhall, and into the broad thoroughfare of Cheapside. The cathedral of St. Paul awaited its moment, and then the great portal of Ludgate, all bedecked with finery. From there, Fleet Street, the Strand, and so down into Westminster, and every step of the way, the citizens of London thronged to see their Queen.

A roar went up as the first members of the procession exited the Tower, temporarily in use once more as a royal residence. By the time the slender figure in cloth of gold and silver came into view, riding in an open-sided litter and waving to her people, the noise was deafening.

The procession made its slow way along the designated route, stopping at predetermined points for pageants that demonstrated for all the glory and virtue of the new sovereign. No passive spectator she, nor afraid of the chill; when she could not hear over the noise of the crowd, she bid the pageant be performed again. She called responses to her loyal subjects, touching strangers for a moment with the honor and privilege of royal attention. And they loved her for that, for the promise of change she brought, for the evanescent beauty that would all too soon fade back to show an architecture of steel beneath.

She reached Westminster late in the day, exhausted but radiant from her ordeal. The night passed: in drunkenness for the people of London, in busy preparation for the great officials in Westminster.

Come the following morning, when she set forth again, a shadow mirrored her elsewhere.

In crimson robes, treading upon a path of blue cloth, one uncrowned woman passed from Westminster Hall to the Abbey.

In deepest black, moving through subterranean halls, a second uncrowned woman passed from the Tower of London to a chamber that stood beneath Candlewick Street.

Westminster Abbey rang with the sonorous speeches and ceremony of coronation. Step by step, a woman was transformed into a Queen. And a few miles away, the passages and chambers of the Onyx Hall, emptied for this day, echoed back the ghostlike voice of a fae, as she stripped herself of one name and donned another.

A sword glimmered in her hand.

The presiding bishop spoke traditional words as the emblems of sovereignty were bestowed upon the red-haired woman. The sound should not have reached the Onyx Hall, any more than the shouts of the crowd should have, but it was not a matter of loudness. For today, the two spaces resounded as one.

Then the fanfares began, as one by one, a succession of three crowns were placed upon an auburn head.

As the Onyx Hall rang with the trumpet's blast, the sword flashed through the air and struck a stone that descended from the ceiling of the chamber.

Drunken revelers in London heard the sound, and thought it a part of the celebrations: the tolling of a terrible, triumphant bell, marking the coronation of their Queen. And soon enough the bells would come, ringing out in Westminster and spreading east to the city, but this sound reached them first, and resonated the most deeply. Sovereignty was in that sound.

Those citizens who were on Candlewick Street at the time fell silent, and dropped to their knees in reverence, not caring that the object they bowed to was a half-buried stone along the street's south edge, its limestone surface weathered and scarred, unremarkable to any who did not know its tale.

Three times the stone tolled its note, as three times the sword struck it from below, as three times the crowns were placed. And on the third, the sword plunged into the heart of the stone.

All mortal England hailed the coronation of Elizabeth, first of her name, by the Grace of God, Queen of England, France, and Ireland, Defender of the Faith, et cetera; and all faerie England trembled at the coronation of Invidiana, Queen of the Onyx Court, Mistress of the Glens and Hollow Hills.

And a dozen faerie kings and queens cried out in rage as their sovereignty was stripped from them.

Half-buried in the soil of Candlewick Street, the London Stone, the ancient marker said to have been placed there by the Trojan Brutus, the mythical founder of Britain; the stone upon which sacred oaths were sworn; the half-forgotten symbol of authority, against which the rebel Jack Cade had struck his sword a century before, in validation of his claim to London, made fast the bargain between two women.

Elizabeth, and Invidiana.

A great light and her great shadow.

# Act Four

O no! O no! tryall onely shewes
The bitter iuice of forsaken woes;
Where former blisse present euils do staine;
Nay, former blisse addes to present paine,
While remembrance doth both states containe.
       — Sir Philip Sidney
          "The Smokes of Melancholy"

$\mathcal{S}$unlight caresses his face with warmth, and grass pricks through the linen of his shirt to tickle the skin inside. He smiles, eyes closed, and lets his thoughts drift on the breeze. Insects sing a gentle chorus, with birds supplying the melody. He can hear leaves rustling, and over the crest of the hill, her laughter, light and sweet as bells.

The damp soil yields softly beneath his bare feet as he runs through the wood. She is not far ahead—he can almost glimpse her through the shifting, dappled emerald of the shadows—but branches keep hindering him. A silly game. She must have asked the trees to help her. But they play too roughly, twigs snagging, even tearing his shirt, leaf edges turning sharp and scoring his face, while acorns and rocks batter the soles of his feet. He leaves a trail of footprints that fill with blood. He does not like this game anymore.

And then he teeters on the edge of a pit, almost falling in.

Below, so far below...

She might be sleeping. Her face is peaceful, almost smiling.

But then the rot comes, and her skin decays, turning mushroom-colored, wrinkling, swelling, bloating, sinking in at the hollows of her face, and he cries out but he cannot go to her—the serpent has him fast in its coils, and as he fights to free himself it rears back and strikes, sinking its fangs into his brow, six stabbing wounds that paralyze him, steal his voice, and she is lost to him.

The fae gathered around laugh, taking malicious pleasure in his blind struggles, but it loses all savor when he slumps into the vines they have bound around him. His dreams are so easy to play with, and the Queen never objects. Bored now by his silent shudders, they let the vines fall away as they depart.

225

*He is left in the night garden, where the plants have never felt neither sun nor breeze. High above, cold lights twinkle, spelling out indecipherable messages. There might be a warning in them, if he could but read it.*

*What good would it do him? He had warnings before, and mis-understood them.*

*Water rushes along at his side. Like him it is buried, forgotten by the world above, disregarded by the world below, chained to serve at her pleasure.*

*It has no sympathy for him.*

*He weeps for his loss, there on the bank of the brook—weeps bloody tears that stain the water for only an instant before dissolving into nothingness.*

*He has lost the sunlit fields, lost the laughter, lost* her. *He shares her grave, here in these stone halls. It only remains for him to die.*

*But he knows the truth.*

*Even death cannot bring him to her again.*

The Angel Inn, Islington: *April 25, 1590*

"We must get you back into the Onyx Hall," Rosamund said to Lune.

Gertrude was in the corner, murmuring to a sleek gray mouse that nodded its understanding from within her cupped hands. Lune was watching her, not really thinking; her thoughts seemed to have collapsed in fatigue and shock after she committed herself to treason. It was a reckless decision, suicidal even; tomorrow morning she would regret having said it.

Or would she? Her gaze slid once more to Deven, like iron to a lodestone. His stony face showed no regrets. She had never expected him to become caught in this net, and could not see a way to free him. However lost he might be right now, he would not back away. Though this pact might benefit Elizabeth, it was also harming her; so Tiresias had said—no, Francis Merriman. The seer had fought so hard to reclaim that self. Having killed him, the least Lune could do was grant him his proper name.

Francis Merriman had believed this pact was wrong. The Goodemeades obviously agreed with him. And Deven's master might well have been murdered at Invidiana's command. She knew him too well to think he would let that pass.

Lune herself had nothing left to lose save her life, and even that hung in the balance. But was that sufficient reason to betray her Queen?

Faint memories stirred in the depths of her mind. The thought, so fleetingly felt, that once things had been different. That once the fae of England had lived warmer lives—occasionally scheming against one another, yes, occasionally cruel to mortals, but not always. Not this unrelenting life of fear, and the ever-present threat of downfall.

Even those who lived far from the Onyx Hall dwelt in its shadow.

The Onyx Hall. Rosamund's words finally penetrated. Lune sat bolt upright and said, "Impossible. I would be executed the moment I set foot below."

"Not necessarily," Gertrude said. The mouse had vanished; now the brownie was prodding the fire, laying an additional log so that bright flames leapt upward and illuminated the room. "I've sent Cheepkin to see if anyone has found Francis's body. So far as we know, that jewel doesn't tell Invidiana when someone dies, so she may not yet know."

Lune's stomach twisted at the mere thought of being in the same room as the Queen when she learned of it. "She will know *how* he died, though. And she will wonder to whom he betrayed her."

Rosamund's nod was not quite complacent, but it didn't show half the alarm Lune felt it should. "Which is why we shall give her another target to suspect. And do you some good in the bargain, I think, as you will be the one to tell her." The brownie's soft lips pursed in thought. "She will be angry regardless, and afraid; how much, she will wonder, did Francis manage to say before he died? But that cannot be helped; we cannot pretend he died by other means. What we must do is make certain she does not suspect *you*."

"Who did you have in mind?" Gertrude asked her sister.

"Sir Derwood Corr. We can warn him to leave tonight, so he'll be well clear of the palace before she tries to arrest him."

Deven was looking at Lune, but she had no more idea than he what the Goodemeades meant. "Who is Sir Derwood Corr?"

"A new elf knight in the Onyx Guard. Also an agent of the Wild Hunt."

Gertrude nodded her approval. "She fears them anyway; it cannot do much harm."

They seemed to be serious. An agent of the Wild Hunt, infiltrating the Onyx Guard itself—and somehow the Goodemeades knew about it, and were eager to get the knight out of harm's way. "Are you working with the Wild Hunt?"

"Not *exactly*," Gertrude said, hedging. "That is, they would like us to be. We choose not to help them, at least most of the time; someone else brought Sir Derwood in. But we do keep an eye on their doings."

Lune had no response to this extraordinary statement. Deven, slouched on his stool as much as his stiff doublet would allow, snorted. "The Principal Secretary said 'twas infamous to use women agents, but I vow he would have made an exception for you."

*They are not spies,* Lune thought. *They are spymasters. With the very birds and beasts of the field their informants.*

"So," Rosamund said briskly. "As soon as Cheepkin reports in, Lady Lune, we shall smuggle you back into the Onyx Hall. You can tell Invidiana that Sir Derwood is an ally of the Wild Hunt; she will discover that he has fled; she will assume Francis spoke to him, and not to you. With any luck, that will sweeten her mind toward you, at least a bit."

Lune did not hold out much hope for that. Was she truly about to return to her rat's life, hiding from Vidar and Dame Halgresta and everyone else who might think to curry favor by harming or eliminating her?

The low, smoldering fire that had lived in her gut since her imprisonment—no, since her inglorious return from the sea—had an answer for that.

Yes, she would. She would go back, and tear every bit of it down.

*Then I am a traitor indeed. May all the power of Faerie help me.*

"Very well," she murmured.

Deven took a deep breath and sat up. "What may I do?"

"No time for that now," Gertrude said. "We must return Lady Lune, before someone finds Francis. Might I ask a favor of you, Master Deven?"

He looked wary. "What is it?"

"Nothing dangerous, dearie; just a bit of dodging around Invidiana. Come with me, I'll show you." Gertrude took him by the hand and led him upstairs.

Lune watched them go, leaving her behind with Rosamund. "Is this safe?" she asked quietly. "I did not think of it before I came, but Invidiana has spies everywhere. She may learn of what we have said here."

"I do not think so," Rosamund said, and now she *did* sound complacent. "We're beneath the rosebush, here—very truly *sub rosa*. Nothing that happens here will spread outside this room."

For the first time, Lune looked upward, to the ceiling of the hidden chamber. Old, gnarled roots spread fingerlike across the ceiling, and tiny roses sprang improbably from their bark, like a constellation of bright yellow stars. The ancient emblem of secrecy gave her a touch of comfort. For the first time in ages, she had friends she could trust.

She should have come to the Goodemeades sooner. She should have asked them about Francis Merriman.

They lied too well, convincing everyone that they stayed out of such matters. But if they did not, they would never have survived for so long.

Lune realized there was something she had not said. The

words came awkwardly; she spoke them so often, but so rarely with sincerity. "I thank you for your kindness," she whispered, unable to face Rosamund. "I will be forever in your debt."

The brownie came over and took her hands, smiling into her eyes. "Help us set this place right," she said, "and the debt will be more than repaid."

A lantern glowed by the door of the inn, and light still showed inside. Lying as it did along the Great North Road, the Angel was a major stopping point for travelers who did not gain the city before the gates closed at dusk, and so there was always someone awake, even at such a late hour.

Deven led his horse toward the road in something of a daze. The part of him that was accustomed to following orders had for some reason decided to obey the little brownie Gertrude, but his mind still reeled. Faeries at court. How many of them? He remembered the rooftop chase, and the stranger that had vanished. Perhaps he had not imagined the flapping of wings.

He mounted up, rode into the courtyard of the inn, and dismounted again, so that anyone inside would hear his arrival. Looping his reins over a post, he stepped through the door, startling a sleepy-eyed young man draped across a table. The fellow sat up with a jerk, dropping the damp rag he held.

"Sir," he said, stumbling to his feet. "Needing a room, then?"

"No, indeed," Deven said. "I have some ways to ride before I stop. But I am famished, and need something to keep me going. Do you have a loaf of bread left?"

"Uh—we should—" The young man looked deeply confused. "You're riding on, sir? At this hour of the night? The city gates are closed, you know."

"I am not going into the city, and the message I bear cannot wait. Bread, please."

The fellow sketched a bad bow and hastened through a door at the far end of the room. He emerged again a moment later with a round, crusty loaf in his hand. "This is all I could find, sir, and 'tis a day old."

"That will do." At least he hoped it would. Deven paid the young man and left before he would have to answer any more questions.

He rode away, circled around, came back to the rosebush. Gertrude had provided him with a bowl; now he set it down by the door of one of the inn's outbuildings, with the loaf of bread inside, and feeling a great fool, he said, "Food for the Good People; take it and be content."

The little woman popped up so abruptly he almost snatched out his blade and stabbed her. The night had not been good on his nerves. "Thank you, dearie," Gertrude said with a cheerful curtsy. "Now if you could pick it up again? We have some of our own, of course, a nice little supply—we so often have to help out others—but if Invidiana finds we've been giving Lady Lune mortal bread...well, we aren't giving it to her, are we? You are. So that's all right and proper. Never said anything about *mortals* giving her bread or milk, and not as if she has any right to tell you what to do. Not that it would stop her, mind you."

Bemused, Deven picked up the bowl and followed the still chattering brownie back to the rosebush, which opened up and let them pass below.

Lune was still in the hidden room, washing her feet in a basin of clear water. She glanced up as he entered, and the sight made his throat hurt; the motion was so familiar, though the body and face had changed. He thrust the bowl at her more roughly than he meant to, and tried to ignore the relieved pleasure on her face as she took the bread. "I shall have to think where to hide this," she said. "You are clever, Gertrude, but Invidiana will still be angry if she learns."

"Well, eat a bite of it now, my lady," the brownie said, retrieving the bowl from Deven. "You could use a good night's sleep here, but we can't risk it; you need to go back as soon as possible. Has Cheepkin returned?"

"While you were out," Rosamund said. "No one has found Francis yet. I've made sure Sir Derwood knows to leave."

"Good, good. Then 'tis time you went back, Lady Lune. Are you ready?"

Deven, watching her, thought that she was not. Nonetheless, Lune nodded her agreement. Holding the small loaf in her hands as if it were a precious jewel, she pinched off a bite, put it in her mouth, chewed, and swallowed. He watched in fascination, despite himself; he had never seen anyone eat bread with such attentive care.

Rosamund said to him, "It strengthens our magic against those things that would destroy it. Traveling through mortal places is dangerous without it."

As he had seen, earlier that very night. No wonder Lune treated it as precious.

"Now," Gertrude said briskly. "Master Deven, would you escort her back to London? 'Twould go faster riding, and unless Lady Lune makes herself look like a man, she should not be traveling alone."

The comment about disguise brought him back to unpleasant matters with a jolt. Lune was toweling her feet dry with great concentration. He very much wanted to say no—but he made the mistake of looking at Gertrude and Rosamund. Their soft-cheeked faces smiled up at him in innocent appeal.

His mouth said, "I would be glad to," without consulting his mind, and thus he was committed.

Lune stood, dropped the towel on her stool, and walked past him. "Let us go, then."

By the time he followed, she was gone from the main room upstairs. He found her outside, waiting with her back to him. Words stuck in his throat; he managed nothing more than a stiff, "My horse is this way." His bay stopped lipping at the grass when Deven took hold of the reins. No footsteps sounded behind him, but when he turned, he found her just a pace away.

Except it wasn't her. She wore a different face, a human one. Not, he was desperately relieved to see, the face of Anne Montrose.

"Who is that?" he said, and could not keep the bitterness out of it.

"Margaret Rolford," Lune said, coolly.

Deven's mouth twisted. "Once a waiting-gentlewoman to Lettice Knollys, as I understand it."

Margaret Rolford's eyes were probably brown in sunlight; at night, they looked black. "I congratulate you, Master Deven. You followed me farther than I realized."

There was nothing he could say to that. Steeling himself, Deven put his hands around Margaret's waist—thicker than Lune's, and Anne's—and lifted her into the saddle; then he swung himself up behind her.

He had not realized, when he agreed to Gertrude's request, that it would mean riding the distance to London with his arms around the faerie woman.

Deven set his jaw, and touched his heels to the flanks of his gelding.

The tiny sliver of a moon had set even before he returned from Mortlake; they rode in complete darkness toward the few glimmering lights of London. Margaret Rolford's body was not shaped like Anne Montrose's — she had a sturdier frame, and was shorter — but still it triggered memories. A crisp, sun-washed autumn day, with just enough wind to lift a maiden's unbound hair. Both of them released from their duties, and diverting themselves with other courtiers. The young ladies all rode tame little palfreys, but Anne wanted more, and so he put her up on the saddle of his bay and galloped as fast as he dared the length of a meadow, her slender body held safely against his.

Silence was unbearable. "Doctor Dee," he said, without pre-amble. "He has nothing to do with it, then?"

She rode stiffly, her head turned away from him even though she sat sideways in the saddle. "He claims to speak with angels. I doubt he would speak with us."

*Us.* She might look human when she chose to, but she was not. *Us* did not include him.

"But you have agents among — among mortals."

"Of course."

"Who? Gilbert Gifford?"

A considering pause. "It depends on which one you mean."

"Which *one*?"

"The Gifford who went to seminary in France was exactly who he claimed to be. The Gifford that now rots in a French jail is someone else — a mortal, enchanted to think himself that man." She sniffed in derision. "A poor imitation; he let himself be arrested so foolishly."

Deven absorbed this, then said, "And the one who carried letters to the Queen of Scots?"

She paused again. Was she doubting her decision to array herself against her sovereign? Deven knew what Walsingham did with double agents who then crossed him in turn. Could he do that to Lune?

"Lord Ifarren Vidar," she said at last. "When he was done, a mortal was put in his place, in case Gifford might be of use again."

Not so long as he was imprisoned in France. Deven asked, "Henry Fagot?"

"I do not know who that is."

How much of this could he trust? She had lied to him for over a year, lied with every particle of her being. He trusted the Goodemeades, but why? What reason had he to trust *any* faerie?

They were nearing the Barbican crossroads. "Where am I going?"

She roused, as if she had not noticed where they were. "We should go in by Cripplegate. I'll use the entrance near to it."

Entrance? Deven turned his horse east at the crossroads, taking them through the sleeping parish of St. Giles. At the gate, he bribed the guards to let them pass, and endured the sly expressions on their faces when they saw he rode with a lady. Whatever the faerie had done to the men at Aldersgate, he did not want to see it happen here.

Then they were back inside the city, the close-packed buildings looming dark and faceless, with only the occasional candle showing through a window. The hour was extremely late. Deven followed Wood Street until she said, "Left here," and then a moment later, "Stop."

He halted his gelding in the middle of Ketton. The narrow houses around them looked unexceptional. What entrance had she meant?

She slipped down before he could help her and made for a narrow, shadowed close. No doubt she would have left him without a word, but Deven said, "'Tis dangerous, is it not? What you go to do."

She stopped just inside the close. When she turned about, Margaret Rolford was gone; the strange, inhuman face had returned.

"Yes," Lune said.

They stared at one another. He should have let her go without saying anything. Now it was even more awkward.

The words leapt free before he could stop them.

"Did you enchant me? Lay some faerie charm upon me, to make me love you?"

Lune's eyes glimmered, even in the near total darkness. "I did not have to."

A moment later she was gone, and he could not even see how. Some door opened—but he could see no door in the wall—and then he was alone on Ketton Street, with only his tense muscles and the rapidly fading warmth along his chest to show there had ever been a woman at all.


The Onyx Hall, London: *April 26, 1590*


A faerie queen did not process to chapel in the mornings, as a mortal queen might, but other occasion was found for the ceremony that attended Elizabeth's devotions. Invidiana left her bedchamber with an entourage of chosen ladies, acquired an escort of lords in her privy chamber, then passed through a long, columned gallery to the chamber of estate, where a feast was laid for her each day. It was an occasion for spectacle, a demonstration of her power, wealth, and importance; any fae aspiring to favor attended, in hopes of catching her eye.

Lune hovered behind a pillar, her pulse beating so loudly she thought everyone must hear it. This was the moment at which she trusted the Goodemeades, or she did not; she put her life in their hands, or she ran once more, and this time did not return.

A rustling told her that the fae in the gallery were withdrawing to the sides, out of the way of the procession that was about to enter. Hunting horns spoke a brief, imperious fanfare. She risked a glance around the pillar, and saw the Queen. Vidar was not with her, but Dame Halgresta was, and Lord Valentin Aspell, Lady Nianna, Lady Carline... did she want to do this so very publicly?

The moment was upon her. She must decide.

Lune dashed out into the center of the gallery and threw herself to the floor. She calculated it precisely; her outstretched hands fell far enough short of Invidiana's skirts that the Queen did not risk tripping over her, but close enough that she could not be ignored. Once there, she lay very still, and felt three trickles of blood run down her sides where the silver blades of Invidiana's knights pricked through her gown and into her skin.

"Your Grace," Lune said to the floor, "I bring you a warning of treachery."

No one had run her through—yet. She dared not breathe. One nod from Invidiana...

The cool, measured voice said, "Would this be your own treachery, false one?"

Obedient laughter greeted the question.

"The Wild Hunt," Lune said, "has placed a traitor in your midst."

The hated, growling voice of Dame Halgresta spoke from behind Invidiana. "Lies, your Majesty. Let me dispose of this vermin."

"Lies hold a certain interest," the Queen said. "Entertain me, worm. Who am I to believe a traitor?"

Lune swallowed. "Sir Derwood Corr."

No voices responded to her accusation. She had the name right, did she not?

One of the blades piercing her back vanished, and then Lune cried out as the other two dug in deeper; someone grabbed her by the tattered remnants of her high collar and wrenched her to her feet. Standing, Lune found herself under the blazing regard of a handsome elf knight, black-haired, green-eyed, and transfigured with fury.

"Lying slut," he spat, twisting his left hand in her battered collar. A sword still hovered in his right. "Do you think to rise from where you have been thrown by accusing me, a faithful knight in her Majesty's service?"

*Sun and Moon. He did not leave.*

Lune dared not look at Invidiana. Even the slightest hint of hesitation... "A faithful knight?" she asked, heavy with derision. "How long have you served the Queen, Sir Derwood? An eyeblink, in the life of a fae. What tests have proved your loyalty to her? Has it been so very strenuous, parading about in your fine black armor, keeping a pleasant smile on your face?" She wished she dared spit, but trapped as she was, it could only go into his face. "Your service is words only. Your heart belongs with the Hunt."

Corr snarled. "Easy enough for a worm to make a baseless accusation. My service may be new, but it is honest. Where is your proof of my guilt?"

"You received a message last night," Lune said. "From outside the Onyx Hall."

For the first time, she saw his confidence falter. "'Tis common enough."

"Ah, but with whom did you communicate? And what answer did you send back?" She saw a crack, and hammered it.

"They say the Hunt is in the north right now. If we send that way, will we find your messenger seeking them? What news does he bear?"

Riders of the Wild Hunt were deadly foes in combat, but they had not the subtlety and nerve to survive in the Onyx Court.

Lune's collar ripped free as she flung herself backward. Not fast enough: the tip of Corr's sword raked across the skin above her breast. One of his fellow guardsmen reached for his arm, meaning to stop him; Invidiana did not tolerate murders in front of her that she had not commanded herself. But Corr was too new, and did not understand that. Metal shrieked as his blade skidded uselessly off the other knight's armor.

Curled up tight to protect herself from the feet suddenly thundering around her, Lune did not see exactly what happened to Corr. The press of bodies was too great regardless, with the fae of the Onyx Guard flocking to protect their Queen, and Sir Prigurd wading in with his giant's fists, his normally placid face showing betrayed anger at the failure of his newest protégé.

Corr did his best to sell his life dearly, but in the end, his was the only body that fell.

*You should have left,* Lune thought, when she heard the rattle of his armor crashing to the floor. *Your true loyalty was too strong. This is no place for faithful knights such as you.*

She did not resist when she was hauled to her feet once more. The guardsman who held her said nothing; he just kept her upright as she lifted her face to Invidiana.

Lune did not see the Queen at first, just the muscled bulk of Dame Halgresta. Then, at an unspoken signal, the Captain of the Onyx Guard stepped aside, abandoning her protective pose, but keeping her wide-bladed sword in hand.

Invidiana's cold black eyes took in the sorry remnants of

Lune's gown, the blood that now coated her breast. "Well, worm," she said. "It seems you spoke true—this time."

Lune could not curtsy, with the guardsman holding her. She settled for inclining her head. "I would not have inflicted my presence upon your Grace without great reason." And that was true enough.

Around the two of them, the array of lords and ladies, guardsmen and attendants waited, every last one of them ready to smile or turn away in disdain, following their Queen's lead in how Lune was to be treated now.

"Release her," Invidiana said to the guardsman, and the hands on Lune's shoulders vanished.

Lune immediately knelt.

"You are filthy," Invidiana said in bored tones, as if the very sight of Lune tasted bad. "Truly like a worm. I do not tolerate filth in my court. Have your wounds dressed, and clean yourself before you show your face here again."

"I will most humbly obey your Majesty's command."

The instant Lune rose to a crouch and backed the requisite three steps away, off to one side, the procession reassembled itself and swept onward down the gallery. Only a few goblins remained behind, to collect and dispose of the corpse of Sir Derwood Corr.

Lune permitted herself one glance down at his slack, blood-spattered face. No one would investigate the message he received last night; they would assume it came from the Hunt. But it seemed he *had* sent a reply, and not to the Goodemeades. What had he told the Hunt? That the Goodemeades were interfering?

She needed to warn them. And to apologize for having brought about Corr's death. Lune did not mourn him, but they would.

The stinging cut across her breast, the smaller wounds along her back, gave her all the cause she needed. Some fae at court practiced healing arts, but no one would think it strange if she went to the Goodemeades.

Corr's body, dragged by the heels, scraped along the floor and out of the gallery, leaving a smear of blood behind. Lune lifted her gaze from it and saw those fae still in the chamber staring at her and whispering amongst themselves.

Invidiana had given her leave to wash and be healed. It was a tiny sign of acceptance, but a sign nonetheless. She was no longer to be hunted.

Bearing her head high, Lune exited the gallery, with all the dignity and poise of the favored lady she no longer aspired to be.


LONDON AND ISLINGTON: *April 26, 1590*

In the morning, it all seemed so terribly unreal.

Colsey's silently disapproving glances chastised Deven for his late return the previous night; the manservant affected to have been asleep when he came in, but Deven doubted it. He had gone to bed straightaway, and suffered uneasy dreams of everyone he knew removing masks and revealing themselves to be fae; now he awoke in brilliant sunlight, with nothing to show for his strange night except a feeling of insufficient sleep.

Had any of it happened?

Deven rose and dressed, then suffered Colsey to shave him, scraping away the stubble Ranwell had left behind. With his face now peeled—Colsey had attended to his task with perhaps a little too much care, as if to show up his upstart fellow—Deven wondered, blankly, what to do with himself.

Whereupon he saw the letter on the windowsill.

Staring at the folded paper as if it were a viper, he did not approach immediately. But the letter stayed where it was, and moreover stayed a letter; at last he drew near and, extending one cautious hand, picked it up.

The top read "Master Michael Deven" in a round, untutored secretary hand. Pressed into the sealing wax was a fragment of dried rose petal.

Deven held his breath and broke the seal with his thumb.

*To Master Michael Deven, Castle Baynard Ward, London, from the sisters Gertrude and Rosamund Goodemeade of the Angel in Islington,* sub rosa, *greetings.*

The paper trembled in his hand. Not a dream, then.

*We hope this letter finds you well rested and in good health, and we beg your presence at the Angel Inn when occasion shall serve, for there are matters we neglected to discuss with you before, some of them of great importance. Speak your name at the rosebush when you arrive.*

Deven exhaled slowly and refolded the paper. Brownies. He was receiving letters from brownies now.

Colsey leapt to his feet when his master came clattering downstairs. "My sword and cloak," Deven said, and the servant fetched them with alacrity. But when Colsey would have donned his own cloak, Deven stopped him with an outstretched hand. "No. You may have another day of leisure, Colsey. Surely after so many days in the saddle, you could do with some time out of it, eh?"

The servant's eyes narrowed. "You're most gracious, master— but no thank you. I'm fit enough to ride some more."

Deven let out an exasperated breath. "All right—I shall be more blunt. You're staying here."

"Why, sir?" Colsey's jaw was set in a determined line. "You know you can trust my discretion."

"Always. But 'tis not a matter of discretion. I simply must go alone."

"You riding to see that necromancer again?"

"There's no evidence of Dee practicing necromancy, and no, I am not going to Mortlake." Deven gave his servant a quelling look. "And you are not to follow me, either."

The disappointed expression on Colsey's face made him glad he'd issued the warning.

Deven hit upon something that would stop him—he hoped. "I am about Walsingham's business, Colsey. And though I trust you, there are others who would not. You will stay behind, lest you foul what I am attempting to do here."

Though Colsey kept the rest of his grumbling objections behind his teeth, Deven imagined he could hear them pursuing him as he rode back out through Aldersgate, retracing the path of black feathers he had followed the night before. Knowing his destination, he rode faster, and came soon to the sturdy structure of the Angel.

He rode past it, tethered his horse, and made his way to the spot behind the inn.

The rosebush was there, looking innocuous in daylight. Feeling an utter fool—but who was there to hear him, if he were wrong?—he approached it, cleared his throat, bent to one of the roses, and muttered, "Michael Deven."

Nothing happened for a few moments, and his feeling of foolishness deepened. But just when he would have walked away, the rosebush shivered, and then there was an opening, with a familiar figure emerging from it.

Familiar, but far too tall. Gertrude Goodemeade arranged her skirts and smiled up at him from a vantage point much closer to his collarbone than his navel. "I am sorry to keep you waiting, but we did not expect you so soon, and I had to put the glamour together."

She still looked herself—just larger. Deven supposed a woman less than four feet tall might attract attention in broad daylight. "Aren't you afraid someone will see us standing here, with the rosebush...open?"

Gertrude smiled cheerily. "No. We are not found so easily, Master Deven." Bold as brass, she reached out and took his arm. "Shall we walk?"

The rosebush closed behind her as she towed him forward. Deven had thought they might go into the woods behind the Angel, but she led him in quite the opposite direction: to the front door.

Deven hung back. "What is in here?"

"Food and drink," Gertrude said. "Since you do not trust our own."

He had slept far later than his usual hour; now it was the noontime meal. Gertrude secured them a spot at the end of one of the long tables, and perhaps some faerie charm gave them privacy, for no one sat near them. "You can drink the mead here," the disguised brownie said. "'Tis our mead anyway—the very same I gave you last night—but perhaps you will trust it when you see others drink it."

A rumbling in Deven's stomach notified him that he was hungry. He ordered sausage, fresh bread, and a mug of ale. Gertrude looked a trifle hurt.

"We have your best interests at heart, Master Deven," she said quietly.

He met her gaze with moderate cynicism formed during his

ride up to Islington. "Within reason. You also wish to make use of me."

"To the betterment of her you serve. But we also wish you to be safe, my sister and I; else we should not have brought you in last night, but left you out where Dame Halgresta could find you." Gertrude lowered her voice and leaned in closer. "That is one thing I wished to warn you of. They know Lady Lune had close dealings with you, and that you served Walsingham; they may yet come after you. Be careful."

"How?" The word came out sharp with resentment. "It seems you can make yourselves look however you wish. Some faerie spy could replace Colsey, and how would I ever know?" The thought gave him a jolt.

Gertrude shook her head, curls bouncing free of the cap on her head. "'Tis very hard to feign being a familiar person; you would know. But 'tis also true that we can disguise ourselves. You have a defense, though." She took a deep breath, then whispered, "The name of your God."

She did not shrink upon uttering the word. Deven took a bite of his sausage, and thought of the bread he had given Lune last night.

"They'll be protected against it, of course," Gertrude said in normal tones. "Most of them, anyhow. But most will still flinch if you say that name, or call on your religion in any fashion. 'Tis the flinch that will warn you."

"And then what?"

The brownie shrugged, a little sheepishly. "Whatever seems best. I would rather you run than fight—many of those she might send against you do not deserve to die—but only you can judge how best to keep yourself safe. And we *do* want you safe."

"Who are 'we,' in this matter?"

"My sister and I, certainly. I have no right to speak for Lady Lune. But I believe in my heart that she, too, wishes you safe."

Deven stuffed a hunk of bread into his mouth, so he would not have to reply.

Glancing around the inn, Gertrude seemed willing to change the subject. "Tell me, Master Deven: what do you think of this place?"

He chewed and swallowed while he considered the room. The day was sunny and warm; open shutters allowed a fresh breeze into the room, while tallow dips augmented the natural light. Dried lavender and other strewing herbs sweetened the rushes on the floor, and the benches and tables were well scrubbed. The ale in his leather jack was good—surprisingly tart—the bread fresh, the sausage free of unpleasant lumps. What reason had she for asking? "'Tis agreeable enough."

"Have you spent any nights here?"

"Once or twice. The beds were refreshingly clear of unwanted company."

"They should be," Gertrude said with a sniff. "We beat them out any night they are not in use."

"You beat..." Deven's voice trailed off, and he set his bread down.

Her smile had a kind of pleased mischief in it. "Rosamund and I *are* brownies, Master Deven. Or had you forgot?"

He had not forgotten, but he had not yet connected their underground home to the inn—and he should have. As he looked around the room with new eyes, Gertrude went on. "We do a spot of cleaning every night—scrubbing, dusting, mending such as needs it—that has been our task since before there was an Angel, since a different inn stood on this site. Even last night, though I don't mind saying we were a bit rushed to get our work done, after you left."

Deven could not resist asking; he had always wondered. "Is it true you leave a house if the owner offers you clothes?" Gertrude nodded. "Why?"

"Mortal clothes are like mortal food," the brownie said. "Or fae clothes and fae food, for that matter. They bring a touch of the other side with them. Wear them, eat them, and they start to change you. Your average brownie, he'll be offended if you try that with him; we're homebodies, and not often keen to change. But some fae crave that which is mortal. It draws them, like a moth to a candle flame."

The solemnity in her voice was not lost on Deven. "Why did you summon me here, Mistress Goodemeade?"

"To eat and drink in the Angel." She held up one hand when he would have said something in retort. "I am quite serious. I wished you to see this place, to see what Rosamund and I make of it."

"Why?"

"To stop you, before you could grow to hate us." Gertrude reached out hesitantly, and took his hands in her own. Her fingers were warm, and somehow both calloused and soft, as if the gentleness of her touch made up for the marks left by lifetimes of sweeping and scrubbing. "Last night you heard of politics and murder, saw Lady Lune as a fugitive, hiding from a heartless Queen and her minions. The Onyx Court hides a great deal of ugliness behind its beautiful face—but that is not all we are.

"Some of us find purpose and life in helping make human homes warm and welcoming. Others show themselves to poets and musicians, giving them a glimpse of something more, adding fire to their art." She met his gaze earnestly, her dark honey eyes beseeching him to listen. "We are not all to be feared and fought."

"Some fae," Deven said in a low voice, so that others would not hear, "play tricks on mortals—even unto their deaths. And others, it seems, play at politics."

"'Tis true. We have pucks aplenty—bogy beasts, portunes, will-o'-the-wisps. And our nobles have their games, as yours do. But the wickedness of some humans does not turn you against them all, does it?"

"You are not human." Yet it was so easy to forget, with her hands gripping his across the table. "Should I judge you by the same standards?"

Somberness did not sit well on Gertrude; her face was meant for merriment. "We follow your lead," she said. "There is a realm of Faerie, that lies farther out—over the horizon, through twilight's edge. Some travel to it, mortal and fae alike, and some fae dwell there always. That realm rarely concerns itself with mortal doings. But here, in the shadows and cracks of your world...when your leaders took chariots into battle, ours soon went on wheels as well. When they abandoned chariots for horses, our elf knights took up the lance. We have no guns among us, but no doubt that will change someday. Even those who do not crave contact with mortals still mimic your ways, one way or another."

"Even love?" He had not meant to say it.

A heartbreaking smile touched Gertrude's face. "Especially love. Not often, but it does happen."

Deven pulled his hands free, nearly upsetting his ale jack. "So you wish me to remember that 'tis your Queen I work against, and not the fae people as a whole." Not Lune. "Is that it?"

"Aye." Gertrude folded her hands, as if she had not noticed the vehemence with which he moved.

"As you wish, then. I will remember it." Deven threw a few coins onto the table and stood.

Gertrude caught up with him at the door. "You should come below for a moment before you leave; I have something for you. Will you do that for me?"

He needed time away from fae things, but he couldn't begrudge the request. "Very well."

"Good." She passed by him, out into the bright sunlight, and called back over her shoulder, "By the by? We also brew their ale."


THE ANGEL INN, ISLINGTON: *April 26, 1590*


"Mistress Goodemeade." Lune nodded her head formally to Rosamund. "At her Majesty's command, I seek healing for these wounds I have suffered. Few if any in the Onyx Court hold any love for me, given my Queen's recent displeasure; therefore I come here, to ask for aid."

"Of course, my lady." Rosamund offered an equally formal curtsy in response. "Please, come with me, and I will tend to you."

They descended the staircase, and then descended again, and the rose-marked floorboards closed behind them.

"My lady!" Formality gave way to distress. "Cheepkin told us some of what passed, but not all. Sit, sit, and let me see to you."

Lune had no energy to disobey, and no desire to. She let Rosamund press her onto the stool Deven had occupied the previous night—it seemed like ages ago. "I am so very sorry. Corr had not left—"

The brownie clicked her tongue unhappily. "We know. Oh, if he had only listened...."

Deft fingers untied those sleeve- and waist-points that

had not already broken, then unlaced her bodice at the back. Lune winced as the material of her undergown pulled free where dried blood had glued it to her skin. She would need to obtain new clothing somehow, or else resort to glamours to cover up her tattered state. People would know she wore an illusion, but at least in the Onyx Hall she need not fear it being broken.

Naked to the waist, she closed her eyes while Rosamund dabbed at her cuts with a soft, wet cloth. "I fear I have put you in danger. With Corr there, I had to cast suspicion on him somehow, and I said he had received a message the previous night. If they trace it back to you—"

"Never you mind," Rosamund said. "We would not be here, Gertrude and I, if we could not deal with little problems like that."

"He also seems to have sent a message out, to the Hunt. At least, he panicked when I accused him of it. But I do not know what it said."

The ministering cloth paused. A heartbeat later, it resumed its work. "Something touching on my sister and me, I expect. We shall see."

Lune opened her eyes as Rosamund began daubing her wounds with a cool, soothing ointment. "Lord Valentin questioned me before I left. Where I had gotten mortal bread—I told him a simple lie—and how I had found out about Corr. They found Francis's body while I was there. I led Aspell to believe the two were connected."

"Then we must be sure they do not catch the messenger. Does this feel better?"

"Very much so. Thank you." The fire seemed to have the knack of warming the room just enough; the cool, damp chill of an underground chamber was perfectly offset, so Lune did not shiver as Rosamund fetched bandages from a small chest. At least not from cold.

The brownie swathed her ribs and collarbone in clean white linen, with soft pads over the cuts themselves. "They should be well in three days," Rosamund said, "and you may take the bandages off after one."

Before Lune could say anything more to that, footsteps sounded above. She had not heard anyone speak through the rosebush, as she had when Dame Halgresta came the previous night. Gertrude, no doubt, but her entire body tensed.

The floor bent open, and the brownie's feet appeared on the top stair, in stout slippers. But a pair of riding boots followed, belonging to someone much larger.

Lune snatched up the bodice of her gown just as Michael Deven came into view.

"Oh!" Gertrude exclaimed, as Deven flushed scarlet and spun about. The floor had already closed behind him; unable to escape, he kept his back resolutely turned. "My lady, I am so very sorry. I did not know you were here."

Lune did not entirely believe her. Irritation warred with an unfamiliar feeling of embarrassment as Rosamund helped her into the stained remnant of her clothing. Fae were often careless of bodily propriety among themselves, particularly at festival time, but mortals were another matter. Especially *that* mortal.

"I just wanted to give Master Deven a token," Gertrude said, opening a chest that sat along one wall. "So our birds can find him if he isn't at home. They will carry messages for you, Master Deven, should you need to send to us. Lady Lune, I would give you one as well—"

"But it might be found on me," Lune finished for her. The sleeves of her dress were not yet reattached, but at least she was covered now. "I quite understand."

"Aye, exactly." Gertrude carried something over to where Deven yet stood on the staircase; it looked like a dried rosebud, but seemed much less fragile. "Here you are."

He moved enough to accept the token and examine it. "Roses again, I see."

Gertrude clicked her tongue. "*I* would have planted something other than a rosebush, but my sister was so very fond of the notion. Now everything we do is roses, and everyone always thinks of her. I should have had a flower in my name."

Rosamund answered her with mild asperity, and the two sisters bickered in friendly fashion while they helped Lune finish dressing. It lowered the tension in the room, as no doubt they intended, and after a few moments Deven risked a glance over his shoulder, saw Lune was decent again, and finally turned to face them all.

"I did not mean to burst in thus," he said to her, with a stiff bow. "Forgive me."

The rote apology hit Lune with far more force than it should have. His eyes were a lighter blue than the seer's had been, and his hair brown instead of black—he had none of the fey look brought on by life in the Onyx Hall—but in her memory, a wavering, nearly inaudible voice echoed him, *"Forgive me."*

"Rosamund," she said, cutting into the amiable chatter of the two sisters. "Gertrude. Last night...I did not think to ask; too much else was happening. But before he died, Tiresias—Francis spoke a name. Begged forgiveness of her. A fae woman, I think. Suspiria."

She expected the brownies would recognize the name. She did not expect it to have such an effect. Both sisters gasped, their faces suddenly stricken, and tears sprang into Gertrude's eyes.

Startled, Lune said, "Who is she?"

Rosamund put one arm around her sister's shoulders, comforting her, and said, "A fae woman, aye. Francis loved her dearly, and she him."

Such romances often ended in tragedy, and more so under Invidiana's rule. "What happened to her?"

The brownie met her gaze gravely. "She sits on a throne in the Onyx Hall."

The notion was so incredible, Lune found herself thinking of the Hall of Figures, trying to recall any enthroned statues there. But Rosamund met her gaze, unblinking, and there was only one throne in all the buried palace, only one who sat upon it.

Invidiana.

The cold, merciless Queen of the faerie court, who could no more love a mortal — love anyone — than winter could engender a rose. Who kept Tiresias as the most tormented of her pets, bound by invisible chains he could only break in death. That Francis Merriman might once have loved her, Lune could almost believe; mortals often loved where it was not wise. But Rosamund said Invidiana loved him in return.

Gertrude said to her sister, through her sniffles, "I told you. He remembered her. Even when his mind was gone, when everything else was lost to him, he did not forget."

Deven was staring at them all, clearly lost. Lune was not certain even she followed it. "If this is true — why did you not speak of it before? Surely this is something we needed to know!"

Rosamund sighed and helped Gertrude onto a stool. "You are right, my lady. But last night, we had no time; we had to get you back to the Onyx Hall, before someone could suspect you of Francis's death. And you were distraught, Lady Lune. I did not wish to add to it."

Lune thought of her confrontation with Invidiana that morning. "You mean, you did not wish me to face Invidiana, try to regain her goodwill, knowing the man who died at my feet had once loved her."

The brownie nodded. "As you say. You are good at dissembling, Lady Lune—but could you have done that, without betraying yourself?"

Claiming a seat for herself, Lune said grimly, "I will have to, now. What have you not said?"

Deven leaned against the wall, arms folded over his chest and that shuttered look on his face; it was a mark of Rosamund's own distress that she did not try to coax him into sitting down, but perched on the edge of one of the beds and sighed. "'Tis a long story; I pray you have patience.

"Gertrude and I once lived in the north, but we came here...oh, ages ago; I don't remember when. Another inn stood on this spot then, not the Angel. The mortals had their wars, and then, when a new king took the throne, the first Henry Tudor, a woman arrived on our doorstep.

"She..." Rosamund searched for words. "We thought she was in a bad way when we saw her. Later, we saw how much worse it could be. Suspiria was cursed, you see, for some ancient offense. Cursed to suffer as if she were mortal. 'Twasn't that she was old; fae can be old, if 'tis in their nature, and yet be very well. She *aged*. She sickened, grew weak—suffered all the infirmity that comes with mortality, in time."

Deven made a small noise, and the brownie looked up at him. "I know what you must think, Master Deven. Oh, how terrible indeed, that one of our kind should suffer a fate every mortal faces. I do not expect you to have much sympathy for that. But imagine, if you can, how it would feel to suffer so, when 'tis a thing *not* natural to you."

Whether he felt sympathy or not, he gave no sign.

Rosamund went on. "She told us she was condemned to

Marie Brennan

suffer thus, until she atoned for her crime. Well, for ages she had thought her suffering *was* atonement, like the penance mortals do for their sins. But she had come to realize that she must do more—that her suffering would continue until she made up for what she had done wrong."

"A moment," Deven said, breaking in. "How elderly was she, if she had suffered 'for ages'? There's a limit to how old one can become. Or was she turning into a cricket, like Tithonus?"

Gertrude answered him, her voice still thick. "No, Master Deven. You are quite right: it cannot go on forever. She grew old, and when the span a mortal might be granted was spent, she...died, in a way. She shed her old, diseased body and came out young and beautiful once more, to enjoy a few years of that life before it all began again."

Lune felt sick to her stomach. It was one thing to don the appearance of mortality, as a shield. To sicken and die like a mortal, though—to crawl out of rotting, degraded, liver-spotted flesh, and know to that she must come again—

"We helped her as best we could," Rosamund said. "But her memory suffered like a mortal's; she could not clearly recall what the cause was for which she had been cursed. She knew, though, that her offense had happened here, in the place that became London, and so she had returned here, to seek out those who might know what she should do." The brownie laughed a little, more as if she remembered amusement than felt it. "We thought her mad when she told us what plan she had formed, to lift her curse."

A hundred possibilities sprang to Lune's mind, each madder than the last. More to stop her own invention than to prod Rosamund onward, she said, "What was it?"

The brownie shook her head, as if she still could not believe it. "She vowed to create a faerie palace, beneath all the city of London."

256

Lune straightened. "Impossible. The Onyx Hall—she cannot have made it."

"Oh?" Rosamund gave her a small smile. "Think, my lady. Where else in the world do you know of such a place? Where else is faerie magic so proof against the powers of iron and faith? Fae live in forests, glens, hollow hills—not cities. Why is there a palace beneath London?"

Rosamund was right, and yet the thought stunned her. Miles of corridor and gallery, hundreds or even thousands of chambers, the Hall of Figures, the night garden, the hidden entrances . . . the magnitude of the task dizzied her.

"She had help, of course," Rosamund said, as if that somehow reduced it to a manageable scale. "Oh, tremendous help—but one person especially."

Gertrude whispered, "Francis Merriman."

Her sister nodded. "A young man Suspiria had come to know. She met him after her body had renewed itself, and she was desperate to keep him from ever seeing her old, to lift her curse before it came to that. But I think he knew anyhow. He had the gift of sight—visions of the future, or of present things kept secret." Her expression trembled, holding back tears. "She often called him her Tiresias."

Deven looked on, not comprehending. Of course: he did not understand how that name had been warped. It wasn't just that Francis Merriman had been obliterated; the man had become one of a menagerie of human pets, a term of love become a term of control.

"So she lifted her curse," Lune said. Gertrude was sniffling again, making the silence uncomfortable.

To her surprise, Rosamund shook her head. "Not then. She created the Hall, but when it was done, Suspiria still aged as she had before. She hid behind glamours, to keep Francis from knowing. And oh, it pained her—seeing him stay young, living as he did in the Onyx Hall with her, while she grew ever older. But he knew, and a good thing, too; 'twas him helped her lift the curse at last, one of his visions. Not long after that Catholic woman took the throne, it was." The look of sorrow was back. "We were all so happy for her."

Deven shifted his weight, and the tip of his scabbard scraped against the plastered wall. "Four or five years later—if my sums are right—you say she formed this pact."

Rosamund sighed. "She did *something*. In one day, not only did she become the only faerie queen in all of England, she erased Suspiria from the world. After her curse was lifted, she had begun to gather a court around her; that, Lady Lune, is when Vidar came to the Onyx Hall. Before she was crowned. But he would no more recognize the name Suspiria than he would remember the court he once belonged to. To him, as to everyone else, there has only ever been Invidiana: the cruel mistress of the Onyx Hall."

Attempting to dry her face with a mostly soaked handkerchief, Gertrude whispered, "But we remember her. And that is why we do not help the Wild Hunt. They would tear down the Onyx Hall, every stone of it, scatter its court to the four corners of England . . . and they would kill Invidiana. And though she is lost to us, we do not wish to see Suspiria die."

Deven straightened and fished a clean handkerchief out of his cuff, offering it to Gertrude. She took it gratefully and repaid him with a watery, wavering smile.

Lune sat quietly, absorbing this information, trying to fit it alongside the things she had seen during her years in the Onyx Court. Fewer years than she had thought. Even the palace itself was new, by fae standards. "You were fond of Suspiria."

"Aye," Rosamund said, unapologetic. "She was warmer then,

and kinder. But all kindness left her that day. You have never known the woman we helped."

Nor the woman Francis had loved.

Deven came forward and placed his hands along the edge of the table, aligning them with studious care. "So how do we break the pact?"

Now Rosamund gave a helpless shrug. "We only just learned of its existence, Master Deven. And I imagine the list of people who know its terms is short, indeed. If Francis knew, he died before he could say."

"Which leaves only two that must know," Lune said. "Invidiana and Elizabeth."

"Assuming we are right to begin with," Deven still had his eyes on his carefully placed hands. "That the pact was formed with her."

"Assuming *you* are right," Lune countered, a little sharply. "You are the one who suggested it last night."

The minuscule slump in his shoulders said he remembered all too well, and regretted it—but his silence told her he had no better explanation to offer in its place.

A muscle rose into relief along his jaw, then subsided. "I do not suppose you could trick your Queen into revealing the terms of the pact?"

The sound Lune made was nothing like a laugh. "You are asking me to trick the most suspicious and politically astute woman I have ever met."

"Elizabeth is the same," he flared, straightening in one fluid motion. "Or do you think my Queen a greater fool than yours?"

Lune met his gaze levelly. "I think your Queen less likely to have one of her courtiers murder you for an afternoon's entertainment."

She watched the contentious pride drain out of his face, one drop at a time. At first he did not believe her; then, as her stare did not waver, he did. And when she saw him understand, an ache gripped her throat, so sudden it brought tears to her eyes. What had life been like, when she lived under a different sovereign? She wished she could remember.

Lune rose to her feet and turned away before he could see her expression break. Behind her back, she heard Deven murmur, "Very well. I will see what I may learn. 'Twill not be easy—" He gave the quiet, rueful laugh she remembered, and had not heard in some time. "Well. Walsingham taught me how to ferret out information that others wish to keep hidden. I never expected to use it against a faerie queen, is all."

"Let us know what you learn," Rosamund said, and Gertrude echoed her after blowing her nose one last time. They went on, but Lune could no longer bear to be trapped in the claustrophobic hidden room with the three of them.

"I should return," she said, to no one in particular. "I have been here too long already." She went up the stairs before remembering the floor was closed above her, but it opened when her head neared its planks, two feminine farewells pursuing her as she went. Lune paused only long enough to restore the glamour she had dropped, and began her journey back to the confines of the Onyx Hall.

MEMORY: *November 12, 1547*

The twisting web of streets, the leaning masses of houses and shops, alehouses and livery halls—it all obscured an underlying simplicity.

In the west, Ludgate Hill. Once home to a temple of Diana,

now it was crowned with the Gothic splendor of St. Paul's Cathedral.

In the east, Tower Hill, the White Mount. The structure atop it had once been a royal palace; now it more often served as a prison.

In the north, the medieval wall, curving like the arc of a bow, pierced by the seven principal gates of the city.

In the south, the string of the bow: the straight course of the Thames, a broad thoroughfare of water.

An east–west axis, stretching from hilltop to hilltop, with temporal power on one end, spiritual power on the other. A north–south axis, barrier in the north, access in the south, with the Walbrook, the *wall-brook,* bisecting the city and connecting the two poles.

The buried waters of the Walbrook ran hard by the London Stone, which lay very near to the center of the city. Near enough to suffice.

A shadow moved through the cloudless autumn sky.

Two figures stirred within the solid earth and stone of the hills. Unseen, their colossal bodies standing where there was no space for them, they reached out and took hold of the power of the earth, which was theirs to command.

Two more stood at the London Stone, blind to the activity of the city around them. A man and a woman, a mortal and a fae.

They waited, as the light around them began to dim.

Slowly, one person at a time, the bustle of the city's streets began to falter and halt. Faces turned upward; some people fled indoors. And the world grew ever darker, as the shadow of the moon moved across the face of the sun, until only a ring of fire blazed around its edge.

"Now," the woman whispered.

The giants Gog and Magog, standing within the hills of Ludgate and the Tower, called upon the earth to obey. The Roman well that lay at the foundations of the White Tower shivered, its stones trembling; an ancient pit used in the rites of Diana opened up once more below the cathedral; and at the bottom of each, something began to grow.

Standing at the London Stone, Suspiria and Francis Merriman reached out and linked hands, mortal and fae, to carry out a working the likes of which the land had never dreamed.

The shadowed light of the sun fell upon the city and cast stranger shadows, a penumbral reflection of London, like and yet unlike. It sprang forth from the buildings, the streets, the gardens, the wells, and sank downward into the ground.

In the earth beneath London, the shadows took shape. Streets became corridors; buildings, great chambers. They transformed as they went, twisting, flowing, settling into new configurations, defying the orderly relations of natural geometry. And then, when all was in place, stone sprang forth, black and white marble, crystal, onyx, paving the floors, sheathing the walls, supporting the ceilings in round half-barrels and great vaulting arches.

Together they made this, Suspiria and Francis, drawing on the fae strength of the giants; the mortal symbolism of the wall; the wisdom of Father Thames, who alone of all beings understood the thing that was London, having witnessed its growth from its earliest days. In the sun's shadowed light, they formed a space that bridged a gap, creating a haven for fae among mortals, from which church bells could not drive them forth.

Their hands came to rest atop the London Stone. The light brightened once more; the moon continued along its course, and normalcy returned to the world.

They smiled at one another, exhausted, but exultant.
"It is done."

PALACE OF PLACENTIA, GREENWICH: *April 28–30, 1590*

Even the sprawling reaches of Hampton Court and White-hall did not have room to house every courtier, merchant, and visiting dignitary that came seeking audience with the Queen and her nobles, especially not with their servants and train. Deven had asked for and received a leave of absence, with the result that when the court removed to Greenwich, he had no lodging assigned to him. He might have troubled Lord Huns-don for one, especially as courtiers retired for the summer to their own residences, but it was simpler to take rooms at a nearby inn. From this staging point, closer to court than his London house but not in its midst, he tried to plan a course of action.

Judicious questions to the right people netted him a fuller story of Elizabeth's coronation, including those who had been involved. Deven could not rule out the possibility that the Queen was not, in fact, the other party to this rumored pact; it might have been another. Lord Burghley leapt to mind. Sir William Cecil, as he was back then, had been a trusted adviser since the earliest days of the reign, and nothing short of the death he had put off for seventy years would make him retire. Moreover, he had taught Walsingham much of what the man knew about how to build an intelligence service.

Burghley was a good candidate. He might do a great deal to ensure his Queen stayed on her throne. But the question remained of how to approach him—or indeed, anyone else—about the matter.

*I most humbly beg your pardon. But did you by any chance form a pact with a faerie queen thirty-one years ago?*

He could not ask that question of anyone.

Deven supposed he had at least one advantage. Lune's bleak eyes had stayed with him, her resigned expression as she spoke so plainly of her Queen's murderous entertainments. Whatever other obstacles he faced—however much Elizabeth might rage and occasionally threaten to chop off someone's head—at least he did not fear for his life when in the presence of his sovereign.

How to do it? For all his fine words about ferreting out hidden information, Deven could not fathom how to begin. He was half-tempted to ask Lune to return to court as Anne Montrose, and let her handle the matter; if people imagined her to be mad, she lost nothing. Deven, on the other hand...he would be lucky if they simply thought him mad. Faeries were plausible; faeries beneath London, less so.

But the true danger would be if they believed him. It was a short step from faeries to devils, from lunacy to heresy. And even a gentleman could be executed for that.

If only he could have discovered this all before Walsingham died! Deven did not know how the Principal Secretary would have reacted, but at least then he could have shared it with someone. Walsingham, he was sure, would have believed, if shown the evidence. But Deven had been too slow; he had not completed the task his master set him until it was too late.

The thought came to him as he walked the bank of the Thames, the river wind blowing his hair back until it stood up in ruffling crests. He had done all of this because Walsingham asked it of him.

And therein lay the opening he needed.

He went to Lord Hunsdon for help. Beale could have done it,

no doubt, using his influence as a secretary to the privy council, but Beale knew too much of what he was about, and would have asked too many questions. Hunsdon's aid was more easily obtained, though he was manifestly curious about Deven's purpose, and his recent absence from court.

A gift for Hunsdon; a gift for the Countess of Warwick; a gift for the Queen. Deven wondered about faerie gold, and whether the Goodemeades could not somehow fund the expense of this work. He was not at all certain he wanted to know.

His opportunity came on a crisp, bright Thursday, when the wind sent clouds scudding across the sun and the Queen rode out to hunt. She was accompanied, as always, by a selection of her ladies, several other courtiers, and servants to care for the hounds and hawks and other accoutrements that attended upon her Majesty; it seemed a great menagerie, when he thought about watching eyes, listening ears. But it was the best he could hope for.

"How stands the Queen's mood?" he asked Lady Warwick, as he rode out with the others into the unreliable brilliance of the morning.

The countess no doubt thought his question had something to do with Anne. "As changeable as the weather," she said, casting one eye skyward, at the racing clouds. "Whatever suit you wish to press, you might consider waiting."

"I cannot," Deven muttered. Even if their situation could wait—which he was not certain it could—his nerve could not withstand delay. "You and Lord Hunsdon have been most generous in arranging this private conference for me. If I do not take my opportunity today, who knows when it will come again?"

"Then I wish you good fortune, Master Deven."

With those reassuring words, the hunt began. Deven did not

devote more than a sliver of his attention to its activity, instead rehearsing in his mind the words he would say. At length the hunt dismounted for a rest, and servants began to erect a pavilion in which the Queen would dine with the Earl of Essex. He saw Lady Warwick approach her, bearing in her hands the small book Deven had obtained from his father, and present it to the Queen. A murmured conversation, and then Elizabeth turned a sharp eye on him, across the meadow in which they rested.

The long-fingered hand beckoned, jewels flashing in the light; he crossed to where she stood and knelt in the grass before her. "Your Grace."

"Walk with me, Master Deven."

The beginnings of a headache were pulsing in his temples, keeping time with his thunderous heartbeat. Deven rose and followed the Queen, one respectful pace behind her, as she wandered the edge of the meadow. There were too many people around, passing into and out of earshot, but he could hardly ask her to withdraw farther; it was favor enough that she was granting him this semi-private audience.

"Lady Warwick tells me you bear a message of some importance," Elizabeth said.

"I do, your Majesty." Deven swallowed, then launched into the words he had rehearsed all morning, and half the day before.

"Prior to his death, Sir Francis set me a task. Were I a cleverer or more talented man, I might have completed it in time to share my discoveries with him, but I am come to my conclusions too late; only in the last few days have I uncovered the information he wished me to find. And in his absence, I have no master to whom 'tis fitting to report such matters. But I swore an oath not to conceal any matters prejudicial to your

Grace's person, and with the loss of the Principal Secretary, my allegiance is, by that oath, to you alone." He wet his lips and went on. "Though it be presumptuous of me, I believe this issue of sufficient import as to be worth your Grace's time and attention, and your wisdom more than sufficient to judge how best to proceed."

Walking a pace behind Elizabeth, he could only see the edge of her face, but beneath the cosmetics he thought he discerned a lively interest. Walsingham to an extent, and Burghley even more, made a practice of trying to keep intelligence from the Queen; they preferred to control the information that reached her, so as to encourage her decisions in directions they favored. But Elizabeth disliked being managed, and had a great fondness for surprising them with knowledge they did not expect her to have.

"Say on," she replied, her tone now more on the pleasant side of neutral.

Another deep breath. "The task the Master Secretary set me was this. He believed he had discerned, within the workings of your Grace's government, the hand of some unseen player. He wished me to discover who it is."

She was too experienced a politician to show surprise. Elizabeth's energetic stride did not falter, nor did she turn to look at him. But Deven noticed that their seemingly aimless wanderings now drifted, ever so slightly, toward a stand of birches that bordered the meadow. Away from those who might listen in.

"And you believe," the Queen said, "that you have discovered some such player?"

"I have indeed, madam. And having done so, I thought it all the more crucial that I convey this information to you alone."

They were far enough away; no one would overhear them. Elizabeth stopped and turned to face him, her back to the white trunks of the trees. Her aged face was set in unreadable lines. A cloud covered the sun, then blew away again, and Deven thought uneasily that perhaps he should have waited to find her in a fairer mood, after all.

"Say on," she commanded him again.

Too late to back out. Deven said, "Her name is Invidiana."

He should have knelt to deliver the information; it would have been respectful. But he had to stand, because he had to be looking her in the face as he said it. This was his one chance to see her reaction, the one time she might betray some hint that would tell him what he needed to know. And even then, he almost missed it. Elizabeth had played this game for decades; she was more talented an actor than most who made their living from it. Only the tiniest flicker of tension at the corners of her eyes showed when he spoke the name: there for an instant, and then gone.

But it was there, however briefly.

Now Deven dropped to his knees, his heart fluttering so wildly it made his hands shake. "Your Majesty," he said, heedless of whether he might be cutting her off, desperate to get the words out before she could say anything, deny anything. "For days now I have thought myself a madman. I have met — people — spoken to them, heard stories that would be incredible were they played upon a stage. But I know them to be true. I have come to you today, risked speaking of this so openly, because events are in motion which could bring an upheaval as great as that threatened by Spain. Consider me a messenger, if you will."

And with that he halted; he could think of nothing more to say. The light shifted around him, and the wind blew more strongly, as if a storm might be on its way.

From above him, Elizabeth's measured, controlled voice. "She sent you to me?"

He swallowed. "No. I represent...others."

Footsteps approached; a rustle of satin, as Elizabeth gestured whomever it was away. When they were alone again, she said, "Explain yourself."

Those two words were very, very cold. Deven curled his gloved hands into fists. "I have come into contact with a group of...these people, who believe that a pact exists between their Queen and someone in your Majesty's own court—perhaps you yourself. The man who told them of this pact was of our own kind, and had long dwelled among them, but he died in the course of confessing this information. He claimed the pact was detrimental to both sides. They wish it to be broken, and have asked me to discover its nature and terms."

How he wished he could see her face! But Elizabeth had not told him to rise, nor did she interrupt his explanation. He had no choice but to continue. "Madam, I know not what to think. They say she is not their rightful Queen, that she deposed many others across England when she ascended to her throne. They say she is cold and cruel—that, at least, I most sincerely believe, for I do not think they could counterfeit such fear. They say their aid has helped maintain your Grace's own safety and security, and perhaps this is true. But if so..." His heart was hammering so loudly, the entire camp must be able to hear it. "I do not know if this pact *should* be broken. Even if I knew its terms, that is not a decision for me to make. All I can do, in good conscience, is lay what I know at your feet, and beg your good wisdom and counsel."

The long speech left his mouth bone dry. How many people were watching them discreetly, wondering what private suit drove him to his knees, with his face so pale? Did Elizabeth show anger, confusion, fear?

He might have just ended his career at court, in one disastrous afternoon.

Deven whispered, "If your Majesty is caught in some bargain from which you would escape, you have but to say so, and I will do everything I may to end it. But if these creatures are your enemies—if they threaten the security of your throne—then bid me stop them, and I will."

The sunlight flickered, then shone down with renewed strength. His linen undershirt was soaked with sweat.

Elizabeth said in courteous, impassive tones, "We thank you, Master Deven, and will take this information under advisement. Speak of this to no other."

"Yes, madam."

"Luncheon is served, it seems. Go you and eat, and send Lord Essex to me."

"I humbly take my leave." Deven rose, not looking at her, backed away three steps, and bowed deeply. Then he fled, wishing it would not be an insult to quit the hunt early, before anyone asked him questions he could not answer.

MOOR FIELDS, LONDON: *May 1, 1590*

The celebrations began in the hours before dawn, and would fade away with the morning light. To dance out here—in the open, under the stars, yet just outside the city walls—was an act of mad defiance, a fleeting laugh at the masses of humanity from which they ordinarily hid, holding their revels underground, or in wilder places. It also required a tremendous outlay of effort.

The laundresses' pegs and the archers' marks that normally dotted the open places of Moor Fields had been cleared away. The grass, trodden into dusty brownness and hard-packed dirt, was briefly, verdantly green, growing in a thick carpet that cushioned the bare feet of the dancers. The dark, somber tones that predominated in the Onyx Hall had given way to riotous color: pink and red and spring green, yellow and blue and one doublet of violent purple. Flower petals, fresh leaves, feathers whose edges gleamed with iridescent light; the garb tonight was all of living things, growing things, in honor of the first of May.

And the fae of the Onyx Court danced. Musicians wove competing tapestries in the air, flutes and hautbois and tabors sending forth sound and light and illusions that ornamented the dance. Orpheus wandered the edges, serenading the many lovers. Blossoms sprang up where he walked. Great bonfires burned at the four corners of their field, serving more than one purpose; they provided heat, light, fire for the festival, and foundation points for the immense web of charms that concealed all this revelry from watching eyes.

When the sun rose, mortals would go forth for their own May Day celebrations. They would pick flowers in the woods, dance around maypoles, and enjoy the onset of benevolent weather. But a few had started early: here and there, a human strayed near enough to the fires to pierce the veils that concealed them, and become aware of the crowds that had overtaken Moor Fields. A young man lay with his head in Lady Carline's lap, eating grapes from her fingers. Another scrambled on the ground in front of her, rump in the air, behaving for all the world like a dog in human form — but for once, those who laughed at him did so without the edge of cold malice their voices would ordinarily have borne. Maidens whirled about the dancing ground with faerie gentlemen who wove blossoms into their hair and whispered sweet nothings into their ears. Nor was everyone young: a stout peasant woman had wandered from her house on Bishopsgate Street to chase a dog not long after sundown on May Eve, and now stamped a merry measure with the best of them, her face red and shining with effort.

Amidst all this splendor, one figure was conspicuous by her absence: conspicuous, but not missed. The Wild Hunt could more easily strike at this open field than at the subterranean confines of the Onyx Hall, and so Invidiana stayed below.

They had more fun without her.

The Queen's absence helped Lune breathe more easily. With wine flowing like water, everyone was merry, and many of them forgot to snub those who deserved snubbing. Nor did the snared mortals have any notion of politics. Shortly after midnight, a young man stumbled up to her, wine cup in hand, mouth languorous and searching for a kiss. He had brown hair and blue eyes, and Lune pushed him away, then regretted the violence of her action. But she did not need the reminder of Michael Deven, and the celebrations Elizabeth's court would engage in today.

Even on a night such as this, politics did not entirely cease. Everyone knew Tiresias was dead; everyone knew the Queen had been little seen by anyone since his body was discovered. A few thought she mourned him. Remembering the Goodemeades' tale, Lune felt cold. Invidiana mourned no one.

But his death created opportunity for those who needed it. Some who questioned Lune thought themselves subtle about it; others did not even try for subtlety. Certain mortals claimed the ability to foretell the future. Were any of them truly so gifted? Lune had lived among the mortal court; she might know something. They pestered her for information. Had she met Simon

Forman? What of Doctor Dee? Did she perhaps know of any persuasive charlatans, who might be put forth as bait to trip up a political rival?

Lune joined the dancing to escape the questions, then abandoned dancing when it turned her mood fouler. There was no surcease for her here. But where would she go? Back down into the Onyx Hall? Its confines were unbearable to her now—and the Queen waited below. To the Angel Inn? She did not dare spend too much time there, and besides, the Goodemeades were here, along with every other fae from miles around. Lune knew the Goodemeades watched her, but she kept her distance.

A golden-haired elf lady she knew by sight but not name waylaid her. Was she familiar with John Dee? Where did he live? Was he old enough that it might not seem suspicious if he died in his sleep?

Lune fled her questioner, heading for one of the bonfires. Arriving at its edge, where the heat scorched her face with welcome force, she found there was one other person gazing into its depths.

From the far side of the bonfire, the hollow-cheeked, wasted face of Eurydice stared at her.

The mortal pet's presence at the May Day celebrations was like a splash of cold water from the Thames. Her black, sunken eyes saw what few others did: the spirits of the dead, those restless souls who had not passed on to their punishment or reward. And this was not All Hallows' Eve, not the time for such things.

But she did more than see. Few fae realized Eurydice was not just a curiosity to Invidiana; she was a tool. She not only saw ghosts: she could bind them to her will. Or rather, the Queen's will.

Lune knew it all too well. Invidiana had formed plans that depended closely on Eurydice's special skill, plans that Lune's disastrous embassy had undone. The folk of the sea wanted for little, and so the things she had gone there to offer them went unremarked. What they had wanted were the spoils of their storms: the souls of those sailors who drowned.

To what use Invidiana would have put such a ghost army, Lune did not know. Had she been aware that her Queen planned to create one, she might have bargained harder; the folk of the sea had no way to bind ghosts to their service. But she thought it a harmless thing, and so she agreed that Eurydice would come among them for a time, provided the ghosts were not turned against the Onyx Court. As long as the ships never reached England's shores, what did it matter?

Invidiana had seen it differently.

Eurydice's mouth gaped open in a broken-toothed, hungry grin. And suddenly, despite the blazing bonfire just feet away, Lune felt cold.

*Ghosts.*

Those who died in the thrall of faerie magic often lingered on as ghosts.

*Francis.*

Somehow, she kept herself from running. Lune met Eurydice's gaze, as if she had no reason to fear. That hungry grin was often on the woman's face; it meant nothing. She had no assurance that Francis Merriman had lingered. After so long trapped in the Onyx Hall, his soul might well have fled with all speed to freedom and judgment.

Or not.

What did Invidiana know?

A chain of dancing fae went past, and someone caught Lune by the hand. She let herself be dragged away, following the line of bodies as they weaved in and out of the crowds of revelers, and did not extricate herself until she was at the far side of the field, safely distant from Eurydice's ghost-haunted eyes.

She should run now, while she could.

No. Running would bring her no safety; Invidiana ruled all of England. And there might be nothing to run from. But she must assume the worst: that the Queen had Francis's ghost, and knew from him what had transpired.

Why, then, would Lune still be alive?

Her mind answered that question with an image: a snake, lying with its jaws open and a mouse in its mouth, waiting. 'Tis safe, come in, come in. Why eat only one mouse when you might lure several? And that meant she could not follow her instinct, to run to the safety the Goodemeades offered. Invidiana could act on suspicion as well as proof, but would want to be sure she caught the true conspirators, and caught all of them. As long as she was not certain...

Lune stayed at the May Day celebrations, though it took all her will. And in the remaining hours of dancing, and drinking, and fielding the questions of those who sought a new human seer, she caught one moment of relative privacy, while Rosamund dipped her a mug of mead.

"He may be a ghost," Lune whispered. It was all the warning she dared give.

PALACE OF PLACENTIA, GREENWICH: *May 2, 1590*

In the days following his audience with the Queen, Deven considered abandoning his lodgings and returning to where Ranwell waited at his house in London. What stopped him was the thought that there, he would be sitting atop a faerie palace.

So he was still at Greenwich, though not at court, when the messenger found him.

He threw Colsey into a frenzy, demanding without warning that his best green satin doublet be brushed off and made ready, that his face needed shaving again already, that his boots be cleaned of infinitesimal specks of mud. But one did not show up looking slovenly when invited to go riding with the Queen.

Somehow his manservant got him out the door with good speed. Deven traversed the short distance to the palace, then found himself waiting; something had intervened, and her Majesty was occupied. He paced in a courtyard, his stomach twisting. Had he eaten anything that day, it might have come back up.

Nearly an hour later, word came that Elizabeth was ready at last.

She was resplendent in black and white satin embroidered with seed pearls, her made-up face and hair white and red above it. They did not ride out alone, of course; Deven might be one of her Gentlemen Pensioners, and therefore a worthy bodyguard, but one man was not sufficient for either her dignity or well-being. But the others who came kept their distance, maintaining the illusion that this was a private outing, and not a matter of state.

Everyone at court, from the jealous Earl of Essex down to the lowliest gentlewoman, and probably even the servants, would wonder at the outing, and speculate over the favor Elizabeth was suddenly showing a minor courtier. For once, though, their gossip was the least of Deven's concerns.

They rode in silence to begin with. Only when they were well away from the palace did Elizabeth say abruptly, "Have you met her?"

He had expected some preface to their discussion; her sudden question took him by surprise. "If you mean Invidiana, your Grace, I have not."

"Consider yourself fortunate, Master Deven." The line of her jaw was sagging with age, but steel yet underlay it. "What do you know of this pact?"

Deven chose his words with care. "Little to nothing, I fear. Only that on your Majesty's coronation day, Invidiana claimed her own throne."

Elizabeth shook her head. "It began well before that."

The assertion startled him, but he held back his instinctive questions, letting the Queen tell it in her own time.

"She came to me," Elizabeth said softly, "when I was in the Tower." Her eyes were focused on something in the distance, and she controlled her horse with unconscious ease. Deven, watching her out of the corner of his eye, saw grimness in her expression. "My sister might have executed me. Then a stranger came, and offered me aid."

The Queen fell silent. Deven wanted to speak, to tell her that anyone might have made the same choice. Years later, there was still doubt in her, uncertainty about her actions. But he dared not presume to offer her forgiveness.

Elizabeth pressed her lips together, then went on. "She arranged my release from the Tower, and a variety of events that helped secure my accession. I do not know how much of that was her doing. Not all, certainly — even now, she does not have that much control. But some of it was hers. And in exchange, when I was crowned, I aided her. My coronation was hers as well." The Queen paused. "I did not know that it deposed others. But I would be false if I said that surprised me."

She hesitated again. At last, Deven prodded her onward. "And since then, your Grace?"

"Since then... it has continued. She has helped remove

threats to my person, my throne, my people." Elizabeth's hands, encased in gray doeskin, tightened on her reins. "And in exchange, she has received concessions from me. Political decisions that suit some purpose of hers. The assistance of—mortals, to manipulate something of importance to her." Her stumble over the word was barely perceptible.

Deven ventured a reminder. "The man who spoke of this claimed, before he died, that it was causing harm to both sides."

For the first time since they rode out, Elizabeth turned her head to face him. The strength of her gaze shook him. It was easy to forget, when one saw her laughing with her courtiers, or smiling coquettishly at some outrageous compliment, that she was her father's daughter. But in that gaze lay all the fabled personality and will of Henry, eighth of that name, King of England. They had stores of rage within them, the Tudors did, and Elizabeth's was closer to the surface than he had realized.

"I do not know," Elizabeth said, "what this pact has cost her side. I do not care. She has often manipulated me, managed me, coerced me into positions I would not otherwise have occupied. Even that, I might have endured, if it meant the well-being of my people. But she went too far with our cousin Mary. I do not know how far back her interference extended, but I know this: were it not for that interference, I might never have been forced to sign that order of execution."

Deven saw, in his mind's eye, the chess pieces with which Walsingham had led him through the story of the Queen of Scots—and the white queen, standing on her own, caught halfway between the two sides.

"Then tell me the terms of your pact," he said quietly, "and I will see it ended."

She turned her gaze back to the landscape ahead, where the

ground rose upward in a rocky slope. The men-at-arms were still all around, maintaining a respectful distance, and Deven was glad for them. He could not both navigate this conversation and keep watch for threats. How easy must it be, for fae to conceal themselves among the green?

"'Twas simple enough," the Queen said. "Do you know the London Stone?"

"On Candlewick Street?"

"The same. 'Tis an ancient symbol of the city, and a stone of oaths; the rebel Jack Cade once struck it to declare himself master of London. At the moment I was crowned, she thrust a sword into that stone, to claim her own sovereignty."

That was most promising; it gave him a physical target to attack. "Will it threaten your own position, if...?"

Elizabeth shook her head. "My throne came to me by politics, and the blessing of a bishop, speaking in God's name. What she has stolen is mine by right."

She spoke with certainty, but he had heard her at court, declaring with swaggering confidence that Spain would not dare attempt another invasion, or that some lord or other would never defy her will. She could feign confidence she did not feel. It felt like a sharp rock had lodged in Deven's throat when he swallowed. Would he help the fae depose Invidiana, only to find his own Queen overthrown?

Elizabeth was willing to risk it, to free herself from the snare that trapped her. His was not to question it.

"If you bring her low," Elizabeth said in a hard, blazing voice, "then I will reward you well for it. She is a cold thing, and cruel in her pleasure. Princes must often be ruthless; this I knew, before I even ascended to my throne. But she has forced matters too far, more than once. There is no warmth in her, no love. And I despise her for it."

Deven thought of the Goodemeades — of Rosamund's story, and the conversation he had with Gertrude — and responded gently. "They tell me she was different once. Before her coronation. When she was still known as Suspiria."

Elizabeth spat, not caring if the gesture was coarse. "I would not know. I never knew this Suspiria."

They had ridden on several paces farther before Deven's hands jerked convulsively on the reins. His gelding short-stepped, then recovered. "Not even when first you met? Not even in the Tower?"

He had drawn level with the Queen again, and she was studying him in wary confusion. "The name she gave me was Invidiana. And I have never known her to show any kindness or human warmth, not since the moment she appeared."

"But —" Deven realized belatedly that he was forgetting to use titles, polite address, anything befitting a gentleman speaking to his Queen. "By the story I was told, madam, she was known as Suspiria until the moment of her coronation, and that while she bore that name, she was not so cold and cruel."

"Your friends are mistaken, or they have lied to you. Although..." Elizabeth's dark eyes went distant, seeing once more into the past. "When I asked her name, she told me 'twas Invidiana. But the manner in which she said it..." The Queen focused on him once more. "It might have been the first time she claimed that name."

Deven was silent, trying to work through the implications of this. His mind felt overfull, too many fragments of information jostling each other, too few of them fitting together.

"I will bear this news to those who work against her," he said at last. If the Goodemeades had lied to him — trustworthy as they seemed, he had to consider it — then perhaps he could provoke some sign out of them. And if not...

If not, then nothing was quite what they had thought.

"You will keep us apprised of your work," Elizabeth said. The familiarity that had overtaken her during the ride, while she spoke of things he was certain she had divulged to no other, was gone without a trace, and in its place was the Queen of England.

Deven bowed in his saddle. "I will, your Majesty, and with all speed."

MEMORY: *January 31, 1587*

The chamber was dim and quiet, all those who normally attended within it having been banished to other tasks. Guards still stood outside the door—in times as parlous as these, dismissing them was out of the question—but the woman inside was as alone as she could ever be.

The cosmetics that normally armored her face were gone, exposing the ravages wrought by fifty-three years of fear and anger, care and concern, and the simple burden of life. Her beauty had been an ephemeral thing, gone as her youth faded; what remained was character, that would bow but never break, under even such pressure as she struggled with tonight.

Her eyes shut and her jaw clenched as the fire flickered and she heard a voice speak out from behind her. Unannounced, but not unexpected.

"You know that you must execute her."

Elizabeth did not ask how her visitor had penetrated the defenses that ringed her chamber. How had it happened the first time? Asking would but waste breath. She gathered her composure, then turned to face the woman who stood on the far side of the room.

Frustrated rage welled within her at the sight. Elaborate gowns, brilliant jewels, and a mask of cosmetics could create the illusion of unchanging beauty, but it was an illusion, nothing more, and one that failed worse with every passing year. The creature that stood before her was truly ageless. Invidiana's face and figure were as perfect now as they had been in the Tower, untouched by the scarring hand of time.

Elizabeth had many reasons to hate her, but this one was never far from her mind.

"Do not," she said in frigid reply, "presume to instruct me on what I must do."

Invidiana glittered, as always, in silver and black gems. "Would you rather be seen as weak? Her guilt cannot be denied—"

"She was *lured into it*!"

The faerie woman met her rage without flinching. "By your own secretary."

"With aid." Elizabeth spat the words. No one ever seemed to hear them, on the infrequent occasions that the two queens came face-to-face; she could shout all she wanted. "How much assistance did you provide? How much rope, that my cousin might hang herself? Or perhaps that was too inconvenient; perhaps 'twas simpler to falsify the letters directly. You have done it before, implicating her in her husband's murder. Had matters gone your way, she would have been dead ere she ever left Scotland."

The black eyes glimmered with cold amusement. "Or dead in the leaving, save that the nucklavee showed unexpected loyalty. I would the monster had drowned her; 'twould have saved much tedious effort on my part. And then your precious hands would be clean."

Words hovered behind Elizabeth's lips, all her customary

oaths, swearing by God's death and his body and countless other religious terms. How fitting it would be, to hurl them now: proof that although Protestant rites might lack the power of Catholic tradition, words of faith yet held some force.

But again, what purpose would it serve? Nothing she said now would save Mary. The Queen of Scots had been proven complicit in a scheme against Elizabeth and England; there was no concealing it. Invidiana had seen to that. Elizabeth's councillors, her parliament, her people—all wished to see Mary gone. Even James of Scotland had bowed to circumstances. His last letter, sitting open on a table nearby, offered no more trouble than the weak protest that his subjects would think less of him if he made no reprisal for his mother's execution.

"And what if I will not do it?" Elizabeth said. "'Tis plain you wish her gone for your own purposes. What if I refuse you? What if, this once, I refused to play a puppet's part?"

Invidiana's lips thinned in icy displeasure. "Would it please you more if I removed my hand from your affairs? Your end would surely then be swift."

Elizabeth almost told her to do it and be damned. The threats to English sovereignty were manifold—they were at war with Spain, and Leicester had bungled the campaign in the Low Countries—but she refused to believe herself dependent upon the faerie queen for her survival. *She* was Queen of England, by God, and needed no shadowy puppeteer to pull her strings.

Yet she could not deny the strings existed. Some of the demands Invidiana made of her seemed innocuous; some were not. The faerie woman had required no devilish rites, no documents signed in blood, but she had imposed a real cost—if a subtle one. A certain ruthless cast to particular affairs, colder and harder than it would otherwise have been. The persistent reminder of her own mortality, more unbearable because of its contrast with the faerie's eternal youth. And, in a blending of the personal and political, solitude.

Once, there had been many suitors for her hand. Leicester, Alençon, even the King of Sweden. None without complications of religion or faction, none without the threat of losing her independence as a ruling queen...but there might have been happiness with one of them. There might have been hope of marriage.

None of it had come to anything. And that, Elizabeth was certain, she could lay at the feet of her dark twin, the loveless, heartless, solitary faerie Queen.

She did not ordinarily resent the price she had been forced to pay, for security on her throne. What Elizabeth resented was the creature to whom she had been forced to pay it.

"You must execute her," Invidiana said again. "However you have come to this pass, no other road lies before you."

True, and inescapable. Elizabeth hated the elfin woman for it.

"Leave me be," she snarled. Invidiana smiled — beautiful, and ever so faintly mocking — and faded back into the shadows, returning whence she had come.

Alone in her bedchamber, Elizabeth closed her eyes and prayed. On the morrow, she would sign the order, and execute her cousin and fellow Queen.

BEER HOUSE, SOUTHWARK: *May 5, 1590*

"The thing to remember," Rosamund said, "is that she's not all-knowing or all-powerful."

The words hardly reassured Lune. All around them the

alehouse was bustling, with voices clamoring in half a dozen languages; the river thronged with travelers, merchants, and sailors from all over Europe, and the Beer House on the south bank attracted its fair share. The noise served as cover, but also made her nervous. Who might come upon them, without her ever knowing?

Rosamund clicked her tongue in exasperation. "She cannot have eyes and ears everywhere, my lady. Even if she has somehow trapped his ghost...." The prospect shadowed her face. "I know we haven't the rose here to protect us, but this will serve just as well. Her attention is bent where 'twill matter, and that is elsewhere."

The brownie was probably right. The greatest threat they faced here was from uncouth men who targeted them with bawdy jests. Lune and the Goodemeades had made certain they were not followed, and with glamours covering their true appearances, there was nothing to draw Invidiana's attention here.

They might as well meet; if Francis were in her clutches, Lune's only hope lay in following this matter through.

Her nerves wound a notch tighter when she saw a familiar head weaving through the noontime crowd. Deven wore a plain woolen cap and clothing more befitting a respectable clerk than a gentleman; Gertrude, who came into view before him, might have been any goodwife of the city. The brownie squeezed herself in next to her sister, leaving Deven no choice but to take the remaining place beside Lune. Rosamund passed them both jacks of ale.

Deven cast a glance around, then said in a voice barely audible through the racket, "Have a care what you say. Walsingham often picked up information from the docks."

Lune gave Rosamund a meaningful look.

He saw it, and an ironic smile touched his lips. For a moment the two of them were in accord; Gertrude, curse her, looked smug. "Escaping both sides at once takes more doing than this, I see. A moment." He vanished into the crowd, leaving behind his untouched ale and a fading warmth along Lune's side, where he'd pressed up against her.

He returned quickly, and gestured for them to follow. Soon they were upstairs, in a private room hardly big enough for the bed and table it held, but at least the noise faded. "Someone may try to listen at the door or through the wall," Deven said, "but 'tis better."

"I can help with that," Gertrude said, straightening up from where she crouched in the corner. A glossy rat sat on its hindquarters in her hands, and listened with a bright, inquisitive manner as she explained what she wanted. Deven watched this entire conference with a bemused air, but said nothing.

When the rat was dispatched to protect them from eavesdroppers, Deven gestured for the women to take the available seats. Lune perched on the edge of the bed—trying not to think about the uses to which it was put, nor what the Beer House's owner thought of the four of them—while the Goodemeades took the two stools.

Deven outlined for them in brief strokes what Elizabeth had said about the London Stone. "But I rode by it coming here," he said, "and saw no sign of a sword."

The fae all exchanged looks. "Have you ever seen it?" Gertrude asked, and Rosamund shook her head.

Lune followed their thoughts well enough. "But who knows every corner of the Onyx Hall? It might be there." Taking pity on Deven's confusion, she said, "The London Stone is half-buried, is it not? The lower end might extend into the palace below. But if it does, I know not where."

"She might well keep it hidden," Rosamund said.

Deven seemed less interested in this than he might have been. His face was drawn into surprisingly grim lines. "There's another problem."

Their speculation halted suddenly.

He looked straight at the Goodemeades. "You spun me a good tale the other day, of curses and lost loves. My Queen tells a different one. She met this Invidiana nearly five years before they were crowned, and says she was no kinder then than she is now, nor did she bear any other name. Have you any way to explain this?"

Lune was as startled as the brownies were. Had the sisters lied? No, she could not believe it. Even knowing they could and did lie with great skill, she did not believe they were feigning their confusion now. Was this some game of Deven's? Or Elizabeth's?

"We do not," Gertrude whispered, shaking her head. "I — that is —"

The unexpected hostility of Deven's tone had distracted Lune, but now she thought about his words. Five years. Her grasp of mortal history was weak, but she thought she remembered this much. "Mary would have been on the throne then. Was that not when Suspiria lifted her curse?"

Rosamund's brow was still furrowed. "I suppose so, near enough. But I do not see —"

Lune rose to her feet. Deven was watching her, with his eyes that kept reminding her of Francis — moreso since she learned what Francis had once been. "Not what *Invidiana* did — what *Suspiria* did. That is what he knew. That is what he was trying to say!"

"What?" Now everyone was staring at her.

She pressed one hand to the stiff front of her bodice, feeling sick. "He was dying, he could barely speak, but he tried to tell me—he could not get the words out—" Her fingers remembered the uncontrollable shaking of his body. Something hot splashed onto her hand. "The last thing he said. 'She is still c—'"

Lune looked down at the Goodemeades' pale faces. *"She is still cursed."*

"But that's impossible," Rosamund breathed. " 'Tisn't a glamour we see now; she is as she appears. Young and beautiful. She *must* have lifted the curse."

"Lifted?" Deven asked, from the other side of the table. "Or changed it somehow? Traded it for some other condition, escaped its terms?" He shrugged when Lune transferred her attention to him. "I know little of these things; you tell me if it is impossible."

"But did it happen before she met Elizabeth?" Rosamund twisted in her seat. "Or after?"

"Before, I think—but not long before. Elizabeth believes their meeting was the first time she claimed the name Invidiana."

Gertrude seized her sister's hand. "Rose, think. 'Twas after that she began gathering a court, was it not? No, she was not as we know her now—"

"But that might have been a mask." All the blood had drained from Rosamund's face; she looked dizzy. "She could have pretended to be the same. Ash and Thorn—that was when Francis began to lose his name. Do you remember? She always called him Tiresias, after that. And he said things had changed between them."

Lune said, "Then it was *not* Elizabeth's doing." Everything she had thought clear was fading away, leaving her grasping at mist. "But he said her pact..."

Into the ensuing silence, Deven said, "Perhaps this is a foolish question. But what certainty have we that she formed only one pact?"

No one seemed to be breathing. They had all leapt so quickly to the thought of Elizabeth and the mortal court—and they had not been wrong. There *was* a pact there. But was that what Francis had meant? Or did he know something they had never so much as suspected?

Lune whispered, "Where do we *begin*?"

"With the curse," Deven said. "Everything seems to have spun out of whatever she did to escape it. Creating the Onyx Hall did not free her, you said. What did?"

"Something Francis saw," Gertrude said. "At least, we think so."

Lune lowered herself slowly back onto the bed. Briefly she prayed that the rats were doing their jobs, and no one was listening to this mad and treasonous conversation. "He said she misinterpreted it. But we cannot know what she did until we know what she was escaping. What crime did she commit, to be cursed in such fashion?"

"We never knew," Rosamund replied, clenching her small hands in frustration. "Even once she knew, she would not tell us. Or even Francis, I think."

"But where did she learn it herself?"

Gertrude answered Deven far more casually than her words deserved. "From Father Thames."

His shoulders jerked. "From *who*?"

"The river," the brownie replied.

"The river." Coming from him, it was an expression of doubt, and he turned to Lune for a saner answer, as if she would be his ally in disbelief.

"The spirit of it," she said; his jaw came just the slightest bit

289

unhinged. Hers felt like doing the same. "She spoke to him? Truly?"

Rosamund shrugged. "She must have done. We were not in London when the curse was laid; 'twas long ago, when we lived in the North. Gertrude told her she must find someone who was here long ago. Who else could she turn to, save Old Father Thames himself?"

Who else, indeed. Lune felt dizzy. Father Thames spoke but rarely, and then to other creatures of the water. She did not know what could possibly induce him to speak to a fae of the land.

But she would have to find out, because they had no one else to question.

"I will try tonight, then," she said, and the Goodemeades nodded as if they had expected nothing else. She met Deven's gaze, briefly, and looked away. This was a faerie matter; he would want none of it.

"We should arrange to meet again," he said into the silence. "Your pigeon was most helpful, Mistress Goodemeade, but I pray you pardon me if I find communicating in such a manner to be...disconcerting." When the sisters smiled understandingly, he said, "There is a tavern along Fleet Street, outside the city's western wall. The Checkers. Shall we find one another there, three days hence?"

Three days. Giving Lune extra time, in case she failed the first night. Did he have so little confidence in her?

The brownies agreed, and they all dispersed, the Goodemeades leaving first. Alone with Deven, Lune found herself without anything to say.

"Good luck," he murmured at last. His hand twitched at his side, as if he might have laid it briefly on her shoulder.

That simple note of friendship struck an unexpected chord.

"Thank you," Lune whispered in response. Perhaps this alliance of theirs was leading him to forgive her—at least a little—for the harm she had done him before.

He stood a moment longer, looking at her, then followed the Goodemeades out the door.

Standing by herself in the center of the room, Lune took a slow, deep breath. Father Thames. She did not know how to reach him, let alone gain his aid... but she had three days to find out.


RIVER THAMES, LONDON: *May 5, 1590*

She had changed her appearance again, but Deven still recognized her. There were certain mannerisms—the way she walked, or held her head—that echoed his memories so powerfully it made him ache inside.

He followed the disguised Lune at a safe distance as she left the Beer House. Doing so required care; she was wary and alert, as if she might be observed or attacked. It was a tension that had not left her since he found her on Cloak Lane, wearing a bad illusion of Anne Montrose. The mere thought of living in such constant fear exhausted him. In comparison with life in her own court, masquerade as a human woman must have seemed a holiday for her.

Not that it excused a year of unending lies.

The crowds on London Bridge helped conceal him from her searching eyes. Disguised as he was, he blended in fairly well. So he followed her through the afternoon as she walked back and forth along the river's bank: first to the Tower of London, with its water port of the Traitor's Gate, then back westward to Billingsgate, the bridge, Queenhithe, Broken

Wharf, pausing each time she passed a river stair, occasionally watching the watermen who rowed passengers from one bank to the other. Her feet at last took her to Blackfriars, on the far side of which the noisome waters of the Fleet poured out into the Thames. Deven, who had been wondering what manner of creature the spirit of the Thames would be, thought he would not want to meet anything that embodied the Fleet.

It seemed that Lune could not make up her mind where to make her attempt. Did it matter so much? Deven could imagine the Thames at its headwaters in the west might be a different being than the Thames where it passed London, but what might distinguish the Blackfriars Thames from the bridge Thames, he had no idea.

That was part of why he followed. Lune had not asked for aid, but his curiosity could not be suppressed. Though it was being sorely tested by all this walking; he had grown far too accustomed to riding.

Night fell, and still Lune delayed. Curfew had long since rung, and for the first time it occurred to him that his sober disguise might pose a problem; with neither horse, nor sword, nor finery, nor anything else save his word that might identify him as a gentleman, he had no excuse for why he might be on the street. The same was true of Lune, but remembering the befuddled guards at Aldersgate the night she fled the city, he was not concerned for her.

When the moon rose into the sky, she made her way back eastward, and Deven at last understood what she had been waiting for.

The tidal waters of the Thames, answering the call of the gibbous moon.

As the river's level rose, he trailed her through the darkness, and mentally rewarded himself the groat he had wagered. Lune was heading for the bridge.

For it, and onto it. The Great Stone Gate on the Southwark end would be closed for the night, but the north end was open. Deven wondered what she was doing, then cursed himself for distraction; he had lost her among the houses, chapels, and shops built along the bridge's length.

Only the scuff of a shoe alerted him. Peering cautiously over the edge in one of the few places it was accessible, he saw a dark shadow moving downward. The madwoman could have hired a wherry to take her there by water—well, perhaps not. Shooting the bridge, passing through the clogged, narrow races between the piers of the arches, was hazardous at the best of times; even the hardened nerves of a London waterman would be tested by a request to drop a passenger off along the way. But that might still have been better than climbing down the side of the bridge.

Lune reached safety below, on one of the wooden starlings that protected the stone piers from collision with debris or unlucky wherries. There was no way Deven could follow her without being heard or seen. He should give up, and he knew it, yet somehow his feet did not move homeward; instead they carried him to the other side of the bridge, one arch farther north, and then his hands were feeling the roughened stone as if this were not the worst impulse he'd had since the night he followed a faerie woman out of the city.

The first part was easy enough, where the pier sloped outward to a triangular point. The second, vertical part was the stuff of nightmares, clinging to crevices where the mortar had worn away, praying he did not fall to the starling below and alert Lune, praying he did not tumble into the Thames and ignominiously drown. But by then it was far too late to turn back.

And then he was safe, and tried not to think about how he would get off the starling again when this was done.

His cap had blown off in the river wind and was lost to the dark water. Shivering a little, though he was not cold, Deven crouched and peeked cautiously around the edge of the pier, looking across the intervening space to where Lune stood on the next platform over. No, not stood; knelt. The sound of the river had faded enough that her voice carried clearly to him.

"Father Thames," she said, respectful and solemn. The glamour that had disguised her all day was gone, but the shadow beneath the arch protected her from prying eyes on the river-bank. Only Deven could see her, a silver figure with her head bowed. "As the moon calls to your waters, so I, a daughter of the moon, call to you. I humbly beseech the gift of your presence and counsel. Secrets lie within your waters, the wisdom of ancient times; I beg you to relate to me the tale of Suspiria, and the curse laid upon her. I ask this, not for myself, but for my people; the good of faerie kind may hang upon this tale. For their sake, I pray you hear my words."

Deven hardly breathed, both from anticipation, and from fear of being overheard. The river licked the planks of the starlings, within arm's reach of the top edges. Every flicker of motion caught his eye—what sign would be returned? A face? A voice?—but it was never more than debris, floating through the narrow gaps of the races.

He waited, and Lune waited, and nothing came.

Then another sound laid itself over the quiet murmur of the water. Only when it recurred could he identify it: not speech, but choked-off breath, the ragged edge of fading control.

"Please," Lune whispered. Formality had failed; now she spoke familiarly. "Please, I beg you, answer me." The river made no reply. "Father Thames...do you wish her power to endure? Or do our acts mean nothing to you? She has warped her court. I can scarce remember where I was before I came here, but I know it was not this cold. I served her faithfully, beneath the sea, in Elizabeth's court, anywhere she has bid me, and now I am hounded to the edge of my life. There is no safety for me now, except in her overthrow. Without your aid, I have nothing. I…"

The words trailed off into another ragged breath. Her shoulders slumped with weariness, abandoning the armor of purpose and drive that ordinarily held her together. Her hands clutched the edge of the starling, white-knuckled in the night.

He should not have followed her. Deven was watching something private, that she would not have shown if she knew he was there. And it stirred something uncomfortable within him, where resentment had lodged itself when first he saw her true face.

That was, after all, the crux of it. Her *true* face. The other was a lie. He knew it, and yet some part of him had still grieved, still resented her, as if she had somehow stolen Anne Montrose from him—as if Anne were a real person, kidnapped away by the faerie woman.

But Anne had never existed. There was only ever Lune, playing a part, as so many did when they came to court.

Yet the part she played was a part of her, too. There had been more truth than he realized to the words she said back then: she could be at ease in his presence, as she could not elsewhere. Perhaps the Lune who existed before the Onyx Court had been more like Anne.

Or perhaps not. He had no way of knowing. But one thing he did know: Lune *was* Anne. He had loved this faerie woman before he knew the truth, and now that he did…

His feelings had not vanished when her mask did.

It might be foolish of him—no doubt it was—but also true.

"You do not have nothing," he murmured, mouthing the words soundlessly to himself. "You have your own strength. And the aid of the Goodemeades. And...you have me."

Slack water had come, the turn of the tide; the river was never more quiet than now. Why, then, did he hear a sound, as if something disturbed its tranquility?

His first thought was that a boat approached; one hand went for his sword, remembered he did not have it, and groped instead for his knife. How would he explain their presence here? But no boat was near, and his fingers released the hilt, suddenly weak with shock.

The water between the two piers was swirling against all nature. The surface mounded, rose upward, then broke, and standing upon the Thames was an old man, broad-shouldered and tall, gray-bearded but hale, with centuries of wisdom graven upon his face.

"Rarely do I speak, in these times that so choke my waters with the passage of ordinary life," the spirit of the river said. His voice was deep and slow, rising and falling in steady rhythm. The murky gray fabric of his robe shimmered with hints of silver in its folds. "But rarely do two call me forth together, mortal and fae. Thus do I come, for the children of both worlds."

Deven froze. Lune's head came up like a doe's when it hears the hunter's step. Could she see him, concealed behind the edge of the pier?

Father Thames was not looking at him, but still he felt shamed. He could not hide from the venerable spirit.

Stepping around the edge, onto the nearer half of the starling, Deven made his most respectful bow, as if he approached the Queen herself. "We are most grateful for your presence." A back corner of his mind worried, *What form of address does one use for a river god?*

Lune rose slowly to her feet, staring at him. She seemed to speak out of reflex. "As he says, Old Father. You honor us by rising tonight."

Deven moved far enough that they both stood before the spirit, on opposite sides of the arch. The fathomless eyes of Father Thames weighed them each in turn. "Daughter of the moon, you spoke the name of Suspiria." Lune nodded, as if she did not trust her voice. "An old name. A forgotten name."

"Forgotten not by all," she whispered. "We seek knowledge of her—this mortal man and I. Can you tell us of her? What wrong did she commit, that she was cursed to suffer as if human?"

The spirit's gaze fixed inexplicably on Deven, who tried not to shiver. "She came to me for this tale, begging every night for a year and a day until I took pity on her and spoke. Her mind was clouded by her suffering. She did not remember.

"'Twas long and long ago. A town stood upon my banks, little more than a village, save that the chieftain of the mortal people dwelt within its palisade, and thereby lent it dignity beyond its size. Within the hollow hills lived the faerie race, and there was often conflict between the two.

"And so a treaty was struck, a bargain to bring peace for both peoples. Faerie kind would walk in freedom beneath the sun, and mortals go in safety beneath the earth. But 'twas not enough simply to agree; the bargain must be sealed, some ritual enacted to bind both sides to honor its terms. The son of the chieftain had gone more than was wise among the faerie people, and seen many wonders there, but one stood high in his mind: the beauty of an elfin lady, who of all things seemed to him most fair.

"Thus was it proposed: that the treaty be sealed by marriage, joining a son of mortality to a daughter of faerie."

The measured, flowing cadence of Father Thames's words carried the rhythm of simpler times. Not the crowded, filthy bustle of London as it was now: the green banks of the Thames, a village standing upon them, a young man dreaming of love.

The river god's eyes weighed Deven, seeing deep into his thoughts, and the admission he had not spoken aloud. Then the spirit continued on.

"But the lady refused her part.

"The dream that might have been was broken. The peace that would have been faded ere it took hold. Spurned, the man cursed her. If she held mortality in such disdain, then he condemned her to suffer its pangs, to feel age and sickness and debility, until she understood and atoned for her error."

Lune whispered, "The Onyx Hall."

At last Father Thames shifted his attention to her. "The time for treaties between the two peoples has passed. The beliefs of mortals are anathema now, and drive fae kind ever farther into the wilderness, where faith and iron do not yet reach. Only here, in this one place, do faeries live so closely with human kind."

"But 'twas not enough, Old Father," Deven said. "Was it? She created the Onyx Hall, and still was cursed. How did she escape it in the end?"

Water rippled around the hem of the spirit's robe. "I know not," he said simply. "That which occurs upon my waters, along my banks, from the dawn of time until now: all that lies within my ken. But that which is done beyond my sight is hidden to me."

In Lune's gaze, Deven read the thoughts that filled his own mind. They still did not have the answer they needed: what pact Suspiria had formed. But this tale mattered, if only because it helped them understand the being that had once stood where Invidiana did now.

"I will bear you safe to shore," Father Thames said, and held out his broad hands.

Without thinking, Deven stepped forward to accept. Only when it was too late did he realize his feet had left the starling. But he did not fall: the surface of the water bore him like a slightly yielding carpet, against all the custom of nature.

Lune took Father Thames's left hand, and then the river flowed beneath them. With gentle motion it carried them out from under the bridge, slantwise across the breadth of the water, until they came to the base of the Lyon Key stair, within sight of the Tower wall. When his feet were securely on the stone, Deven turned back.

Father Thames was gone.

Then he looked at the rippling surface, and understood. The river god was never gone.

"Thank you," he murmured, and Lune echoed him, her own words no louder than his.

BRIDGE AND CASTLE BAYNARD WARD, LONDON: *May 6, 1590*

Lune realized, as if through a great fog, that she stood openly on the bank of the Thames, her elfin form undisguised, Michael Deven at her side.

Summoning a glamour took tremendous effort. She should not have let her guard down, out there on the starling; not only had Deven been listening—why had he followed her?—but allowing herself to relax her control had been a mistake. Weariness dragged at her like leaden chains, and she could not focus.

What face could she wear? Not Anne Montrose. Not Margaret Rolford. Her first attempt failed and slipped, without even being tested. She took a deep breath and tried again. The illusion she created was a poor one, unnaturally generic; it would seem strange, like a badly crafted doll, if anyone looked at her closely. But it was the best she could do.

She surfaced from her concentration to find Deven watching her with an odd expression.

"Have you somewhere safe to go?" he asked.

Lune forced herself to nod. "There's a chamber in the Onyx Hall I have been permitted to claim as my own."

He bit his lower lip, apparently unconscious of the gesture. "But will you be safe there?"

"As safe as I may be anywhere at court." It sounded stiff even to her; she did not want to appear like she sought pity. "We should part. 'Tis not safe for you to be seen with me."

They still stood a little below the surface of the wharf, not that it would protect them much. Deven gave her a frank appraisal. "And if you go there now, tired as you are, will I be any safer? Weariness can drive any man to error." His mouth quirked wryly. "Or any woman. Or faerie."

Lune did not want to hear of the risk. She had measured it herself, time and again, even before she fell out of favor. It was the way of the Onyx Court. One mistake, one wrong word . . . she was so very tired of that world.

"Come," Deven said, and took her by the hand.

She followed him in a daze, too tired to ask questions. He led her through the streets, and it seemed like they walked forever before they arrived at a house. Lune knew she should protest — her absence might raise suspicion — but pathetic as it was, the thought of spending even one night outside the Onyx Hall was enough to make her weep with relief.

A single candle lit their way, kindled from one by the door; up the stairs they went, and then something made an appalling amount of noise as Deven dragged it from under the bed and out the chamber door. "Sleep here for tonight," he said, before he left her. "I'll keep near."

That was not safe. But Lune was well past the point of arguing. She collapsed onto the bed, barely pausing to pull a blanket over herself, and slept.

When morning came, she found herself in a small, moderately appointed bedchamber. On the floor beside her was a large, empty box; the noise must have been Deven dragging a mattress free of the truckle bed.

Her glamour had faded while she slept. It had been too long since she ate from that loaf of bread. Lune closed her eyes and rebuilt it, far better this time, making herself into an auburn-haired young woman with work-roughened hands, then pinched off another bite from the lump she carried with her. She dared not leave it behind in the Onyx Hall.

In the neighboring chamber, the mattress lay on the floor; Deven she found downstairs. Pausing at the door, Lune looked around at the modest pewter plate on the sideboard, the cittern in one corner, with two of its strings broken. She had thought briefly last night that the place might belong to some former agent of Walsingham, and had been both right and wrong. "This is your house."

He'd glanced up at her approach. "Yes." After a pause, he added, "I know. I should not have brought you here. But I was tired, too, and did not know where else to go; it seemed unkind to put my father in danger. We shall not do it again."

It was too late to undo. Lune came forward a few steps, smoothing the apron over her skirt. She looked like a maidservant for the house. "I'll take my leave, then."

"They know about me, do they not?" The room was dim, even though it was morning; Deven had kept the windows shuttered, and only a few lights burned. They accentuated the hollows in his face. He had not been sleeping well.

"Yes," Lune said. Taking a deep breath, she added with sincerity, "I am sorry for it. I cannot play the part of a man, and Walsingham would not take a woman into his confidence. The only course open to me was to attach myself to someone in his employ." That skirted too close to the wound between them. "They knew you were my contact in his service."

He was dressed once again as a gentleman, though not completely; his servants were nowhere in evidence. The sleeves of his doublet lay across his knees, and the aglets of his points dangled loose from his shoulders. "Would I still be in danger, had it ended at that?"

"Yes." He deserved honesty. "They would kill you, to make themselves safe."

"Well." Deven's fingers brushed over the vines embroidered on one sleeve, then stilled. "My Queen has commanded me to break her pact with yours. Even if that is a separate thing from this other one we are chasing, we need each other's aid. But I do not know how one might escape a curse."

The door was behind Lune, a silent reminder that she should leave. Doing so would only slow their progress, though; the only true safety lay in completing their task. Hoping she was not making a terrible mistake, Lune sat.

"Nor I. A curse may only be ended on its own terms. But Suspiria tried that, and failed. I do not think anyone could absolve her of it. The man who laid it might have lifted it, but he is long dead. And Tiresias—Francis—believed it still bound her."

"He had some vision, the Goodemeades said. Did he never speak of it to anyone else?"

Lune shook her head, more in bafflement than confident denial. "If 'twere part of the binding she laid on him—she has this jewel, that she can use to place commands on others, so they must obey or die. She might have bound him not to speak of that vision. But even if she did not . . . he died before he could tell me."

"And he never mentioned it at other times."

"How could I know?" Frustration welled up; Lune forced herself not to turn it on him. "You must understand. Dwell among fae for long enough, drink our wine, eat our food . . . it changes a man. And he had been there for years. He raved, he lived in dreams; nine-tenths of what he said was madness, and the other tenth too obscure to understand. He might have told a dozen people the content of his vision, and we would never know."

"Did he never say anything else?" Deven leaned forward, elbows on knees, face earnest and alert. "Not of the vision specifically. Anything touching on Suspiria, or curses, or the Onyx Hall . . . he would not speak entirely at random. Even madmen follow a logic of their own."

It might be true of ordinary madmen, but Tiresias? Under Deven's patience gaze, Lune disciplined her mind. When else had he spoken to her of the past?

When he told her to find him.

"He remembered his name," she murmured, recalling it. "Before I came to Elizabeth's court. He bade me find Francis Merriman; not until later did I realize he had forgotten who he was."

"Begin with that," Deven said. They had not worked together like this, piecing together an image from fragments, in months. And this time she was on his side. "He wanted you to find him. When you did . . ."

"He died." Deven had never known Francis; she could tell him what she could not tell the Goodemeades, who had loved the mad seer. "I forced him. He was afraid to speak, but I would not let him back away; I thought finding him would better my position in the Onyx Court." Quite the opposite, and the memory left a bitter taste in her mouth. "I demanded he tell me what he knew. And so he died."

She could not look away from his intent blue eyes. Speaking softly, Deven said, "Did you rack him? Put him to the question? Of course not. You kept him from fleeing at the last, perhaps, but unless there is something you have not told me, he chose to speak."

She would not cry. Lune turned her head away, by sheer force of will, and studied the linen-fold paneling of the wall until she had her composure again.

Deven granted her that space, then spoke again. "Go back to when he bade you find him. What precisely did he say?"

What *had* he said? Lune tried to think back. She had been wondering how to regain Invidiana's favor. Tiresias had been in her chamber. She had mortal bread....

"He spoke of Lyonesse," she said. "The lost kingdom. Rather, he looked at my tapestry of Lyonesse, and spoke of errors made after it sank." Or had he been speaking of other things? The Onyx Hall, perhaps? She could see him in her mind's eye now, a slender, trembling ghost. "He did not want to dream. I know he thought of his visions as dreams... then he said something about time having stopped."

This made both of them sit more sharply upright. "So it had, for Suspiria," Deven said. Excitement hummed in his voice, held carefully in check.

But there had been something before that. *If I should find this Francis Merriman, what then?*

He had sounded so lucid, yet spoken so strangely. Lune echoed his words. "'Stand still, you ever-moving spheres of Heaven....'"

Deven's breath caught. "What?"

She had not expected such a reaction. "'Tis what he said, when I asked him what I should do. '*Stand still, you ever-moving spheres of Heaven*—'"

"—*that time may cease, and midnight never come.*"

"He did not use those words. But 'twas then he said time had stopped." Deven's expression baffled her. "What is it?"

He answered with half a laugh. "You never go to the theater, do you."

"Not often," she said, feeling obscurely defensive. "Why? What are those words?"

"They come from a play." Deven rose and went to the cold fireplace, laying one hand on the mantel, chin tucked nearly to his chest. "The man who wrote them... he has served Burghley in the past, but he's more a poet than a spy. Sir Francis's cousin is a friend of his. I met him once, at dinner." He turned back to face her. "Is the name Christopher Marlowe familiar to you?"

Lune's brow furrowed. "I have heard it. But I do not know him."

"Nor his work, 'twould seem. The lines are from his play *Doctor Faustus*."

She shook her head; the title meant nothing to her.

Deven's jaw tensed, and he said, "The story is of a man who makes a pact with the devil."

Lune stared up at him, utterly still.

"Tell me," Deven said. "Have your kind any dealings with Hell?"

She spoke through numb lips, as if someone else answered for her. "The Court of Thistle in Scotland tithes to them every seven years. A mortal, not one of their own. I do not know how they were bound into such obligation. But Invidiana— Suspiria—surely she..."

"Would not have done so?" Deven's voice was tight with something: anger, fear, perhaps both. "By what you said, your own people would have no way to restore her beauty without lifting her curse. And she is still cursed. Some other power *must* have aided her."

Not a celestial power; an infernal one. What had she offered them in return? Any kindness she had once possessed, it seemed. And to fill that void, she craved power, dominion, control. She made of the Onyx Court a miniature Hell on earth; Tiresias had said often enough that it was so.

And he had told her what to do.

"Sun and Moon," Lune breathed. "We must break her pact with Hell."

# Act Five

Ah, Faustus,
Now hast thou but one bare hower to liue,
And then thou must be damnd perpetually:
Stand stil you euer mouing spheres of heauen,
That time may cease, and midnight neuer come!
— Christopher Marlowe
The tragicall history of D. Faustus

*T*he long gallery is lined from end to end with tapestries, each one a marvel of rich silk and intricate detail, limned in gold and silver thread. The figures in them seem to watch, unblinkingly pitiless, as he stumbles by them, barefoot, without his doublet, his torn shirt pulled askew. His lips ache cruelly. There is no one present to witness his suffering, but the embroidered eyes weigh on him, a silent and judgmental audience.

He spins without warning, shoulders thrown back, to tell the figures in the tapestries they must leave him be—but the words never leave his mouth.

The scene that has arrested his attention might depict anyone. Some faerie legend, some ancient lord whose name has escaped his mind, slipping through the cracks and holes like so much else. But his eye is transfixed by the two central images: a lone swordsman in a field, gazing at the moon high above.

His bruised lips part as he stares at those two. The broken spaces of his mind fill suddenly with a barrage of other pictures.

He sees another Queen. A canopy of roses. A winter garden. A stool, alone in a room. Lightning, splitting the sky. A loaf of bread. A sword, clutched in a pale hand. Two figures on a horse.

Shattered crystal, littering the floor, and an empty throne.

He presses one hand to his mouth, trembling.

He has seen it before. Not these same images, but other possibilities, other people. They have not come to pass. But who knows how far in the future a vision may lie? Who is to say whether one might not yet become true?

Some of those he has seen lie dead now. Or so he thinks. He has lost all grip on time; past, present, and future long since ceased to

309

*hold any meaning. He does not age, and neither does she, and it is always night below. There is no anchor for his mind, to make events proceed in their natural order, first cause, then effect.*

*It may be nothing more than the desperate hope of his heart. But he clings to it, for he has so little else. And he will bury this new one with the others, so deep that even he will not recall it, for that is the only way to keep such things from her.*

*She has gotten some of them. Or will get them. That is why those people are dead, or will be.*

*But not him. Never him. She will never let him go.*

*He tugs the tattered remains of his shirt about himself and hurries away from the tapestries. Must not be seen looking at them. Must not give her that hint.*

*Someday, perhaps, he will see one of these visions come to pass.*

St. Paul's Cathedral, London: *May 6, 1590*

Deven thought, a little wildly, *God have mercy. I'm bringing a faerie woman to church.*

By her expression, Lune might have been thinking the same thing. Mindful of how the stone would carry her voice, she murmured acidly, "Do you expect some priest here to stop her?"

"No. But at the very least, we are less likely to be overheard within these walls." One hand on her elbow, he pulled her farther down the nave. Outside, the churchyard echoed with its usual clamor, booksellers and bookbuyers and men looking for work. The vaulting interior of the cathedral somehow remained untouched by it all, a small island of sanctity in the midst of commerce.

"We can still come inside, when prepared; you yourself have seen me at chapel."

"True. But I doubt your kind wander in idly." Deven broke off as one of the cathedral canons passed by, giving him an odd look.

Without realizing it, he had led them to an all-too-familiar spot. Lune was not paying attention; she did not seem to notice that the magnificent tomb nearby contained not just Sir Philip Sidney, but his erstwhile father-in-law Walsingham.

Deven pulled up short, turning her to face him. "Now, tell me true. Do you think it mere chance, that your seer spoke that line? If you have *any* doubts..."

Lune shook her head. She still appeared a common maidservant, but he no longer had any difficulty imagining her true face behind it, silver hair and all. "I do not. I even thought, at the time, that he sounded sane...I simply could not make sense of the words. And I know of no power our kind possess to effect such a change, against the force of the curse."

He had hoped she would say it was a lunatic idea. Hoped for it, but not expected it.

"How do we break such a pact?" she whispered. She looked lost, stumbled without warning into a realm alien to her faerie nature. "Mere prayer will not do it. And I doubt she would stand still for an exorcism — if such would even touch her."

Despite his resolution not to draw her attention to his dead master, Deven found himself looking at the tomb that held Walsingham's body. Puritan belief was strong against them, Lune had said; Puritan, and Catholic. He was not on good terms with any Catholics. And he could not possibly ask Beale for help with this.

No, not Beale. The realization came upon him like a blessing from God.

"Angels," Deven said. "To break a pact with the devil...one would need an angel."

Lune's face paled as she followed his logic. "Dee."

The old astrologer, the Queen's philosopher. How many of the stories were true? "They say he speaks with angels."

"Or devils."

"I do not think so," Deven replied, soberly. "Not from what I saw of him...he might have feigned piety, of course. But can you think of one better?"

She wanted to; he could see her trying, calling up and then discarding names, one by one. "No."

Now Deven regretted his contrived visit of a few weeks before; how would he look, a supposedly lovestruck fool, coming back and asking for aid against a faerie queen? His audience with Elizabeth would seem simple by comparison. But Dee had been a faithful supporter of Elizabeth since even before her accession; it should be possible to convince him to act against her enemy, however strange that enemy might be. And Walsingham had set him on this road—though the Principal Secretary could not have guessed where it would lead.

"I'll go to him," Deven promised. "Without delay. You. . ."

"Will warn the Goodemeades."

He could not quite suppress his ironic smile. "They have set a few pigeons to shadow me; one should be at my house. 'Twill carry a message, if you can find paper—"

Her own mouth quirked, and he remembered what lay outside the cathedral doors.

"'Twill carry a message to them," he finished lamely.

Then they stood in awkward silence, the shared tomb of Sidney and Walsingham a mute presence beside them.

At last Lune said, the words coming out stiffly, "Be careful as you ride. They know who you are."

"I know," he replied. They stood only a step apart; the intervening space was both a yawning gulf, and intimately close. He would have taken Anne's hands, but what would Lune make of such a gesture? "Have a care for yourself. 'Tis you who must go into the viper's den, not I."

Lune smiled grimly and moved past him, heading for the cathedral doors. "I have lived with the viper for years. And I am not without my own sting."

Queenhithe Ward, London: *May 6, 1590*

Only after Lune was gone did Deven realize he had left his sleeves behind at the house. No wonder the canon had stared.

He needed to put himself together properly if he was to visit Dee. He needed Colsey; he needed his horse. The previous day had left the pieces of his ordinary life scattered around London like debris after a storm.

Assembling himself again took until the afternoon. Colsey was mutinously silent while tending his master, no doubt anticipating what would come; he did not even blink when Deven said, "I must go alone."

"Again."

"Yes." Deven hesitated. How much could he say? Not much. He laid one hand on Colsey's shoulder and promised, "This will be over soon."

Ranwell had readied his black stallion for some reason; the warhorse stood rock still as he mounted. The day was half-spent. He would spend the other half getting to Mortlake, and hope Dee granted him an audience at the end of it. At least he would be out of London, with no faerie palace lurking beneath his feet.

The congestion of the city's streets had never irritated him so much. He should have gone west, made for the horse ferry at Fulham, but by the time he thought of it he was halfway to the bridge, with no point in backtracking. A cart in the process of unloading had mostly blocked Fish Street ahead of him; standing briefly in his stirrups, Deven scowled at the ensuing knot, as people tried to edge by. Then he cast a sideways glance at a narrow, lamp-lit lane whose name he did not recall. If memory served, it ran through to Thames Street.

Turning the black stallion's head, he edged behind a heavily laden porter and into the lane.

Lamplight marked his way through the shadows. The lane brought him into a small courtyard, not Thames Street, but on the far side there was an archway, and his horse paced toward it without needing to be nudged. The lamp hovered above that arch, but did nothing to touch the darkness within. . . .

"Master! *Don't follow the light!*"

Irritation seized him. What was Colsey doing, following against his orders? He turned in his saddle to reprimand the servant, and found himself crying out instead. "*Ware!*"

Colsey leapt to the side just in time to dodge the grasping hands of the man behind him. A strange man, clad in nothing more than a brief loincloth and sandals, but broad-shouldered and muscled like a wrestler. He was unarmed, though, and in the close confines of the courtyard, he would be easy enough to ride down.

Except that Deven's horse stood like a rock when he jerked at the reins, heedless of his master's command.

And when he tried to swing his leg over the saddle, to go to Colsey's aid, he found himself rooted as if his feet were tied to the stirrups.

The strange, eldritch light hovered and pulsed as he fought to free himself. Across the way, Colsey slashed out with his knife at the half-naked stranger, who parried his blows and stalked him with hands spread wide. Christ above, the horse wasn't his; how had he ever mistaken it for his own stallion?

Christ. "In the name of the Lord God," Deven snarled, "release me!"

The animal bucked with apocalyptic force, hurling him through the air and into the wall of a neighboring house. All the air was driven from Deven's lungs, and he crashed heavily to the dirt below. But he untangled himself and lurched to his feet in time to see the creature shuddering and writhing into a two-legged shape, a man with a shock of black hair and large, crushing teeth.

The stranger fighting Colsey was blocking the exit to Fish Street—Deven no longer felt the slightest urge to go through the black archway at the other end—and as he looked, the man seized Colsey's knife hand and twisted it cruelly. The servant cried out and dropped his dagger.

Deven charged toward them, but his sword was only half-clear of its sheath when something cannoned into him from the side. The horse-thing knocked him into the wall again, and Deven gasped for air. Reflex saved him; he kept drawing and now had three feet of steel to keep the creature from him. It danced back, suddenly wary.

Colsey had broken free, but now he was unarmed. "Get to the street!" Deven shouted, or tried to; the words rasped painfully out of him. If Colsey could rouse some kind of aid—

Except that Colsey shook his head and backed up two steps, retreating toward Deven's side. "Damn your eyes," Deven snarled, "do as I say!"

"And leave you with yonder two? With the greatest respect, master, shove it." Colsey made a swift lunge, but not toward their opponents. Deven's own knife whisked clear of its sheath, into the servant's hand.

They had another weapon, though, better than steel. "By the most Holy Trinity," Deven said, advancing a step, "by the Father, the Son, and the Holy Spirit—"

He got no farther. Because although the horse-thing shrank back and the hovering light snuffed out as if it had never been, the strange man charged in without flinching.

His bulk bowled Colsey away from Deven's side, dividing them again. Deven lunged, but retracted it as the stranger whirled to grab for his arm; he dared not lose hold of his sword. Then the horse-thing was there again, kicking out and getting stabbed for his pains, and Colsey circled with his opponent, slashing with the knife to keep him at bay.

But not well enough. The stranger stepped in behind a slash, closing with the servant. A swift kick to the back of the leg dropped Colsey to one knee, and then the broad, hard hands closed around his head.

The crack echoed from the walls of the small courtyard. Deven crossed the intervening space in an eyeblink, but too late; Colsey's limp body dropped to the ground even as his master's blade scored a line across the back of his murderer. And the stranger did not seem to care. He turned with a feral grin and said, "Come on, then," and spread his killing hands wide.

The horse-thing faded back, clutching his wounded side and seeming glad to leave this fight to its partner. Deven focused on the man before him. The tip of his blade flickered out, once, twice, a third time, but the stranger dodged with breathtaking speed, more than a fellow of his size should possess. "Drop the sword," the stranger suggested, with a grin of feral pleasure. "Face me like a proper man."

Deven had no interest in playing games. He advanced rapidly, trying to pin the man against a wall where he could not dodge, but his opponent sidestepped and moved to grab his arm again. Deven slammed his elbow into the other man's cheek, but the stranger barely blinked. Then they were moving, back across the courtyard, not so much advancing or retreating as whirling around in a constantly shifting spiral, the stranger trying to close and get a hold on him, Deven trying to keep him at range. He wounded the man a second time, a third, but nothing seemed to do more than bleed him; the grin got wilder, the movements faster. Jesu, what was he?

They were almost to the courtyard entrance. Then Deven's footing betrayed him, his ankle turning on an uneven patch of ground, and what should have been a lunge became a stagger, his sword point dropping to strike the dirt.

And a sandaled foot descended on it from above, snapping the steel just above the hilt.

A calloused hand smashed into his jaw, knocking him backward. Deven punched out with the useless hilt and connected with ribs, but he had lost the advantage of reach; an instant later, the man was behind him, locking him into a choke hold. Gasping, Deven reversed his grip and stabbed blindly backward, gouging the broken tip into flesh.

The stranger ignored that wound, as he had ignored all others.

The world was fading, bright lights dancing with blackness. The hilt fell from his nerveless fingers. Deven reached up, trying to find something to claw, but there was no strength in his arms. The last thing he heard was a faint, mocking laugh in his ear.

TURNAGAIN LANE, BY THE RIVER FLEET: *May 6, 1590*

The sluggish waters of the Fleet reeked, even up here by Holborn Bridge, before it passed the prison and the workhouse of Bridewell and so on down to the Thames. It was an ill-aspected river, and always had been; again and again the mortals tried to cleanse it and make its course wholesome once more, and always it reverted to filth. Lune had once been unfortunate enough to see the hag of the Fleet. Ever since then, she kept her distance.

Except when she had no choice.

The alehouse her instructions had told her to find was a dubious place in Turnagain Lane, frequented by the kind of human refuse that clustered around the feet of London, begging for scraps. She had disguised herself as an older woman, and was glad of her choice; a maiden wouldn't have made it through the door.

She had been given no description, but the man she sought

was easy enough to find; he was the one with the wooden posture and the disdainful sneer on his face.

Lune slipped into a seat across from him, and wasted no time with preliminaries. "What do you want from me?"

The glamoured Vidar tsked at her. "No patience, and no manners, I see."

She had barely sent word off to the Goodemeades when Vidar's own messenger found her. The added delay worried her, and for more than one reason: not only might Invidiana wonder at her absence, but the secrecy of this meeting with Vidar meant he had not called her for official business.

She had not forgotten what she owed him.

But she could use that to her advantage, if only a little. "Do you want the Queen to know of this conference? 'Tis best for us both that we be quick about it."

How had he ever managed his extended masquerade as Gilbert Gifford? Vidar sat stiffly, like a man dressed up in doublet and hose that did not fit him, and were soiled besides. Lune supposed the preferment he got from it had been motive enough to endure. Though he had been squandering that preferment of late; she had not seen him at court in days.

Vidar's discomfort underscored the mystery of his absence. "Very well," he said, dropping his guise of carelessness. What lay beneath was ugly. "The time has come for you to repay that which you owe."

"You amaze me," Lune said dryly. She had made no oath to be polite about it.

He leaned in closer. The face he had chosen to wear was sallow and ill shaven, in keeping with the tenor of the alehouse; he had forgotten, however, to make it smell. "You will keep silent," Vidar growled, "regarding any other agents of the Wild Hunt you may uncover at court."

Lune stared at him, momentarily forgetting to breathe.

"As I kept silent for you," he said, spitting the words out one by one, "so you shall for me. Nor, by the vow you swore, will you let any hint of this matter leak to the Queen—by *any* route. Do you understand me?"

Corr. No wonder Vidar had been so absent of late; he must have feared what Invidiana would uncover about the dead knight... and about him.

Sun and Moon—what was he planning?

Lune swallowed the question, and her rudeness. "I understand you very well, my lord."

"Good." Vidar leaned back and scowled at her. "Then get you gone. I relish your company no more than you relish mine."

That command, she was glad to obey.

FARRINGDON WARD WITHIN, LONDON: *May 6, 1590*

Her quickest path back to the Onyx Hall led through Newgate, and she walked it with her mind not more than a tenth on her surroundings, working through the implications of Vidar's demand.

He must have formed an alliance with the Hunt. But *why*? Had he given up all hope of claiming Invidiana's throne for himself? Knowing what she did now, Lune could not conceive of those exiled kings permitting someone to take the usurper's place. If he thought he could double-cross them...

She was not more than ten feet from the Hall entrance in the St. Nicholas Shambles when screeching diverted her attention.

Fear made her heart stutter. In her preoccupation, someone might have crept up on her with ease, and now her nerves all leapt into readiness. No one did more than eye her warily, though, wondering why she had started in the middle of the street.

The noise didn't come from a person. It came from a jay perched on the eave of a building just in front of the concealed entrance. And it was staring straight at her.

Watching it, Lune came forward a few careful steps.

Wings flapped wildly as the jay launched itself at her face, screaming its rasping cry. She flinched back, hands coming up to ward her eyes, but it wasn't attacking; it just battered about her head, all feathers and noise.

She had not the gift of speaking with birds. It could have been saying anything, or nothing.

But it seemed very determined to keep her from the entrance to the Onyx Hall—and she did know someone who might have sent it.

Lune retreated a few steps, ignoring the staring butchers that lined both sides of the shambles, and held up one hand. Now that she had backed away, the jay quieted, landing on her outstretched finger.

Something in her message must have panicked the Goodemeades. But what?

She dared not go to them to ask. She had to hide herself, and then get word to the sisters. Not caring how it seemed to onlookers, Lune cupped the bird in her hands, closing her fingers around its wings, and hurried back out through Newgate, wondering where—if anywhere—would be safe.

THE ONYX HALL, LONDON: *May 7, 1590*

Instinct stopped him just before he would have moved.

He could feel ropes binding his ankles together, his arms

behind him. The stone beneath him was cold and smooth. In the instant when he awoke, before he shut his eyes again, he saw a floor of polished black and white and gray. The air on his skin, ghosting through the rents in his clothing, was cool and dry.

He knew where he was. But he needed to know more.

Footsteps tapped a measured beat on the stone behind him. Deven kept his body limp and his eyes shut. Let them think him still unconscious.

Then he began to move, without a single hand touching him.

Deven felt his body float up into the air and pivot so that he hung upright, facing the other direction. His arms ached at the change in position, cold and cramped from the ropes and the stone. Then a voice spoke, as cool and dangerous as silk over steel. "Cease your feigning, and look at me."

For a moment he considered disobeying. But what would it gain him?

Deven opened his eyes.

The breath rushed out of him in a sigh. *Oh, Heaven save me....* They had spoken of her beauty, but words could not frame it. All the poetry devoted to Elizabeth, all the soaring, extravagant compliments, comparing her to the most glorious goddesses of paganism—every shred of it should have been directed here, to this woman. Not the slightest imperfection or mark interrupted the alabaster smoothness of her skin. Her eyes were like black diamonds, her hair like ink. High cheekbones, delicately arched brows, lips of a crimson hue both forbidding and inviting...

The words tore their way free of him, driven by some dying instinct of self-preservation. "God in Heaven..."

But she did not flinch back. Those red lips parted in an arrogant laugh. "Do you think me so weak? I do not fear your God, Master Deven."

If she did not fear the Almighty, still His name had given Deven strength. He wrenched his gaze away, sweating. They had spoken of Invidiana's beauty, but he had imagined her to be like Lune.

She was nothing like Lune.

"You are not surprised," Invidiana said, musingly. "Few men would awake in a faerie palace and be unamazed. I took you for bait, but you are more than that, are you not, Master Deven? You are the accomplice of that traitor, Lune."

How much did she know?

How much could he keep from her?

"Say rather her thrall," Deven spat, still not looking at her. "I care nothing for your politics. Free me from her, and I will trouble you no more."

Another laugh, this one bidding fair to draw blood by sound alone. "Oh, indeed. 'Tis a pity, Master Deven, that I did not have Achilles steal you sooner. A man who so readily resorts to lies and deception, manipulation and bluff, could well deserve a place in my court. I might have made a pet of you.

"But the time for such things has passed." The idle amusement of her voice hardened. "I have a use for you. And if that use should fail . . . you will provide me with other entertainment."

Deven shuddered uncontrollably, hearing the promise in those words.

"You are my guest, Master Deven." Now it was mock courtesy, as disturbing as everything else. "I would give you free run of my domain, but I fear some of my courtiers do not always distinguish guests from playthings. For your own safety, I must take precautions."

The force that held him suspended now lowered him. The

toes of his boots touched the floor; then she pushed him farther, until he knelt on the stone, arms still bound behind his back.

His head was dragged forward again; he could not help but look.

Invidiana was lifting a jewel free of her bodice. He had a glimpse of a black diamond housed in silver, edged with smaller gems; then he tried to flinch back and failed as her hand came toward his face.

The metal was cool against his skin, and did not warm at the contact. An instant later Deven shuddered again, as six sharp points dug into his skin, just short of drawing blood.

"This ban I lay upon thee, Michael Deven," Invidiana murmured, the melody of her voice lending horror to her words. "Thou wilt not depart from this chamber by any portal that exists or might be made, nor send messages out by any means; nor wilt move in violence against me, lest thou die."

Every vein in his body ran with ice. Deven's teeth clenched shut, his jaw aching with sudden strain, while six points of fire fixed into the skin of his brow.

Then it was gone.

Invidiana replaced the gem, smiling, and the bonds holding him fell away.

"Welcome, Master Deven, to the Onyx Hall."


DEAD MAN'S PLACE, SOUTHWARK: *May 7, 1590*

There was something grimly appropriate, Lune thought, about hiding a stone's throw from an Episcopal prison full of heretics.

But Southwark was a good place for hiding; with its stews and bear-baiting, its prisons and general licentiousness, a woman on her own, renting out a room for a short and indefinite period of time, was nothing out of the ordinary way. Lune would simply have to be gone before her faerie gold — or rather, silver — turned back to leaves.

Had the jay in truth belonged to the Goodemeades? Or had it taken her message to another? Would the Goodmeades come? What had happened, that they were so determined to keep her from the Onyx Hall?

Footsteps on the stair; she tensed, hands reaching for weapons she did not have or know how to use. Then a soft voice outside: "My lady? Let us in."

Trying not to shake with relief, Lune unbarred the door.

The Goodemeades slipped inside and shut it behind them. "Oh, my lady," Gertrude said, rushing forward to clasp her hands, "I am so sorry. We did not know until too late!"

"About the pact?" Lune asked. She knew even as she said the words that wasn't it, but her mind had so fixated on it, she could not think what Gertrude meant.

Rosamund laid a gentle hand on her arm. The touch alone said too much. "Master Deven," the brownie said. "She has taken him."

There was no refuge in confusion, no stay of understanding while Lune asked what she meant. Fury began instantly, a slow boil in her heart. "I trusted you to warn him. He's as much in danger as I; why did you warn only me?"

The sisters exchanged confused looks. Then Rosamund said, "My lady … the birds stopped you of their own accord. Her people ambushed him on the street yesterday. We did not even know of it until later. We sent birds some time ago, to watch you both. They had lost you, but when one saw him taken, they chose to watch the entrances and stop you if they could."

Lost her. Because she had tried so very hard to keep anyone

from following her when she went to meet Vidar. Where had she been, when they attacked him? Had Vidar distracted her on purpose?

"Tell me," Lune said, harsh and cold.

Gertrude described it softly, as if that lessened the dreadfulness of what she said. "A will-o'-the-wisp to lead him astray. A tatterfoal, to replace his own horse and carry him into the trap." She hesitated before supplying the last part. "And Achilles, to bring him down."

One tiny comfort Lune could take from that: Invidiana must not mean to have Deven battle to the death, or she would have saved Achilles for later, and sent Kentigern instead.

"There's more," Rosamund said. "His manservant Colsey was following him, it seems. I do not know why, or what happened... but he's dead."

Colsey. Lune had met him, back when they were all at court, and her greatest concern had been how to evade Deven's offer of marriage without losing his usefulness to her. She had liked him, and his close-mouthed loyalty to his master.

Gone, that easily. And Deven...

Lune turned away and walked two paces. She could go no farther; the room she had rented was scarcely larger than a horse's stall.

The lure was plain. The question was whether she would take it.

It hardly mattered whether Invidiana had Francis Merriman's ghost. The Queen knew enough. Would Lune now walk into her trap?

Without thinking, one hand dropped to touch the purse that held the last of the loaf Deven had given her. Mortal bread. She had consumed so much of it, since she met him. Not enough to make her human, but enough to change her.

Michael Deven loved her. Not Anne Montrose, but *Lune*. She knew it the night he led her to his house. What did that love mean to her?

Would she spurn it, and flee to save herself?

Or would she accept it—return it—despite the cost?

She had never felt that choice within her before. Too much mortal bread; it brought her to an unfamiliar precipice. Her mind moved in strange ways, wavering, uncertain.

"My lady?" Gertrude whispered from behind her.

Lune's hands stilled on her skirt. She turned to find the two brownies watching her with hesitant expressions. It was the first time she had seen them show fear. They had spent years opposing Invidiana; now, at long last, their game might be at an end.

"The London Stone lies within the Onyx Hall," Lune said. "So does Invidiana, who made a pact with Hell. And so does Michael Deven.

"I will do what we had intended. I will seek out Doctor Dee."

MEMORY: *Long and long ago...*

*T*here was a beauty of night, pale as the moon, dark as her shadow, slender and graceful as running water. A young man saw her dancing under the stars, and loved her; he pined and sighed for her, until his mother feared he would waste away, lost in dreams of love. For that happened at times, that folk should die for love of the strangers under the hills.

Such was not this young man's lot. A plan was formed, wherein he would have the beautiful stranger to wife. Great preparations were made by his people and by hers, a glorious

midsummer wedding on the banks of the river, a little distance
from the village where the young man's father ruled. There
would be music and dancing, good food and drink, and if the
maidens and youths of the village fell in love with their guests
from the other side, perhaps this wedding would be only the
first of many. And when it was done, the young man would
have a fine house to share with his wife, in time succeeding his
father as chieftain and ruling in his place.

So it was planned. But it did not come to pass.

The guests gathered beneath the twilit summer sky. On the
one side, the weathered faces of the villagers, tanned by the sun
in their labors, the old ones wrinkled, the young ones round-
cheeked and staring at the folk across the field. There stood
creatures tall and tiny, wide-shouldered and slender, some with
feathers, hooves, tails, wings.

The one the young man loved looked at her people, in all
their wild glory, and even their ugliness was more beautiful to
her, because it was what they were and always would be.

Then she looked at the people of the village, and she saw
how accidents marked their bodies, how they soon crumbled
and fell, how their houses stood on bare dirt and they scratched
out their living with toil.

And she asked herself: *Am I to go from this to that?*

So she fled, leaving the young man alone beneath the rising
moon, with his heart broken into pieces.

He sickened and died, but not for love. Yet he took strange
pride in his illness, laughing a mad laugh that grieved his
mother unbearably. *You see, we prove her right. We die so soon,
so easily; she will remain long after I am gone. I do not mourn the
mayfly, nor yoke my heart to its; why should it be different with
her?*

Bitterness poisoned the words, the terrible knowledge that

his love was as nothing to the immortal creature upon whom it had fixed.

The moon waned and waxed, and when it was full once more, the young man died. On his deathbed he spoke his last words, not to his family, but to the absent creature that had been the end of him. *May you suffer as we suffer, in sickness and age, so that you find no escape from that which you fled. May you feel all the weight of mortality, and cry out beneath your burden, until you atone for the harm you have done and understand what you have spurned.*

Then he died, and was buried, and never more did the villagers gather in harmony with the strangers under the hills.

MORTLAKE, SURREY: *May 7, 1590*

The house, with all its additions and extensions, was like an old man dreaming in the afternoon sunlight, relaxed into a sprawling doze. Yet to Lune it seemed more foreboding than the Onyx Hall: a lair of unknown dangers.

Be it angels or devils he summoned inside, it was not a place a faerie should go.

Lune put her shoulders back and approached the door with a stride more resolute than she felt.

She was a woman on her own, with no letter of introduction to smooth her way. But the maidservant was easy enough to charm, and Dee's wife proved sympathetic. "He's at his studies," the woman said, shifting the infant she held onto her other hip. The small creature stared frankly at Lune, as if it could see through the glamour. "But if 'tis urgent..."

"I would be most grateful," Lune said.

Her reception was warmer than expected. "You will forgive

my frankness in asking," Dee said, once the formalities were dispensed with, "but has this anything to do with Michael Deven?"

This was not in the mental script Lune had prepared on her journey to Mortlake. "I beg your pardon?"

A surprising twinkle lightened the astrologer's tired eyes. "I am not unaware of you, Mistress Montrose. Your lady the Countess of Warwick has been kind to me since my return, and I had the honor of friendship with Sir Francis Walsingham. When Master Deven came to my door, asking for aid in the matter of a young gentlewoman, 'twas not difficult to surmise whom he meant."

No magic, just an observant mind. Lune began to breathe again. "Indeed, Doctor Dee—it has everything to do with him. Will you aid me?"

"If I can," Dee said. "But some things are beyond my influence. If he is in some political difficulty—"

Not of the sort he thought. Lune clasped her hands in her lap and met the old man's gaze, putting all the sincerity she could muster into it. "He is in great peril, and for reasons I fear must be laid at my feet. And it may be, Doctor Dee, that you are the only man in England who could help us."

His face stilled behind its snowy beard. "And why would that be?"

"They say you speak with angels."

All pleasantness fell away, but his eyes were as bright and unblinking as a hawk's. "I fear, Mistress Montrose, that you may have an overly dramatic sense of his danger, my abilities, or both. Angels—"

"I am not overly dramatic," she snapped, forgetting in her distress to be polite. "I assure you. The tale is a complex one, Doctor Dee, and I have not the time to waste on it if at the end you will tell me you can be of no aid. Do you hold conference with angels, or not?"

Dee rose from his seat, ink-stained fingers twitching his long robe straight. Turning away to pace across the room, he spoke very deliberately. "I see that you are distraught, Mistress Montrose, and so I will lay two things before you. The first is that angelic actions are no trivial matter, no miracle that can be summoned at a whim to solve worldly ills.

"The second..." He paused for a long time, and his hands, clasped behind his back, tightened. Something hardened his voice, lending it an edge. "The second is that such efforts require assistance — namely, the services of a scryer, one who can see the presences when they come. My former companion and I have parted ways, and I have found no suitable replacement for him."

The first point did not worry her; the second did. "Can you not work without such assistance?"

"No." Dee turned back to face her. His jaw was set, as if against some unhappy truth. "And I will be honest with you, Mistress Montrose. At times I doubt whether I have *ever* spoken with an angel, or whether, as they accuse me, I have done naught but summon devils, who play with me for their own amusement."

Her mouth was dry. All her hope crumbled. If not Dee, then who? A priest? Invidiana had destroyed priests before. And Lune did not think a saint would answer the call of a faerie.

"Mistress Montrose," Dee said softly. Despite the lines that had sobered his face, his manner was compassionate. "Will you not tell me what has happened?"

A simple question, with a dangerous answer. Yet some corner of Lune's mind was already calculating. If he were not the sorcerer she had expected, then a charm might bedazzle him long enough for her to escape, should all go poorly. She would be destroying Anne Montrose, but no life remained for that woman regardless....

She truly was thinking of doing it.

"Can I trust you?" Lune whispered.

He crouched in front of her, keeping space between them, so as not to crowd her. "If it means no harm to England or the Queen," Dee said, "then I will do my best to aid you in good faith."

The door was closed. They were private.

Lune said, "I am not as I seem to be." And, rising to her feet, she cast aside her glamour.

Dee rose an instant later, staring.

"The Queen of faerie England," she said, every muscle tensed to flee, "has formed a pact with Hell. I need the aid of Heaven to break it. On this matter rests not only the safety of Michael Deven, but the well-being of your own kingdom and Queen."

He did not shout. He did not fling the name of God up as defense. He did nothing but stare, his eyes opaque, as if over-taken by his thoughts.

"So if you cannot summon angels," Lune said, "then tell me, Doctor Dee, what I should do. For I do not know."

Within the mask of his beard, his mouth was twitching; now she read it as a kind of bitterness, surprising to her. "Did you send him?" he asked abruptly.

"Michael Deven?"

*"Edward Kelley."*

The name ground out like a curse. Where did she know it from? She had heard it somewhere....

"When he came to me," Dee said coldly, "he offered to fur-ther my knowledge in magic with faeries."

Memory came. A human man with mangled ears; she had seen him once or twice at court—her own court—and heard his name. She had never known more. "I did not send him," Lune said. "But someone may have. Who was he?"

"My scryer," Dee replied. "Whom I have long suspected of deception. He came to me so suddenly, and seemed to have great skill, but we so often fought...." Now she recognized the note in his voice; it was the sound of affection betrayed. This Kelley had been dear to him once.

"He is gone now?" Lune asked.

Dee made a cut-off gesture with one hand. "We parted ways in Trebon. He is now court alchemist to the Holy Roman Emperor."

Then he truly was out of reach. Lune said, "Please, Doctor Dee. I beg you." Never in all the ages she could remember had she knelt, as a fae, to a mortal, but she did it now. "I know I am no Christian soul, but Michael Deven is, and he will die if I cannot stop this. And does not your God oppose the devil, wherever he may work? Help me, I beg. I do not know who else to ask."

Dee gazed blindly down at her, distracted once more. "I have no scryer. Even Kelley may have given me nothing but falsehoods, and I myself have no gift for seeing. It may be that I have no more power to summon angels than any other man."

"Will you not try?" Lune whispered.

With her eyes fixed on him, she saw the change. Some thought came to him, awakening all the curiosity of his formidable mind. The expression that flickered at the edge of his mouth was not quite a smile, but it held some hope in it. "Yes," Dee said. "We will try."

THE ONYX HALL, LONDON: *May 8, 1590*

Thirst was the greatest threat.

Deven tried to distract himself. The room, he came to

realize, was Invidiana's presence chamber. Larger by far than Elizabeth's, it had an alien grandeur a mortal queen could only dream of, for in this place, fancies of architecture could truly take flight. The pillars and ribs that supported the arching ceiling were no more than a decoration born from some medieval fever dream; they were not needed for strength. The spaces between them were filled with filigree and panes of crystal, suspended like so many fragile swords of Damocles.

Beneath and among these structures wandered fae whom he presumed to be the favored courtiers of this Queen. They were a dizzying lot: some human-looking, others supernaturally fair, others bestial, and clad in finery that was to mortal courtiers' garb as the chamber was to mortal space. They all watched him, but none came near him; clearly word had gone around that he was not to be touched. How much did they know of who he was, and why he was there?

Lacking an answer to that question, Deven decided to test his boundaries. He tried to speak to others; they shied away. He followed them around, eavesdropping on their conversations; they fell silent when he drew near, or forwent the benefit of being so near the Queen and left the chamber entirely. The fragments he overheard were meaningless to him anyway.

He spoke of God to them, and they flinched, while Invidiana looked on in malicious amusement.

She was less amused when he decided to push harder.

Deven took up a position in the center of the chamber, facing the throne, and crossed himself. Swallowing against the dryness of his mouth, he began to recite.

"Our father, which art in Heaven, hallowed be Thy Name. Thy kingdom come. Thy will be done in earth, as it is in Heaven. Give us this day our daily bread, and forgive us our trespasses, as we forgive them that trespass against us. And lead us not into temptation, but deliver us from evil. Amen."

The chamber was half-empty before he finished; most of those who remained were bent over or sagged against the walls, looking sick. Only a few remained untouched; those, he surmised, had eaten of mortal food recently. But even they did not look happy.

Nor did Invidiana. She, for the first time, was angry.

He tried again, this time in a different vein, dredging up faded memories of prayers heard from prisoners and recusants. *"Pater noster, qui es in caelis: sanctificetur Nomen Tuum..."*

This time even he felt its force. The hall trembled around him; its splendor dimmed, as if he could see through the marble and onyx and crystal to plain rock and wood and dirt, and all the fae stood clad in rags.

Then something slammed into him from behind, knocking him to the floor and driving all breath from him. His Catholic prayer ended in a grunt. A voice spoke above him, one he knew too well, even though he had heard scarcely a dozen words from it. "Should I cut out his tongue?" Achilles asked.

"No." If the Latin form had shaken Invidiana, she gave no sign. "We may yet need him to speak. But stop his mouth, so he may utter no more blasphemies."

A wad of fabric was shoved into Deven's mouth and bound into place. His thirst increased instantly as every remaining bit of moisture went into the cloth.

But his mind was hardly on that. Instead he was thinking of what he had seen, in that instant before Achilles took him down.

Invidiana's throne sat beneath a canopy of estate, against the far wall. Under the force of his prayer, it seemed for a moment that it masked an opening, and that something lay in the recess behind it.

What use he could make of that knowledge, he did not know. But with his voice taken away, knowledge was his only remaining weapon.

MORTLAKE, SURREY: *May 8, 1590*

"You are mad," Lune said.

"Perhaps." Dee seemed undisturbed by the possibility; no doubt he had been accused of it often enough. "But children are ideal for scrying; children, and those who suffer some affliction of the mind. Kelley was an unstable man—well, perhaps that is no recommendation, if in truth he did naught but deceive me. Nonetheless. The best scryers are those whose minds are not too shackled by notions of possibility and impossibility."

"You yourself, then."

He shook his head. "I am too old, too settled in my ways. My son has shown no aptitude for it, and we have no time to find another."

Lune took a slow breath, as if it would banish her feeling that all this had taken a wrong turn somewhere. "But if you question whether you have ever spoken with an angel before, what under the sun and moon makes you believe one will answer to a *faerie*?"

They were in his most private workroom, with strict orders to his surprisingly large family that under no circumstances were they to be disturbed. Lune hoped it would be so; at Dee's command, she had eaten no food of any kind since the previous day—which meant no mortal bread.

He knew quite well what that meant, for she had told him.

At great length, when she began to understand what he had in mind. And that was *before* he voiced his decision to use her as his scryer.

The philosopher shook his head again. "You misunderstand the operation of this work. Though you will be a part of it, certainly, your role will be to perceive, and to tell me what you see and hear. The calling is mine to perform. I have been in fasting and prayer these three days, for I intended to try again with my son; I have purified myself, so that I might be fit for such action. The angel—if indeed one comes—will come at my call."

Now she understood the fasting. But prayer? "I have not made such thorough preparations."

The reminder dimmed his enthusiasm. "Indeed. And if this fails, then we will try again, three days from now. But you believe time to be of the essence."

Invidiana had the patience of a spider; she would wait three years if it served her purpose. But the longer Deven remained in the Onyx Hall, the greater the likelihood that the Queen would kill him—or worse.

*Worse* could take many forms. Some of them were the mirror image of what Lune risked now. Baptism destroyed a fae spirit, rendering it no more than mortal henceforth. Dee had not suggested that rite, but who knew what effect this "angelic action" would have?

That frightened her more than anything. Fae could be slain; they warred directly with one another so rarely because children were even more rare. But death could happen. Nor did anyone know what if anything lay beyond it, though faerie philosophers debated the question even as their human counterparts did. The uncertainty frightened Lune less than the certainty of human transformation. 'Twas one thing to draw close to them, to bask in the warmth of their mortal light. To *be* one...

Marie Brennan

She had already made her choice. She could not unmake it now.

Lune said, "Then tell me what I must do."

Dee took her by the hand and led her into a tiny chapel that adjoined his workroom. "Kneel with me," he said, "and pray."

Her exposed faerie nature felt terrifyingly vulnerable. With mortal bread shielding her, she could mouth words of piety like any human. But now?

He offered her a kindly smile. If her alien appearance disturbed him, he had long since ceased to show it. "You need not fear. Disregard the words you have heard others say—Catholic and Protestant alike. The Almighty hears the sentiment, not the form."

"What kind of Christian are you?" Lune asked, half in astonishment, half to stall for time.

"One who believes charity and love to be the foremost Christian virtues, and the foundation of the true Church, that lies beyond even the deepest schism of doctrine." His knobbled hand pressed gently on her shoulder, guiding her to her knees. "Speak in love and charity, and you will be heard."

Lune gazed up at the cross that stood on the chapel's wall. It was a simple cross, no crucifix with a tormented Christ upon it; that made it easier. And the symbol itself did not disturb her—not here, not now. Dee believed what he said, with all his heart. Without a will to guide it against her, the cross was no threat.

Speak in love and charity, he had said.

Lune clasped her hands, bent her head, and prayed.

The words came out hesitantly at first, then more fluidly. She wasn't sure whether she spoke them aloud, or only in her mind. Some seemed not even to be words: just thoughts, concepts, inarticulate fears, and longings, set out first in the manner of a

338

bargain — *help me, and I will work on your behalf* — then as justifications, defenses, an apology for her faerie nature. *I know not what I am, in the greater scope of this world; whether I be fallen angel, ancient race, unwitting devil, or something mortals dream not of. I do not call myself Christian, nor do I promise myself to you. But would you let this evil persist, simply because I am the one who works against it? Does a good deed cease to be good, when done by a heathen spirit?*

At the last, a wordless plea. Invidiana — Suspiria — had taken this battle into territory foreign to Lune. Adrift, lost in a world more alien than the undersea realm, she could not persevere without aid.

So far did she pour herself into it, she forgot this was preparation only. She jerked in surprise when Dee touched her shoulder again. "Come," he said, rising. "Now we make our attempt."

The workroom held little: a shelf with a few battered, much-used books. A covered mirror. A table in the center, whose legs, Lune saw, rested upon wax rondels intricately carved with symbols. A drape of red silk covered the tabletop and something else, round and flat.

Upon that concealed object, Dee placed a crystalline sphere, then stepped back. "Please, be seated."

Lune settled herself gingerly on the edge of a chair he set facing the sphere.

"I will speak the invocation," he said, picking up one of the books. Another bound volume sat nearby, open to a blank page; she glimpsed scrawled handwriting on the opposite leaf, that was evidently his notes, for he had ink and a quill set out as well.

She wet her lips. "And I?"

"Gaze into the stone," he said. "Focus your mind, as you did when you prayed. Let your breathing become easy. If you see aught, tell me; if any being speaks to you, relate its words." He smiled at her once more. "Do not fear evil spirits. Purity of purpose, and the formulas I speak, will protect us."

He did not sound as certain as he might have, and his hand tightened over the book he held, as if it were a talisman. But Lune was past the point of protest; she simply nodded, and turned her attention to the crystal.

John Dee began to speak.

The first syllables sent a shiver down her spine. She had expected English, or Latin; perhaps Hebrew. The words he spoke were none of these, nor any language she had ever heard. Strange as they were, yet they reverberated in her bones, as if the sense of them hovered just at the edge of her grasp. Did she but concentrate, she might understand them, though she had never heard them before.

The words rolled on and on, in a sonorous, ceaseless chant. He supplicated the Creator, Lune sensed, extolling the glory of Heaven and its Lord, describing the intricate structure of the world, from the pure realms of God down to the lowliest part of nature. And for a brief span she perceived it as if through his eyes: a beautifully mathematical cosmos, filled with pattern, correspondence, connection, like the most finely made mechanical device, beyond the power of any mind save God's to apprehend in its entirety, but appreciable through the study of its parts.

To this, he had devoted his life. To understanding the greatest work of God.

In that moment, all the aimless, immortal ages of her life seemed by comparison to be flat and without purpose.

And then she felt suffused by a radiance like that of the moon, and her lips parted; she spoke without thinking. "Something comes."

Dee's invocation had finished, she realized, but how much time had passed, she did not know. A soft scratching reached her ears: his quill upon paper. "What do you see?"

"Nothing." The sphere filled her vision; how long since she had last blinked?

"Speak to it."

What should she say? Her mind was roaringly empty of words. Lune groped for something, anything. "We—I—most humbly beseech your power, your aid. The Queen of the Onyx Court has formed a pact with Hell. Only with your power may it be broken. Will you not help us?"

Then she gasped, for the crystal vanished; she saw instead a figure, its form both perfect and undefinable. The table was gone, the chair was gone; she stood in an empty space before the terrible glory of the angel, and sank to her knees without thinking, in respect and supplication.

As if from a great distance, she heard Dee utter one word, his own voice trembling in awe. *"Anael."*

Her spirit lay exposed, helpless, before the angel's shining might. With but a thought, it could destroy her, strip all faerie enchantment from her being, leave her nothing more than a mortal remnant, forever parted from the world that had been hers. She was no great legend of Faerie to defend herself against such, and she had laid herself open to this power of her own free will.

All that defended her now was, as Dee had said, charity and love.

She trembled as the figure drew closer. The strength might have crushed her, but instead it held her, like a fragile bird, in the palm of its hand. Lune felt lips press against hers, and the cool radiance flooded her body; then they were gone.

*"Bear thou this kiss to him thou lovest,"* the angel Anael said,

its words the true and pure form of the language Dee had spoken, a force of beauty almost too much to bear.

Then the light receded. She was in her chair; the crystal was before her; they were alone once more in the room.

Dee murmured a closing benediction, and sank back into his own chair, from which he had risen without her seeing. The notebook sat next to him, hardly touched.

Lune's eyes met the philosopher's, and saw her own shock echoed there.

He, who had no gift for seeing, had seen something. And he knew, as she did, that it was a true angelic presence, and it had answered her plea.

*Bear thou this kiss to him thou lovest.*

She had made that choice. What it meant, she did not know; she had never given her heart before. How a kiss would aid her, she could not imagine. It seemed a weak weapon against Invidiana.

But it was Heaven's response to her plea. For Michael Deven's sake, she would go into the Onyx Hall, and somehow win her way through to him. She would bring him Anael's kiss.

What happened after that was in God's hands.

THE ANGEL INN, ISLINGTON: *May 8, 1590*

"She must be distracted," Lune said. "Else she will place all her knights and guardsmen and other resources between me and Deven, and I will stand no hope of reaching him. They will kill me, or they will bind me and drag me before her; either way, I will not be able to do what I must."

The Goodemeades did not question that part of it. Lune had told them in brief terms of what had passed in Mortlake — brief not because she wished to hide anything from them, but because she had few words to describe it. Their eyes had gone round with awe, and they treated her now with a reverent and slightly fearful respect that unnerved her.

Not so much respect, though, that they didn't question certain things. "My lady," Gertrude said, "she will be expecting you to do exactly that. You have not come back, which means you know of your peril. If you are not simply to walk into her claws, then you must try to draw her attention away. But she will recognize any diversion as just that—and ignore it."

From across the rose-guarded room, Rosamund, who had been silent for several minutes, spoke up. "Unless the diversion is something she cannot ignore."

"The only thing she could not ignore would be—"

"A real threat," Lune said.

Something Invidiana truly did have to fear. A war on her very doorstep, that she must send her soldiers to meet, or risk losing her throne.

The list of things that fit that name was short indeed.

Gertrude's face had gone white, and she stared at her sister. Grimness sat like a stranger on Rosamund's countenance, but if a brownie could look militant, she did. "We could do it," she said. "But, my lady, once such a force is unleashed, it cannot be easily stopped. We all might lose a great deal in the end."

Lune knew it very well. "Could anything stop them?"

"If she were to draw the sword out again—perhaps. That, more than anything, is what angers them. They might be satisfied, if she renounced it."

"But Invidiana would never do it," Gertrude said. "Only Suspiria, and perhaps not even her." She stared up at Lune, her eyes trembling with tears. "Will we have her back, when you are done?"

The unspoken question: *Or do you go to kill her?*

Lune wished she could answer the brownie's question, but she was as blind as they. The angel's power waited within, alien and light, but she did not know what it would do. Could a faerie spirit be damned to Hell?

Her reply came out a whisper. "I can make no promises."

Rosamund said heavily, "With that, we must be content. We have no other choice."

"You must move with haste." The knot of tension in Lune's stomach never loosened, except for a few timeless moments, in the angel's presence. "Use Vidar."

"Vidar?"

"Corr was his agent, or at least an ally. He bade me be silent about any others I might find at court. I do not know his scheme, but there must be one; we can make use of it." Her vow did not prevent her from telling the Goodemeades; the last person in creation they would share the information with was Invidiana. But she had never expected to use such a loophole.

Rosamund came forward, smoothing her apron with careful hands, and put an arm around her white-faced sister. "Make your preparations, my lady. Gertrude and I will raise the Wild Hunt."

THE ONYX HALL, LONDON: *May 9, 1590*

The sun's heat baked his shoulders and uncovered head. His ride had been a long one, and he was tired; he swung his leg over the saddle and dropped to the ground, handing off his reins to a servant. They were gathered by the riverbank, an elegant, laughing crowd, playing music, reciting poetry, wagering at cards. He longed to join them, but ah! He was so thirsty.

A smiling, flirtatious lady approached him, a cup of wine in each hand. "My lord. Will you drink?"

The chased silver was cool in his fingers. He looked down into the rich depths of the wine, smelling its delicate bouquet. It would taste good, after that long ride.

With the cup halfway to his lips, he paused. Something...

"My lord." The lady rested one hand gently on his arm, standing closely enough that her breasts just touched his elbow. "Do you not like the wine?"

"No," he murmured, staring at the cup. "That is..."

"Drink," she invited him. "And then come with me."

He was so thirsty. The sun was hot, and the wine had been cooled in the stream. He had not eaten recently; it would go to his head. But surely that did not matter — not in this gay, careless crowd. They were watching him, waiting for him to join them.

He brought the cup to his lips and drank.

The liquid slid down his throat and into his belly, chilling him, making all his nerves sing. No wine he had ever drunk tasted thus. He gulped at it, greedy and insatiable; the more he drank, the more he wanted, until he was tipping the cup back and draining out the last drops, and shaking because there was no more —

There was no sunlight. There was no meadow by the stream. There were courtiers, but the faces that watched were wild and inhuman, and all around him was darkness.

The lush faerie lady stepped back from him, her face avid with delight, and from some distance away Invidiana gave sardonic applause. "Well done, Lady Carline. Achilles, you need not restore his gag." The Queen smiled across the chamber at Deven, letting all her predatory pleasure show. "He will speak no names against us now."

The cup fell from Deven's hand and clanked against the stone, empty to the dregs. Faerie wine. He had refused all food, all drink, knowing the danger, but in the end his body had betrayed him, its mortal needs and drives making it an easy target for a charm.

Even if Lune came for him now, it was too late.

He reached for the names that had been his defense, and found nothing. A mist clouded his mind, obscuring the face of . . . what? There had been something, he knew it; he had gone to church, and prayed. . . .

But the prayers were gone. Those powers were no longer within his reach.

Laughter pursued him as he stumbled away, seeking refuge in a corner of the chamber. Now, at last, the stoicism he had clung to since his capture failed him. He wanted more; his body ached with the desire to beg. Another cup — a sip, even —

He clenched his hands until his knuckles creaked, and waited, trembling, for the next move.

LONDON: *May 9, 1590*

The moon rose as the sun set, its silver disc climbing steadily into the sky.

The curfew bells had rung. London was abed — or ought to be; those who were out late, the drunken gentlemen and the scoundrels who waited to prey on them, deserved, some would say, whatever happened to them.

On the northern horizon, without warning, storm clouds began to build.

They moved from north to south, against the wind, as clouds should not have done. In their depths, a thunder like the pounding of hoofbeats against the earth, up where no earth was. A terrible yelping came from the clouds, that more skeptical minds would dismiss as wild geese. Those who knew its true source, hid.

Brief flashes of lightning revealed what lay within the clouds.

The hounds ran alongside, leaping, darting, weaving in and out of the pack. Black hounds with red eyes; white hounds with red ears; all of them giving that terrible, belling cry, unlike any dog that ever mortal bred.

Horses, shod with silver and gold, flaring with spectral light. Formed from mist, from straw, from fae who chose to run in such shape, their headlong gallop brought them on with frightening speed. And astride their backs rode figures both awful and beautiful.

Stags' horns spiked the sky like a great, spreading crown. Feathered wings cupped the air, pinions whistling in the storm wind. Their hair was yellow as gold, red as blood, black as night; their eyes burned with fury, and in their hands were swords and spears out of legend.

The forgotten kings of faerie England rode to war.

It went by many names. Wisht Hounds, Yeth Hounds, Gabriel Rachets, Dando and His Dogs. A dozen faces and a dozen names for the Wild Hunt, united now in a single purpose.

They would not involve mortals in their war, and for decades their enemy had lain safe behind that shield. But something else was vulnerable, could not be hidden entirely away; to do so would negate its very purpose, and break the enchantment it held in trust. And so it stood in the open, unprotected, on Candlewick Street.

The Wild Hunt rode to destroy the London Stone.

St. Paul's Cathedral, London: *May 9, 1590*

The wind was already stirring, fleeing before the oncoming storm, when Lune reached the western porch of St. Paul's Cathedral.

"The entrances will be watched, my lady," Gertrude had said, when word came that the irrevocable move was made, the Wild Hunt was alerted to the secret of the London Stone, and the battle would take place under the full moon. "But there's one she cannot guard against you."

St. Paul's and the White Tower. The two original entrances to the Onyx Hall, created in the light of the eclipse. The latter lay within the confines of a royal fortress, and would have its own protection below.

But the former lay on Christian ground. No faerie guard could stay there long, however fortified with mortal bread he might be. None had passed through it since Invidiana had confined Francis Merriman to the chambers below.

The only question was whether it would open for Lune.

She passed the booksellers' stalls, closed up for the night. The wind sent refuse rattling against their walls. A snarl split the air, and she halted in her tracks. Light flashed across the city, and then from the sky above, a roar.

She glimpsed them briefly, past the cathedral's spire. Dame Halgresta Nellt, towering to a height she could never reach in the Onyx Hall. Sir Kentigern, at his sister's right hand, howling a challenge at the oncoming storm. Sir Prigurd, at the left, his blunt features composed in an expression of dutiful resolution. She had always liked Prigurd the best. He was not as brutal as his siblings, and he was that rarity in the Onyx Hall: a courtier who served out of loyalty, however misplaced.

They stood at the head of the Onyx Guard, whose elf knights blazed in martial glory. Their armor gleamed silver and black and emerald, and their horses danced beneath them, tatterfoals and brags and grants eager to leap into battle. Behind stood the massed ranks of the infantry, boggarts and barguests, hobyahs and gnomes, all the goblins and pucks and even homely little hobs who could be mustered to fight in defense of their home.

The Onyx Hall. It *was* their home. A dark one, and twisted by its malevolent Queen, but home nonetheless.

Before the night was done, the Wild Hunt might reduce it to rubble.

But if Lune let herself question that price, she would be lost before she ever started.

The great doors of the western porch swung open at her approach. Stepping within, she felt holiness pressing against her skin, weirdly close and yet distant; the waiting tension of the angel's kiss thrummed within her. Like a sign shown to sentries, it allowed her passage.

She did not know what she sought, but the angel's power resonated with it, like a string coming into tune. *There.* A patch of floor like any other in the nave; when she stepped on it, the shock ran up her bones.

Here, faerie magic erupted upward. Here, holy rites saturated the ground. Here, London opened downward, into its dark reflection.

Lune knelt and laid one hand against the stone of the floor. The charm that governed the entrance spoke to her fingers. Francis had prayed, the words of God bringing him from one world to the other without any eyes seeing him. For her, the angelic touch sufficed.

Had any observer been there to watch, the floor would have

remained unchanged. But to Lune's eyes, the slabs of stone folded away, revealing a staircase that led downward.

She had no time to waste. Gathering her courage, Lune hurried below—and prayed the threat of the Hunt had done its job.

THE ONYX HALL, LONDON: *May 9, 1590*

The marble walls resonated with the thunder above, trembling, but holding strong.

Seated upon her throne, Invidiana might have been a statue. Her face betrayed no tension—had been nothing but a frozen mask since a hideous female giant brought word that the Wild Hunt rode against London.

Whatever he might say against her, Deven had to grant Invidiana this: she was indeed a Queen. She gave orders crisply, sending her minions running, and in less time than he would have believed possible, the defense of the Onyx Hall was mustered.

The presence chamber was all but empty. Those who had not gone to the battle had departed, hiding in their chambers, or fleeing entirely, in the hope of finding some safety.

Most, but not all. Invidiana, motionless upon her throne, was flanked by two elf knights, black-haired twin brothers. They stood with swords unsheathed, prepared to defend her with their lives. A human woman with a wasted, sunken face and dead eyes crouched at the foot of the dais.

And Achilles stood near Deven, clad only in sandals and a loincloth, his body tense with desire to join in the slaughter.

The thunder grew stronger, until the entire chamber shook. A crashing sound: some of the filigree had detached from between the arches, and plummeted to the floor. Deven glanced up, then rolled out of the way just in time to save himself as an entire pane of crystal shattered upon the stones.

Achilles laughed at him, fingers caressing the hilt of the archaic Greek sword he wore.

Where was Lune, in it all? Up in the sky, riding with the Hunt to save him? Battling at some entrance against guards that would keep her from the Onyx Hall?

Would she bring the miracle he needed?

He hoped so. But a miracle would not be enough; when she arrived, Achilles and the two elf knights would destroy her.

His sword was gone, broken in the battle against Achilles; he had not even a knife with which to defend himself. And he had no chance of simply snatching a weapon from the mortal or the knights. While he struggled with one, the others would get him from behind.

His eye fell upon the debris that now littered the floor, and a thought came to him.

They said Suspiria had called her lover Tiresias, for his gift. She had clearly continued the practice, naming Achilles for the great warrior of Greek legend.

Deven glanced upward. More elements of the structure were creaking, cracking; he dove suddenly to one side, as if fearing another would fall on him. The movement brought him closer to Achilles, and when he rose to a kneeling position, a piece of crystal was cold in his palm, its razor edges drawing blood.

He lashed out, and slashed the crystal across the backs of Achilles's vulnerable heels.

The man screamed and collapsed to the floor. Downed, but not dead, and Deven could take no chances. He seized a fragment of silver filigree and slammed it down onto his enemy's

*Marie Brennan*

head, smashing his face to bloody ruin and sending the muscled body limp.

He got the man's sword into his hand just in time to meet the rush of the knights.

The palace groaned and shook under the assault of the battle above. How long would the Nellt siblings and their army hold off the Wild Hunt?

She ran flat out for the presence chamber. The rooms and galleries were deserted; everyone had gone to fight, or fled. Everywhere was debris, decorations knocked to the floor by the rattling blasts. And then the doors of the presence chamber were before her, closed tight, but without their usual guard. She should pause, listen at the crack, try to discover who was inside, but she could not stop; she lacked both the time and the courage.

Lune hit the doors and flung herself into the room beyond.

A wiry arm locked around her throat the instant she came through, and someone dragged her backward. Lune clawed behind herself, arms flailing. Fingers caught in matted hair. *Eurydice. Sun and Moon, she knows....*

Achilles lay in a pool of his own blood along one wall. Sir Cunobel of the Onyx Guard groaned on the floor not far away, struggling and failing to rise. But his twin Cerenel was still on his feet, and at the point of his sword, pinned with his back to a column, Michael Deven.

"So," Invidiana said, from the distant height of her throne. "You have betrayed me most thoroughly, it seems. And all for *this*?"

Deven was bruised and battered, his right hand bleeding; great tears showed in his doublet, where his opponents had nearly skewered him. His eyes met hers. They were not so very far apart. If only she could get to him, just for an instant—

352

One kiss. But was it worth them both dying, to deliver it? What would happen, once their lips met?

Lune forced herself to look at Invidiana. "You mean to execute us both."

The Queen's beauty was all the more terrible, now that Lune knew from whence it came. Invidiana smiled, exulting. "Both? Perhaps, and perhaps not...he has drunk of faerie wine, you see. Already he is becoming ours. Once they take the first step, 'tis so easy to draw them in further. And you have deprived me of two of my pets. It seems only fitting that one, at least, should be replaced."

She saw the signs of it now, in the glittering of his eyes, the hectic flush of his cheeks against his pale skin. How much had he drunk? How far had he fallen into Faerie's thrall?

Some. But not, perhaps, enough.

Lune faced the Queen again. "He is stubborn. 'Tis a testament to your power that he drank even one sip. But a man with strong enough will can cast that off; he may refuse more. I know this man, and I tell you now: you will lose him. He will starve before he takes more from your hand, or from any of your courtiers."

Invidiana's lip curled. "Tell me now what you think to offer, traitor, before I lose patience with you."

Eurydice's bony arm threatened to choke her. Lune rasped out, "Promise me that you will keep him alive, and I will convince him to accept more food."

"I make no *promises*," Invidiana spat, her rage suddenly breaking through. "You are not here to bargain, traitor. I need do nothing you ask of me."

"I understand that." Lune let her weight drop; Eurydice was not strong enough to keep her upright, and so she sagged to her knees on the floor, the mortal now clinging to her back.

Bowing her head against the restricting arm around her throat, Lune said, "With nothing left to lose, I can only beg, and offer my assistance — in hopes of buying this small mercy for him."

Invidiana considered this for several nerve-racking moments. "Why would you wish for that?"

Lune closed her eyes. "Because I love him, and would not see him die."

Soft, contemptuous laughter. Invidiana must have guessed it, but the admission amused her. "And why would he accept from you what he would not take from us?"

Her fingernails carved crescents into her palms. "Because I placed a charm on him, when I went to the mortal court, that made his heart mine. He will do anything I ask of him."

The battle still shook the walls of the presence chamber. Most of what could fall, had fallen; the next thing to go would be the Hall itself.

Eurydice's arm vanished from her throat.

"Prove your words true," Invidiana said. "Show me this mortal is your puppet. Damn him with your love. And perhaps I will hear your plea."

Lune pressed one trembling hand to the cold floor, pushed herself to her feet. She found Eurydice offering her a dented cup half-filled with wine. She took it, made a deep curtsy to the Queen, and only then turned to face Michael.

His blue eyes stared at her unreadably. There was no way to tell him what she intended, no way to tell him her words were a lie, that she had placed no charm upon him, that she would see him dead before she left him to be tormented by Invidiana, as Francis had been. All that would have to come later — if there was a later.

All that mattered now was to get close to him, for just one heartbeat.

Sir Cerenel sidestepped as she approached, but kept his blade at Deven's throat, and now a dagger flickered out, its point trained on her. Lune drew close, raised the cup, and leaned in just a fraction closer, so she could smile into his eyes, as if drawing upon a charm. "Drink for me, Master Deven."

His hand dashed the cup to the floor, and the instant it was gone from between them, she threw herself forward and kissed him.

As their lips met — as Lune kissed him as herself for the first time, with no masks between them — a voice rang out in the Onyx Hall, high and pure, speaking the language that lay beyond language.

*"Be now freed all those whose love hath led them into chains."*

Fire burned again on Deven's brow, six points in a ring, and he cried out against Lune's mouth, thinking himself about to die.

But it was a clean fire, a white heat that burned away whatever Invidiana had left there, and it caused him no pain; when it ended, he knew himself to be free.

Nor was he the only one.

The elf knight staggered away, dropping his weapons, hands outstretched, as if the power of that angelic presence had blinded him. The mortal woman collapsed on the floor, mouth open in a silent scream.

And in the center of the chamber, in the very place Deven had stood to pray, he saw a slender, dark-haired man with sapphire eyes.

Francis Merriman stood loose and straight, his shoulders unbowed, his chin high, his eyes clear. Deven could see a shadow falling away from him, the last remnant of Tiresias, the maddened reflection that wandered lost in these halls for so many years. But it was a shadow only: death had freed him from the grip of dreams, and restored the man Suspiria once loved.

And Invidiana's icy calm shattered beneath his gaze.

"Control him!" she screamed at the woman on the floor, her fingers clutching the arms of her throne. "I did not summon him—"

"Yet I am come," Francis Merriman said. His voice was a light tenor, clear and distinct. "I have never left your side, Suspiria. You thought you bound me, first with your jewel, then by Margaret's arts—" The mortal woman gasped at the name. "But the first and truest chains that bound me were ones I forged myself. They are my prison, and my shield. They protected me against you after my death, so that I told you nothing I did not wish you to know. And they bring me to you now."

"Then I will banish you," Invidiana spat. Rage distorted the melody of her voice. "You are a ghost, and nothing more. What Hell waits for your unshriven soul?"

She should not have mentioned Hell. Francis's face darkened with sorrow. "You need not have made that pact, Suspiria. Nor need you have hidden from me. Did you think me, with my gift, blind to what you were? What you suffered? I stayed with you, knowing, and would have continued so."

"Stayed with me? With what? A shriveling, rotting husk—you speak of prisons, and you know nothing of them. To be trapped in one's own flesh, every day bringing you closer to worms—a fitting fate for you, perhaps, but not for me. I did what he demanded, and yet to no avail. Why should I go on trying? I would endure his punishment *no more.*"

Then her voice dropped from its heightened pitch, growing cold again. "Nor will I endure you."

She raised her long-fingered hands, like two white spiders in the gloom. Deven's entire body tensed. A darkness hovered at the edge of his vision, deeper than the shadows of the Onyx Hall, and more foul. A corruption to match the purity that had touched him with Lune's kiss. It but waited for someone to invite it in.

Francis stopped her. He came forward with measured strides, approaching the throne, and despite herself Invidiana shrank back, hands faltering. "You did not give them your soul. You were never such a fool. No, you sold something else, did you not?" His voice was full of sorrow. "I saw it, that day in the garden. A heart, traded for what you had lost."

Her mouth twisted in fury: an open admission of guilt.

The man who had been her lover watched her with grieving eyes. "You bartered away your heart. All the warmth and kindness you could feel. All the love. Hell gained the evil you would wreak, and you gained a mask of ageless, immortal beauty.

"But I knew you without that mask, Suspiria. And I know what you have forgotten."

He mounted the steps of the dais. Invidiana seemed paralyzed, her black eyes fixed unblinking upon him.

"You gave your heart years before you sold it to the devil," Francis said. "You gave it to me. And so I return it to you."

The ghost of her love bent and kissed her, as Lune had kissed Deven moments before.

A scream echoed through the Onyx Hall, a sound of pure despair. The flawless, aching beauty of Invidiana shriveled and decayed, folding in upon itself; the woman herself shrank, losing her imposing height, until what sat upon the throne seemed like a girl, not yet at her full growth, sitting upon a chair too large for her. But no girl would ever have looked so old.

Deven flinched in revulsion from the ancient, haggard thing Invidiana had become.

As the pact with Hell snapped, as the Queen of the Onyx Court dwindled, so, too, did the ghost of Francis Merriman fade. He grew fainter and fainter, and his last words whispered through the chamber.

*"I will wait for you, Suspiria. I will never leave you."*

The last wisp of him disappeared from view.

*"Please — do not leave me."*

Deven and Lune were left, the only two still standing, before the throne of the Onyx Hall.

A sound pierced the air, faint but passionate: part snarl, part shriek. The creature before them should not have been able to move, but she shifted forward, rising to her feet, and she had not lost the force of her presence; hatred beat outward like heat from a forge. Her voice was a shredded remnant of itself, grinding out the accusation. *"You brought this upon me!"*

Lune opened her mouth, her eyes full of urgency. But Deven stepped forward, interposing himself between his lady and the maddened shell of the Queen. He recognized what he saw in her eyes. Fury, yes, but fury to cover what lay beneath: a bottomless well of pain. She had her heart again; with it must have come all the emotions she had lost. Including remorse, for what she had done to the man she loved.

He had to say it now, before it was too late; the chance would not come again.

"Suspiria." It was important he use that name. The pieces had fallen together in the depths of his mind; he spoke from instinct. "Suspiria — *I know why you are still cursed.*"

The withered hag twitched at his words.

"You had so much of it right," he said. Lune came forward a step, moving to stand at his side. "You atoned for your error. The Onyx Hall was a creation worthy of legend — a place for fae to live among mortals in safety, a place where the two could come together. You had so much of it right. But you did not *understand.*

358

"The chieftain's son loved you. But you disdained mortality, did you not? You could not bear to join yourself to it. And so you cast him aside, cast his love aside, as a thing without value, for what can it be worth, when it dies so soon? But the ages you endured after that must have taught you something, as they were intended to do; else you would not have made this great hall. And you would not have loved Francis Merriman."

He could feel the presence still. The ghost was gone, but Francis was not. The man had said it himself. He would never leave her. The love he felt joined them still.

And he had restored *her* ability to love.

"You did everything right," Deven said. "Your mistake came when you did not trust it. Faced with a future alongside the man you loved—suffering a sort of mortality, yes, aging while you watched him stay eternally young—you let your fear, your disdain, triumph again. You cast aside his love, and the love you felt for him. You failed to understand its worth."

A heart, traded for what she had lost. Youth. Beauty. Immortality. The answer had been in her hands, had she but accepted it.

*Do not leave me,* Francis had said.

"You face that decision again," Deven whispered. "Your true love waits for you. Honor that love as it deserves. Do not cast it aside a third time." This world operated by certain rules he did not have to explain to her or Lune. What was done a third time, was done forever.

For the first time since she bargained with Invidiana, Lune spoke. "Once we love, we cannot revoke it," she said. "We can only glory in what it brings—pain as well as joy, grief as well as hope. He is as much a fae creature now as a mortal. Where you will go, I do not know. But you can go with him."

Suspiria lifted her wasted face, lowering the clawlike hands that had risen to hide it. Only after a moment did Deven realize she was crying, the tears running down the deep gullies of her wrinkles, almost hidden from sight.

Invidiana had been evil. Suspiria was not. His heart gave a sharp ache, and a moment later, he felt Lune's hand slip into his own.

The change happened too subtly to watch. Without him ever seeing how, the wrinkles grew shallower, the liver spots began to fade. As age had shriveled her a moment ago, now it acted in reverse, all the years lifting away, revealing the face of the woman Francis had loved.

She had the pale skin, the inky hair, the black eyes and red lips. But what had been unnerving in its perfection was now mere faerie beauty: a step sideways from mortality, enough to take the breath away, but bearable. And *right*.

A last, a crystalline tear hovered at the edge of her lashes, then fell.

"Thank you," Suspiria whispered.

Then, like Francis Merriman, she faded from view, and when the throne was empty Deven knew they were both gone forever.

For a moment they stood silently in the presence chamber, with the corpse of Achilles, the huddled forms of Eurydice and the two elf knights, while Lune absorbed what she had just seen and done.

Then a pillar cracked and split in two, and Lune realized the thunder had not stopped. It had drawn nearer.

And Suspiria was gone.

Deven saw the sudden panic in her face. "What is it?"

"The Hunt," she said, unnecessarily. "I was to ask Suspiria— the Stone—they think the kings might relent, if she relinquished her sovereignty—but what will happen, now that she is gone?"

He took off before she even finished speaking, flying the

length of the presence chamber at a dead run, heading directly for the throne. No, not directly; he went to one side of it, and laid hold of the edge of the great silver arch. "Help me!"

"With *what*?" She came forward regardless. "The throne does not matter; we have to find the London Stone—"

"'Tis here!" Tendons ridged the backs of his hands as he dragged ineffectually at the throne. "A hidden chamber—I saw it before—"

Lune stood frozen for only a moment; then she threw herself forward and began to pull at the other side of the seat.

It moved reluctantly, protecting its treasure. "Help us!" Lune snapped, and whether out of reflexive obedience or a simple desire not to die at the hands of the Hunt, first Sir Cerenel and then Eurydice picked themselves up and came to lend their aid. Together the four of them forced it away from the wall, until there was a gap just wide enough for Lune and Deven to slip through.

The chamber beyond was no more than an alcove, scarcely large enough for the two of them and the stone that projected from the ceiling. A sword was buried halfway to the hilt in the pitted surface of the limestone, its grip just where an extremely tall woman's hand might reach.

Lune did not know what effect the sword had, now that one half of its pact had passed out of the world, but if they could take it to the Hunt, as proof of Invidiana's downfall ... a slim hope, but she could not think of anything else to try.

Her own fingers came well short of the hilt. She looked at Deven, and he shook his head; Invidiana had been even taller than he, and he looked reluctant to touch a faerie sword regardless.

"Lift me," Lune said. Deven wrapped his bloodstained hands about her waist, gathered his strength, and sent her into the air, as high as he could.

Her hand closed around the hilt, but the sword did not pull free.

Instead, it pulled her upward, with Deven at her side.

CANDLEWICK STREET, LONDON: *May 9, 1590*

She understood the truth, as they passed with a stomach-twisting surge from the alcove to the street above. The London Stone, half-buried, did not extend downward into the Onyx Hall. The Stone below was simply a reflection of the Stone above, the central axis of the entire edifice Suspiria and Francis had constructed. In that brief, wrenching instant, she felt herself not only to be at the London Stone, but at St. Paul's and the Tower, at the city wall and the bank of the Thames.

Then she stood on Candlewick Street, with Deven at her side, the sword still in her hand.

All around them was war. Some still fought in the sky; others had dragged the battle down into the streets, so that the clash of weapons came from Bush Lane and St. Mary Botolph and St. Swithins, converging on where they stood. Hounds yelped, a sound that made her skin crawl, and someone was winding a horn, its call echoing over the city rooftops. But she had eyes only for a set of figures mounted on horseback that stood scant paces from the two of them.

She thrust the sword skyward and screamed, *"Enough!"*

And her voice, which should not have begun to cut through the roar of battle, rang out louder than the horn, and brought near-instant silence.

They stared at her, from all around where the fighting had raged. She did not see Sir Kentigern, but Prigurd stood astraddle the unmoving body of their sister, a bloody two-handed blade in his grip. Vidar was missing, too. Which side did he fight on? Or had he fled?

It was a question to answer later. In the sudden hush, she lowered the tip of the sword until it pointed at the riders — the ancient kings of Faerie England.

"You have brought war to my city," Lune said in a forbidding voice, a muted echo of the command that had halted the fighting. "You *will* take it away again."

Their faces and forms were dimly familiar, half-remembered shades from scarcely forty years before. Had one of them once been her own king? Perhaps the one who moved forward now, a stag-horned man with eyes as cruel as the wild. "Who are you, to thus command us?"

"I am the Queen of the Onyx Court," Lune said.

The words came by unthinking reflex. At her side, Deven stiffened. The sword would have trembled in her grasp, but she dared not show her own surprise.

The elfin king scowled. "That title is a usurped one. We will reclaim what is ours, and let no pretender stand in our way."

Hands tensed on spears; the fighting might resume at any moment.

"I am the Queen of the Onyx Court," Lune repeated. Then she went on, following the same instinct that had made her declare it. "But not the Queen of faerie England."

The stag-horned rider's scowl deepened. "Explain yourself."

"Invidiana is gone. The pact by which she deprived you of your sovereignty is broken. I have drawn her sword from the London Stone; therefore the sovereignty of this city is mine. To you are restored those crowns she stole years ago."

A redheaded king spoke up, less hostile than his companion. "But London remains yours."

Lune relaxed her blade, letting the point dip to the ground, and met his gaze as an equal. "A place disregarded until the Hall was created, for fae live in glens and hollow hills, far from mortal eyes—except here, in the Onyx Hall. 'Twas never any kingdom of yours. Invidiana had no claim to England, but here, in this place, she created a realm for herself, and now 'tis mine by right."

She had not planned it. Her only thought had been to bear the sword to these kings, as proof of Invidiana's downfall, and hope she could sue for peace. But she felt the city beneath her feet, as she never had before. London was *hers*. And kings though they might be, they had no right to challenge her here.

She softened her voice, though not its authority. "Each side has dead to mourn tonight. But we shall meet in peace anon, all the kings and queens of faerie England, and when our treaty is struck, you will be welcome within my realm."

The red-haired king was the first to go. He wheeled his horse, its front hooves striking the air, and gave a loud cry; here and there, bands of warriors followed his lead, vaulting skyward once more and vanishing from sight. One by one, the other kings followed, each taking with them some portion of the Wild Hunt, until the only fae who remained in the streets were Lune's subjects.

One by one, they knelt to her.

Looking out at them, she saw too many motionless bodies. Some might yet be saved, but not all. They had paid a bloody price for her crown, and they did not even know why.

This would not be simple. Sir Kentigern and Dame Halgresta, if they lived—Lady Nianna—Vidar, if she could find him. And countless others who were used to clawing and biting their way to the top, and fearing the Queen who stood above them.

Changing that would be slow. But it could begin tonight.

To her newfound subjects, Lune said, "Return to the Onyx Hall. We will speak in the night garden, and I will explain all that has passed here."

They disappeared into the shadows, leaving Lune and Deven alone in Candlewick Street, with the sky rapidly clearing above them.

Deven let out his breath slowly, finally realizing they might—at last—be safe. He ached all over, and he was light-headed from lack of food, but the euphoria that followed a battle was beginning to settle in. He found himself grinning wryly at Lune, wondering where to start with the things they needed to say. She was a *queen* now. He hardly knew what to think of that.

She began to return his smile—and then froze.

He heard it, too. A distant sound—somewhere in Cripple-gate, he thought. A solitary bell, tolling.

Midnight had come. Soon all the bells in the city would be ringing, from the smallest parish tower to St. Paul's Cathedral itself. And Lune stood out in the open, unprotected; the angel's power had gone from her. The sound would hurt her.

But it would destroy something else.

He had felt it as they passed through the London Stone. St. Paul's Cathedral, one of the two original entrances to the Onyx Hall. The pit still gaped in the nave, a direct conduit from the mortal world to the fae, open and unprotected.

In twelve strokes of the great bell, every enchantment that bound the Onyx Hall into being would come undone, shredded by the holy sound.

"Give me your hand." Deven seized it before she could even move, taking her left hand in his left, dragging her two steps sideways to the London Stone.

"We will not be safe within," Lune cried. Her body shook like a leaf in the wind, as more bells began to ring.

Deven slapped his right hand onto the rough limestone surface. "We are not going within."

It was the axis of London and its dark reflection, the linchpin that held the two together. Suspiria had not made the palace alone, because she *could* not; such a thing could only be crafted by hands both mortal and fae. Deven would have staked his life that Francis Merriman was a true Londoner, born within hearing of the city bells.

As Deven himself was.

With his hand upon the city's heart, Deven reached out blindly, calling on forces laid there by another pair before them. He had drunk of faerie wine. Lune had borne an angel's power. They had each been changed; they were each a little of both worlds, and the Onyx Hall answered to them.

The Thames. The wall. The Tower. The cathedral.

As the first stroke of the great bell rang out across the city, he felt the sound wash over and through him. Like a seawall protecting a harbor in a storm, he took the brunt of that force, and bid the entrance close.

A fourth stroke; an eighth; a twelfth. The last echoes of the bell of St. Paul's faded, and trailing out after it, the other bells of London. Deven waited until the city was utterly silent before he lifted his hand from the Stone.

He looked up slowly, carefully, half-terrified that he was wrong, that he had saved the Hall but left Lune vulnerable, and now she would shatter into nothingness.

Lune's silver eyes smiled into his, and she used their clasped hands to draw him toward her, so she might lay a kiss on his lips. "I will make you the first of my knights—if you will have me as your lady."

The man walked down a long, colonnaded gallery, listening to his boot heels click on the stone, trailing his fingers in wonder across the pillars as he passed them by. It was impossible that this should all be here, that it should have come into being in the course of mere minutes, and yet he had seen it with his own eyes. Indeed, it was partly his doing.

The thought still dizzied him.

The place was enormous, far larger than he had expected, and so far almost entirely deserted. The sisters had chosen to stay in their own home, though they visited from time to time. Others would come, they assured him, once word spread farther, once folk believed.

Until then, it was just him, and the woman he sought.

He found her in the garden. They called it so, even though it was barely begun: a few brave clusters of flowers—a gift from the sisters—grouped around a bench that sat on the bank of the Walbrook. She was not seated on the bench, but on the ground, trailing her fingers in the water, a distant expression on her face. The air in the garden was pleasantly cool, a gentle contrast to the winter-locked world outside.

She did not move as he seated himself on the ground next to her. "I have brought seeds," he said. "I have no gift for planting, but I am sure we can convince Gertrude—since they are not roses." She did not respond, and his expression softened. He reached for her nearer hand and took it in his own. "Suspiria, look at me."

Her eyes glimmered with the tears she was too proud to shed. "It has accomplished nothing," she said, her low, melodic voice trembling.

"Did you hear that sound, half an hour ago?"

"What sound?"

He smiled at her. "Precisely. All the church bells of the city rang, and you did not hear a thing. This is a haven the likes of which has *never* existed, not even in legend. In time many fae will come, all of them dwelling in perfect safety beneath a mortal city, and you say it has accomplished nothing?"

She pulled her hand from his and looked away again. "It has not lifted the curse."

Of course. Francis had known Suspiria far longer than his appearance would suggest; he had not dwelt among mortals for many a year now. This hall had been an undertaking in its own right, a challenge that fascinated them both, and they had many grand dreams of what could be done with it, now that it was built. But it was born for another purpose, one never far from Suspiria's mind.

In that respect, it had failed.

He shifted closer and put gentle pressure on her shoulder, until she yielded and lay down, her head in his lap. With careful fingers he brushed her hair back, wondering if he should tell her what he knew: that the face he saw was an illusion, crafted to hide the age and degeneration beneath. The truth did not repel him—but he feared it would repel her, to know that he knew.

So he kept silent as always, and closed his eyes, losing himself in the silky touch of her hair, the quiet rippling of the Walbrook.

The gentle sound lifted him free of the confines of his mind, floating him into that space where time's grip slackened and fell away. And in that space, an image formed.

Suspiria felt his body change. She sat up, escaping his suddenly stilled arms, and took his face in her delicate hands. "A vision?"

He nodded, not yet capable of speech.

The wistful, loving smile he knew so well softened her face.

He had not seen it often of late. "My Tiresias," she said, stroking his cheekbone with one finger. "What did you see?"

"A heart," he whispered.

"Whose heart?"

Francis shook his head. Too often it was thus, that he saw without understanding. "The heart was exchanged for an apple of incorruptible gold. I do not know what it means."

"Nor I," Suspiria admitted. "But this is not the first time such meaning has eluded us—nor, I think, will it be the last."

He managed a smile again. "A poor seer I am. Perhaps I have been too long among your kind, and can no longer tell the difference between true visions and my own fancy."

She laughed, which he counted a victory. "Such games we could play with that; most fae would believe even the strangest things to be honest prophecy. We could go to Herne's court and spread great confusion there."

If it would lighten her heart, he would have gladly done it, and risked the great stag-horned king's wrath. But sound distracted him, something more than the gentle noise of the brook. Someone was coming, along the passage that led to the garden.

Suspiria heard it, too, and they rose in time to see the plump figure of Rosamund Goodemeade appear in an archway. Nor was she alone: behind her stood a fae he did not recognize, travel-stained and weary, with a great pack upon his back.

Francis took Suspiria's hand, and she raised her eyebrows at him. "It seems another has come to join us. Come, let us welcome him together."

WINDSOR GREAT PARK, BERKSHIRE: *June 11, 1590*

The oak tree might have stood there from the beginning of time, so ancient and huge had it grown, and its spreading branches extended like mighty sheltering arms, casting emerald shadows on the ground below.

Beneath this canopy stood more than two score people, the greatest gathering of faerie royalty England had ever seen. From Cumberland and Northumberland to Cornwall and Kent they came, and all the lands in between: kings and queens, lords and ladies, a breathtaking array of great and noble persons, with their attendants watching from a distance.

They met here because it was neutral ground, safely removed from the territory in dispute and the faerie palace many still thought of as an unnatural creation, an emblem of the Queen they despised. Under the watchful aegis of the oak, the ancient tree of kings, they gathered to discuss the matter—and, ultimately, to recognize the sovereignty of a new Queen.

It was a formality, Lune knew. They acknowledged her right to London the moment they obeyed her command to leave. Her fingers stroked the hilt of the sword as one of the kings rolled out a sonorous, intricate speech about the traditional rights of a faerie monarch. She did not want to inherit Invidiana's throne. It carried with it too many dark memories; the stones of the Onyx Hall would never be free of blood.

But that choice, like others, could not be unmade.

The orations had gone on for quite some time. Lune suspected her fellow monarchs were luxuriating in the restoration of their dignity and authority. But in time she grew impatient; she was glad when her own opportunity came.

She stood and faced the circle of sovereigns, the London Sword sheathed in her hands. The gown she wore, midnight-blue silk resplendent with moonlight and diamonds, felt oddly conspicuous; she still remembered her time out of favor, hiding in the corners of the Onyx Hall, dressed in the rags of her own finery. But the choice was deliberate: many of those gathered about her wore leather or leaves, clothing that less closely mirrored that of mortals.

Lune had a point to make. And to that end, she lifted her gaze past those gathered immediately beneath the oak, looking to the attendant knights and ladies that waited beyond.

Lifting one hand, she beckoned him to approach.

Standing between the Goodemeade sisters, Michael Deven hesitated, as well he might. But Lune raised one eyebrow at him, and so he came forward and stood a pace behind her left shoulder, hands clasped behind his back. He, too, was dressed in great finery, faerie-made for him on this day.

"Those of you gathered here today," Lune said, "remember Invidiana, and not fondly. I myself bear painful memories of my life under her rule. But today I ask you to remember someone else: a woman named Suspiria.

"What she attempted, some would say is beyond our reach. Others might say we *should not* reach for it, that mortal and faerie worlds are separate, and ever should stay so.

"But we dwell here, in the glens and the hollow hills, because we do not believe in that separation. Because we seek out lovers from among their kind, and midwives for our children, poets for our halls, herdsmen for our cattle. Because we aid them with enchantments of protection, banners for battle, even the homely tasks of crafting and cleaning. Our lives are intertwined with theirs, to one degree or another—sometimes for good, other times for ill, but never entirely separate.

"Suspiria came to believe in the possibility of harmony between these two worlds, and created the Onyx Hall in pursuit of that belief. But we do wrong if we speak only of her, for that misses half the heart of the matter: the Hall was created by a faerie and a mortal, by Suspiria and Francis Merriman."

Reaching out, Lune took Deven by the hand, bringing him

forward until he stood next to her. His fingers tightened on hers, but he cooperated without hesitation.

"I would not claim the Onyx Hall if I did not share in their belief. And I will continue to be its champion. So long as I reign, I will have a mortal at my side. Look upon us, and know that you look upon the true heart of the Onyx Court. All those who agree will ever be welcome in our halls."

Her words carried clearly through the still summer air. Lune saw frowns of disagreement here and there, among the kings, among their attendants. She expected it. But not everyone frowned. And she had established her own stance as Queen—her similarity to Suspiria, her difference from Invidiana—and that, more than anything, was her purpose here today.

The day did not end with speeches. There would be celebrations that night, and she would take part, as a Queen must. But two things would happen before then.

She walked with Deven at twilight along the bank of a nearby stream, once again hand in hand. They had said many things to one another in the month since the battle, clearing away the last of the lies, sharing the stories of what had happened while they were apart. And the stories of what had happened while they were together—truths they had never admitted before.

"Always a mortal at your side," Deven said. "But not always me."

"I would not do that to you," Lune responded, quietly serious. "'Twas not just Invidiana's cruelty that warped Francis. Living too long among fae will bring you to grief, sooner or later. I love the man you are, Michael. I'll not make you into a broken shell."

He could never leave her world entirely. The faerie wine he drank had left its mark, as Anael's power had done to her. But it did not have to swallow him whole.

He sighed and squeezed her hand. "I know. And I am thankful for it. But 'tis easy to understand how Suspiria came to despair. Immortality all around, and none for her."

Lune stopped and turned him to face her, taking his other hand. "See it through my eyes," she said. "All the passion of humanity, all the fire, and I can do no more than warm myself at its edge." A presentiment of sorrow roughened her voice. "And when you are gone, I will not grieve and recover, as a human might. I may someday come to love another—perhaps—but this love will never fade, nor the pain of its loss. Once my heart is given, I may never take it back."

He managed a smile. "Francis gave Suspiria's heart back."

Lune shook her head. "No. He shared it with her, and reminded her that she loved him, still and forever."

Deven closed his eyes, and Lune knew he, like her, was remembering those moments in the Onyx Hall. But then an owl hooted, and he straightened with a sigh. "We are due elsewhere. Come—she does not like to be kept waiting."

WINDSOR CASTLE, BERKSHIRE: *June 11, 1590*

When all the attendants and ladies-in-waiting had been dismissed, when the room was empty except for the three of them, Elizabeth said, "I think 'tis time you showed me your true face, Mistress Montrose."

Deven watched Lune out of his peripheral vision. She must have been half-expecting the request, for she did not hesitate. The golden hair and creamy skin faded away, leaving in their place the alien beauty of a faerie queen.

Elizabeth's mouth pressed briefly into a thin, hard line. "So. You are her successor."

"Yes." Deven winced at Lune's lack of deferential address, but she was right to do it; Elizabeth must see her as a fellow queen, an equal. "And on behalf of my people, I offer you a sincere apology for the wrongs your kingdom suffered at the hands of Invidiana."

"Is that so." Elizabeth fingered her silken fan, studying Lune. "She did much that was ill, 'tis true."

Deven could not make up his mind which queen to watch, but something in Elizabeth's manner sparked a notion deep within his brain. "Your Majesty," he asked, directing the words at the aging mortal woman, "how long did you know Anne Montrose was not what she seemed to be?"

Elizabeth's dark gaze showed unexpected amusement, and a smile lurked around the corners of her mouth, proud and a little smug. "My lords of the privy council take great care to watch the actions of my royal cousins in other lands," she said. "Someone had to keep an eye on the one that lived next door."

This *did* startle Lune. "Did you—"

"Know of others? Yes. Not all of them, to be sure; no doubt she sent temporary agents to manipulate my lords and knights, whom I never saw. But I knew of some." Now the pride was distinctly visible. "Margaret Rolford, for one."

Lune gaped briefly, then recovered her dignity and nodded her head in respectful admission. "Well spotted. I would be surprised you allowed me to remain at court—but then again, 'tis better to know your enemy's agents and control them, is it not?"

"Precisely." Elizabeth came forward, looking thoughtful. She stood a little taller than Lune, but not by much. "I cannot say I will like you. There is too much of bad blood, not so easily forgotten. But I hope for peaceful relations, at least."

Lune nodded. Looking at the two of them, Deven marked their choice of color: Lune in midnight blue and silver, Elizabeth in russet brocade with gold and jewels. Neither wore black, though Elizabeth often favored it. For the striking contrast with her auburn hair and white skin, or out of some obscure connection to or competition with Invidiana? Either way, it seemed both were determined to separate themselves from that past, at least for today.

Elizabeth had turned away to pace again; now she spoke abruptly. "What are your intentions toward my court?"

This was the true purpose of the meeting, the reason why "Mistress Montrose" had made a visit to Windsor Castle. Deven and Lune had talked it over before coming, but neither could guess what answer Elizabeth wanted to hear. All they could offer was the truth.

"'Tis a delicate balance," Lune said. "Invidiana interfered too closely, appropriating your actions for her own ends, and treading upon your sovereign rights. I have no wish to imitate her in that respect. But we also have no interest in seeing England fall to a Catholic power. I do not speak for all the faerie kingdoms, but if there is need of defense, the Onyx Court will come to your aid."

Elizabeth nodded slowly, evaluating that. "I see. Well, I have had enough of pacts; I want no swords in stones to bind us to each other. If such a threat should arise, though, I may hold you to your word."

Then she turned, without warning, to Deven. "As for you, Master Deven—you offered to free me from that pact, and so you did. What would you have of me in return?"

His mind went utterly blank. How Colsey would have laughed to see him now, and Walsingham, too; he had come to court with every intention of advancing himself, and now that his great opportunity came, he could not think what to ask. His life had gone so very differently than he expected.

Kneeling, he said the first thing that came into his head. "Madam, nothing save your gracious leave to follow my heart."

Elizabeth's response was cool and blunt. "You cannot marry her, you know. There's not a priest in England that would wed you."

John Dee might do it, but Deven had not yet worked up the courage to ask. "I do not speak only of marriage."

"I know." Her tone softened. Deep within it, he heard the echo of a quiet sorrow, that never left her heart. "Well, it cannot be made official—I would not fancy explaining it to my lords of the council—but if our royal cousin here finds it acceptable, you shall be our ambassador to the Onyx Court."

He could almost hear Lune's smile. "That would be most pleasing to us."

"Thank you, madam." Deven bowed his head still further.

"But there is one difficulty." Elizabeth came forward and put her white fingers under his chin, tilting his head up so he had no choice but to meet her dark, level gaze. "'Twould be an insult to send a simple gentleman to fill such a vital position." She pretended to consider it, and he saw the great pleasure she took in this, dispensing honors and rewards to those who had done her good service. "I believe we shall have to knight you. Do you accept?"

"With all my heart." Deven smiled up at one of his queens, and out of the corner of his eye, saw his other queen echo the expression.

It was a divided loyalty, and if a day should come that Elizabeth turned against Lune, he would regret occupying such a position.

But he could not leave the faerie world, and he could not leave Lune. So together, they would ensure that day never came.

# Epilogue

RICHMOND PALACE, RICHMOND: *February 8, 1603*

The coughing never went entirely away anymore. They sent doctors to pester her; she mustered the energy to drive them out again, but every time it was harder. The rain beat ceaselessly against the windows, a long, dreary winter storm, and it was easy to believe that all the world had turned against her. She sat upon cushions before the fire, and spent many long hours staring into its depths.

Her mind drifted constantly now, forgetting what it was she had been doing. Cecil came occasionally with papers for her to sign; half the time she was surprised to see it was Robert, William's hunchbacked little son. The wrong Cecil. Burghley, her old, familiar Cecil, had died...how long ago now?

Too long. She had outlived them all, it seemed. Burghley, Walsingham, Leicester. Her old enemy Philip of Spain. Essex, executed on Tower Hill—oh, how he had gone wrong. She could have handled him differently, perhaps, but when all was said and done he would never forgive her for being an old woman, too proud to give in, too stubborn to die. She was approaching seventy. How many could boast reaching such a great age?

She could think of some, but her mind flinched away. Those thoughts were too painful, now that illness and the infirmity of old age were defeating her at last.

"But I have done well, have I not?" she whispered to the fire. "I have done well. 'Twas not all because of her."

She glanced behind her, half-expecting to see a tall figure in the shadows, but no one was there. Just two of her closest maids, keeping weary vigil over their crabbed old queen, periodically trying and failing to convince her to go to bed. She looked away again, quickly, before they could raise their incessant refrain again.

Sometimes she could almost believe she had imagined it all, from her visitor in the Tower onward. But no—it had been real. Invidiana, and all the rest.

So many regrets. So many questions: What would have been different, had she never formed that pact? Would the Armada have reached the shores of England, bearing Parma's great army to overrun and subjugate them beneath the yoke of Spain? Or would she never have gotten that far? Perhaps she would have died in the Tower, executed for her Protestant heresy, or simply permitted to perish from the damp cold there, as she was perishing now. Mary Stewart might have had her throne, one Catholic Mary to follow another.

Or not. She had survived thirteen years without Invidiana, through her own wits and will, and the aid of those who served her. She was the Queen of England, blessed by God, beloved of her people, and she could stand on her own.

"And I have," she whispered, her lips moving near-soundlessly. "I have been a good queen."

The rain drumming against the windows made no reply. But she heard in it the cheers of her subjects, the songs in her honor, the praise of her courtiers. She had not been perfect. But she had done her best, for as long as she could. Now the time had come to pass her burden to another, and pray he did well by her people.

Pray they remembered her, and fondly.

Gazing into the fire, Elizabeth of England sank into dreams of her glorious past, an old woman, wrinkled and ill, but in her mind's eye, now and forever the radiant Virgin Queen.

# EXTRAS

www.orbitbooks.net

# About the Author

Perry Reichanader

**Marie Brennan** holds an undergraduate degree in archaeology and folklore from Harvard and is now pursuing a PhD in anthropology and folklore at Indiana University.

To find out more about Marie and our other Orbit authors, register for the free monthly newsletter at www.orbitbooks.net

*An interview with*
# MARIE BRENNAN

**Why did you choose the Elizabethan period as your focal point for Midnight Never Come?**

At a guess, I'd have to say my interest started with Shakespeare; I've always loved certain of his plays. (Surprise, surprise.) But it grew past that about ten or twelve years ago, when I read *Shakespeare of London* by Margaret Chute; that book approaches him as a working member of a company rather than as a great literary genius, and it may have been my first introduction to the world of Renaissance London. I fell in love pretty fast. It's a fascinating period all over Europe, really — ferocious religious tension and conflict, and yet despite that (or because of it?) such a vibrant time culturally. It offers the prospective author a lot to play with.

And Elizabeth herself is interesting because even in her own time, they deliberately built her up as this iconic figure, as a means of legitimizing her rule as a Protestant and a woman on the throne. It explains a lot of her cult following even today. I'm not as much of an idolater as I used to be; these days, I've done enough research to recognize her flaws. But I still have a lot of respect for her, and for the people around her. There are a lot of great names from her reign: Walsingham, Burghley, Ralegh, Drake, Dee, Marlowe, Shakespeare, and so on.

Plus, I like the clothes. Though I could do without the extremes of fashion: oversized cartwheel ruffs, enormously padded sleeves, and all the rest. Give me a streamlined Elizabethan look, thank you. (Which is more or less what I put the fae in.)

**This novel grew out of your experience with a role-playing game. How did that drive you to create the novel?**

Some time ago, White Wolf published a game system called *Changeling: The Dreaming*, which is about playing faeries in the modern world. I ran a game of my own in that system during 2006, but it ended up being pretty non-standard, starting with the fact that it went through six hundred and fifty years of English history — *backward*. (I called it "Memento," after the similarly-structured movie of the same name.) The Elizabethan segment of the game, originally set in 1589, grew like kudzu; it sprouted backstory starting in the mid-fourteenth century and repercussions going all the way to 2006, and more to the point, *it wouldn't leave my mind*. Specifically, Francis and Suspiria wouldn't leave my mind.

So I did some narrative surgery, lifting that part of the story out of the broader context of *Changeling* and Memento, and reworked it as a novel. A few key points of the plot are drawn from the game, but since we had only three evening sessions in which to play it, I had to do a *lot* of expanding, and things don't happen exactly the way they did the first time. I also had to do some work to remove the *Changeling*-specific elements, but not as much as I expected; when you get right down to it, both the game designers and I were working from the same source, namely, real-world faerie lore. If you still see some similarity, that's why.

**What types of media influenced this story?**

Shekar Kapur's movie *Elizabeth* left a strong imprint in my mind (and I'm delighted to see he's made a sequel). I recognize the liberties he's taken with history, but Cate Blanchett makes a *fantastic* Elizabeth, and Geoffrey Rush ain't bad as Walsingham, either. The Onyx Court owes a lot to that film; Kapur's vision is very rich and dark.

I also think Invidiana's the conceptual daughter of Maleficent in Disney's *Sleeping Beauty*, though I'd written the whole novel before I noticed that.

Music was a huge part of writing this book. Since I made "soundtracks" (i.e. mix CDs) for my game, I started off with some songs already chosen; I also made playlists for different moods—the mortal court, the Onyx Court, confrontations, romantic/sad scenes (funny how those two go together), church scenes, and tavern/city scenes. Those were playing on shuffle while I wrote, and then in the end, for the first time ever, I went the extra step and made a "novel soundtrack." You can see the full listing on my website, and if you have a good film score collection, you can reconstruct most of it for yourself.

**What can you tell us about your faerie research?**

Without realizing it, I set myself a big challenge at the outset: keeping it English. Most of the faerie fantasy I've read, especially the modern urban fantasy, takes a globalizing approach, where a redcap and a kitsune and a leshy might all rub shoulders. That approach has a lot of fun potential, but for a story set in the sixteenth century, I decided I wanted to preserve regionalism as much as I could.

Which turns out to be harder than you might think: many of the most famous bits of faerie lore (like the *sidhe,* or the Seelie and Unseelie Courts) turn out to be Irish or Scottish. If you strip those away, then the next biggest category is probably Welsh. Strip *that* away, and you find yourself looking at Cornwall and Yorkshire. We've got precious little surviving faerie lore from central and southern England. But although it's a lot of work,

I'm glad I did it; my own setting felt more real to me because I could talk about continental fauns and muryans from Cornwall and redcaps along the Border, and how the Goodemeades are from the North originally, because that's where stories of brownies come from.

I'm deeply indebted to the folklorist Katherine Briggs. Not only does she have two very useful books on general British faerie material (*British Folk-Tales and Legends*, and *The Faeries in Tradition and Literature*), she wrote one called *The Anatomy of Puck* that's specifically about the lore of Shakespeare's time. I couldn't have asked for a better resource.


**What about the historical research?**

There was a *lot* of it.

I ended up with nearly three shelves of the small bookcase in my office devoted to nothing more than the books I was using to write this novel. Biographies, books about London, some literature from the time period, architectural histories…the list seemed endless. Like an optimistic fool, I believed at first that a time would come when I would say "okay, that's it for the research" and be done. God only knows where I got that idea; maybe my subconscious was in denial. Research never ends. There's always two or three more books that will be the last, you swear. I think I was reading William Tighe's dissertation on the Gentlemen Pensioners while I was in revisions.

But the good news is, it's fun. I can't remember where I came across this line, but someone once said history was a cross between a disaster movie and a celebrity tabloid; I love that description. The further I got into the biographies, the more people came to life, with all kinds of quirks and warts and behaviors that make you think, humans haven't fundamentally changed. The surface details, sure, but where it really counts, they're not so different from us.

So I guess what I would say is, it's a tremendous amount of work, but the payoff is worth it. As long as you enjoy history, anyway, and if you don't, what are you doing writing a historical novel? There are easier ways to go crazy.

**How was writing this book different from others?**

Not since the first novel I wrote (which was not *Witch*) has a project eaten my head so thoroughly. Part of it, I'm sure, was the necessity of research; when I wasn't writing, I was eyeball-deep in nonfiction. I've done spot research before—reading up on poisons for *Warrior*, for example—but never on anything like this scale, because I was never representing a real time period and place before. But I think it was more than that.

Like I said above, certain key events in the plot came from the game Memento. That served as a kind of outline for me, and normally, I'm not an outlining kind of writer. Between that and my own growth in the craft, I found myself going through this book less asking myself, "how is this going to get resolved?" and more "how can I make the resolution of this *more awesome*?" Add in the richness of the history and backstory, and the greater number of pieces on my mental chessboard...you get the idea. Pretty much every aspect of this book, down to the words I used to tell it, really challenged me. And you don't meet a challenge firing on only half of your cylinders. I said in a post on my journal that this was the fourteen-year-old boy of books: it ate everything I fed it and demanded more.

**Would you write a historical fantasy again? If so, what time period?**

I'm pondering this very question right now, actually.

If anybody had asked me right after I finished the draft, I

would have screamed "HELL NO" and dived for cover under the bed. But people were smart and didn't ask me. Now that I've had some time to recover, the answer is "maybe, if I get an idea that grabs me." I found it deeply satisfying, slipping my story into the cracks and open spaces of history, and as I said, the research was fun. But, as I also said, it was a huge amount of work, so it isn't the kind of thing that I'd enter into lightly.

The question of time period is pretty wide open. If I were smart, I'd do more with the Elizabethan period, so I can make use of the research I've already done. Unfortunately, I'm *not* smart, and so I'm likely to skip off to a different century entirely. Running Memento introduced me to a broad swath of English history; I might latch onto any part of it. Of course, then there's the rest of the world—who says it would have to be England? But I boggle at the thought of setting something in a country where the best research materials wouldn't be in English. Knowing me, I'd feel like I ought to get fluent in Arabic or whatever before I try to write the thing.

But all that is dancing around the question. Honestly? Right now the nineteenth century is trying to look enticing. I've got a couple of ideas, unrelated to each other, that would all benefit from me knowing more about that era—even if some of them are modeled on that culture rather than being set in it. Only time will tell which ones will struggle to the top of the heap in my head and make it out into the light of day.

*These questions were collected from Marie Brenan's online fan community. If you would like to read more about Marie Brennan and the world of* Midnight Never Come, *please visit her website at www.mariebrennan.net*

If you enjoyed
*Midnight Never Come,*
look out for

# BLACK SHIPS

by

Jo Graham

You must know that, despite all else I am, I am of the People. My grandfather was a boatbuilder in the Lower City. He built fishing boats, my mother said, and once worked on one of the great ships that plied the coast and out to the islands. My mother was his only daughter. She was fourteen and newly betrothed when the City fell.

The soldiers took her in the front room of the house while her father's body cooled in the street outside. When they were done with her she was brought out to where the ships were beached outside the rig of our harbor, and the Achaians drew lots for her with the other women of the City.

She fell to the lot of the Old King of Pylos and was brought across the seas before the winter storms made the trip impossible. She was ill on the vessel, but thought it was just the motion of the ship. By the time she got to Pylos it was clear that it was more than that.

King Nestor was old even then, and he had daughters of the great houses of Wilusa to spin and grind meal for him, slaves to his table and loom. He had no use for the daughter of a boatbuilder whose belly already swelled with the seed of an unknown man, so my mother was put to the work of the linen slaves, the women who tend the flax that grows along the river.

I was born there at the height of summer, when the land itself is sleeping and the Great Lady rules over the lands beneath the earth while our world bakes in the sun. I was born on the night of the first rising of Sothis, though I did not know for many years what that meant.

My mother was a boatbuilder's daughter who had lived all her life within the sound of the sea. Now it was a morning's walk away, and she might not go there because of her bondage. Perhaps it was homesickness, or perhaps something in the sound of my newborn mewing cries, that caused her to name me Gull, after the black-winged seabirds that had swooped and cried around the Lower City.

By the time the autumn rains came, I was large enough to be carried in a sling on my mother's back while she worked.

I know it was not that year, but it is my first memory, the green light slanting through the trees that arched over the river, the sound of the water falling over shallow stones, the songs of the women from Wilusa and Lydia as they worked at the flax. I learned their songs as my first tongue, the tongue of the People as women speak it in exile.

There were other children among the linen slaves, though I was the oldest of the ones from Wilusa. There were Lydians older than I, whose mothers had come from far southward down the coast, and a blond Illyrian from north and west of Pylos. Her name was Kyla; she was my childhood friend, the one who paddled with me in the river while our mothers worked. At least until she was also put to work. I knew then what my life would be – the steady rhythm of beating the flax, of harvest and the life of the river. I could imagine no more. The tiny world of the river was still large enough for me.

The summer that I was four was the summer that Triotes came. He was the sister-son of the Old King, tall and blond and handsome as the summer sun. He stopped to water his horses, and talked with my mother. I thought it was odd.

A few days later he came again. I remember watching them talking, Triotes standing at his horses' heads, ankle deep in the river. I remember thinking something was wrong. My mother was not supposed to smile.

He came often after that. And sometimes I was sent to sleep with Kyla and her mother.

My fifth summer was when my brother was born. He had soft, fair baby hair, and his eyes were the clear gray-blue of the sea. I looked at my reflection in the river, at my hair as dark as my mother's, eyes like pools of night. And I understood something new. My brother was different.

Triotes threw him high in the air to make him laugh, showed him to his friends when they led their chariots along the road. He was barely a man himself, and he had no son before, even by a slave. He brought my mother presents.

One night I heard them talking. He was promising that when my brother was older he would bring him to the palace at Pylos, where he would learn to carry the wine cups for princes, where he would learn to use a sword. He was the son of Triotes, and would be know as such.

Later, when he had gone, I crept in beside my mother. My brother, Aren, was at her breast. I watched him nurse for a few minutes. Then I laid down and put my head on my mother's flat fair stomach.

"What's the matter, my Gull?" she said.

"I am the daughter of no man," I said.

I do not think she had expected that. I heard her breath catch. "You are the daughter of the People," she said firmly. "You are a daughter of Wilusa. I was born in the shadow of the Great Tower, where the Lower Harbor meets the road. I lived my whole life in the sound of the sea. Your grandfather was a boatbuilder in the Lower City. You are a daughter of Wilusa." My mother stroked my hair with her free hand, the one that did not support Aren.

"You were meant to be born there. But the Gods intervened."

"Then won't the Gods intervene again and take us back?" I asked.

My mother smiled sadly. "I don't think the Gods do things like that."

And so I returned to the river. I was old enough to help the women with the flax in the cool twilight along the water. And this, I knew, was where I would spend my life.

I don't remember the accident that changed all that.